Beyond the S

T0160353

This was really good! This is the third book in Miller's Manhattan Sloane Thriller series and is the best written book of the series. I was caught up in the mystery, it kept me turning the pages, but so did the romance.

-Lex Kent's Reviews, *goodreads*

I loved the first two novels, but I think this one might be the best yet...I've enjoyed all the mystery, excitement, action, and intrigue in the plots of these books, but I've fallen in love with these characters, and want to know what's happening in their lives. This is the mark of an exceptionally talented author.

-Betty H., *NetGalley*

From the Ashes

I have been looking forward to reading *From the Ashes* by Stacy Lynn Miller since I read her first Manhattan Sloane novel back in April. I fell in love with Sloane, Finn, and all the other characters in this story while reading the first book, and I wanted more, especially since the story didn't completely end with the first novel. I'm happy to say I loved this book as much as the first one.

In this second tale, we find Sloane still struggling with her grief over her wife's death as she also deals with her growing love for Finn. Nothing is ever easy for Sloane and Finn, since the head of the drug cartel they battled in the first book is now looking for revenge, and he's quite willing to target Sloane and Finn's loved ones.

This is an action-packed story with a complex plot. Most of the characters in this book were introduced in the first one, so they are already well developed and we learn more about the different members of the drug cartel and their motivations. This is definitely a character-driven tale, and Ms. Miller has done an excellent job of creating realistic characters, both good and bad.

I enjoyed seeing the romance grow between Sloane and Finn, even with all the obstacles that could come between them. The author did a wonderful job weaving this romance into all the action and suspense in the overall story.

As I mentioned above, this book is the second in the Manhattan Sloane series and takes up where the first novel, *Out of the Flames*, ended. These books really need to be read together and in order to get the most enjoyment out of the story. I highly recommend both novels, though, so get them both. You won't be disappointed.

-Betty H., NetGalley

This was the sequel to this author's very good debut book, *Out of the Flames*.

I enjoyed how the author developed this sequel with realistic problems the characters faced after the loss of loved ones. The author also provided more answers to the car accident that killed Sloane's parents. This was a very emotional moment for those involved. The way it was described, I couldn't help but feel for those characters.

Similar to the previous book, there was a lot of drama when the characters dealt with the cartels. These scenes quickened the pace of the story and allowed for more anxious moments. The secondary characters, both good and bad, increased this story's emotional depth.

Since this was a sequel, I recommend reading the first book to get an overall understanding of the characters and their backgrounds. The author did allow some past events to resurface, but the emotional scenes from the first book were too good not to read and experience.

This book was very engaging with tense moments, emotional breakdowns and recovery, and most of all, tender loving scenes.

-R. Swier, NetGalley

From the Ashes is the sequel to *Out of the Flames* with SFPD Detective Manhattan Sloane and DEA Finn Harper. They're chasing after a Mexican drug cartel that is ultimately responsible for killing Sloane's wife. Sloane and Harper had a connection in high school but they were torn apart after Sloane's parents were killed in a car accident. Then they were thrown together on this case as the drug cartel seeks revenge for the death of one of their own. Miller is a wonderful storyteller and this story had me sitting on the edge of my seat from start to finish. The first book in the series, *Out of the Flames*, was a 5-star read and *From the Ashes* is the same as it ducks and weaves and thrills and spills all the way to the end. The chemistry between Sloane and Harper is palpable…Miller certainly knows how to write angst into her characters. This book is a thrill a minute and I can't wait for the next one.

-Lissa G., NetGalley

I read Stacy Lynn Miller's debut novel *Out of the Flames* back in May, and couldn't wait to read the sequel to learn what happens to San Francisco police detective Manhattan Sloane and DEA Agent Finn Harper's relationship as well as the drug cartel they were chasing. *From the Ashes* resumes from the point that *Out of the Flames* ended.

The book was fast-paced with quite a few anxious and emotional moments. I don't think that you have to read the first book to enjoy this one, but I recommend it since it is a good story and it will introduce the background and characters in a more complete manner. I'd definitely recommend both books to other readers.

-Michele R., NetGalley

Firstly, if you've not read Stacy Lynn Miller's debut novel and first in the series of 'A Manhattan Sloane Thriller'… give it a read. It's called *Out of the Flames* and I can guarantee you will not regret it and be hooked like many of us who are now following her work.

From the Ashes follows on from the first book, you don't really need to read the first BUT PLEASE DO! Its fast-paced action keeps you on your toes and includes romance! What's not to love?

-Emma S., *NetGalley*

This is one amazing follow up to book one. The characters grow very well together, even though there are still mafia issues going on around them. I felt that the plot to resolve all issues was nicely provided. The finish was wonderful, and I feel like there will be a new set of stories (or so I hope) for the main characters to decide on their new adventures.

-Kat W., *NetGalley*

One of the things that Stacy Lynn Miller is skilled at is breathing life into her characters. Even important secondary characters. They all stand up as themselves, and there's never any difficulty remembering who is who. This is as true for Miller's previous book as this one. In fact, when I read the final passage, my first thought was for the future of a secondary character! Who worries what kind of future the daughter of a criminal will have? Me, apparently.

There is danger here, passion, secrets…all of the things that keep me reading long into the night. But this book wormed its way into me and wouldn't let up. I was quite literally unable to sleep because I was worried about one of the secondary characters—an autistic young man. I had to pick the book back up and finish it just so I knew what happened to him.

Miller wrapped up questions left dangling in the first book that I didn't know I had. There was a satisfying sense of completion and closure, and yet…there is still room for more stories to come from this fictional world. I do hope the author is interested in bringing us more from this made-up world of hers because I'll be among the first in line with my money out.

-Carolyn M., *NetGalley*

Out of the Flames

This is the debut novel of Stacy Lynn Miller and it's very, very good. The book is a roller coaster of emotion as you ride the highs and lows with Sloane as she navigates her way through her life which is riddled with guilt, self blame, and eventually love. It's easy to connect with all the main characters and sub-characters, most of them are all successful strong women so what's not to love? The story line is really solid.

-Lissa G., NetGalley

If you are looking for a book that is emotional, exciting, hopeful, and entertaining, you came to the right place. There are characters you will love, and characters you will love to hate. And the important thing is that Miller makes you care about them so, yes, you might need the tissues just like I did. I see a lot of potential in Miller and I can't wait to read book two.

-Lex Kent's 2020 Favorites List.
Lex Kent's Reviews, *goodreads*

If you are looking for an adventure novel with mystery, intrigue, romance, and a lot of angst, then look no further.

...I'm really impressed with how well this tale is written. The story itself is excellent, and the characters are well-developed and easy to connect with.

-Betty H., *NetGalley*

DESPITE
CHAOS

STACY LYNN MILLER

More Bella Books by Stacy Lynn Miller

A Manhattan Sloane Thriller
Out of the Flames
From the Ashes
Beyond the Smoke

About the Author

A late bloomer, Stacy Lynn Miller took up writing after retiring from the Air Force. Her twenty years of toting a gun and police badge, tinkering with computers, and sleuthing for clues as an investigator form the foundation of her Manhattan Sloane romantic thriller series. Visually impaired, she is a proud stroke survivor, mother of two, tech nerd, chocolate lover, and terrible golfer with a hole-in-one. When you can't find her writing, she'll be golfing or drinking wine (sometimes both) with friends and family in Northern California.

For more information about Stacy, visit her website at stacylynnmiller.com. You can also connect with her on Instagram @stacylynnmiller, Twitter @stacylynnmiller, or Facebook @ stacylynnmillerauthor

DESPITE
CHAOS

STACY LYNN MILLER

BELLA BOOKS
2022

Bella Books, Inc.
P.O. Box 10543
Tallahassee, FL 32302

Printed in the United States of America on acid-free paper.

First Edition - 2022

Editor: Medora MacDougal
Cover Designer: Heather Honeywell

ISBN: 978-1-64247-334-6

PUBLISHER'S NOTE

Acknowledgments

Thank you, Jacky Abromitis, proprietor of LesFan.com, for providing a place for amateur fanfiction writers like me to spread my writer wings.

A special thanks goes to Barbara Gould, who stuck with me through writer infancy and let me bounce ideas off her until she was black and blue.

Thank you, Louise, Kristianne, Diane, Sue, and Sabrin, for reading my rough-as-sandpaper draft and giving your unvarnished critique. Every thumbs up and down whipped this story into shape.

Thank you, Linda and Jessica Hill, for believing in my work and giving me a platform to share it with the world.

Thank you, Medora MacDougall, for your endless hours of elbow grease that put the final shine on my first baby.

Finally, to my family. Thank you for doing the shopping and dishes so I could stay in the writing groove.

Dedication

To Leslie Miller
My daughter and co-owner of my heart.
My world forever changed for the better the day I first
held you in my arms.

PROLOGUE

Long Beach, New York, July 1979

Rebecca Castle swallowed the cold, hard truth—cancer had won. Two years of treatments more painful than the rot consuming her breasts had failed, succeeding only in stripping her of energy and hope. Now she'd come to a crushing conclusion—her twins would be motherless beyond the age of five. Alexandra and Andrew didn't know it, but today's trip to the beach would be their last chance to form memories of the mother Rebecca wanted them to look back upon—a woman full of smiles and enough love to last them a lifetime.

By late morning, the Castle family had staked out a prime spot on the white sand in advance of the forecasted afternoon winds and unbearable heat and humidity. Steadied by the folding chair her husband, William, had brought, Rebecca covered her feeble legs with her grandmother's hand-knitted blanket. Refusing to dwell on a fate she couldn't change, she trusted her mother's 1957 Leica M3 camera to chronicle this precious day and snapped photo after photo of Alex and Andrew while they splashed and built sandcastles along the shoreline. She couldn't remember the last time she'd run through four rolls of film in one sitting, but capturing the perfect moment was essential.

At the first hint of a stiff breeze, Rebecca recognized the signs that Andrew had become impatient. He kicked and flattened the masterpiece he and his sister had spent the better part of an hour building, sending Alex crying into Rebecca's reassuring arms. As early as in the crib, Andrew was always the first to grow tired of the toys provided there, preferring to explore beyond the confines of the playpen. For being twins, her children couldn't be more different. Her son would likely turn out to be a thrill-seeker, while she was convinced Alex would forever be her father's little girl, favoring order over chaos.

"It's all right, Alex." Rebecca used her soothing voice as she cradled her daughter in her lap. "I took a picture of your beautiful sandcastle. When we get home, we can make a print of it just like the ones in your album. Would you like that?"

Alex nodded up and down, slowing her tears to match her occasional sniffle. "Yes." She cocked her head to one side and pointed at Rebecca's Leica. "The picture is in there?"

"Yes. It's called film." Rebecca showed Alex the different features of her camera and explained the concept of photography as best she could to a five-year-old. "See here? If you look through the viewfinder, you can see what you want to take a picture of. This long cylinder on the front is called a lens. It makes things appear bigger and closer than they really are. When you press this button, a little door inside the camera called a shutter opens and lets light through the lens and it hits a small square of the film. The film remembers what the lens was just pointed at." Rebecca let Alex look through the camera viewfinder and fumble with a few of the dials. "When we get home, we can transfer what's on the film to shiny paper and make the photograph."

"So, it's magic?" Alex asked.

"I like to think that every photograph is magical. But no, honey, photography is not magic. It's art rooted in science." Rebecca recognized Alex's knitted brow. She wouldn't let correctness ruin a nearly perfect day. "But we can call it anything we want. How about we rename my darkroom the Magic Room?"

Alex clapped her hands and squirmed in her mother's arms. "Magic Room! Let's go make magic, Mommy."

Without question, Rebecca's prized Leica needed to end up in Alex's hands. She made a mental note to add that provision to her will and hoped William would see to it. If not him, surely her dear Abby would.

Besides not living long enough to see her children grow up, Rebecca had one other regret about dying young: Abigail Spencer. She'd told Abby only a year ago that her affection had grown into attraction during their six-year friendship and then into romantic love. Her regret now was based not on disappointment that Abby hadn't returned her feelings, but on the sad reality that Abby had reciprocated them tenfold. The year of clarity that came next through a handful of clandestine encounters in an era when lesbianism was socially unacceptable wasn't nearly enough time for Rebecca to discover her true self fully. She hoped that after she was gone, Abby would live long enough to see a time when women like them could live an authentic life without fear. The kind of life Rebecca wished she could have experienced in her final year.

CHAPTER ONE

New Haven, Connecticut, Spring 1994

Alexandra Castle's destiny was written the day she was born—a path from private school to prep school to Ivy League university. Before this week, she had welcomed the family legacy and the expectations of her to live up to it. One day it would all be worth it. It was all written in stone. She and her two siblings would take the Castle empire of luxury hotels over from their father, William Castle, a man who was loving in his own way but controlling.

Her father wasn't always that way. Her earliest memories of him, following her mother's death, were marked by sadness. He'd spend hours alone in his study, playing the same Platters' song over and over again. But when he'd come out, he'd hug and kiss her good night. When she was fifteen, he changed. She thought perhaps his Parkinson's diagnosis then and the prospect of facing a lifelong debilitating disease was the cause, but his transformation went beyond self-pity. She had yet to discover why he suddenly began rationing out love to her, Andrew, and their much older half sister, acting as if they were lost in a desert and he had but a single precious canteen of water to offer them.

As his disease progressed, meeting his standards had become the only way to earn his approval. This was easier said than done. It was a lesson she learned through her twin brother, Andrew. His risk-taking, corner-cutting personality flew in the face of everything their father expected of them. Andrew would blow it off as if he didn't care, but as his twin, she knew better and felt it was her job to give him the love their father wouldn't. Protecting her brother had become second nature.

Since setting foot onto Yale's sacred grounds a year and a half ago, Alex had stayed the course expected of a Castle, maintaining a rigorous schedule of studies and athletics. Equally gifted academically, she and her brother had seesawed for the top two grades in each class they had in common. The only edge she had over Andrew when it came to earning their father's hard-earned approval was running track. She was faster in comparison to her female contemporaries than he was to his male ones.

All of that didn't matter as much as it once did, though. Not after she fell prey to an unexpected yet welcomed temptation—a liaison that her father would never condone because of the whispers it might generate in his Manhattan social circles.

Inhaling the fresh spring air, Alex extended a hamstring to its maximum against the plush infield grass of Yale's running track. The shorts of her track team uniform inched up, no doubt exposing the faint tan line on her warm, beige-toned skin. She'd been self-conscious about that, but a few more hours poolside in a bathing suit and that line would be invisible. Between stretches, she tightened her long brown ponytail. Then, unable to resist, she stared not at the coach directing their pre-meet warm-up but at her teammate, Kelly Thatcher. Eyeing the tall, athletic, and smart blonde had become a guilty pleasure, one Alex couldn't bring herself to regret even if her father learned of it. For weeks, Kelly had increasingly regarded her as if she were a fine cut at Wolfgang's Midtown. Her attention had brought to the surface a craving within Alex which previous male suitors had never inspired. For the first time, she felt downright sexy.

On and off the track, Kelly had become a distraction that William Castle wouldn't approve of on any level. For starters, she was a scholarship student, unable to afford the hefty Yale price tag. According to William, anyone with South Philly roots was beneath any Castle with an ounce of self-respect. Then there was the bigger issue. Her brother's daily lusting after Kelly's long legs was terrible enough, but in her father's world, Alex doing the same was an unforgivable sin—an attitude she never fully understood, considering his longstanding support of progressive charities like the ACLU and Habitat for Humanity.

"Thinking about taking a dip into the lady pond?" Andrew plopped down next to Alex, his gaze dissecting Kelly's features from head to toe with the thoroughness of a surgeon.

"And if I were?" Alex glanced at him. Andrew used to be her mirror image. He was taller than her now with a stronger chin, slightly thicker nose, and more pronounced brow.

"Considering how you fixate on Madonna and the Divine Miss M, it wouldn't surprise me."

She gave him a sturdy shoulder shove. Andrew had a finely honed sixth sense about her. He was often sure of Alex's feelings before she was, which made keeping secrets from him a monumental task. He could ferret out deception like a police dog alerting to the scent of a drug mule.

"I don't know, Andrew." She cocked her head, studying Kelly's teasing form. "I've only dated men." If she were honest, she'd tell him she was questioning why Kelly's seductive gazes made her breath hitch and why a bend at the waist made her heart beat wildly out of control. Since sophomore year in high school, Alex had found herself drawn to girls, but she had yet to explore the likelihood she might not be straight. As a Castle, being open about such an indulgence was not only stupid but dangerous. Her father would never accept it.

"And the men you date are either vacuous or more feminine than you."

"They are not." Although his assessment of her last two failed dating escapades was spot-on, she shot her brother a mind-your-own-business stare.

"Other than Father finding out, what does it matter?"

"You have a point." Alex tossed her hesitation—and the witless and effeminate men she'd been drawn to—in the trash heap of regrets for not taking this leap sooner. Harley Spencer, her only confidant on the topic since high school, would say, "It's about damn time. Welcome to the sapphic club."

"It appears we have another competition on our hands," he said.

Alex followed his stare. Deep into a hamstring stretch, Kelly had dipped deep enough that her college track uniform precisely accentuated every curve, revving Alex's pulse. A rush of warmth radiated up her cheeks, setting off a three-alarm fire. "You're on."

"Then I better up my game." Andrew bounced to his knees to engage in a vigorous hip-flexor stretch.

Alex joined him, but her stretching effort was half-hearted. "Game? Brother, you have no game."

"Don't look now, but Father is here. If you expect to win the 5K today like I'm going to"—Andrew waved a disparaging finger at Alex and her lack of effort—"you better do a better job of warming up."

Alex shook her head. Her brother had yet to figure out their father. William Castle was not capable of showing unconditional love, only praise when his conditions were met. "Haven't you learned by now that you can't win his approval by winning races?"

"That's rich coming from you. You always win, and you've always been Father's favorite." Andrew's expression matched his bitter words.

"My winning has nothing to do with it. I've learned what he respects."

"Which is…?"

"Public conformity. Father cares foremost about image. You getting busted by the campus police for gambling and binge drinking didn't exactly meet the William Castle standard of behavior."

"It seems you are considering a rebellion of your own." He jutted his chin toward Kelly, the one person who made her want to do anything but conform.

She focused on the body that made her want to buck everything Castle. To forget the pile of academic awards and trophies in her bedroom that rivaled the collection compiled by Syd, her older half sister. To follow her brother's example of taking chances and living on the edge.

Wanting to break her father's rules, though, didn't mean she was ready for the consequences. If he discovered her secret revolt, he'd react in authentic Castle form—dignified yet sure and swift. He'd say the entire Castle legacy rested on what she did in public, and if she chose not to live up to it, she was not a true Castle. Some days, she longed for the father she had before his diagnosis, the one who cared more about making her happy than about what others thought.

Alex's stare followed Kelly as she sprang from the turf and made her way toward the water cooler. Her brief contemplation of defiance evaporated when her father, looking every bit the part of a Manhattan business mogul, came into view in the stands. Not even a weekend athletic event could persuade him to dress informally. He stood out in the casual crowd with his distinctive, tailored double-breasted navy-blue suit and the crisp white collar contrasting against his golden-toned skin. She attributed his devotion to proper attire, at least in part, to his compensating for his disease. "The correct blazer," he'd noted, "can hide the most noticeable flaw."

"Of course, she would come." Andrew's taut tone snapped Alex out of an internal battle between daring and cowardice. She followed his gaze into the grandstands, focusing on Harley Spencer, her best friend, who was standing to her father's left as a buffer between him and Harley's mother.

At forty-four, Abigail Spencer, New York City philanthropist, epitomized elegance. Thick, wavy auburn hair, immaculately trimmed to the trailing edge of the collar on her tailored suit jacket, framed prominent cheekbones, highlighting skin the color of pale linen. Unlike William, she was dressed for the outdoors, pairing her silk blouse and floral scarf with formfitting jeans and sensible yet chic walking shoes. Abby could make any pair of Levi's look like they had cost a thousand dollars.

"She made it." Alex waved until she received a reciprocal gesture. She grinned so hard her cheeks hurt. "Abby!"

"Always Abby. Sometimes I think you're more of a Spencer than a Castle." Andrew's disapproving tone on the topic of Abigail Spencer had escalated along with their father's, reaching a tiresome level by their final year in high school.

"Not this again."

"Can you blame me?"

"Yes, I can. Abby has been our surrogate mother since we were six."

If not for Abby, the cancer that took their mother would've also taken Alex's spirit, especially after her father's diagnosis and transformation for the worse. Abby offered Alex the same love she showed her own daughter, Harley. She showed the same to Andrew, but he had shied away from it as he grew older.

"To you, but not to me." Andrew's habitual sneer was pronounced today.

"Abby treated you the same. Her standing invitation was for both of us. You're the one who stopped coming."

"What did you expect? Father made it clear when we were fifteen that he didn't like her, but you continued going. That's when you stopped being my best friend. Sometimes I think Harley is more your twin than I am."

"You know that's not true." Though Andrew had a point, Alex gave him a playful shoulder shove. Three months older than them, Harley shared more in common with Alex, but she lacked one fundamental attribute—Castle blood. Blood trumped friendship. "You're my twin. We may not have played together every day of our lives, but you've been my bestest friend since we were in a crib."

Behind those brown eyes, identical to her own, his cocky sparkle had faded, replaced by a look of defeat. "I may be your twin, but I've never been your equal in Father's eyes. You'll always be his favorite." Before she could respond, he bounced to his feet and took off down the track in a slow jog.

Students, friends, family, and alumni cheered on athletes from Yale for the next three hours as they battled Harvard in an evenly matched event. Tradition and pride, rather than setting records, marked the day. William Castle beamed when he joined the other parents and competitors on the infield. He still walked strongly, though more slowly than he had at her high school graduation two years ago.

"There are my stellar athletes." William gave Alex a hearty hug before shaking Andrew's hand. His hand twitched ever so slightly. Her father could still hide the effects of his Parkinson's to most, but not to Alex, who looked for it regularly. "You two gave Harvard a good trouncing, just like your old man did back in the day."

Andrew's face lit up. "Yes, sir, we sure did. Those pilgrims didn't stand a chance."

"Well, Andrew, that Harvard man was right on your tail. If not for his slight stumble at the end, you might have come in a sad second." Andrew's shoulders slumped, making his disappointment palpable. William turned toward Alex, his grin increasing twofold. "But, Alexandra. Now that's how to win a race, a full ten seconds ahead. You must have trained hard, young lady."

Despite Andrew's earlier digs, he still deserved her backing, especially following their father's not-so-subtle jab. "Thank you, Father, but Andrew—"

"But nothing." William dismissively swept his hand. "You did the Castles proud."

Abby joined the group, a disarming smile highlighting her face's fine lines. She said, "They both did," essentially settling the argument. William returned her polite nod with the contemptuous cast of his chin that he had resorted to every time she'd entered his orbit for the last five years. Their previously cordial friendship had turned into a cold war, a transition Alex never understood and one neither Abby nor her father had cared to explain.

Harley followed behind her mother. Her hair, dark and flowing, differed from Abby's short and graying blond strands, but she looked and carried herself like her mother—polished and sophisticated. They both gave Andrew and Alex kisses on the cheek. Andrew rolled his eyes as he did every time they showed him affection, while Alex returned Abby's kiss and whispered into her ear, "Thank you. Andrew needed a pick-me-up."

"I could tell," Abby whispered before pulling away.

"I thought you had business in New York today," Alex said.

"I wouldn't have missed this for the world, dear. Family tradition and all hanging in the balance."

"A Castle family tradition." William followed his retort with a brief but stern glare at Abby. His disapproving eyes were the least frightening part of his expression.

"Father." Alex sharpened her response enough to make her disappointment in him clear but not so much as to earn his ire.

"It's all right, Alex. William is right. It is a wonderful Castle tradition." Abby smiled as only she could, gently brushing a hand down Alex's forearm. Her trademark charm put the gruffest of Manhattan's elite at ease at lightning speed. William Castle, one of those self-made elites, had been immune since his diagnosis. "I believe today is cause for celebration."

"I agree, Mother. The entire team made a wonderful showing," Harley said. "We should invite them all to our beach house tonight to celebrate."

"Really, Harley?" Abby raised an eyebrow. "A college party in the Hamptons? What kind of mischief do you have in mind?"

"I'm hurt." Harley's movie star dramatics, while humorous, couldn't offset their memories of her rich history of misbehavior. "You should come too, Mother."

"Oh, no." She shook a reproving finger Harley's way. "I'm much too old to chaperone a bunch of wild Ivy Leaguers. I'll alert Sonja to expect you. She has a standing order to report back to me if anything gets too out of hand."

"Thank you, Mother." Harley kissed her on the cheek before turning toward the twins. "Alex. Andrew. Both of you are coming to the party, aren't you?"

"I don't know, Harley." Alex weighed her academic responsibilities against the prospect of watching her best friend engage in another weekend of debauchery. The last Spencer beach house party, while epic, had put her days behind in her studies.

"Did I hear 'party'?" Kelly halted on her way to the locker rooms, her ponytail slowing its sway. Her body drew Alex's undivided attention instantly.

Harley turned. "Yes, the entire team is invited to our beach house tonight."

"Are you going?" Kelly turned her gaze on Alex, starting at her toes and settling on her eyes. If not for her father standing five feet away, Alex would've let the spark of desire she felt build into an illicit fantasy.

Harley stepped beside Alex, shoulder to shoulder, and linked an arm with hers. "Of course, she's going. As is Andrew."

"Well, I'll definitely be there then." Kelly gave Alex a suggestive wink, then continued on her way.

"It's settled," Harley said.

Nothing on earth could make Alex say no if Kelly was going. "Yes, settled." Alex's head tilted as her eyes followed the progression of Kelly's mesmerizing backside.

"I guess we're going to a party." Andrew's shrug earned William's disapproving gaze again. Her brother was right. She was "daddy's favorite."

* * *

The quarter-mile buffer between Southampton estates made the Spencer beach house the ideal location for one of Harley's legendary parties. Tonight, a light breeze whisked fresh salt air into the lush, well-lit seaside yard, providing the perfect setting. Blood-pumping music and free-flowing beer and mojitos fueled the loud mischief of a hundred drunk Ivy Leaguers and their friends.

Alex stood alone poolside, engaging in people-watching and concluding that she was one of the few sober people there. Though tequila was more to her liking, she'd settled on beer. In order to appear to be keeping up with the other partygoers, she took a micro-sip from a bottle that had lost its chill half an hour ago. She had decided at Harley's first wild party in the fall that losing control in a rowdy crowd where the ratio of men to women was about even had no appeal. The only fascinating thing at this party was the tall, mini-skirted blonde from the wrong side of Philly. The one that Alex had been eyeing all night.

"Ready to trade that swill for tequila?" Andrew appeared from behind her and extended hands filled with what seemed to be shot glass peace offerings. He knew her all too well.

"I'm good." Alex raised her half-full bottle. She returned her stare to where she last had spied Kelly, but she had disappeared.

Despite the ensuing silence between them, so deafening that it drowned out the music and poolside chatter, Alex was having difficulty reading Andrew. Before today, she would've said she knew her twin as well as she knew herself. Sadly, their earlier argument over Abby made her wonder if the symbiotic connection she thought they shared—in sync with every childhood need, want, and emotion—had lost its potency.

"I'm sorry about earlier today." He withdrew his offering, chugging the clear liquid in each of the glasses before placing them on the nearby stone retaining wall.

"I'm sorry, too." Alex turned toward him. She'd made it her job to make him feel loved and wanted, but she'd failed. The hardest thing to swallow now was that she had no do-overs. "Are you still pissed?"

"When am I not pissed about how Father favors you? That will never change. Because he won't." Regrettably, Andrew was correct. Alex couldn't envision a day when their father would stop putting conditions on his favor. Instead, she saw him getting more controlling as time and his disease marched on. He'd continue to ride Andrew harder for not meeting his expectations.

Andrew scanned the crowd. "I'm off to find Kelly. That's one competition I still have a chance of winning." He walked away, blending into the drunken crowd.

You've already lost, Brother, she thought. His defeatism about their father was providing the final push she needed to take chances of her own.

Minutes later, the voice that had seduced Alex the first time she heard it floated behind her. "You were wonderful out there today."

Alex didn't have to turn to know who had paid her the compliment. That sultry tone, despite being expressed at high volume in order to pierce through the loud music, had become a drug, intoxicating her. She twisted to face the speaker.

"Thanks, Kelly. You did well yourself, placing third in the mile. If memory serves, that was your best time."

"It was. Thanks for noticing." Kelly's penetrating stare raised the heat. The desire that had simmered in Alex for weeks came to a boil.

Without breaking her stare, Alex lowered her voice to a tantalizing tone. "That pool looks especially inviting tonight. Would you like to swim?"

"Do you have anything to wear? I didn't bring anything."

"I spend a lot of time here." Alex inspected every curve from thigh to chest, mentally salivating about everything in between. "We're about the same size. I'm sure I can find something."

"Great, let's go." Without a moment of hesitation, Kelly grabbed Alex's hand and dragged her toward the main house at a brisk pace.

Inside, Alex took the lead, guiding Kelly toward the guest room Abby had set aside for her years ago. Not one of the young men she'd led down this hallway before had had her heart beating as fast as it was doing now. Debating whether she was straight, gay, or bi seemed unnecessary at the moment. If she'd correctly read Kelly's flirting all these weeks, Alex would soon determine which labels to rule out.

Alex rummaged through a dresser drawer, keeping one eye on the mouthwatering distraction standing near the bed. Her breath turned ragged at the sight of Kelly undoing one blouse button and then a second to reveal an exquisite gap between her breasts. *Father definitely wouldn't approve. Not at all.*

"Red or black?" Alex held up two skimpy selections, hoping she'd choose neither.

"Which one would you like to see me in?" Kelly's tone turned low, and its cadence slowed to a seductive pace. Unhurriedly, she removed her cotton blouse and skirt, exposing sheer black lace, top and bottom.

"Definitely black." From toned legs to curved hips to flat stomach to appetizing breasts, every inch of Kelly boosted

Alex's craving to an unfamiliar level. Not even Todd Hamilton, the boy who took her virginity, had had her this revved.

"Are bathing suits necessary?" Kelly reached behind her back and loosened her bra, causing each strap to inch lower. The garment fell to the wood floor without fanfare, turning Alex's legs into Jell-O.

Weeks of dressing in front of each other in Yale's field house among a flock of other team members hadn't prepared Alex for this moment. She'd stolen a few glimpses in the crowded locker room, but she hadn't the courage before now to soak in the allure of Kelly's naked, addictive shape. And what a fool she was for wasting every opportunity to send her pulse into overdrive.

"Only if we want to go swimming." Alex licked her lips, hoping Kelly had changed her mind.

"I'm not sure I want to spend our time together doing that." Kelly ran a fingertip from a clavicle to the top of a breast. A pulse pounded in Alex's folds faster than in every previous encounter she had with a man. "Would you like to kiss me, Alex?"

"God, yes." Alex's chest heaved as she gulped in a robust breath. The prospect of losing an inheritance she didn't particularly care about seemed like a small price to pay to make weeks of fantasizing come true.

Kelly took several long, sexy strides toward Alex, stopping when her bare breasts pushed against the thin fabric of Alex's top and bra. A touch never felt so good. So erotic. So dizzying. Kelly wrapped her arms around Alex's neck and pressed their lips together in a fiery kiss. Endorphins must've kicked in because a runner's high swept through Alex. This was how a kiss was supposed to feel—soft lips with the taste of cherry.

Self-control evaporating, Alex tossed the Castle standard of behavior to the wayside. Unable to stop herself, she let her hands roam the taut back muscles lying beneath Kelly's soft skin. Strong yet feminine. It was a combination she never knew she craved. Her center clenched with the force of a vise when she moved her hands forward and her fingertips grazed the swell of an ample breast.

Coherent thought left in a whirlwind as a carnal instinct took over. The need to touch and be touched hit Alex like a loaded eighteen-wheeler careening out of control. She shifted into high gear and hurried Kelly back toward the bed until they bounced on the mattress. Clothing flew in random directions until not a stitch remained. Their bodies entwined. Hands roamed patches of exposed smooth, sweaty flesh. Never had she responded so quickly, so intensely. She understood why. Straight or bi would never again be in her lexicon.

CHAPTER TWO

Sacramento, California, Fall 1994

Tyler Falling had a dream—to be running her own graphic design firm by the age of thirty. She had three years to make it happen. The catch: how to simultaneously hold down a hair-pulling, full-time graphic artist job at the state's top advertising company, complete a graduate degree, and mother a feisty preschooler. Her meager pay, along with her husband's paltry salary as a cop, had dictated her reasoning. If she were to put her daughter through college and hopefully another child or two, she had to think big.

Her ambitious plan had taken its toll. Salty or high-carb snacks had substituted for meals more times than she cared to count, and the new graphic design software in class had her more confused than she cared to admit. If not for the sterling midterm grade she'd earned in class tonight, she'd regret those few extra pounds and the nights lost tucking Erin into bed.

Tyler allotted herself five minutes of solitude in the ladies' restroom to celebrate her hard-earned accomplishment. Sadly, the reflection in the mirror told her it had come at a price. Black circles had taken up permanent residence under her eyes, and the low lights of her chin-length blond hair had long disappeared. *You've earned a spa day.* Moments like this revealed the wisdom of her mother's caution against spreading herself too thin.

Half-filled with cars but void of other people, the dimly lit state college student parking lot had Tyler on alert, as it had twice each week for the last two months. She was well prepared, clutching her weapons of choice in the dark. She silently thanked her husband for the gift of mace and a lesson on using the ragged edge of a house key as a makeshift dagger.

Leaves on the ground near a tree suddenly rustled. A shadowy figure about the size of her shoe darted toward the safety of a nearby SUV, bringing Tyler to a dead halt. She gasped, her heart hammering wildly. "Damn squirrels." That was the third time those pesky rodents had scared the life out of her.

Behind her, she heard a rapid thumping of rubber soles against pavement. As it drew closer, she spun around and extended her hand chin-high, thumb pressed against the mace button. The tall, dark figure stopped a yard shy of her.

"Holy fuck, Tyler."

"You scared the shit out of me, Paul." She lowered her primary weapon. In the faint amber glow of the streetlamps, she recognized his frumpy figure. If she'd run across a man on the street with the same shaggy red hair and baggy, unmatched clothes, she would've given him a wide berth. But this particular parents' basement dweller had done her the biggest favor of her graduate school career. For that, she could forgive the fright and the fashion faux pas.

"Sorry about that." His breathing was labored, a sure sign he spent more time in front of a glowing monitor than at the gym. His pudgy gut was another. But it was all that computer time and his willingness to pass along his expertise over the last month while working on their joint midterm project that had earned Tyler's gratitude.

"It's okay, but you shouldn't sneak up on a woman in the dark." She eased her tone and momentarily placed a hand on his forearm.

"Lesson learned." Paul's smile contained an extra pep. He was clearly still riding high from tonight's surprise. "I can't believe we earned the top grade in the class."

"Thanks to you. I don't think I could've pulled my weight if you hadn't helped me learn Corel so fast." His after-class tutoring sessions at IHOP had paid off in spades, making it easier to forgive his misguided, clumsy flirting. Tyler felt sorry for him. He just needed someone to give him pointers on transforming his lackluster, somewhat juvenile exterior into something more artful. Maybe then, his awkward advances might be believable.

"You're incredibly smart," he said. "You would've picked it up without my help."

"Maybe."

"Definitely. We need to celebrate." He puffed out his chest, nearly bringing it even to his round belly. His boldness was growing. "How about we go hit Fridays' for a drink?"

"I should get home and relieve the babysitter."

"Oh, come on, Tyler. One drink. You earned it."

Tyler glanced at her watch. It was nine o'clock. Her husband wasn't due home for hours. Erin should already be in bed, and the babysitter was likely engrossed in her favorite television show. When she thought of the hours spent on their project, not to mention the hours spent fretting about it, she decided she deserved an hour to unwind, an indulgence she hadn't considered in months. "Why not? I have the babysitter for another hour."

* * *

One drink, he said. An hour, I said. What was I thinking?

Regret had set in when Paul insisted on a second drink for himself while she still nursed her first. Impatience took root during the drinking contest between him and the college football star for the third and fourth. The last thing she wanted to do late on a weeknight was to roll a drunk yet polite manboy safely into his bed, but it appeared that was where things were heading. The annoying competition had, at least, provided Tyler with a needed escape from him schooling her on the particulars of video gaming, which wasn't her idea of unwinding.

Tyler's mother had taught her, "friends don't let friends drive drunk," so, here she was, three hours after agreeing to one drink, with one of Paul's arms slung over her shoulder, pounding on the front door of his childhood home, the smell of stale whiskey making her nose curl. She hoped his mother would take over and give him a piece of her mind. Plainly, the kind of woman who ringed the front yard tree with fresh annuals wouldn't put up with a drunk, failure-to-launch son throwing up on her carpet.

"No one's home. Mom and Dad are addicted to the slots and went to Reno." Paul slurred his words and swayed.

"Please tell me you have a key."

"Yep." After missing twice, Paul stuffed a hand into his front pocket and proudly pulled out a set of keys. He held them for a three-count before letting them freefall into a pot of flowers.

Tyler mumbled an obscenity on a loop, one she'd been trying hard to eliminate from her vocabulary since it had rolled out of Erin's mouth at the grocery store. "Which key is it?" She blew off clumps of potting soil, eyeing a collection of keys any janitor in the state would be proud to possess.

"The gold one." Paul plopped against the wall, his head bouncing off the stucco. *Good. That should leave a knot.*

"They're all gold in this light."

"Yoshi."

"I should've guessed." His obsession with video games permeated every aspect of his life—the definitive mark of a manchild. After using the key topped with a bright green and white cap and rounded ears, Tyler slung Paul's arm back over her shoulder and guided him through the entryway of the 1970s ranch-style house. "Which way?"

"In the back, on the right."

A few steps in, Tyler flipped on the hallway light switch and tossed Paul's keys in the bowl centered on a three-foot-high bookcase. Illumination from the single ceiling light showed the way to the back of the house. The living room had signs of a woman's touch, but the stretched canvas paintings on nearly every wall were signs of a dedicated patron of art. As they passed through, Paul stumbled into a table and then a wall, knocking down one of those paintings and ensuring several bruises were in his future. *Serves him right.*

"My sitter is going to kill me." Tyler had some serious groveling ahead of her. She'd never been more than an hour late. "I can't believe you talked me into staying while you engaged in a drinking contest."

"Sorry, Tyler." Paul straightened the best a drunk could do and puffed out his chest again. If the chest thing was his signature move, it wasn't working. "But he challenged my manhood. I had no choice."

"Yeah, yeah, yeah, you're all man, Paul. Now let's get you into bed before you pass out or throw up on the floor." Pushing with an outstretched palm, Tyler tipped him onto the bed before starting to remove his shoes.

"You think I'm all man, huh? Am I man enough for you?"

The question stood the hairs on the back of Tyler's neck on end and demanded a response that would knock some sense into this drunk schlub. "My husband is a police officer. He's all the man I need."

In one swift tug, he pulled Tyler onto the bed, rolled on top, and slurred, "You're so beautiful." The smell of cheap whiskey and sour sweat turned her stomach.

She felt like a trapped animal, the instinct to flee exploding like a bomb. Tyler's father had been right years ago—boys, girls, and alcohol were a disastrous mix. She kicked herself for not listening closer to his and her husband's self-defense tips.

"Don't, Paul. Don't. Let me go." Tyler's voice turned brittle with panic. Weaker. Smaller. She couldn't break free. The weight of his body crushed her against the worn mattress. Paul squeezed her arms tighter and went in for a kiss. Not tender and loving like her husband's, but sloppy and forceful. She thrashed her head left and right. One swipe popped his cheek and nose.

He stopped, eyes sobering in an instant. They burned with a fire she'd never seen before, sending a chill down her spine. For the first time, she feared for her life.

"You bitch." Spit landed in her eyes. He balled a fist and smashed it into her face. A crack. Pressure. A sharp, prickling sting. A second punch. A third. Liquid tracked down her upper lip, leaving a growing coppery taste in her mouth.

He clawed at her clothing until nothing covered her breasts and abdomen. She'd never felt more exposed, more cold. Tyler let a few quiet sobs escape when a dry, chapped hand squeezed a breast. Every muscle stopped twitching. Frozen nerve endings stopped firing. Her eyes focused on nothing, the entire room blurring into space. The musty smell of dog wafting from the bedding triggered a thought. Did he have a dog? Small or large? He seemed more like the lapdog type, someone who would coo at his pet as if it were his only friend in the world.

He rustled above her for some time, for how long and for what purpose she couldn't determine. Cool air tickled her hips, legs, and feet, reminding her of a recurring dream—her in her high school science classroom, naked and unprepared for a test worth half her grade. She snapped her eyelids shut, disengaging. Disassociating.

When she opened her mind's eye, instead of the classroom, she was sitting against a mature oak as it stood sentinel over a slow-moving creek. She knew this creek. It wasn't far from her childhood home. Clear water trickled over the smooth rocks that filled the stream's bottom, creating a soothing, rhythmic sound, threatening to put her to sleep. But sleep, she feared, was her enemy. Keeping the water in her sight would keep her safe, of that she was sure.

The oak she was propped against was one of many that lined the water on either side for as far as her eyes could see. Its bark poked her shoulder blade, forcing her to adjust until the pain stopped. She glanced at her hand, not realizing how hungry she was until she focused on the sandwich she was holding in it. She took a bite. Yum. Peanut butter—a childhood favorite. It was the taste of carefree summer days, the flavor of innocence. She nibbled at a slow pace because once the savory taste was gone, she'd have to leave this place where the trees protected her from the blistering sun and formed a sturdy wall from the outside world.

The water slowed until the flow stilled and receded into the rocks, revealing silt and weeds from years of neglect. She willed the water to return, but it stubbornly refused. She left the protection of her oak, turning her back to the once soothing creek bed. A well-worn foot-trail led her through the army of mighty oaks, which protected her as she passed. Soon she stood at the edge of the tree line, staring into a black abyss, waiting for a sign. A light grew in the distance, and she stepped through.

The rancid smell of vomit forced Tyler's eyes open to a near-darkness. Her surroundings gradually came into focus. Her gaze followed the smooth ceiling to a wall lined with a cluttered, rickety dresser. Motion to her other side brought her exploration to an abrupt halt. As she slowly craned her neck, the scent of bile grew stronger. The left side of her face throbbed as she turned, her breathing hastening and growing shallow at the sight of the man lying next to her on the mattress, unclothed from what she could tell. A flash of memory explained the pain in her cheek, but her mind refused to recall what had happened beyond that point.

Self-inspection confirmed a growing fear—she was naked and sore all over. She couldn't tell in the dark, but she predicted bruises and marks everywhere she ached. Deducing that Paul had passed out, she gathered her clothes, most of which were torn beyond usefulness. She stumbled out of the room, past the fallen painting, through the living room, her foot catching on a coffee table. She fell. The jolt hurt, but not as much as the reality she was refusing to accept. She picked herself up and ran out the door, clutching her clothes to her with a death grip, as if they'd protect her from the truth.

Out on the street, she spotted her car, but she had no keys. She'd forgotten her purse. Her heartbeat picked up tenfold. Trembling, she turned toward the house, but going back in was not an option. She turned again and ran down the sidewalk. Her bare feet slapped the hard cement at a pace she couldn't maintain for long, but she needed to put as much distance between her and the unbearable truth as fast as she could.

She turned the corner, hoping to run across a pedestrian or traveler, but the suburban neighborhood was like a ghost town at this time of night. Even the birds were asleep in their nests. She continued to run until her lungs burned and her side cramped so hard that she fell to her knees. They scraped on the rough cement, which was still radiating the last echoes of the day's heat, but they didn't hurt as much as reality. Clutching her tattered clothes, she crawled over landscaping rock until she reached grass, collapsing onto the soft, damp blades of a lawn that sloped up to a house. A dog's muffled but vigorous barking came from within it, followed by a porch light coming to life. Without the energy to cover herself from the cold, she curled into a ball, shivering and hoping someone inside that house would come find her. Someone kind.

CHAPTER THREE

Manhattan, New York, 2007

If not for Andrew Castle's penchant for gambling and women looking for hookups, not relationships, the Flatiron District would not have been on his radar. He preferred the liveliness of Tribeca or the chaos of Hell's Kitchen, which fed his need to not only be part of the action but its centerpiece. The one thing going for Flatiron, besides the plethora of models calling the neighborhood home, was Arthur's Alley, a decent sports bar and pool hall even by Andrew's lofty standards. It had been Manhattan's premier upscale sports bar for several decades. Upscale, though, didn't mean upstanding. The bar attracted sports lovers loaded with money, which in turn attracted polished, sophisticated bookmakers willing to part those patrons from their cash. That topped Andrew's agenda tonight—finding his bookie.

The familiar gaudy, bright-yellow neon sign came into view from the back seat of the cab, signaling that Arthur's was less than a block away. That meant he had only a moment to brush off his overly efficient assistant. He gripped his Blackberry extra hard, cursing the day last month when Human Resources had assigned this stickler for details to his staff. "Damn it, Darcy. I don't have time for this. Just process the invoices I gave you."

"But a cash withdrawal of that size should go through Mr. Castle."

"I told you. The contractor has a cash flow emergency. I can't risk his crew walking off the job. I'll make sure my father knows about this on Monday."

"But a hundred thousand dollars. Mr. Castle will have my head."

"Darcy, while I appreciate your proclivity for doing things by the book, this one is on me. You let me worry about my father." His cab came to an abrupt stop a few yards shy of a neon sign big and bright enough to hail the International Space Station. "I gotta go. I'll see you on Monday."

He disconnected the call, hoping he'd done enough to get Lassie off the scent of little lost Timmy. He tossed the cabbie a healthy tip and exited without a word of thanks. He rarely had time for pleasantries, and tonight was no different. He strode past the outdoor seating area. It was closed for the season, but even when open, the area was for amateurs. Inside was the place to be.

Andrew was a regular at the bar; the hostess at the entrance paid little attention when he walked past her. Further in, hundreds of patrons cheered on games and races of all sorts, displayed on large-screen televisions lining each wall. Undoubtedly, dozens of side bets, most likely related to which teams were going to win conference titles in the run-up to March Madness, were resting on what was playing out on the TV screens, but that wasn't where the real action lay. That took place in an area nestled between the bar and the billiards room. A regular heavy hitter, Andrew expected to breeze past the unofficial bouncers guarding the space. Instead, he was greeted with a stiff arm.

"Whoa." Andrew stopped in his tracks, waiting for the six-foot-six blob of muscle and a few too many pizzas to lower the virtual crossing-arm. He'd encountered this goon dozens of times, but he'd never before felt threatened by him. "I'm here to see Victor."

"Unless you have his money, Victor doesn't want to see you." Rolls of fat popped over the collar of the white shirt beneath the bouncer's ill-fitting dark suit.

Andrew tapped his breast suit pocket with a confident flair. "I have it."

The thick-as-a-house guard signaled over his shoulder toward Arthur's Alley's inner sanctum with a nod—Andrew's cue to step inside. The man's steely eyes followed Andrew as he passed, sending the loud and clear message that a double-cross could be hazardous to his health.

Andrew's eyes took several seconds to adjust to the dimly lit private party room. Wall Street types, trust fund babies, and their dates filled a dozen curved red leather couches fronted by low cocktail tables. He locked his sights on the man who had fed his living-on-the-edge cravings for the past year. To the world, Victor Padula presented himself as a New York businessman with perfectly trimmed black hair, manicured nails, a tailored suit, and, despite his street roots, no splashy bling. In reality, he was bookie to Manhattan's elite. Until tonight, he had given Andrew the impression he was his favorite client.

Andrew approached the booth of power, humbler than in his previous meetings with Victor. Tension sitting heavy in the back of his throat, he forewent his usual open-arm greeting and bright smile, choosing to stand silent at the table's edge. He waited for Victor to finish his conversation with two female tablemates and a man whom Andrew assumed was a VIP client like himself.

Victor sipped from the tumbler that had been resting on the table. He gave it a good swirl before staring Andrew in the eye with the intensity of a tiger sizing up its prey. "You're late."

Andrew lightly patted his breast pocket, this time with modesty. "I have what you asked for." Victor whispered left and right to his tablemates, who rose and left in unison. A jutting of his chin signaled Andrew to take a seat on the curved couch.

Andrew slid two unsealed two-inch-thick letter-sized envelopes across the table. "This should settle my tab."

After inspecting the contents, Victor snapped his fingers and handed the envelopes to a second goon flanking the back of the curved couch. His icy stare sent chills down Andrew's spine. "You're two weeks late. Broken bones have been inflicted for less."

"I'm sorry about that, but it couldn't be helped." Victor's tough talk never used to bother Andrew. The rumors of what happened to clients who failed to pay up had been enough motivation to keep him in line. Enough so that he had drained his trust fund and mortgaged the loft his father gifted him for earning a Yale MBA before resorting to siphoning company funds. Despite how his father treated him, betraying him hadn't come easy. Andrew couldn't help it, though. One sure bet would put him back on the plus side.

"You know what your problem is?" Victor paused at Andrew's cautious headshake. "You're a trust-fund baby who thinks he can buy his way out of trouble. No one crosses Victor Padula."

Andrew had spent a decade dealing with small-time bookies, each of whom had demanded prompt payment. It took months to find someone who could accommodate his growing paycheck, along with his growing need. It took even longer to cultivate a level of trust with Victor that allowed him to establish a tab. That had been his downfall. He'd let himself get in deep. Before this, deceit had never been in his wheelhouse. He'd discovered, though, that desperation made it easy for him to bend his morals into an unrecognizable mess.

"You never want me to come looking for you," Victor said. "It won't end well."

"I always pay my bill." A lump reemerged in Andrew's throat. He needed to get a handle on his gambling, of that he was sure, but first...

"Now that we're square, I'd like to put twenty large on the Knicks."

* * *

Five Days Later

Had Harley declared a promotion or a birthday as the occasion for tonight's celebration of her flavor of the week? Frankly, it didn't matter to Alex because she hadn't come for the jubilee. Since her father privately announced that he could no longer hide his Parkinson's symptoms and would retire this summer, Alex had become more focused on his needs—and on winning the competition he had kicked off between her and Andrew. She had had neither the time nor the inclination for clubbing. Within months, William would select one of them to take his place as the Chief Executive Officer and the other as the Chief Financial Officer of Castle Resorts. She was determined to fill his shoes.

It was the choice of venue that swayed her decision when Harley begged her to come. The Pegu Club had been added to her bucket list of Greenwich Village cocktail cathedrals following its remodel. This would be one rare, well-spent hour away from work.

From the moment Alex stepped over the threshold, the place didn't disappoint. An updated blend of luxury and southeast Asian flair struck the right balance between opulence and theme. Maybe an hour wouldn't be enough. A proper exploration might require two. After checking her coat in at the front, she navigated the thick Tuesday night crowd, zipping through a half-dozen roughly hewn wood tables. Smooth jazz music played in the background.

"Ms. Castle."

Alex stopped in mid-stride and turned toward the familiar male voice that had come from a table she'd passed a moment earlier. She should've recognized her assistant's metrosexual hairstyle, razored on the sides with frosted short tips gelled into spikes on the top, but seeing him out of his signature office three-piece had thrown her off. "Robbie. It's good seeing you out having fun."

Robbie gestured to his immediate left. "Ms. Castle, I'd like you to meet Darcy. She works at the Times Square Resort."

"Of course. I never forget a face. You work for my brother, right?" Alex shook her hand. She'd seen Darcy several times on her walkthroughs of the resort back offices. Though Alex and Robbie never discussed his personal life, she sensed he and Darcy had been a thing for a while. She seemed perfect for him—around the same age in her early twenties, hip, cute, and the same brown hair.

"Yes, Ms. Castle. It's a pleasure." Darcy's timid voice didn't match her external vibe of confidence.

"Despite what Robbie might tell you, I promise I don't bite."

"Um." Darcy's eyes widened to the size of hockey pucks.

The smooth way Robbie placed an arm across the back of Darcy's chair confirmed this wasn't their first date. "Don't listen to her. She bites my head off daily."

"We'll discuss your talking out of school tomorrow." Alex playfully waved a finger at Robbie before softening her expression. "You two enjoy your evening."

Alex continued her trek to the back of the restaurant. Near the far end of the bar, she spotted a distinctively dark, curly mid-length mane, the bearer of which was gently caressing a creamy, mini-skirted thigh. Her gaze focused on that hand, lingering beyond what would've qualified as innocent gawking. It bordered on envy. She envied how Harley hid none of herself from the world. Why would she? The lesbian sweet sixteen party Abby had hosted for her had made Harley the most out and proud socialite on the island.

Alex raised her gaze to eye level, meeting Harley's grin with one of her own. *A redhead? I thought you were dating a blonde.* Harley kissed the woman she'd been stroking like a pet Siamese. The kiss was the kind that said one of them would make the walk-of-shame not long after daybreak.

Harley joined Alex. Her grin took on the look of satisfaction. "Darling, you're late."

"Couldn't be helped." Alex kissed her on both cheeks. "With that late winter storm blanketing northern Japan, their supply chain is a mess. I had to nail down a different liquor distributor for the Tokyo resort."

"Sweet Alex, do you ever not work?" At Alex's hard "no," Harley gestured toward the opposite end of the bar. "Let's congratulate the birthday girl. Then we can get you a drink."

"Wait." Alex grabbed Harley by the arm before she could escape the inquisition. She nodded in the other direction. "The redhead isn't your girlfriend-slash-birthday girl?"

Harley glanced over her shoulder. "Who? Jordi? I have no idea if today is her birthday, but she's in the running in terms of girlfriend," she said with an exaggerated wink.

"Harley, do you ever stop playing the field?"

"Does the sun stop rising in the morning?" Harley placed a hand on Alex's forearm. "So many beautiful women. So few days to explore them."

"Maybe if you considered a woman for what's between her ears and not her legs, you might not feel the need to change them out more often than you do your razor blades."

Harley dramatically clutched her chest. "The women I date are not disposable."

"Really? You're ready to trade in a blonde for a redhead and on her birthday of all days." As far back as Alex could remember, no one woman could satisfy her best friend. She suspected Harley's philandering was a defense mechanism. Having been burned three times, she could never be sure if a woman loved her or her money, so she ended things before it became an issue.

"Perhaps you're right." Harley pursed her lips, producing her trademark pout. "Doing this on her birthday *is* poor form. Would you like a shot at the redhead?"

Alex scanned Jordi from head to toe. Redheads weren't typically on her radar, but ever since the corporate competition between her and Andrew had kicked into high gear, her already less-than-stellar sex life had taken a back seat. The long hours spent putting out one fire after another at their international resorts had her tight as a spring. Unwinding between a pair of creamy legs for a few hours had the potential of sustaining her for another month.

"The suggestion is appealing, but Robbie is here."

"I wish you'd muster the courage to stop considering William's needs over your own." Harley touched Alex's arm until their eyes met.

"You know I made a promise. Keep my private life out of the rags, and he'd overlook my sexuality."

"He ignores his part of the deal, dear. You're a nearly thirty-three-year-old lesbian who he is still trying to set up with rich, male suitors. When are you going to call enough enough?"

Alex let out a heavy sigh. If she were honest, she'd say that she'd had enough years ago. But she loved him and the legacy he'd built from the ground up, one her mother had helped expand before she died. She wanted to be the one to take up the mantle of what they'd created.

"He's depended on me since Syd married John and went off to make wine in Napa."

"It's not like he doesn't have another heir to take over the reins of Castle Resorts."

"I love my brother dearly. I've looked out for him since we were kids. But would you trust Andrew as CEO?"

Harley rolled her eyes. "You have a point. He has a head for numbers but not for people. Maybe he should have majored in humanities and not economics like you did. Then again, his wild streak by no means makes him CEO material. When will this silly competition be over, so William can finally stop treating you two like chess pieces? I need my best friend back."

"Hopefully, by summer."

"That's months away. Who's winning?"

"I'm happy to report the San Francisco renovations are on schedule and under budget, and a new marketing strategy I'm piecing together should cover the costs in three years."

"And Times Square?"

Alex snickered. "Andrew has some great marketing ideas, but my sources tell me he is woefully over budget."

"Good. Maybe then William will finally realize you're the only one qualified to take over." Harley gestured toward the bar. "Now, how about Jordi?"

Alex returned her stare to the redhead, who already had her juices flowing. A little more unwinding couldn't hurt. "Make the introductions." She touched Harley's arm. "But be discreet."

"I've been your wing-woman for years. Discreet is my middle name."

CHAPTER FOUR

Alex sat at her desk inside her sleek office suite at Castle Resorts Headquarters, unable to remember when she had last felt more focused. Even the never-ending refurbishing in the building's lobby and stairwells didn't bother her this morning. Last night's excursion with the redhead had gone better than expected, erasing months of built-up tension. She made a mental note to never again let this competition between her and Andrew deprive her of releases like those she had enjoyed overnight.

Following a short, annoying buzz from the intercom on her desk phone, a confident, male voice announced, "Ms. Castle, you have a call on line one."

Alex pressed the intercom button with a little extra zest. "Who is it?"

"Um." Robbie's collected tone wavered, a sure sign he was moments away from complicating the first worry-free day she'd had in months. "She wouldn't say, but she mentioned it was an urgent personal matter."

Alex sighed. "Fine, I'll take it." After Robbie disconnected, she pressed line one. "Alex Castle."

"Hello, Alex." The voice was playful and had a quality that Alex thought she should've recognized but didn't.

"I'm sorry. Who's calling?"

"I'm hurt, Alex. There was a time when you'd recognize my voice in an instant."

The sultry tenor clicked then. That voice used to have her tongue-tied, throbbing with a single syllable and blowing off midterms, workouts, and weekend trips home with a single word. But not anymore.

"Kelly." Her voice was flat.

"You remembered. I'm flattered."

How could Alex forget? Kelly was the only one she'd let close enough to break her heart, a painful ordeal she never wanted to repeat. "What do you want, Kelly?"

"My dear Alex, you're still hurt."

"Hurt? No. Indifferent? Yes."

"You cut me to the quick. I'm so sorry for how I ended things. Trust me when I say that I still care for you very much."

Alex laughed. "Breaking up with me over the phone to chase a bigger trust fund showed me your true colors. I wouldn't trust you to tie my shoelaces."

"Come now. As much as I enjoyed our hot-as-hell affair, you and I both know that you would never have gone public. Not as long as the great William Castle was still breathing."

"So at the earliest opportunity you run after the first swinging dick with an extra zero in his bank account."

"It wasn't only about the money. Douglas Pruitt wasn't ashamed of our relationship."

"I'm sure the fact that he was one of the Boston Pruitts didn't hurt. But you overshot there, didn't you? I read on Page Six back then that your engagement was called off within months."

"As soon as Mother Pruitt realized I came from the wrong side of the tracks, she put the kibosh on the engagement." Not surprisingly, Kelly's voice didn't contain the distinct pain of heartbreak. It had the distasteful sound of someone discussing a missed business opportunity.

Alex harrumphed, loud and clear. "Karma is a bitch. Why did you call, Kelly?"

"Can't a girl catch up with an old friend?"

"We're not friends. Now, if you don't mind, I really have to go."

"Please, Alex, I wouldn't have called if it wasn't important."

"What do you want?"

"I read the article in the *Financial Times* about Castle Resorts' expansion. Congratulations."

"Spit it out, Kelly."

"I need a job."

"There's no way in hell I'm giving you a job."

"Please, give me a chance, Alex. I'm sorry about how I left things with you. My scholarship ran out, and I'd racked up a pile of student debt. You know the old saying, 'If you aren't born with money, you either make it or you marry it.' I tried to take the easy way out."

Alex had gotten over feeling hurt and broken because of Kelly a long time ago, but forgetting didn't mean forgiving. "And what? I'm supposed to feel sorry for you?"

"Think of this as a 'do-over.' It's not like I'm not qualified. I was smart enough to get into Yale." *But not smart enough to stay in*, Alex thought. "And I have a bachelor's degree in business. I just need to get my foot in the door to prove my worth. And who knows, maybe this could rekindle our friendship."

"Are you nuts? I'm not a masochist."

"You might want to reconsider."

"Is that right?" Alex suspected either backstabbing or a scam was on the horizon.

"If you want to keep your father happy, you will."

"What are you inferring?"

"I don't think you want our lesbian college fling becoming the lead story in the *Post*. Do you?" Kelly had honeyed her last two words, but Alex wasn't buying it. Nothing about Kelly Thatcher was sweet.

"I can't believe I once loved you."

"I'm desperate, Alex."

"How much will it take to be rid of you?" Money was the only language Kelly understood.

"One."

"Thousand?"

"Million."

"You *are* nuts."

"A girl has to survive. It's your choice, Alex. A job or one million dollars, or proof of our often-wild fling hits the checkout stands. I really would like the opportunity to work with you, but it appears money and our photo collection from back in the day will have to sustain me."

"You kept those?"

"I'm a girl with needs. You used to fulfill them so well, but I'll have to settle for Plan B. Think about it, Alex. I'll give you one week. Expect my call."

Alex slammed the phone down. Her father would never forgive her for embarrassing the family, as he would label it. The company she loved would end up in the hands of her brother, a boy who had yet to outgrow his rebellious streak.

Her intercom buzzed again, the grating sound irritating her more than before. "Ms. Castle, do you have time to take a short meeting?"

She'd prefer to hear nails raking across a chalkboard than accommodate an unscheduled intrusion at this point. Her world was about to crash around her, and she needed time to think about how to cut Kelly off at the knees before she ruined her not-so-ideal life. "Can this wait, Robbie? I'm in the middle of something."

"Normally, I wouldn't press, but I think you'll want to take this meeting, Ms. Castle." Robbie had been Alex's personal assistant for the last three years, and his judgment as a gatekeeper had proven impeccable. His pressing the issue meant this meeting would likely be worth her time.

"All right, you win. Send them in."

Moments later, Robbie appeared in the doorway, which was alarming. Unless a visitor was a VIP, Alex never required Robbie to show them in. Behind him was Darcy, who was clutching a manilla folder to her chest as if it were a shield. Having seen her a handful of times at Andrew's office and last night at the Pegu Club, Alex had little basis on which to form an opinion, but the woman looked rattled.

"Come in, Darcy." Robbie ushered her in with haste and closed the door behind them.

"What's going on, Robbie?" Alex asked.

He tugged Darcy toward the front of Alex's sleek desk. "It'll be fine, Darcy. You can trust Ms. Castle. She'll sort this out."

If Darcy was nervous walking in, her trembling hands suggested downright panic the moment she moved forward. Alex rounded her desk and steered the shaky woman toward the nearby white leather couch and matching armchair. Once seated, Alex used a calm, reassuring tone. "Whatever this is, you won't be in any trouble. Robbie is my right hand. If he thinks this is important, I'm sure I will too."

Darcy lowered the folder she'd been gripping, placing it on a coffee table that matched Alex's desk, a combination of dark rich wood accented by polished steel. "As you know, Ms. Castle"—Darcy's voice was shaky—"I took over as young Mr. Castle's personal assistant last month."

"A well-deserved promotion. I'm told you proved your worth in Logistics. Mr. Barlow was sorry to see you go."

"Thank you, Ms. Castle. I hate to bring this up, but I can't account for the irregularities."

"What irregularities?"

Darcy spread out the papers that had been hidden inside the folder. "I discovered several expense reports that didn't match the originals submitted by the contractors at the Times Square hotel."

Alex briefly studied the documents. "Have you brought this up with my brother?"

"I did, but he didn't seem concerned, which troubled me. I'm no accounting expert and wasn't sure what I was looking at, but things weren't adding up. So I did a little digging, going back several months." Darcy pulled out another set of papers. "These are expense reports for maintenance and supplies from two different companies for the same month. We never do business with more than one company for those items at a time, and it seemed very odd."

Alex rubbed her chin, trying desperately to make sense of what Darcy was saying. "As part of the remodeling, we had to change several vendors. There could be some overlap."

"I concur, but for six months?"

"Six months? That can't be."

"That's what I thought. Normally, I would forward my findings to Accounting, but after last week's significant cash withdrawal without prior authorization, I didn't know what to think."

A pit formed in Alex's stomach as a vague suspicion took shape. She didn't want to believe her brother capable of this kind of dishonesty, but the evidence was mounting. "How much?"

"One hundred thousand."

Alex drew in a sharp breath. Amounts that large required special checks and authorizations to ensure accountability. Alex hated to think it, but she feared Andrew had finally gotten in over his head with his gambling. "Thank you, Darcy. It took some courage to bring this to my attention. Trust me, I'll sort this out."

Alex redirected her attention. "Robbie, I need you to pull every document associated with Times Square financials for the past year. Oh, and book me a flight to Sacramento for tomorrow."

"You got it, Ms. Castle." Robbie covered Darcy's hands with his own. "See? I told you everything would be all right."

After Robbie and Darcy left, Alex stood at the panoramic window, staring at the Manhattan jungle below. Confused, alarmed, and numb, she was reeling from the sucker punches she'd received—a blackmail scheme that threatened to position her brother, a gambler and probable embezzler, to take over the reins of the company she loved. Equally disappointing to her was the fact that though she was supposed to watch out for her twin, she'd obviously failed him.

Alex needed to regroup this weekend. She needed her sister and the help that only she could provide.

CHAPTER FIVE

Napa, California

Ashamed to admit she hadn't been down this narrow, private road in almost two years, Alex coasted her rented SUV to a stop a few feet short of the eight-foot-tall dual-paneled gate. Flanked by two finely crafted stone-faced pillars, the gate posed a formidable barrier between the Barnette Winery and the rest of the world. She chided herself for needing to glance at her cell phone to confirm the security code before entering it into the keypad. If she were a good sister, she should've set that code to memory from frequent visits. It would not be something she had to ask for and jot down. She had plenty of reasons she hadn't used it in years, all of them connected to her father and the business. None of her dysfunctional family dynamics added up to an acceptable excuse, however.

She pulled through the gate, keeping her window and speed down to take in the unique blend of coastal and valley smells. Now she knew why her sister loved it here—no winters or summers, only spring or fall year-round. On both sides of the meandering asphalt, red-hued manzanita bushes contrasted brightly against well-aged live oak trees and other vegetation, painting a majestic sunset landscape. After the first bend, the scene changed to one of row after row of Napa Valley's finest Cabernet Sauvignon grapevines beginning to bud. Only the sound of tires rolling over the occasional twig or pebble broke the serenity of the quaint, isolated vineyard.

This was exactly what Alex needed, a calm place far away from her controlling father, a place where she could enlist her sister's help. Having been out from under William's thumb for three years now meant Syd could assist her, with their father none the wiser.

Once the road surface changed from asphalt to concrete, it widened comfortably to the width of two to three cars. If memory served, the main house was one curve in the road away. Alex pulled into the circular turnout used for guest parking and walked toward the main house. Her guilty conscience eased when the front yard appeared as she remembered. A single large oak tree still sat in the center of a perfectly manicured lawn outlined by colorful annuals.

The moment she turned up the walkway leading to the front door, a thundering, familiar voice boomed from the covered patio. "Baby sis."

When she approached, Alex matched her sister's broad smile and open arms. "Syd, you're a sight for sore eyes." Syd's long, tight hug meant she had already forgiven Alex's lengthy absence, a gift she didn't deserve. When she pulled back, Alex focused on Syd's muscular arms, the white tank top straps contrasting with her tanned, firm skin. Syd was eleven years older, but she looked as young as Alex and was much prettier, she thought. "Working in the vineyard has transformed you into a chiseled, bronze goddess."

"I'm in the best shape of my life." Syd rubbed Alex's arms, the type of tender touch that said she'd missed her more than she'd ever let on. She gestured toward a set of cushioned wicker chairs. "First, how's Father? Has he gotten worse since my visit over the holidays?"

Alex gave her a bleak nod. "He's slowing down. I hate to say this, but I think his retirement is well-timed."

"That's what I thought. He'd never willingly walk away from Castle Resorts." Syd patted her on the knee. "Enough about him. It's been too long since you've been here."

"I'm the worst sister in the world. First, I miss your wedding because of a damned flight delay from Tokyo. Then I don't visit for two years while you come out every summer and Christmas." Alex took a seat close to her sister on the wicker loveseat but dared not lean back into its comfort. If she did, the eight hours she'd spent in her flight from LaGuardia would win.

"Nonsense. It's not as if I gave you a lot of notice for our wedding. Plus, I know how Father has become." Syd patted Alex's knee, conveying a mutual understanding of William's commanding character. He was a force of nature and had increasingly demanded nothing less than full measure from his children. As far as Alex could tell, that was a big part of Syd's leaving. "I'm sure ever since he privately announced his retirement and started this successor rivalry, he's had you and Andrew jumping through hoops to test your mettle."

Unfortunately, William's hoops were the least of her problems. Despite her brother's flaws, which were plentiful and more deep-rooted than she had previously thought, she still loved him. The last thing she wanted was for Andrew to give their father one more reason to be disappointed in him or, worse, to end up in prison. But after yesterday's circus, she was more convinced she needed to craft a plan to save both the company and her misguided twin.

She'd take that up with Syd later. For the moment, she settled for simply saying, "The competition has been brutal with the long hours, but not as draining as that flight."

"You look tired. How about we get you settled in, so you can take a nap?"

"That sounds heavenly. Then we need to talk."

Syd furrowed her brow, the lines that came with being eleven years Alex's senior deepening. "You sounded worried over the phone."

"I am, and I need your help."

"This must be serious if you'd fly three thousand miles just to get my advice."

"It is, but I'm too exhausted to think right now."

When Alex's head hit the pillow, she had had no intention of sleeping the evening away. Still, the next time she opened her eyes, she realized she'd done precisely that. The window revealed morning light filtered by coastal fog. If not for a queasiness brought on by hunger pangs, it would've been a perfect start to the day. Mornings at the Barnette Winery weren't anything like those in Alex's West Village neighborhood. They were much better. There were no wailing sirens, no parade of honking horns, only the moist Napa Valley air mixing with the quiet like a Sunday mimosa, chilly and relaxing.

If she remembered correctly from two years ago, Syd and John had likely been up for hours. By now, they'd be working in fields where the fog hung like a blanket for hours following sunrise, protecting the delicate vines from the outside world. She'd already wasted a good ten hours by her estimate, and the dilemma that had brought her here wouldn't solve itself. She needed coffee, food, and her sister, in that order.

Alex rolled out of bed, put on the white cotton robe Syd had left in the guest bath, and went in search of a strong cup of coffee to knock out the cobwebs of jet travel. She strolled into the Tuscan kitchen, warm and inviting for both cooking and conversation. Windows from the neighboring breakfast area bathed the room in warm light, highlighting a plate of store-bought pastries in the center of the granite countertop island. Syd had left Alex's favorite peach jam there and a handwritten note that made her feel her night as Sleeping Beauty wasn't a wasted exercise.

After filling a mug from the countertop coffeemaker, she helped herself to several doughy sweets, double the amount she typically allowed herself, to make up for the missed dinner. She then headed to the true heart of the home, the covered back patio. This was the space where everything meaningful happened. Multiple seating and dining areas with big screens, couches, and tables flanked a stone cooking area. A grill and an oven were on one side, and a wood-burning floor-to-ceiling stone fireplace was on another.

Alex sat in a west-facing chair, the patio pillars perfectly framing a breathtaking view of the rolling vineyard hills and lush green coastal mountains. In record time, she devoured the pastries and then let herself sink into the plush cushion, eyes closed, listening to the singsong of the nearby birds. Their soft, rhythmic chirping cleared her head of all thoughts Kelly and Andrew, and for the first time since she left New York, she didn't feel the walls closing in on her. Coming here was the right decision. With the help of her sister, she'd devise a plan.

Footsteps, crunching against the gravel path, broke the tranquility. Syd's voice sang out, outstripping the songbirds. "Good morning, sleepyhead."

Alex pried her eyes open. "Sleepyhead? It's barely past sunrise."

"Around here, we get up before the birds." Syd removed her well-worn work gloves, one at a time. She did her best to tame her mussed chin-length brown hair and swiped at the beads of sweat glistening on her forehead. "Wine doesn't make itself."

"Sit with me." Alex gestured to the matching patio chair to her right.

Syd walked to the outdoor kitchen and retrieved a cold water bottle from the refrigerator before plopping down. She inspected the contents of Alex's mug and plate, both of which were empty. "It looks like someone was hungry after missing dinner."

"Sorry about that. I didn't realize how tired I was until I crawled into bed." Alex fixed her gaze on the beautiful mountain vista. The fog had thinned, as had the gloom that had followed her on the plane. "This place is so beautiful. It's nothing like Manhattan."

Syd took an ample swig of water and waited until Alex returned her gaze to the mountains to say, "And it doesn't have Father."

"As horrible as it sounds, I'm starting to consider that as a good thing."

"Leaving was the best decision of my life. I needed to get away from his toxicity."

"I know you did. Still, I cried for days after you left." Alex turned her gaze toward the woman who had been more role model than a sister for as far back as she could remember. She couldn't blame Syd for leaving. In their father's eyes, a vintner would never be good enough for his oldest child, but Syd didn't let that stop her. "Sometimes, I wish I had your courage."

"I'm about to break my rule and be a little judgy." Syd shifted to face Alex eye to eye. "You date women in secret to keep up appearances for Father's sake. He's not worth putting your life on hold. You deserve to be with someone you love, and that will never happen with a series of one-night stands."

"Until he retires and Castle Resorts is in good hands, I can't chance it. Andrew—" Alex paused when gravel crunched again beneath approaching feet.

"There's my beautiful wife." John appeared from the gravel pathway, entering the seating area beneath the patio cover. His neatly trimmed salt-and-pepper hair and sun-soaked skin were exactly as Alex remembered. He'd put on about ten pounds since she last saw him, though. His fifties were catching up with him. "Morning, Alex. Ready for some manual labor? We have to finish checking the ties on the north end today and could use an extra pair of hands if you're up to it."

"Now, John. She's our guest. Besides, we just started talking." Syd glanced at Alex, her eyebrows arched high. That meant one thing—she wanted to hear more.

"The rest can wait until later." Alex slapped her knees and stood. A discussion about their brother's exploits and Kelly's blackmail would have to wait until she and Syd were alone. "How about I get dressed so we can get to work on those vines?"

Six hours later, any illusions Alex may have had that running two miles three times a week equated to being in top shape were crushed like the grapes fermenting in the Barnette Vineyard barrels. Working the day away in the north field with a small seasonal crew had her arms feeling like rubber. *What the hell was I thinking?*

It was nearly two o'clock when Alex made her way into the main house through the mudroom. She struggled to remove her dirty shoes, while John and Syd had taken theirs off with ease and were already washing up at the twin sinks. "No wonder your arms and shoulders are so well defined, Syd. I never knew growing grapes was such hard work. I'm exhausted."

John wiped his hands dry, moved behind Syd, and caressed her toned arms. "And how beautiful they are. I'll go shower and get the grill going. Chicken or pork for supper?"

Syd looked back over her shoulder, answering her husband with a smile. "I already marinated the pork loin in the oyster sauce you like so much. Can we eat around four?"

"Yum, you do love me." John gave Syd a quick kiss. "Four it is." As Alex lumbered to the unoccupied sink, he said, "I'd be happy to put you to work, Alex, and beef up those skinny runner's arms of yours."

Alex opened the faucet to wash her mud-caked hands. "Thanks, but I think I'll stay in my lane with the hotel business. If today was an accurate barometer, Syd might be the only Castle cut out for the wine business."

"We'll make a winemaker out of you yet." John teasingly wagged a finger at Alex before giving Syd a frisky swat on the butt. "All right, ladies, I'm outta here." He strolled down the hallway leading to the master suite with Syd eyeing his backside until he disappeared around the corner.

Envy came to mind. Alex wanted the type of lively play Syd and John shared with a life partner of her own, but her self-imposed residence in the closet put that possibility out of reach. She'd never find that level of happiness with a string of clandestine fuck buddies and one-night stands. "I like John. He's the perfect husband."

"He's far from perfect, but he's perfect for me." Syd grabbed the other hand towel and mischievously flicked Alex on the butt. "Now, let's get those chicken wings of yours all cleaned up and go fix dinner."

Alex dried her hands before pursing her lips and flexing and inspecting each arm. "I do not have chicken wings."

Two hours later, following supper, Alex curled up in the same comfortable patio lounge chair she had sat in this morning, but this time with a glass of Barnette cabernet, to wait for her sister. The sun had begun its slow retreat, barely creeping above the coastal mountains to the west, painting a pleasing mix of purple, blue, and orange on the horizon. A few more sips of wine warmed her cheeks against the rapidly cooling air. A few feet to her left, the cozy fire John had built in the outdoor fireplace before he went inside warmed the rest of her.

Alex studied the flames as they danced in and out of the charred oak logs. Mimicking her life, they hid behind barriers for short periods and reappeared fully energized to face the world. *Four more months*, she thought. All she had to do was hold out four more months, possibly fewer, and she could stop hiding behind walls. She sighed. If she didn't deal with Kelly first, those four months wouldn't matter. Her father, in his state, would send her packing, and Andrew would assume the reins of Castle Resorts.

The sliding door sounded as it skimmed across the bottom rail. Syd appeared at Alex's feet. "I'll trade you that second glass of wine for this birthday present."

"That sounds like an even trade, but my birthday isn't for two months." Alex accepted a beautifully wrapped box the size of a soccer ball before handing Syd the glass she'd poured for her minutes earlier. "Thanks, Syd. I'll open it up on my birthday."

"Oh, no, you don't." Syd sat sideways on the neighboring lounge chair, facing Alex. "This might be my only chance to see you before your birthday. I want to see the look on your face when you open it."

"You have me curious now." Alex shifted on the lounger, carefully unwrapped the box, and discovered an antique leather camera case. She lifted the case out and read the etched letters on the front. It read *Leica*. Alex's heart fluttered with anticipation. She lovingly grazed her fingertips over the letters before unsnapping and removing the top flap. When she did, she exposed a mint-condition Leica M3 Double Stroke 35mm camera. She fought to hold back the tears pooling in her eyes. It was the spitting image of her mother's old Leica, the one she had learned photography on as a teenager. The same one she had lost during a move from Yale.

"It's not your mother's 1957, but I found a 1965 model. The salesman told me it has the same features and works virtually the same." Syd sipped on her wine.

"It's beautiful, Syd." Tears fell, one after another, as Alex examined the camera and played with the settings. Not since losing her mother's Leica had she picked up a film camera. She had kicked herself for months, unable to forgive herself for misplacing her mother's prized possession. Sure, she still had her mother's photographs, but she didn't feel as connected to them as she had to that Leica. Once she'd lost it, she realized that she'd never again look through the same viewfinder, adjust the very lens, nor depress the actual shutter her mother had. She couldn't bring herself to use another, opting for digital. But this was so similar, Alex could feel her mother's approval.

"I loaded it with a roll of black and white T-Max four-hundred," Syd added.

"You remembered." Alex maneuvered the camera, pointing it toward the rolling vineyard, lit by the intense orange glow of the early evening sun. She hovered her right index finger over the shutter button while using her left hand to adjust the lens to focus on a hilltop on the horizon. It was like reacquainting herself with an old friend.

"I remember how upset you were when you lost your mother's Leica. I've been looking for a replacement for years and finally came across this one. It's not hers, but I hope you'll like it just the same."

"I love it, Syd." Alex returned the camera to its case and placed it on the lounge chair beside her. She reached for her sister's hand and gave it a long, tight squeeze. "This means so much to me. Thank you."

"I'm so glad you like it." After sipping more of her cabernet, Syd asked, "Care to come with me into town? I have to drop off a case of wine at my friend's restaurant."

"Sure. Why not? Maybe I can take a few pictures." Alex retrieved her wine, taking a giant swig and debating how much, if anything, to reveal about their foolish brother. She'd only scratched the surface of his pilfering and had yet to determine when it had started. If she were to upset her sister, she first wanted to have all the facts. News of Andrew's disappointing behavior would have to take a backseat to that of Kelly and her primary threat.

"Syd, before we go, I need to tell you that Kelly Thatcher is blackmailing me. She has pictures of us having sex in college and has threatened to make them public if I don't give her a job or a butt ton of money."

Syd narrowed her eyes like a gunslinger preparing to pull the trigger in a duel. "That little hussy."

"Syd?" Her voice ended in a sharp, surprised uptick. Before she moved away, name-calling hadn't been her sister's trademark; she'd preferred employing razor-like wit.

Syd narrowed her eyes again. "Would you prefer I call her a floozy? How about tramp? Jezebel? Trollop? Or vixen?"

"Will you stop with the synonyms?" Alex let a grin materialize on her lips. "Though, I must say, trollop is my favorite."

"Mine too." Syd offered a wink filled with complicity. "So, what's your plan? How are you going to stuff that trollop back under the rock she crawled out from?"

Alex snickered so hard her wine splashed over the glass's rim. Insults at this point were appropriate and had the added benefit of making her feel good. Making this moment sweeter— Syd's newfound affinity for mudslinging. Alex had John to thank for her sister's refreshing transformation. He had swept Syd off her feet after landing an exclusive wine contract with Castle Resorts and whisked her away from the proper life expected of a Castle. Alex envied Syd's ability to walk away from years of being groomed by their father to take over Castle Resorts. She had forfeited her interest in the business without blinking an eye. No such option was available to Alex. Andrew was the only other heir, and she was not about to put the company she loved in his hands.

"Seriously, what about that trollop?" Syd asked.

"That's why I'm here," Alex said. "I need John's help."

"John? How can he help?"

"I need to fight fire with fire. The last time you two visited, John mentioned his cop cousin moonlighted as a private investigator and did a bang-up job conducting background checks on prospective investors. I need someone we can trust to do some discreet digging."

"Wonderful idea. If anyone can find the dirt on Kelly Thatcher, it's Ethan." Syd offered a confident nod before retrieving her cell phone from the small table between them. "Let's call him."

CHAPTER SIX

Sacramento, California, three days earlier

Triangles of diffused light, one after another, illuminated the gloomy street, speeding by faster and faster in rhythm to the thumping of her bare feet on pavement. Covered by not a stitch of clothing, she should've been shivering from the crisp night air, but she was too numb. Pebbles and broken glass shredded the pads of her feet. It should've slowed her pace, but fear pushed her forward. A painful spasm in her chest made her struggle for air, threatening to break her stride, but she couldn't slow. Not yet. Her life depended on it. If she slowed by even a fraction, the danger would catch up with her.

Hands grabbed her shoulders from behind and gripped her tighter and tighter until they brought her to an abrupt stop. They squeezed out what little air was left in her lungs, forcing a panicked gasp. She opened her mouth but couldn't scream. Thrashed but couldn't break free.

Beep, beep, beep, beep.

The daily morning ruckus snatched Tyler from the terrifying dream she'd endured most nights for the past thirteen years.

She turned toward her nightstand and slammed a hand atop the alarm clock to make that damn thing stop. Annoying or not, being awake was better than being asleep. During the day, she controlled where her thoughts wandered by staying busy. Asleep, her unconscious mind inevitably relived the terror of that horrible night with the regularity of Brady Bunch reruns— always on and in vivid color. Morning meant she was in control and could wash off her nightmare sweats to begin the day of raising two girls.

Tyler rolled out of bed. The other side had gone cold hours earlier when her husband woke for an early stakeout in the gang-ridden Arcade area. The one good thing about the irregularity of a police officer's schedule, something which became even more so after he became a detective, was that it provided a ready-made excuse for their lackluster sex life. Since the rape, she'd become adept at avoiding emotional dialog about either their predicament or its provenance. She learned early on that such discussions picked at a wound that never seemed to heal. Compartmentalizing her emotions became vital. She kept the memory of that dreadful night locked in a box, refusing to recall details beyond what she couldn't control in her dreams. She was in denial, but that was the only way she had found to live the semblance of a normal life.

Her eat-in kitchen provided a big part of that normalcy. As was the case every weekday, she was down first. Which meant she was free to curse their cheap coffeemaker, which was as reliable as the Ford Edsel. It was not filled this morning with a steaming pot of her favorite french roast, the timer having apparently failed to kick in. "Today of all days."

She had an hour to get two daughters off to school—one too young and the other too lazy to cook for herself—and get to the office in time for a momentous day. Years ago, to make her mornings easier, Tyler and her girls had struck a compromise based on the premise that "the cook don't clean." Anyone thirteen or older who did not have a hand in preparing a meal was in charge of cleaning up after said meal. In less than three months, both of her daughters would be old enough and would share the duties. By default, Tyler served as head cook. This morning fried eggs, toast, juice, and sliced bananas would have to suffice.

"Morning, Mom." Twelve-year-old Bree scampered into view. An overloaded backpack slung over one shoulder hid most of the light blue hoodie she was wearing. She served as trivia buff most mornings, opting to share the latest gem learned from watching an old episode of *Full House*. "Did you know that *Charlotte's Web* is Stephanie's favorite book?"

Tyler stopped plating the food to give her daughter her full attention. "I didn't know that. Aren't you reading *Charlotte's Web* in school?"

"I am." Bree swung back her shoulder-length red locks and stood taller. "I think I like the book now."

"Well, that's good news. I'm glad you and Stephanie have something in common."

"Not *Full House* again?" The grumpy greeting meant seventeen-year-old Erin had stayed up late texting or calling friends. Senior-itis had set in before the school year started, and this academically talented young woman had taken a liking to showing her independence.

"Yes, *Full House* again." Bree flicked her gaze upward, a quirk she picked up from her father.

"Come now. I remember another young lady who used to love *Full House*," Tyler said.

"That was until syndication ruined it. One can put up with Uncle Joey for only so long."

"I see your point." For years, Tyler had taken pride in how much she and Erin had in common. Besides the same short stature, straight-as-an-arrow dark blond hair, and athletic body type, they were both book and life smart. Erin's sharp wit, though, was something she had developed all on her own. That trait would carry her far and forever make her mama proud.

After stuffing down her breakfast, Tyler checked the clock on the oven. If she hurried, she could drop Bree off at school, pick up coffee on the way, and still make the first appointment.

She placed her dishes on the counter and reminded Erin, "Please make sure the sink is cleared before heading off to school."

"As if I could forget." Erin's eye roll was born out of repetition. Not one day had passed since she was tall enough to reach the faucet that Tyler hadn't made that request. A dirty sink represented a thing left undone when order and accomplishing simple tasks kept Tyler's demons at bay.

Soon, Tyler's plan of getting to work on time hit a major snag. Acquiring two piping hot tall lattes—no fat, no foam—seemed like a weak reason for nearly being late on the most important day of her professional career. She paused, though, for an extra second at the office door emblazoned with the words "Creative Juices," soaking in its significance. Two years ago, she and her best friend had busted their butts to fulfill her dream of running her own graphics design firm. It happened later than planned due to her dropping out of grad school for nearly a decade. But one of their designs had won a national award late last year, bringing in more work than they could handle. They needed to grow the business. This morning, they would interview and hopefully hire their first apprentice graphic designer.

She took in a deep, satisfied breath. With a laptop satchel slung over a shoulder and those hard-earned hot cardboard coffee cups in hand, she pushed through the door with a hip into the tiny reception area that doubled as their break room and conference room. *We're small but growing*, she reminded herself.

Tyler eyed the woman and the man seated in the guest chairs. *Must be the first of the applicants.* "Good morning, folks. We'll get going as soon as I set up."

Receiving polite nods, Tyler rushed down the short hallway and slipped inside her not-a-thing-out-of-place office—their agreed-upon interview room. "I'm so sorry, Maddie." Tyler did a double take. It had been months since she'd seen her friend done up at the office. Maddie regularly dressed in nice slacks or skirts, but her hair and makeup were an afterthought on most days. "Wow. You look nice."

"Thanks." Maddie primped chestnut hair that she had had freshly cut into a collar-length A-line. She'd finished her fresh look with modest makeup and an aqua cardigan layered over a white silk blouse. "I want our applicants to think we're a professional outfit."

"We *are* professional." Tyler handed Maddie her latte and gave her a reassuring pat on the hand. They'd poured their life's blood into Creative Juices, often referring to it as their baby. Hiring the right person this morning would be the critical first step in watching it grow. "Though my showing up five minutes late for the first interview might make them think otherwise. I'm sorry about that."

"Thanks for calling to alert me." Maddie shook her head. "There's no accounting for idiots milking the last drop of gas out of their tank before filling up."

"If those college guys hadn't pushed that damn Beetle out of the drive-thru, I'd still be stuck in line." Before Tyler sat next to Maddie at her desk, which was doubling today as their makeshift interview table, she gazed at the framed photo on the wall behind it. Christmas at the Falling household was always magical, even after her daughters outgrew Santa. Each year, the most recent photo of the family sitting in front of their lit tree made it to the wall behind her desk so it was the first thing she saw every time she walked in. They were the reason she worked so hard.

Tyler placed her purse on the floor near her feet, shook off the guilt she felt from arriving late, and focused on the objective of the day—helping their baby grow. "I really appreciate you taking the lead on fielding résumés and scheduling these interviews, Maddie. Between work, Bree's softball practices, and keeping Erin sane until she hears about her college applications, I'm slammed for time. I haven't even had time to review the résumés you emailed me." Expanding their staff couldn't come quick enough.

"I'm glad to do it." Maddie gave her a wink. Without complaint, she'd taken on the lion's share of the managerial duties in recent weeks to lighten Tyler's load. They'd met only three years ago at an elementary school event when Bree and Maddie's son were in the same class, but they acted more like lifelong friends. So much so that Maddie, who was in grad school for website design, had inspired Tyler to return to school for graphic arts. Tyler couldn't have chosen a better business partner.

The next few hours proved fruitful, with one standout candidate so far. Tyler was more than confident they'd make an offer to someone by the end of the day. At the next break, she checked the day's growing "to-do" list on her desktop computer. She had to finish the logo and website design for Capitol Landscaping—*they're going to love the leaves as the call buttons*. She had to drop her tax returns at the post office by four, and she had to buy Bree a pair of socks for her first softball game next week. *Dinner? Did I take the chicken out this morning?*

"I'm really looking forward to this last guy," Maddie said. "On paper, he's the best qualified. He has a graduate degree in graphic arts like you and worked in his family's graphics business until his parents sold it last month." Maddie pushed her chair back and stepped toward the office door. "I'll escort him back."

Tyler responded with a non-committal "Uh-huh" while she scanned the subject lines of her unopened emails. Moments later, faint voices from the hallway, Maddie and a man's, grew stronger, prompting Tyler to wrap up her administrative housekeeping. When their chatter became clear, Tyler looked up. In an instant, every muscle turned rigid. A predator had her in his crosshairs. Fight or flight? He stood between her and the single avenue of escape, limiting her options.

He looked nothing like he had the last time she saw him. The trim torso, sharply tailored dark blue business suit, and "high and tight" haircut with a touch of dark red curls on top made him appear all grown up. That, to Tyler, made him even more threatening.

On instinct, she sprang from her chair and sought the safety of the furthest corner. How did he find her? They said she'd never see him again, but he was now within striking distance. They lied. Heat filled her chest and cheeks as her rage grew. Her hands trembled, stress building like a pressure cooker about to lose its seal. One motion in her direction, one noise to break the dead silence, and she'd blow.

"Tyler?" Maddie's voice barely registered.

The image of him pawing at her clothing hit her like a tidal wave. The memory of fleeing naked in the night—terrified, bloodied, and numb—pummeled her until she couldn't breathe. She crossed her arms and pressed them high across her chest, forming a protective shield. "Get out! Get out! Get out!"

"I didn't know, Tyler." He raised a hand in a failed, calming motion.

"Get the fuck out!" She raised her voice high enough to rattle the rafters. The strain left her heart pounding wildly out of control.

"Okay." He raised his hands in surrender.

"Out!" Tyler balled her hands into fists and snorted like a dragon preparing to blast an enemy with a wall of fire. She wouldn't let him win again. Wouldn't let him beat her into a bloody mess. Wouldn't let him take what he wanted by force, leaving her broken for years.

"What in the hell is going on?" Maddie closed the distance, positioning herself between Tyler and the threat. Her eyes searched Tyler's with a mix of concern and confusion. "Are you okay?"

Tyler was far from all right. This animal had done unspeakable things to her thirteen years earlier, irrevocable damage that had been seared into her trembling bones. But she couldn't voice the very thing she'd consciously avoided facing for years. Maddie gently gripped Tyler's upper arms, sending the message she wouldn't let him hurt her, but she was thirteen years too late.

"Tyler, I'm going to send him away. Okay?"

Tyler offered a slow, uncertain nod—the best she could muster.

Maddie turned toward Tyler's worst nightmare. "I don't know what happened between you two, but if you ever come back, I'm calling the police." Once he left, she locked the door and returned to Tyler, worry etched on her face. "Can I get you some water?"

Tyler shivered, her quivering head her only response. Her skin crawled at the thought of still being trapped. She needed her safe place. She frantically shoved her things inside her purse and stepped toward the door, but Maddie grabbed her arm.

"I have to go."

"Not until you tell me what's going on."

"I can't stay here." Tyler threw off her grip before snatching her purse and clutching it to her chest. She stepped forward again, but Maddie beat her to the door.

"Talk to me, Tyler. What did he do to you?"

Tears burned Tyler's eyes. The truth gripped her by the throat. She hadn't uttered the three words since her husband held her hand in the emergency room that night. She'd locked them away and buried them so deep that no one would ever find them. Today, though, the ugly past had caught up with her, forcing her to repeat them.

"He raped me."

* * *

Tyler needed the singsong of birds calling to one another from the naked branches of mature oaks and cottonwoods, a cool breeze tickling her cheeks, and the sweet scent of wild primrose. She craved the soothing sight and sound of clear water trickling over smooth rocks. Her safe place along the slough, reachable only by foot or bicycle, offered all those things.

For the last thirteen years, Tyler had come here for comfort. She sat on her favorite large flat rock along the slough's upper bank and wrapped her folded knees against her chest. Closing her eyes, she willed this place to erase the day's unnerving encounter.

A question rattled in her head so loudly that it drowned out the soft noises around her: *How much does he know?*

More questions popped up fast. Had he stalked her all this time? Or, as Maddie suggested before she left, was it a cruel, cosmic joke that had brought him back into her life after all these years? Now that he'd found her, would he come again? Should she relocate the office that had taken months for Maddie and her to find? Did he know where she lived? Should she uproot the family and move to another city?

The more questions that went unanswered, the more she realized that the one spot where she felt the safest in the world couldn't bring her the peace of mind she desperately needed today.

"Tyler?" Despite its soft tone, her husband's voice startled her. She flinched and gasped. "I thought I'd find you here."

"He found me." She kept her stare at the slow-moving water, her focus following a lone leaf making its trek downstream. On a zigzag course, it snagged on a section of rocks. Tyler felt like that leaf—stuck between her past and present, unable to move forward or backward.

"I know. Maddie called." Ethan took a seat next to her on the neighboring rock. Too tall to bend his knees to a comfortable position, he crossed his bent legs at the ankles and lowered them until they touched stone. "Are you okay?"

"No, I'm not. How did he find me?"

"I don't know, but I'm sure as hell going to find out."

Tyler's chest tightened. The last thing she wanted was to give that bastard a reason to take out his anger on her again. She turned to her husband, pleading with her eyes as well as her voice. "Please don't make things worse. Don't make him mad."

The veins in his neck popped, reddening his skin there to the shade of a fire truck. "Five years wasn't nearly enough for what he did to you."

"This isn't helping."

"I'm sorry. What do you need from me?"

"I don't know yet." Though he didn't move a muscle, the two decades they'd spent as a couple told her he was resisting the instinct to take her into his arms. During the first half of their marriage, he'd do that every time she felt broken or like a failure. But the rape changed her. Her husband's touch, though it remained unaltered, no longer comforted her. Whether it was offered as an overture to sex or as a tender gesture, her skin no longer tingled when he ran a hand up and down her back. Instead, it felt as if troops of cockroaches were marching across her body. She had no explanation and had wasted no time attempting to figure out the reason for her changed reaction.

Tyler still loved him, of that she was sure, but she couldn't bring herself to melt into his touch as she once did.

"I need to know. Did he touch you?"

"No." She shook her head, infusing the gesture with the vigor of pure relief. "I didn't let him get close enough."

"Did he try?"

"No. He left without making a scene."

"That tells me he didn't know you were there."

"So Maddie was right. This was some cruel, cosmic joke."

He raised his hand as if to comfort her but drew it back. "I'll have a talk with him. Make sure he knows to stay away."

"Please don't, Ethan. If this was a coincidence, I don't want to exacerbate things. Let's let it go. I'd rather forget it ever happened."

Forgetting was what Tyler did best. The quicker she could lock away the memories again, the faster she could put this behind her.

CHAPTER SEVEN

Napa, California

"How cute," Maddie cooed, stopping in front of the outdoor entrance to the riverside hotel spa and the casually dressed mannequin guarding it.

"Yes, it is." Three days ago, Tyler would have been the first to notice the floppy sun hat and beautifully handwritten welcome sign slung around the mannequin's neck. She might have insisted on the two of them taking a selfie with it. But not today. She was still jittery from the encounter with her rapist.

Tyler thought she'd found a way to handle the self-blame, the sense of helplessness, and her fear of being alone with a man that had plagued her since the rape. But the ease with which those destructive things had returned after she came face-to-face with the man who had stolen her carefree life convinced her that there was much heavy lifting in store for her. Reburying the past wasn't ideal, but if she ignored the insomnia, high blood pressure, and sexual dysfunction that had plagued her for the last thirteen years, it would work for her.

That bastard had invaded her workplace, though—one of her safe spaces—which meant Tyler would have to work twice as hard to put the genie back in the bottle. That would start, at Maddie's urging, with a girls' spa day in Napa.

Maddie slung an arm around Tyler's shoulder. "Ready for the royal treatment?"

"Days ago."

Inside, aromatic lavender diffusers complimented soft, calming instrumental music. If any place could unwind her tension, Tyler thought, this would be it. She couldn't remember the last time she indulged in a spa day, except that Bree was still in diapers when it had happened.

An hour later, she and Maddie lay face down atop neighboring massage tables. A perky blond masseuse worked on Maddie, while Tyler was more than happy to draw Jessica, a tall, thirty-something brunette. She was athletic, with curves in all the right places, and her firm touch was giving Tyler the relief she desperately needed.

Tyler had all but forgotten what a woman's touch felt like, simultaneously strong and soft, not calloused or with chapped skin. Her mind relaxed, focusing on nothing other than the sensations. *No wonder people pay hundreds of dollars every month for this kind of personal service*, she thought. She vowed to never again consider such vital things an indulgence.

"Oh my God, this is better than sex," Maddie mumbled through the donut-hole face cradle. "And it lasts longer."

Giggles all around ended with a witty reply from the curvy brunette. "You've never slept with a woman, have you? My girlfriend and I make it last for hours."

"I envy you." Tyler's core awoke with a whisper at the question. She'd never seriously entertained being with a woman, but now that Jessica had put it into her head, the notion didn't seem absurd. Sex had taken a permanent backseat in her marriage. Hell, she and her husband had put sex on blocks and tarped it over in the driveway—an eyesore that both parties ignored.

Tyler poked her head up from the cradle and turned it toward her very talented and very intriguing masseuse. "So, what comes after this?"

"The Royal Treatment is our top-shelf package. Next is our signature grape seed foot treatment and full body exfoliation, followed by a hydrating body wrap. We'll finish with our deeply clarifying antioxidant facial."

"It sounds like an army will work on me."

"No such luck. I'm afraid you're stuck with me for the next four hours."

No luck? Based on how good those hands were making her feel, Tyler would say she was the luckiest one in the room. In that instant, the massage took on a new tenor in her head. While the masseuse maintained the same motion and pressure, the clinical touch she'd enjoyed for the last hour had made her skin tingle in a way it hadn't in years. Without a doubt, she was enjoying it more than she should have. "I don't think I'll ever want to leave."

"Very few do." Jessica added a flirtatious wink.

Following four glorious hours under Jessica's expert care, Tyler was exploring the revitalized downtown Napa riverfront with Maddie. Its distinctive shops, boutiques, and eateries combined with the warmth accompanying the rapid approach of spring had attracted a robust weekend crowd, amplifying the urban feel. Wandering into a quaint designer-shoe store, Tyler eyed their unique selection, which ranged from sandals to stilettos. She had never understood why some women tortured themselves by attaching six-inch pegs to their heels, but she respected those who mastered the seductive hip sway that resulted from wearing them. She walked out of the shop with an extra pair of sensible flats for the office.

"I'm so sorry about Paul Stevens, Tyler," Maddie said as they continued their stroll down the riverfront.

Tyler glanced at her. She knew where this was going but was wholly unprepared for dealing with it. That bastard had exhumed the past and put it on full display for her business partner and best friend to see. Until three days ago, the only other person in her life who knew she'd been raped was her husband, and he had stopped raising the topic years ago. Talking about it with Maddie now was as good an idea as putting maple syrup on a hot dog.

"There's no way you could've known. It's not something I talk about."

"I can't imagine what you went through." Maddie brought them to a halt by resting a hand on Tyler's forearm, telegraphing her intention to pursue the issue. "But I know PTSD when I see it. Jim suffered from it for years after the Gulf War."

"Then you know this is something I don't want to discuss."

"You won't until you're ready. But understand this. When you are, I'll be there, ready to listen without judgment. Without prying."

It became hard to swallow. Someone Tyler had kept in the dark for too long—her best friend—was offering to help her face the demons that plagued her, and on her own terms. Maybe it was time. And maybe this time the heavy lifting that needed to be done involved facing her past, not ignoring it. She caressed Maddie's arm, acknowledging her kindness.

"Thank you," she said, turning to resume their stroll. The move put her directly in the path of a woman walking in the opposite direction. They collided lightly, and she dropped her shopping bag, spilling its contents on the cement. Simultaneously, she and the other woman knelt to retrieve her things. Their hands touched.

Under any other circumstance, Tyler would have exercised social politeness and pulled back from the uninvited contact, but the soft and slender hand seized her attention. A woman's touch, she had learned over the past four hours, had felt more natural to her than that of the man she'd been married to for nearly two decades. Years of wondering what was wrong with her now surfaced. Had her schoolgirl crush on a classmate in pigtails been an accurate barometer reading of her sexual identity? Was she bisexual? Or gay and in denial?

She looked up to learn who was attached to the hand that had her reevaluating her entire identity, something she hadn't done since high school. Flowing, dark hair framed a striking face. Full, rounded lips gave way to a scooped nose and mesmerizing eyes that were the color of dark almonds. They looked right through her. Could they tell she was living a lie? Could they see the attraction she was feeling? The curiosity? The desire?

"I'm so sorry." The stranger's melodic voice was as soft as her hand and as soothing as an evening cocktail after an exasperating day.

Tyler didn't pull back her hand, willing their connection to grow. Refusing to break eye contact, she blindly fumbled for her shopping bag with her other hand. One word tumbled from her lips. "Hi."

"Hi," the striking stranger replied as she slowly rose from her crouch, pushing back the camera case she had slung over a shoulder. Formfitting bootcut jeans and a modest black silk short-sleeved blouse completed the appealing picture.

Tyler returned her new shoes to the bag and stood. The stranger was a few inches taller, but the difference in their height seemed complementary. From somewhere behind her, a voice shouted, "You coming, baby sis?"

The stranger angled her head ever so slightly toward the voice without breaking her gaze on Tyler. "I'll be right there." She smiled at Tyler. "You're not hurt, are you?"

"No, I'm fine," Tyler replied, not bothering to take an inventory. Her skin was flushed from head to toe, but that was an indicator better left unreported.

"All right then, I guess we're both no worse for the wear." The stranger nodded her head toward the voice that had called for her. "My sister has the worst timing. I should get going." She pointed at the bag Tyler was holding and said before walking in the opposite direction, "Hope your shoes are okay too."

Don't go, Tyler wanted to say. Turning toward her, she settled on, "Thank you."

The stranger stopped after a few steps and turned. "Cute shoes. You can't go wrong with Aquatalia." She resumed walking at a fast clip, traveling toward her sister, Tyler assumed, and calling out, "Wait up."

Tyler kept her stare on the stranger, the camera case bouncing against her backside. Who the hell was that? Better yet, what the hell just happened? She'd never been more fascinated by another person, not even her husband when she first laid eyes on him.

"Earth to Tyler." Maddie playfully shoved Tyler's shoulder, breaking the trance.

"What was that for?"

"You tell me," Maddie quipped. "Who was that?"

"I have no idea." As Tyler watched the stranger step further away until disappearing around a corner, a tingle radiated in her chest, exciting her more than receiving an unexpected gift. She had the same question: *Who was that?* More importantly, why did she feel like slowly unwrapping the stranger, one inch at a time?

CHAPTER EIGHT

Sacramento, California

A week had gone by since Tyler's past had caught up with her and invaded her waking thoughts as well as her unconscious ones. Four days had gone by since she'd bumped into the mysterious woman in Napa who had left her thinking that her having crushes on both boys and girls during her teen years suddenly was making sense. Not a day had gone by when she didn't fixate on both unsettling encounters. Staying busy at work helped, and with the new hire not expected to come on board for two more days, Tyler was swamped.

When she and Maddie formed Creative Juices, they had divided the work along the lines of personal strength. Tyler brought the artistic creativity, while Maddie brought the tech juice as they designed the hottest graphics and web pages for small businesses in northern California. Maddie had been holding up her end, but Tyler had fallen days behind schedule. She was in danger of missing a client's deadline if she couldn't find the handwritten notes she'd placed somewhere on her desk.

"Damn it. Where did I put them?" Tyler pushed herself back in the chair so hard it almost toppled to the ground with her in it. She raked her hands down her cheeks equally hard, likely leaving stretch marks to match the ones on her abdomen that she'd earned in the course of giving birth twice.

Maddie peeked into Tyler's office. "Hey, I need to head out early today. Derrick forgot his baseball cleats at home again, and practice starts in an hour." Her expression turned from lightheartedness to concern before she stepped inside. "Are you okay?"

"I can't find my notes for the walk-a-thon fundraiser. I had them this morning."

"You gave them to me after lunch so I could work on the webpage while you worked on the posters." She tapped an index finger on her temple. "You said that you had it all up here."

"That's right." Tyler's shoulders slumped. Stress had gotten to her at both work and at home. Last night, until Bree's worried phone call, she'd forgotten it was her turn to pick up her and her friend from softball practice. If things didn't change, it wouldn't be long until she cracked.

She considered taking Maddie up on her offer to act as a sounding board, but that posed a bigger problem. Maddie's family and hers were intertwined. Her daughter and Maddie's son were in the same grade and spent more time at each other's house than at school. Her husband and Maddie's were golf buddies, and they double dated as couples once a month. The last thing she could discuss with Maddie was her shifting sexual identity.

"Do you need me to stay? We can knock it out in an hour," Maddie asked.

Tyler couldn't let her problem become Maddie's. She needed to pull it together like she had following the rape and compartmentalize her emotions. "No, please go. Baseball is important to Derrick. I won't be long."

Maddie stepped further inside and rested a hip against the desk. "I'm worried about you, Tyler. I thought our girls' trip to Napa would help, but you still seem rattled." She dug into her purse and handed Tyler a business card. "I think you need to see someone. This therapist helped Jim deal with his PTSD. She could help you, too."

"I don't know, Maddie. A therapist?"

"She's expecting your call." Maddie tapped the card with a finger, her look of quiet concern convincing Tyler it was time. "Sure you don't mind locking up tonight?"

"Go." Tyler playfully shooed her friend out the door. Maybe Maddie was right. Dealing with this on her own wasn't working this time. Perhaps she needed help to sort through her thoughts and feelings, especially those surrounding that mystery woman.

Within an hour, Tyler had completed enough of the project to justify going home for the evening. As she packed up her things, she heard the distinct chime alerting her that someone had entered the offices through the front door. She turned her office light off and made her way to the front. "I'm sorry, but we're closing up for the—" Tyler froze, then instinctively clutched her purse to her chest and backed up against the wall.

"She's mine, isn't she?" The bastard remained near the door with his hands in his pockets. If he intended to look less intimidating, it didn't work.

"What?" The thumping of her heart had muffled his voice, making it difficult to pick up more than every other word.

"I saw the red hair in the picture behind the desk. She'd be what, twelve?"

Skin flushed. Breathing shallowed. Tyler's pulse raced to the dizzying point. "I don't care what you think. She is not your daughter. She never has been and never will be. You need to leave. Now!"

"I have a right to know if she's mine."

Her breathing grew faster. She clenched her fists against her purse. "Don't talk to me about rights. What right did you have to beat and rape me? Do you have any idea what you did to me? You destroyed me. Rights? You have no fucking rights here."

"Look, Tyler, I have no right to be a father to her, but if she's mine, I'd like to support her."

"You're damn right. You'll never be a father to her. Now leave." Tyler's heart rate went into overdrive. She no longer controlled her breathing. Her legs became wobbly, and she reached out for the credenza to her left to brace herself.

"Are you all right?" He took a few steps in her direction, sending Tyler's fight-or-flight instinct into high gear.

"Stay away!" The room spun. Her knees buckled. On her way to the floor, her head bounced off a piece of furniture. Groggy, she shifted on the cold linoleum but hadn't the strength to lift herself. A sharp pain pierced her temple.

The bastard appeared at her side. "Tyler, you're bleeding." He propped something soft under her head, easing the awful pain in her head. Opening her eyes to a blurry room, she struggled to make out what he was saying. She thought she heard the word "ambulance." Relief took shape. He must have called for help, or so she hoped.

He touched her head again, this time wrapping what felt like fabric around it. She assumed he'd crafted a makeshift bandage and was oddly comforted at the thought he didn't leave her there to die.

He leaned closer. When his warm breath tickled Tyler's ear, she trembled. She couldn't defend herself if he tried to kiss her. Or touch her. Or force himself inside. She was at his mercy. His moist breath penetrated her ear again, turning her stomach. It had found its way into her and made her sick. He whispered, "I'm sorry, Tyler, but this isn't over. I know she's mine."

The next moment he was gone, and the room went black.

* * *

He was five minutes late for his meeting. Ethan Falling had no real excuse for that other than that his mind had been on his wife, not his moonlighting private-eye gig. Ever since that asshole had reentered the picture, Tyler had been more distant than she had been following the rape itself. Sure, she was functioning, getting most things done around the house, but the twinkle in her eye had disappeared.

She needed more time, he reasoned, but at what point should he step in and voice his concern? He'd done his research years ago to understand the psychological impact of rape on victims and had learned his wife presented as a classic case of post-traumatic stress disorder. Ethan loved her enough to not judge and loved her too much to not consider leaving her because of how she dealt with it—by ignoring both the trauma and their sex life.

Jogging through the crosswalk near Land Park's south end, he predicted his client would excuse his tardiness without a fuss. After all, they were family. Another few minutes wouldn't matter. He slowed his pace to take in the warm, early appearance of spring in Sacramento.

He caught sight of Syd near the doorway of The Spot, his favorite place for soup and signature sandwiches. Clad in jeans and a lightweight plaid shirt, sleeves rolled to the elbows, she appeared beautiful and ready for a day of labor in the vineyard.

"Sorry I'm late," he said. "Hope I didn't keep you waiting." After greeting her with a warm hug, Ethan used one hand to open the restaurant door while holding a folder in the other.

"Not at all. I just got here myself."

Inside, they perused the extensive menu board mounted on the wall behind the service counter and then took part in the magic. The choices seemed endless, but by the time Ethan and Syd reached the end of the production line, they'd created masterpieces to their personal liking.

Trays in hand, they weaved their way toward the empty tables along the far wall. As she seated herself, Syd said, "It's been a while since you and Tyler have been to the winery. You should come up for a visit."

"Between our two careers and raising two girls, our schedules have been crazy. But now that her graphic and web design company is thriving, I'm sure she would welcome the time away. I'll mention it."

Ethan chose a table for two. He sat and unbuttoned his tailored dark gray suit jacket, exposing a star-shaped detective badge and the Glock service pistol attached to his belt. After a few bites of his sandwich, he handed Syd a rust-colored folder containing dozens of documents organized into sections. He'd fastened each sheet widthwise across the top.

"My, you work fast. You should start doing this full time."

"I hope to by the end of the year. I plan to retire at my twenty-year point. If I don't get picked up by one of the big private firms, I might form one of my own with a few colleagues."

"Well, anyone who passes you up is about as smart as a box of rocks."

"Thanks for the vote of confidence."

Syd flipped through the pages, her brow narrowing. "What am I looking at?"

"The information you and Alex provided over the phone was an excellent starting point. It didn't take long to learn that Kelly Thatcher is quite a number," Ethan said. "First, I know why she's hitting Alex up for money."

"I'll bite."

"Her name popped up on a foreclosure and bankruptcy filing. She's not only flat broke, she's in debt up to her knees." After taking a sip of his soda, he continued, "She didn't lie about a business degree, but she was at the bottom of her class at West Chester. She held a few entry-level management positions in Philly but never stayed in one place for more than a year. It seems she has a history of trying to make a quick buck. She had a string of rich boyfriends who bankrolled what she called 'surefire investments.' All were dismal failures except one."

"Why doesn't any of this surprise me? How on earth did you find out about her sugar daddies?"

"Alex mentioned on the phone that Kelly had dumped her to marry Douglas Pruitt, a trust fund baby from Boston, but his family put a stop to it. Lucky for us, Mother Pruitt wasn't all too pleased when her little Douglas came home with a Philly girl. She was a wealth of information."

Syd snickered. "What about this investment?"

"I called in a favor from a friend who works with the IRS. Two years ago, Kelly somehow turned a tidy profit on a stock purchase. She bought ten thousand dollars of stock in an energy drink company weeks before the public announcement that PopCo would acquire it. She sold the stock a month later for one hundred thousand dollars."

Syd whistled. "You're thinking insider trading."

"Either she became a genius investor overnight, or she had a tip. My guess is it came from one of those sugar daddies Mother Pruitt mentioned. That's all I could find by the deadline Alex gave me. I don't think this is enough to quash Kelly's threat, but if she wants me to continue digging, I'm sure I can get her a name."

"Definitely keep digging. We need something to knock Kelly back to Tuesday."

Ethan laughed. A buzzing vibration from his inside breast pocket alerted him to an incoming call. He raised a finger in the air when he recognized the caller as his wife. "I have to take this, Syd." He accepted the call. "Hi, sweetheart... Tyler, what's wrong?"

* * *

The Emergency Department glass doors at Sutter Hospital swooshed open to a pleasant surprise. Years as a cop in Sacramento had led Ethan to expect virtual anarchy in this hospital, but today it was relatively calm. Patients and visitors occupied a quarter of the seats, with most people hypnotized by a pretty blond anchor on the TV, droning on about the day's news and proving the adage "If it bleeds, it leads." A handful of adults were failing miserably to control a collection of toddlers playing smash-up with toy fire trucks in a corner.

There was no line at the reception desk; Ethan would get answers sooner than he expected. He flashed his detective's badge to the nurse. "Paramedics brought in my wife, Tyler Falling, with a head injury."

The nurse scanned her computer terminal, searching for the intake record. "Your wife is stable and assigned to bed eleven, but she's in X-ray at the moment. If you have a seat, we'll get you when you can see her."

Ethan scanned the waiting area and picked a seat furthest from anyone who appeared the least bit contagious. No sense in catching anything, especially if he needed to care for Tyler for a few days. Hell, he had no idea what was in store. All he knew from Tyler's groggy phone call was that she'd hit her head at work and an ambulance took her here.

Soon, a male nurse appeared through the double doors leading to the heart of the Emergency Department. "Falling. Family for Falling?"

Ethan buttoned his suit jacket and followed the nurse through the corridors, past several stations packed with doctors, nurses, and paramedics. At bay eleven, the nurse swung the curtain open, revealing Tyler asleep atop a gurney. A white blanket covered most of her, but experience told him the hospital gown she was in meant doctors had already examined her and scans were already done or ordered and waiting for analysis. Ethan expected the IV attached to her left arm, but not the cardiac monitor with the multiple leads taped to her torso. Under any other circumstance, the large bandage covering her swollen right temple would've disturbed him the most. Her pale complexion, however, stood out as the primary worry marker.

"What the hell happened to her?" he asked the nurse.

Before the man could answer, a trim woman dressed in dark blue hospital scrubs entered the bay. "You must be Mr. Falling. I'm Doctor Ahmed." Ethan gave a quick "yes" after shaking her hand. "Your wife has had quite the scare."

"How is she? Is she conscious?"

"She should be fine. After she called you, your wife became agitated, so we gave her a mild sedative."

"She was vague over the phone and told me nothing more than she hit her head. Can you tell me what happened?"

"Paramedics reported that when they found your wife she was unconscious, suffering from an apparent head wound. She came to at the scene but experienced pronounced disorientation. X-rays show no bone fractures, but a CT scan showed signs of a mild concussion, so we stitched up her wound." Doctor Ahmed's expression and inflection remained unchanged, the trademark of a well-trained trauma doctor. "She's stable now, but during my initial exam, I detected a mild irregular heartbeat. Does she have a history of arrhythmia?"

"No, she doesn't. Is this life-threatening?"

"It can be if left untreated. But arrhythmia is common and can easily be managed with medication and a healthy lifestyle."

"This is a lot to take in." Ethan locked his stare on Tyler, his legs going weak. He'd wrapped his entire life around this woman. They'd spent twenty-two years as a couple, eighteen of those married. Everything he did was for her or because of her. Their marriage wasn't ideal, but love was at its core. He could hardly bear seeing this woman lying in a hospital bed again. He didn't think he'd survive if something worse happened to her.

"This isn't a death sentence. She's otherwise strong and healthy and should recover in a few weeks. I want to keep her overnight, and if there are no further complications, I don't see why she can't go home tomorrow."

"Does anyone know how she hit her head?"

"She hasn't said. When paramedics arrived, her head was already wrapped with a makeshift bandage, but no one else was there."

"Someone did this to her?" Ethan's gut told him Stevens was involved. Who else would give her first aid and leave?

After the doctor left, Ethan sat beside the gurney, inhaling the hospital's palpable antiseptic scent and listening to the rhythmic beeping of machines monitoring Tyler's vital signs. Her injuries and heart condition weren't his primary concern at the moment. For a week now, she had been pulling away. He feared that Stevens' return had brought something to a head in her and that once she faced whatever had her in knots, their marriage, already strained, wouldn't be the same.

Within an hour, Tyler's eyes fluttered open. Ethan squeezed her hand. *Thank goodness.* She grimaced and touched the bandage covering her head injury with her free hand.

"Sweetheart, it's Ethan."

"Ooohhh. I feel like I have the worst hangover ever."

"The doctor said you'll have a headache for a while, but you should be fine. Do you remember what happened?"

"The bastard came to the—"

"I knew it." Ethan dropped Tyler's hand and formed his fingers into fists, ready to pummel the son of a bitch like a punching bag. His shirt collar tightened so much the top button threatened to pop. "He'll get more than five years this time. I'll see to it."

Tyler shook her head from side to side once, her face contorting in undeniable pain. "It's not what you think."

"What I think is that son of a bitch tried to rape you again."

"No." Tyler reached out for Ethan. He grabbed her trembling hand. "He didn't hurt me. He scared me, and I passed out." She swallowed hard. "Ethan, he knows about Bree."

Ethan's heart skipped a beat. For twelve years, biology hadn't mattered. He was Bree's father in every sense of the word, never considering her as anything other than his daughter. He ran both hands down his face to a breathy exhale. "How did he find out?"

"He saw the Christmas photo behind my desk and put it together."

Ethan dipped his head at the realization that by some quirk of fate Tyler's rapist was now poised to throw his family into a tailspin. Again. "We knew this could happen. Thankfully, the laws have changed since Bree was born. We need to take him to family court and terminate his parental rights."

"I had hoped this day would never come, but now that it has, you're right. We have to get him out of our lives forever."

"I'll call Scott and get the ball rolling." If Ethan had his way, he'd lock that bastard up and throw away the key. More than a court order would be needed to make sure Bree never found out about that animal. A private conversation with him was in order, one Tyler best not know about. He sat on the bed and caressed his wife's arms. "Tyler, we have to talk about your heart."

CHAPTER NINE

Manhattan, New York

Tired and beaten down by last week's turn of events, Alex barely had the strength to push open the heavy front door of her West Village townhouse. Inside, she dropped her purse at the entry table. Without pausing, she started the long walk past the wasted space of her father's gift for graduating from Yale business school—the formal main floor. She silently vowed her next home would be for living in, not entertaining the Manhattan elite, something she avoided like brussels sprouts.

Descending to the garden floor and her modern eat-in kitchen, she glanced out the two-story-high windows. At the far end of the lush rectangular courtyard was the charming carriage house she once had sworn to convert into a darkroom and photography studio with the idea of following in her mother's footsteps. That was one of many pet projects that had taken a backseat to her demanding job.

Herbal tea to help her sleep would've been more prudent, but nothing about Andrew's embezzlement and the ultimatum from Kelly deserved a pragmatic choice. Tonight's unusually mild weather called for a healthy dose of the night sky and a

Barnette cabernet to help her wait out Syd's update. After igniting the nearby patio heaters, she dragged herself, bottle and glass in hand, to her favorite recliner in her private urban oasis. As she poured her second glass, the glass door leading from the kitchen slid on its track, ending in a loud thud. That meant one of two things: an adept burglar had found his way inside or Harley had used her key.

"You're drinking and didn't call me? I'm hurt." Harley plopped down in the recliner next to Alex and extended an empty wine glass she'd liberated from her kitchen wine bar.

"Busy day." Alex half-filled Harley's glass and resumed her star gazing.

"I'm buying that excuse like you buy single-ply tissue— never."

"At least I do my own shopping."

"One of the many benefits of living in Mother's penthouse." Harley spun in the recliner until she faced Alex. The grilling was about to commence. "Now, spill. You've been avoiding me since your evening with Jordi. Did she bring the U-Haul?"

"No, nothing like that. Though it was better than expected." Alex smiled inwardly, recalling the pleasurable moment she discovered Jordi was a natural redhead.

"Then what happened? You haven't answered my calls, and your one text was sophomoric in the brush-off department."

"Kelly Thatcher happened."

Harley squirmed in her seat, her eyes glowing fiercely enough to illuminate Times Square. "You didn't go retro, did you? I thought we marked her as persona non grata."

"God, no." That Alex ever had loved that conniving, self-centered wretch of a woman boggled her mind. The thought of "going retro" with her churned the fine cabernet in her stomach. "You made me throw up a little in my mouth."

"Then spill it. Why has Godzilla come out of hibernation?"

"She's threatened to splash photos of us in the rags if I don't give her money or a job."

"I knew she was trouble, but a blackmailer? Why didn't I see that coming?"

"I never should've taken pictures of us together." Alex shook her head in disbelief of her younger self and youthful foolhardiness. "I did this to myself."

"You were in love."

"Stupid in love."

"What's your plan?" Harley leaned in as if they were about to plan the jewel heist of the century. "I've never known Alex Castle to not have a well-crafted strategy to counter anyone's gambit. How will you draw her in for the kill?"

Alex swung her feet to the brick pavers and sat up to face her co-conspirator. "Well—"

Her cell phone buzzed, announcing an incoming call. The screen lit up, displaying her sister's name. She gestured with an index finger. "Hold that thought. This call should give me the answer you seek, grasshopper." She swiped her phone alive. "Syd, please tell me you have some good news."

"I wish I did, baby sis." Syd's melancholy tone wasn't what Alex had hoped for. Her shoulders slumped. "Ethan dug up quite a bit on that harlot, but not anything that we can use against her yet."

"What do you mean by 'yet'?" Alex asked. After Syd explained about the shady stock sale, Alex focused on the next move. Placating Kelly into complacency appeared to be her only option to buy the time they needed. "How confident is Ethan that he'll find proof?"

"Very. And he's like a dog with a bone. If he says he'll find it, he will."

"Well, she's not getting one red cent from me. That leaves me one option until Ethan comes through."

"Father won't be happy to have that vixen on the payroll," Syd said.

"I'll come up with something." Better yet, Alex hoped, he wouldn't find out.

"Are you sure you don't want to give her the money and be rid of that bimbo?"

"No. Not one penny. And again, with the synonyms?" Alex liked this new playful side of her sister. John had been so good for her.

"I can't help it. She's made it to the top of my naughty list."

"Remind me to never get on your bad side, Syd."

Alex finished the call. Before she could utter a single syllable, Harley filled in the gaps from her side of the conversation. "If Kelly Thatcher is a stock market genius, I'm Jennifer Lopez."

"You're much prettier than JLo."

"Thank you." Harley smiled and primped her long brown locks with pride. She arched an eyebrow. "What position do you have planned for her? Licking the ashtrays clean?"

"Don't I wish." A corner of Alex's mouth quirked up at the image of Kelly on her knees, licking— *Scratch that.* No matter how demeaning it would be, she couldn't stomach any thought of Kelly on her knees. "She expects a management position."

"Dust off your dancing shoes, Alex. How do you plan to pull this off?"

"I'm not sure yet." Alex let out a fluttering sigh. Explaining to her father why she hired the woman he blamed for turning his daughter gay would prove more than tricky. She needed to keep an eye on Kelly but keep her far away from William. Very far. Another continent would be preferable.

CHAPTER TEN

Sacramento, California

The world's worst headache and the lousiest breakfast of her life since a failed Mother's Day offering by the girls weren't the best things to wake to. The plain oatmeal, canned pears, barely toasted wheat bread, and coffee that could pass for screen door lubricant fell dismally short of Tyler's idea of a delicious meal. Nibbling at her soupy oatmeal would pass the time until Ethan could spring her from this place, but it did little to help her choose which disturbing turn of events she should address first. The deep, dark family secret on the verge of being exposed had her on edge. A vivid dream last night about making love to the mysterious woman from Napa was equally unnerving. Both had earth-shattering implications, neither of which she was prepared for.

She and Ethan had told anyone who asked, including Bree, that her red hair stemmed from a recessive gene on Bree's father's side. Telling an outright lie would have been more convenient perhaps, but the partial truth was much easier to justify in Tyler's head. The partial truth had the added benefit of strengthening the bond between Bree and Ethan. Bree was Daddy's little girl through and through, but if the bastard followed through with his threat, he would alter that bond forever.

Then there was her husband. She'd loved Ethan since she was a teenager. That would never change. But since the rape, how she loved him had. No matter how much she tried and how loving he was in return, she was no longer capable of feeling romantic love for him. Despite that difficulty, their marriage had remained a true partnership. They were equals in terms of income, household chores, and parental responsibilities, which made questioning her sexual identity that much harder.

She could chalk up the dream to the pain medication, but she'd be lying. With each passing day, that woman in Napa had invaded her thoughts with increasing frequency, to the point it had become hard to concentrate. Even more alarming, last night marked the first time she'd dreamed vividly about anything other than the night that had haunted her for years. And when she woke this morning, one thought overwhelmed her—she wanted to find this woman. Needed to.

Ethan appeared from behind the partially drawn privacy curtain, prompting Tyler to sit up straighter in the bed and tuck away thoughts about a tall, striking brunette. He snickered. "I see they brought your favorites."

"I should've asked for a menu." Tyler tossed her spoon on the tray and rolled the bedside table past her knees.

"Which is why I made a stop on the way here." Ethan held up a sack from Tyler's favorite bakery-café.

"You didn't?" A smile built on Tyler's lips when a faint whiff of bacon tickled her nose.

"I did." He winked and replaced the hospital food with Tyler's favorite breakfast sandwich and Greek yogurt parfait, heaven in a bag.

"You know me so well."

"I should." He moved closer and hovered his lips an inch from hers. "I've been in love with you since you were eighteen." He gave her a brief yet sweet kiss.

"Thank you." Tyler wished she could say the same thing, but that would be a lie. She was a master at half-truths but not of outright lies, not unless she counted her "I'm fine" polite responses to the Target cashier's robotic greeting. Most days, she appeared fine on the surface, but below her public facade she was a mess, a mass of denial. No wonder she had a heart condition. Waking in a hospital bed signaled it was time to make some changes in her life.

Tyler took several bites wrapped in awkward silence before pushing her plate away. "I'm scared."

"What are you scared about?" Ethan sat on the corner of the mattress, carefully avoiding Tyler's legs.

She wanted to tell him about the mysterious woman and that she was afraid of what her dream meant for their marriage, but she wasn't sure what any of it meant. Until she was, more half-truths would have to suffice.

"I'm afraid Bree will find out about him. That he won't give up and will always be a part of our lives."

Ethan straightened his back and drew a deep breath. His eyes narrowed the way they did when he'd decided he was done arguing. "I'll take care of everything, sweetheart."

Tyler offered him a nod. They were out of choices and had to make their position clear. "Please don't risk your job."

"You know me better than that." Ethan gave her hand a reassuring squeeze. She knew that doing the right thing was his trademark, though that sometimes meant bending the rules. Ironically, the last time he admitted to rule-bending was when he told her he had looked the other way when the father of a thirteen-year-old rape victim beat her rapist to within an inch of his life. His report read that the suspect had resisted arrest. Stevens' return was personal to Ethan. Would he become like that heartbroken father, unable to control himself? She didn't know. Frankly, she didn't want to. All she wanted was to have that animal out of their lives.

"You know what?" His smile meant he was pivoting the conversation and nothing more about the bastard needed to be said. "I think you and I need to get away for a few days. When I met with John's wife yesterday, she said it had been too long since we'd come for a visit. Would you like to go for a weekend getaway?"

Tyler's mind went into overdrive. The winery meant Napa, and Napa meant the mysterious woman. Before she could think about the kids' schedules or how much work had piled up the last few days at the office, one word flew from her mouth. "Yes."

Once she said it, she'd never felt more guilty in her life. Whatever she was feeling about this woman, or generally about women, she needed to sort through it and be honest with Ethan. Deep in her heart, she was sure that even on her worst day she'd never act on those feelings, but saying yes made her a horrible person and an even worse wife. He deserved better. He deserved the same love and respect he'd shown her since the first time he asked her out.

"Good. I'll take care of everything." His relieved expression turned up the volume on Tyler's shame. Maddie was right. She needed to see a therapist.

* * *

After nineteen years and ten months on the job, half of that time dealing with guns, drugs, prostitutes, pimps, and gangbangers, Ethan wasn't one to stand by when someone close to him was hurt or needed his help. That was why he had called in favors to help Syd run down the dirt on Kelly Thatcher. It was also why he and his partner, Marco Banuelos, were now parked on the edge of the Bell Street hooker stroll between the Polynesian Apartments and a strip mall decorated in barbed wire and metal bars. For eight hours, the backseat of their unmarked Chevy Impala police sedan had served as a trash bin. The rolled-up fast-food wrappers, tall paper cups, and plastic straws were a stark difference from the sterile hospital room where he'd visited his wife yesterday.

Most law-abiding citizens didn't recognize the 9C1 Impala as an undercover vehicle, but the clientele Ethan regularly dealt with in the seedier areas of North Highlands and Watt Avenue did. Ethan was betting that Stevens was too much of an idiot to recognize an undercover sedan on stakeout, even one parked in front of his run-down one-bedroom apartment.

Ethan and Marco, both introverts happy with silence, had an unspoken agreement during stakeouts—keep conversation to a minimum unless it involved their mutually favorite topic of baseball. "I'm telling you," Ethan said, "the Dodgers are going to take the NL West this year. The entire division sucks this preseason, but if last year was any indicator, they should have the strongest bullpen."

"Are you kidding me?" Marco challenged. "They stunk on the road, and the middle of their lineup was so weak against lefthanders."

"True, but—"

Ethan stopped in mid-sentence. Three passengers were exiting the blue, white, and yellow public bus that had pulled curbside across the street. The first two were not distinctive to the rest of the world, but to Ethan, the last one stuck out like a street hooker in a church. He'd found the redheaded sperm donor he'd come to loathe more than the Golden State Killer and every other serial rapist combined. The little shit was thinner than when Ethan last saw him, having finally lost his baby fat.

"It's him."

When Marco reached for the driver's door handle, Ethan said, "This is something I have to do myself."

"Ten minutes." Marco's tone was firm, signaling that the time limit was nonnegotiable. In their four years as partners, not once had they stepped beyond the boundaries of the law. On Day One, they had agreed that neither of them would. "After that, I'm coming in."

"Don't worry." What Ethan had in mind wouldn't take ten minutes. He'd be sorely disappointed in himself if he couldn't get his message across in less than two. He slid out of the passenger seat and held the open car door with a hand. "I'm just going to have a little talk with the dirtbag."

"Keep it that way."

Ethan nodded and shut the door. Each step toward the apartment complex made this more personal. The last time he had faced Stevens was in a courtroom when, in exchange for receiving a sentence of only five years behind bars, he'd pled guilty to brutally raping Tyler. The sentence wasn't nearly enough, but it had meant Tyler didn't have to testify and relive the worst day of her life.

Stevens disappeared inside his second-floor apartment. Ethan followed him up the exterior stairs, his back teeth grinding so hard he'd probably need to make an appointment with his dentist. He stood out of the view of the peephole and knocked firmly without pounding so as not to frighten off the little shit. He needed Stevens to open the door, not cower behind it like a gutless lowlife. In less than a minute, the deadbolt clicked, and the knob slowly turned. When the door was pulled ajar, Ethan barreled through, leading with a shoulder. Stevens stumbled backward into the apartment. Ethan closed the door and covered the distance between him and Stevens like a raging bull.

"Hello, Paul." Four inches taller and twenty pounds heavier, Ethan towered over the gulping coward. He resisted the urge to choke the life out of him. "Remember me? I'm the man whose wife you raped thirteen years ago. The same woman you beat up yesterday."

"I didn't touch her."

"Didn't touch her?" The horrid thirteen-year-old image Ethan had conjured up of his wife enduring the unthinkable returned with the power of a locomotive. He drew an arm back and clenched a fist so tightly his short nails bore into his palm. Then, for the first time in his career, Ethan was the first to let a punch fly, a stomach blow that had been thirteen years in the making. Stevens doubled over, sucking in ragged breaths between groans. "You raped her."

Stevens popped up, his eyes wide. "Is that what she said? All I did yesterday was call 9-1-1, make sure she didn't bleed out, and then I left. I did nothing wrong. I helped her."

Years of interviewing witnesses and suspects made Ethan believe that Stevens' shocked reaction might mean he was telling the truth. But he didn't want to believe a word he said. "Binding a wound that you caused doesn't make you a hero. It makes you an asshole trying to avoid a murder wrap. If you did nothing wrong, why did you run?"

"I knew how it would look. The cops would figure out who I was. Then it would've been the same old story with every ex-con. Cuffs first. Questions later."

"You have yourself to blame for that." Ethan rolled his neck, trying to tamp down the storm brewing inside him. For nearly twenty years as a cop, he'd kept his cool with every perp and suspect, even with the two dozen who had pushed him to his limits. Right now, standing two feet from the man who violated his wife in the worst imaginable way, tested every moral belief he had. Ethan swallowed his anger and disgust. "Do you know why I'm here?"

The asshole nodded, slow but sure. "I have a daughter."

Ethan closed in, toe to toe, smelling his nervous sweat. The scent sickened him. This scum may have provided the sperm that made his daughter, but that in no way made him a father. "Get this straight. You are not her father. I am."

"I have a right to know if she's mine."

Ethan straightened Stevens' shirt collar before patting him on the shoulders with too much vigor for it to be mistaken as friendly. "The law says you have no rights. I'm here to make sure you fully understand and follow the law. Are we on the same page here, Paul?"

He nodded again.

"Nothing good will come if you pursue this. Now, two things are going to happen. First, when family court notifies you about terminating your parental rights, you will not fight it. You will accept it and go on your merry way. Second, and this is very important, Paul. Are you listening?"

Stevens' nod was faster this time.

"Second, you will never again contact Tyler or anyone else in my family. If you do, I'll make it my life's purpose to put you back in prison until the day you die. If you ever come within fifty feet of my wife or my family again, I guarantee that will be the last time you ever see daylight. Are we clear?"

"Crystal." Stevens' caved-in posture served as a white flag. Perhaps he wasn't as stupid as Ethan first thought and prison had knocked some sense into him. Perhaps. Ethan wasn't taking any chances. His job was to keep his family safe, and this piece of work was its greatest threat.

Descending the stairs, Ethan took pride in what he'd done. He'd kept it to one punch. Anyone with an ounce of compassion would agree Stevens had had it coming, perhaps more. He hadn't disgraced the badge or himself.

Marco started up the engine and shifted the car into drive. As he pulled away from the curb, he asked, "All good?"

"All good." *But only if Stevens does as he's told.*

CHAPTER ELEVEN

Manhattan, New York

An afternoon summons from William Castle meant lunch at the Key Grill would include business. Located across the street from Castle Resorts headquarters, a particular booth there had been the site of virtually every landmark business deal William had ever made. Alex predicted this would be the spot where he would announce his successor to the Castle Resorts throne.

The summons to her and her brother didn't bother her as much as its timing. Her father had a way of discovering most things of importance in his children's lives, no matter how hard they tried to hide them.

Had he come across Andrew's pilfering? Alex wouldn't blame her father if he used today's meeting as a pretense for a public dressing down. She'd barely scratched the surface of the Times Square financials Robbie had gathered. Already she'd identified two things—strange purchase patterns with two questionable companies and the fact that his embezzlement had surpassed two hundred thousand dollars.

Or had William unearthed Kelly's blackmail? Would this be the unforgivable embarrassment he had warned her against? If so, Alex hadn't adequately prepared herself for it. She hadn't thought past countering Kelly's demand, and she should've. The time had come to consider a life where Castle Resorts wasn't at its heart.

Shrugging off her multilayered trepidation, Alex pushed open the glass and brass door leading into the Key Grill. Not two steps in, a tuxedo-clad host snapped to attention. "Welcome, Ms. Castle. Your table is waiting. May I take your coat?"

Shedding her light outer layer and reshouldering Syd's precious gift, she asked, "Is my father here yet?" The question was asked out of courtesy. William had held business lunches here with her and Andrew for years, and not once had he arrived before her. He'd taught her when she was a teenager that if "you're not ten minutes early, you're late." Her personal cushion was fifteen.

"No, miss. You're the first to arrive." He gestured toward the dining room. "I'll take you to your table."

Alex waved him off when two businessmen entered behind her. "Thank you, but I know my way. Our usual table, right?"

Following an affirmative nod, Alex weaved her way through the dining room, taking in the distinctly stately atmosphere she associated with her father. The dark woods, white tablecloths, dim lighting, and tufted leather booths had an impressive appeal. She preferred, however, the clean lines, modern theme, and muted earth tones she'd picked for the San Francisco renovation. She hoped her choices would become Castle Resorts' signature look.

At William's preferred corner booth, a spot that offered a bird's-eye view of the entire dining floor, Alex considered ordering her usual lunchtime Pellegrino. Instead, with the prospect of her life unraveling looming, when the server asked for her order, she replied, "Tequini. Straight up."

Taking her first sip, Alex assessed her situation. She prided herself in having realized early on that as part of the disease ravaging him, her father had turned into a man with little patience or compassion for misfortune. For thirteen years, since she'd agreed to hide the best part of herself from public eye for his sake, she'd planned for his foreseeable wrath, building a personal net worth beyond a trust fund she refused to touch. She'd given herself a cushion for the day William might cut her out of Castle Resorts and his life.

On her second sip, she contemplated several career options. The hotel business was in her blood, but only if it was Castle Resorts. She couldn't see herself being happy at the helm at any place that didn't have her parents' fingerprints on it. Maybe she should take John's suggestion and become a winemaker. Syd could teach her the ropes with the added plus of lots of "sister" time. Or maybe she should take up photography professionally and follow in her mother's footsteps. The photography and art history courses she had taken at Yale had been by far her favorites. She had discovered she had a genuine talent for it. She removed Syd's gift from its case and compared its similarities to her mother's Leica, then snickered out loud. Her love of taking pictures was what had gotten her into this mess.

"What's so funny?"

Alex shifted her gaze toward the voice that had matched hers before Andrew transitioned through puberty. She gestured toward the camera. "Just thinking about Mother. Syd's birthday present was so thoughtful, but I wish I still had her original Leica."

"That old thing?" Andrew slid into the booth directly across from her. "Losing it gave you the excuse to go digital, a much better medium."

"It had sentimental value."

"Father has more of her old cameras. I'm sure he'd give you one." He signaled the server, who scurried over. "Scotch. Neat."

"It's not the same." Alex studied her twin brother's body language. His subdued attitude told her he might be as much in the dark about things as she was. "Do you know why Father asked us here?"

"Not a clue, but it wouldn't surprise me if he were to move the goalposts again."

"Your response tells me I should've called this meeting weeks ago." The deep, matter-of-fact tone was unmistakable. Alex and Andrew turned their heads toward it.

"Father." Andrew reacted the same way every time their father caught him speaking out of school, blushing slightly.

Alex moved to the center of the curved leather bench to give William an end seat—a change since last year. Shimmying across a booth had become increasingly difficult with his muscles stiffening, often without warning. The day Andrew had had to help him out of the booth likely marked the day their father first considered retiring.

Within seconds, a server arrived with a tall Manhattan, William's drink of choice. Alex couldn't remember the last time her father had had to resort to placing a drink order here. Key Grill's staff had been well-trained to anticipate every VIP's needs, and William was the most "VIP" of the lot.

She sat back, knowing that William never discussed business until servers removed the lunch plates. Today was no exception. Andrew initiated a short but lively discussion on the Yankees' dismal performance so far during spring training. He didn't say it, but she suspected Andrew, a lifelong Yankees fan, had lost a bundle because of it.

After staff cleared and swept the table for stray crumbs, William dabbed each corner of his mouth with the white cloth napkin. He turned toward Alex. "I trust your impromptu escape to wine country recharged your batteries."

"It did." That wasn't a complete lie. When she left, the prospect of turning the tables on Kelly had given her a burst of energy. Subsequent days of worry, however, had erased it and then some. She pointed to the camera sitting on the table between her and William. "Syd gave me this beautiful Leica for my birthday to replace the one I lost."

"Perhaps you'll be more respectful of it than you were of your mother's."

That was an interesting choice of words, Alex thought, but she had no intention of letting this camera out of her sight. "I will. Syd and John were hoping we could all make it out there over the summer this year."

"I'm afraid you won't have the time, Alexandra. I need to make some immediate changes, and I'm counting on you to do the heavy lifting."

"How so?"

"Have you looked at the last quarterly report for Times Square?"

"Only a surface glance. Three consecutive quarters in the red looks bad, but I'm confident Andrew will pull it together in the end."

"Your optimism is misguided." William sipped the remaining liquid from his cocktail glass, his hand shaking more perceptibly than it had at their last luncheon. "I started this competition to see which of you had the foresight necessary to take over the company I built from nothing. The answer has become abundantly clear."

Andrew's posture stiffened. Alex's did, too. There was no way to tell how much her father knew. If there was one thing he had taught her, though, it was to never show her hand. Case in point, William's current unchanging, stoic expression could mean he knew everything about Kelly and Andrew or that his seared filet was giving him indigestion. Except for moments of sheer delight, which were rare, he was hard to read.

"Andrew has a sound plan. Given time, I'm sure—" Alex stopped in mid-sentence when her father dismissed her statement with a wave of a hand.

"New projections show we won't start showing a profit for five years. Times Square was my first resort. I will not retire before I'm confident it's out of trouble."

"I didn't realize things had gotten that out of hand." Alex glanced at her brother. Other than a single bead of sweat and a twitch of his jaw muscles, his expression remained substantially unchanged. Two crucial questions came to mind: How much had he stolen? And for how long? Her recent review of the Times Square financials had given her a leg up on the general situation, though. "I have a few ideas that could get the budget in the black in two years."

"I knew I could count on your creativity and innovation. Your brother has made a mess of things, so I need you to clean up after him. You'll have complete control because I'm naming you the next CEO."

That wasn't merely music to her ears, it was three three-hour-long Melissa Ethridge, Cindi Lauper, and Joan Jett concerts all rolled into one. The next sound, though, was that of breaking glass. Andrew had gripped his near-empty tumbler so tightly that it had shattered, sending shards across the table. Blood trickled to the white tablecloth, leaving a pattern of red dots.

"Andrew, you've hurt yourself." Alex wrapped her cloth napkin around his hand to stem the light bleeding. Andrew's death stare, however, signaled that this cleaning up of his mess would be her last. That they were done.

"You always win." Andrew jerked his hand back.

"Insolence, Andrew." William pounded his fist atop the table. He grimaced and then inspected his hand. He had cut it on one of the glass shards. Drops of blood were streaking toward Alex's beautiful new-old camera.

"Father, you're hurt too."

"It's just a scratch. I'll be fine, but your brother won't be if he continues to act like a petulant child."

William pitting one twin against the other was damaging enough. Now that he'd crowned Alex the winner and was treating Andrew like an eight-year-old, she feared he'd severed forever the connection she shared with her brother.

"He's rightly upset." Alex briefly glanced at Andrew, setting soft eyes on him. "Why don't I get the lay of the land and have a proposal to you by the end of the week before you make your final decision?"

"You misunderstand, Alex. Speed is of the essence."

"By the end of tomorrow, then."

"That's my girl." He patted her hand with his uninjured one. "But my decision is final."

CHAPTER TWELVE

For one evening, Alex basked in the most gratifying news of her life. As her father's successor, she'd be free to implement her vision of transforming Castle Resorts into an innovative luxury resort chain. Guests would come for unique experiences, not merely amenities. But she needed to get past the first hurdle—proposing a bulletproof marketing plan to put the Times Square resort in the black.

The following day she returned to her office, rolled up her sleeves, and studied the marketing proposal she'd worked on for months and refined overnight. Though tailored for the San Francisco resort, the tweaks she had added to it before dawn made it ideal for Times Square and the New York market. The only thing left was to fold in the few good ideas her brother already had in the works, and she'd have a solid plan.

Despite having her dream of running the company within reach, Alex tempered her enthusiasm. Kelly's threats still had teeth. For now, she'd play along and give Kelly what she wanted. But once Castle Resorts was hers or Ethan came through, Alex would insist on a ringside seat when security perp-walked her out of the building. She looked at her calendar. *Timing is everything*, she thought. Her week was up, and that witch was her next appointment.

"I hope you're happy." Andrew burst through her office door, bouncing it off the wall with a thud. Alex made a mental note to dock his pay for damages.

"I'm sorry, Ms. Castle." Robbie appeared steps behind Andrew, wearing a terrified look that suggested he expected to be in the unemployment line by the end of the day. "Mr. Castle refused to wait so I could announce him."

"It's all right, Robbie. My brother is in the grip of another of his tantrums." From behind her desk, Alex shot her assistant a reassuring wink, hoping to convey the message that he could throw out any thought of having to file for unemployment. After Robbie closed the door behind himself, she turned her attention to Andrew. The daggers he was shooting her way could've sliced and diced a five-pound bag of potatoes in seconds.

"You need to whip out a mirror if you're looking for someone to blame, Andrew."

"You always get what you want, no matter who you have to walk over."

"That's not fair. You created this mess all by yourself." She decided to table her suspicions about the cost overruns until she had all her ducks in a row. "You know what? I really don't care what you think. Father asked me to mop up after you, and that's exactly what I'm going to do. You're a decent manager, but you don't have the strategic vision or gut instinct to be a leader in this business. There's nothing wrong with that, but it's about time you settle into a position within your wheelhouse."

"Well, there she is, the same old smug Alex, who gets off on telling me how to live my life. Well, no, thank you. I don't plan on giving you the satisfaction of throwing in the towel. I have as much right to this company as you do." Gearing up for battle, Andrew straightened his tie in the same fashion as their father when he was about to take down a business adversary. "Prepare yourself for a fight."

"Bring it, Brother." Alex circled her desk, strode to the door, and yanked it open. "I have bigger things to worry about than your bruised ego." *Kelly being the biggest.*

Andrew turned on his heel, assuming the perfect, arrogant Castle posture. When he pulled up even with her, he shot Alex another look. "Don't write me off yet, Sister."

"Why, if it isn't the lovely Castle twins. You both look positively delicious."

Alex snapped her head toward the voice. Her heart sank. "Bad timing" had become the phrase of the day. Though it had been thirteen years since she'd seen Kelly Thatcher, there was no mistaking the flamboyant dress, makeup, and accessories. She looked as if she was ready to walk down the red carpet. She had abandoned the curls of youth, opting for a straight tapered look. Dirty-blond hair framed the angled features of a face that had not aged particularly well—the sign of a hard life. Her body was still trim, perhaps curvier, lending to it an even sexier look than it had had during their college days. Alex shivered at the thought. *Don't even go there.*

"Hello, Andrew. Nice to see you again." Kelly offered her hand, but he ignored it. That was the first thing he had done since barging in that Alex appreciated. The thought of him getting that close to Kelly made her breakfast churn with a vengeance. His curiosity would run amuck.

Alex whispered under her breath, "Fucking great."

"Kelly? What the hell are you doing here?" Andrew's expression suggested he suspected something scandalous was going on. Why did he have to be so good at reading between the lines?

"I'm here to see Alex about a business proposal."

"Is that what they call it these days? Are you still batting for both teams, Kelly?"

"Andrew!" Alex brayed. "Enough. It's time for you to leave. Some of us around here have to work for a living."

"This isn't over. Not by a long shot." Before he left, Andrew cocked his grin to one side, which wasn't a good sign. Alex had no doubt he would sniff around until he got to the bottom of Kelly's sudden reappearance.

"What's wrong with him?" Kelly sauntered into the office, coming dangerously close to brushing against Alex in the process. The kindergartner in Alex shuddered at the thought of catching her cooties.

She retreated to the safety of the leather chair behind her desk, giving Kelly a wide berth. "Nothing of your concern."

Kelly walked the room's perimeter, taking in the elegant touches Alex had added to the suite. When Kelly breathed in the fresh flowers Alex had brought in Monday to fill the crystal vase Abby had given her for her thirtieth birthday, Alex felt invaded. When she stopped to admire the framed unpublished black and white photos from Alex's mother's portfolio of their last family beach vacation, she felt exposed. Her life was on display to this poor excuse for a woman. When, however, Kelly paused at the stretched canvas prints of a promising young abstract painter with whom Alex had shared an incredible week in Milan, Alex smirked. Those few days of unbridled passion had outstripped all of those in the months she had shared with Kelly.

Kelly sat on one end of the leather couch, leaning back slowly. She crossed her legs at the knees with the same seductive tempo. In their college days, that would've been enough to trigger a steamy, on-the-verge-of-getting-caught fuck, but now it turned Alex's stomach.

"It's been a week, Alex. Have you considered my proposal?" She posed her question as if blackmail were a simple business proposition.

"I have." Alex steepled her fingers, resisting the urge to slap the satisfied grin off Kelly's face. "But what guarantee do I have if I give you what you want, you won't make those pictures public?"

"Dear, dear Alex." Kelly laughed. "You have none. If you don't give me what I want, though, I guarantee they will find their way to the *Post* or the *Enquirer*."

"Honestly, I don't know what I ever saw in you."

"You saw the same thing I saw in you. You were sexy as hell, and I knew you would be a hot fuck."

"Well, I was young and stupid back then." Alex paused at Kelly's frown. It seemed she'd hit a sore spot. Maybe this blackmailing scheme wasn't solely about money. "All right. I'm not giving you a red cent, but I will give you a job and make you work for it. I'm taking over the Times Square Resort. Stop by in the morning, and we'll find you a position."

"Not just any position, Alex. I want a minimum of six figures, and I want to work directly for you, starting today."

"Fine, I'll walk you down to Human Resources." Alex felt cornered.

"I'm glad you see things my way."

"I'd be lying if I said likewise." Alex stood and stepped toward the door. "Let's get this over with."

"Why so fast? It's been such a long time. I'd like to hear what you've been up to."

"Look, Kelly, we're not going to catch up and reminisce about old times over afternoon tea. We made a deal. I give you a job, and you keep your mouth shut."

"You know, Alex, we once were terrific together." Kelly recrossed her legs, hiking up the hem of her skirt. "And we could be again."

If Alex wasn't ready to throw up in her mouth before, she was now. "You are delusional. There is no way that"—she pointed back and forth between herself and Kelly—"will ever happen again. I was a fool to have fallen in love with you. I was an even bigger fool to have taken those pictures of us. You are a heartless gold digger out to make a quick buck. I am never going back there again."

"I'm not talking about love, Alex. I'm talking about sex. Admit it. We were good in bed together."

"I will admit no such thing." Alex's frustration and disgust had reached a crescendo. She needed to put a stop to Kelly's advances quickly. "We need to set some ground rules. We will never again be lovers. We will never again be friends. This is a business arrangement, nothing more."

"All right, Alex, we'll play it your way for now."

Alex added extra seriousness to her tone. "One more thing. This is a place of business, not the Oscars. Tone down the makeup and attire." That generated another grimace, one that Alex thoroughly enjoyed causing. She extended her arm, pointing her out the door. "Now, I'll introduce you to our director of HR."

She took one step into her outer office and came to a halt, a knot the size of New Jersey forming in her gut. Andrew stood, a hip leaned against Robbie's unoccupied desk, arms crossed in front of his chest. Kelly had had Alex so flustered when she arrived, she hadn't closed the door after her brother left. He likely sent her trusty assistant on an errand, and from the grin plastered on his face, he'd gotten an earful.

Shit!

* * *

As if her day weren't bad enough, Alex felt woefully underprepared for this evening's meeting with her father. Her plan to get Times Square in the black had good bones, but she hadn't the time to flesh out the marketing minutia fully. Most days, William Castle wasn't a details man, but in those rare instances when he was, whoever was on the receiving end had better have answers to his questions or be prepared to dust off their résumé.

A return trip to the Key Grill for dinner meant the meeting's sole focus was business. She intended to keep the discussion short. She arrived early to ensure staff had reserved William's favorite table and had two Pellegrinos waiting, not tap water.

"Alexandra, always early, I see." William unbuttoned his navy tonal Brioni windowpane suit jacket and took his now traditional position facing the wall of windows.

"Always, Father." Alex smiled. "I took the liberty of ordering your favorite."

"The sea bass is back in season, I take it. You know your old man." Moments later, the waiter delivered their plates along with William's Manhattan cocktail. "So, tell me about your plan to clean up your brother's mess."

"I've poured over the last twelve months of operational and financial reports of the resort and analyzed Andrew's original business plan, along with the schedule and expenditures. I also compared the ongoing renovations of the San Francisco resort to Times Square."

"You have been a busy little bee." That was as close to a compliment William had ever given her without seeing bottom-line results.

"You're counting on me, Father. I don't take that lightly." Alex reached for her Burberry leather briefcase and pulled out the file she'd assembled. "When I talked to the contractor today, I learned the bulk of the delays were because of late modifications of the architectural plans, which required additional permits and inspections. With a few minor changes, we can align the renovations with the San Francisco remodel with a minimum of additional expenses. I expect completion around Mother's Day. I'm still poring over the financials. Some numbers don't add up, but I'll continue digging."

She couldn't say that Andrew was at the center of the missing money. Wouldn't. At least not yet. First, she didn't know the extent of his embezzlement. And second, despite their recent falling out, she didn't want to see her brother hurt.

"I'm feeling confident already, but what about projected revenue? When will we be in the black?"

"Andrew was right. This market is ripe for another luxury destination for special events. He just needed a unique hook to attract high-end clientele in greater numbers, including an affordable option. That's why I'm proposing partnerships with a select number of topflight businesses. For example, I have a tentative agreement with Christie's art auction house to host special auctions and exhibitions at the resort. I'm exploring exclusive agreements with Chanel, Prada, and Saint Laurent to sell certain pieces in our hotel store with discounts for resort guests. I've also looked into a partnership with a local private jet company to offer *Fly & Stay* packages from Europe and Asia with both the Times Square and San Francisco resorts as destinations."

"Ambitious. I like it."

"If we want to attract more high-end customers, our hook should be our exclusive partnerships with high-end businesses and designers. If my projections are right, Times Square should show a profit in three to six quarters."

"I knew I could count on you. Now I have to figure out what to do with Andrew."

"He was on to something and got in way over his head. He's a good manager, but he doesn't have the best strategic vision for this business." She hoped saying that would be enough to keep Andrew out of an autonomous position of trust.

"I'd have to agree with you." William offered a slight nod. "Perhaps I should groom him for the CFO track."

"I'm not sure if that's the right fit. Maybe lower-level operations or marketing. Andrew would have an expert team around him in either case."

"I won't have a Castle buried five layers deep. He's always been good with numbers, so CFO it is. Now, I like what you've laid out so far. I expect a formal proposal in two weeks."

No, no, no, no, no. As the next CEO, she couldn't tolerate having a Chief Financial Officer with his finger in the till. That left two choices: tell her father about her suspicions or confront her brother. Both would fracture an already dysfunctional family, but only one would allow Andrew to save face. *You're lucky I still love you, Andrew.* Undoubtedly, gambling was at the root of his stealing, but she needed to know how deep it went before confronting him. In other words, she needed someone she could trust to be discreet to look into a few names.

"Of course. I'll have to survey the San Francisco remodel so I can perfectly align both projects. I'll fly out this weekend."

CHAPTER THIRTEEN

Napa, California

Tyler had been pulling away from Ethan for years. Today she finally understood why. There was an unnerving reason behind the other day's very enthusiastic "yes" to revisiting the city where she'd encountered her mystery woman, she realized: her hope for another chance meeting. The appointment next Monday with a psychologist was well-timed. She had a lot to sort through.

In the meantime, a long weekend at this calm place of refuge was precisely what the doctor ordered. A few days strolling the vineyard and quaint Napa shops should make the mystery woman, the bastard, and the family court proceedings scheduled a week from Monday far-off thoughts.

Ethan turned their SUV onto the half-mile-long private road leading up to John and Syd's winery, coasting to a stop at the gate. After entering the security code into the keypad, he pulled forward, and the magic began. Acres of rolling hills with row after row of grapevines came into view.

Tyler gasped. "I forgot how beautiful this place is. It's like a magazine cover."

"Isn't it? It's even better in the summer."

Years had passed since she'd last visited the Barnette Winery, so many that she couldn't be sure when she was last there. Raising two girls and expanding Creative Juices had been her excuse, but she realized there was more to it. John and Syd were lovely, welcoming people, and she'd enjoyed both previous visits, especially the one after Syd joined the family. If she loved Ethan the way he deserved, the way she desperately wanted to, she would embrace everything and everyone important to him, including his extended family. She hoped John and Syd hadn't picked up on her pulling away from them too.

"This was your grandfather's, right? Something about Prohibition."

"Excellent memory. It originally belonged to my great-grandfather. He bought the land in the late 1920s when several wineries went bankrupt during Prohibition. John's side of the family took it over in the seventies, which is why I used to visit here almost every summer when I was a kid."

"You two are more like brothers."

"My gosh, the trouble he and I used to get into. It's a wonder his mother kept asking me back."

"Why haven't I heard this before?" Tyler licked her lips, relishing the thought of hearing about the shenanigans her husband had gotten into as a boy.

"Man code. What happens in Napa stays in Napa."

"Well then, John and I will have to have a long talk." Tyler smiled, conjuring up a strategy to get Ethan's cousin to spill the beans. Without a doubt, it would involve lots of wine.

"Good luck. But I guarantee he'll never break the code."

"You and your man code." Tyler gave him a playful shove on the shoulder.

Ethan parked and retrieved their overnight bags from the rear compartment while Tyler gathered her purse and the floral arrangement she'd picked up for Syd. A voice boomed from the covered patio, beckoning them closer. "There you two are. Do you need help with anything?"

"Thanks, but we have it all." Ethan put the bags down past the first patio step and gave Syd a warm hug. "Syd, you remember my wife, Tyler."

"Of course." Syd pulled Tyler into a sincere hug, the type of embrace reserved for family. In Tyler's book, the wife of her husband's first cousin barely qualified as family, but apparently, Syd defined family in simpler terms. Tyler's feelings of guilt grew from concerning to downright crushing.

Syd pulled back and accepted the bright, aromatic bouquet. "Thank you. These are beautiful. Let's get you all settled in, so I can show you around. So much has changed since you were here last."

Ethan grabbed their bags again and followed Syd and Tyler into the main house and toward the guest wing. "Syd, are we still on for tomorrow?"

"We sure are. She should be here around ten but can't stay for long. Maybe an hour or two."

"That should be plenty of time." Ethan threw the bags on the bed before turning his attention to Tyler. "Are you sure you don't mind me taking a business meeting tomorrow?"

"An hour won't ruin our weekend getaway. Maybe I'll drive into town and do a little shopping while you're meeting."

"You're the best." He kissed her on the cheek, quickly but with passion. Over the years, each kiss, especially the daily hover over her lips following a long shift one, gave her the sense they stemmed from love, not obligation. This one was no exception, giving her more reason to sort out her feelings sooner than later.

"The weather will be perfect tomorrow," Syd said. "You should use my bicycle. We finished paving a trail that cuts through the vineyard and ends near Old Town. It's only a two-mile ride."

"That sounds perfect." Tyler took in Syd's spacious guestroom. It was different from the last time she stayed in it. The linens and drapes all had warm, inviting yellow and cream tones. A sliding glass door led to the wraparound outdoor patio, which, if memory served, was the heart of the home. "You redecorated. This is incredible, Syd. You're going to spoil me." "That's the whole idea. I want you and Ethan to enjoy your stay with us. Why don't you two get settled in? Then we can tour the winery. And if you're recovering well from your head injury, we can put you to work."

"Ooohhh. Stomping grapes like Lucy and Ethel? I could do that all day long."

Syd laughed. "Not quite, but if we're not back by six, I *will* have some 'splainin' to do.' John has a special dinner planned."

Hours later, John had prepared a delicious barbecued tri-tip roast, fast smoking it with a generous amount of red oak chips. He'd topped it off with a Santa Maria pinquito bean relish and added grilled artichokes, Syd's fresh tossed green salad, and grilled french garlic bread on the side. With all the smokey tastes, dinner was a five-star meal.

Ethan leaned back in his chair at the outdoor dining table, rubbing his stomach with both hands. "It doesn't get more Californian than that, John. Excellent meal. I think you grill better than your old man."

"I learned from the master." John leaned back in his chair as well, loosening his belt a notch. "My dad put together a feast every Sunday. I remember the summers during our high school days. You and I would polish off everything at dinner. Then raid the fridge in the middle of the night for my mom's apple pie."

Ethan gave a belly laugh. "She'd get so mad at us and then shoo us back into your room, swearing we had hollow legs because she didn't know where we put all that food."

"I remember my dad catching us staring endlessly into the fridge. He'd say, 'You're gonna get frostbitten ears if you don't close that damn door.'"

The laughter around the table was exactly what Tyler needed. She'd spent the better part of two weeks in a state of heightened anxiety. Her rational side told her the bastard was no longer a physical threat, yet her emotional side couldn't shake the terror he'd subjected her to for thirteen years. His return had undone years of successfully compartmentalizing her past from her present. Tonight offered a much needed distraction.

"So, John," Tyler said. "Ethan tells me you two used to get into a lot of trouble."

"Oh gosh, there was this one time when Ethan found this foot-long lizard and—"

Ethan cleared his throat loudly. "I have two words for you, John—Francis Boyle."

His cousin's eyes shot wide open, and his face took on a "you wouldn't dare" expression. Ethan nodded. John sprang from his chair and began clearing the table. "My, my, look at the time. We better get these dishes cleared if we're gonna catch the end of the Warriors game."

Man code, my ass. More like mutually assured destruction by means of embarrassing childhood tales. Tyler silently vowed to pry stories out of them someday. If Syd's exaggeratedly narrowed eyes were any indication, she intended to do so too.

After everyone pitched in to clean the dishes, Syd poured the after-dinner coffee. Ethan and John escaped to the media room to watch the basketball game, and Tyler eagerly accepted Syd's invitation to return to the outdoor patio. The cool, moist, nearly spring air was a refreshing departure from the dry valley.

Tyler settled into a plush chair next to Syd. "Is it always this nice here?"

"Pretty much. Perfect temps. Low humidity. So unlike New York. When I lived there, I'd work up a sweat walking to the mailbox."

"That's right. Weren't you in the hotel business? That's quite the leap to running a winery."

"Not as much as you think. Once I learned the winemaking process, the rest was easy. Managing a business is fairly universal."

"Which hotel did you manage?"

"Not one hotel. My family owns Castle Resorts."

"Get outta town!"

Syd gave a quick shrug as if owning a multi-billion-dollar international business was nothing. "Frankly, as one who doesn't like change, I don't miss it. I left before the technology boom, and now all the resorts have been playing catch-up with major renovations and technology upgrades. The winemaking process changes very little. The only variable is Mother Nature from year to year. My blood pressure has never been better." Syd sipped on her coffee. "What about you, Tyler? Ethan tells me you started your own business."

"I did." Tyler smiled broadly. Her trauma and inability to focus on her own needs might have delayed her dream of owning her own business by several years, but the wait had made it much more satisfying. "Two years ago, my best friend and I started a graphic and web design company. We make a good team. She's the techie, and I'm the creative one."

"So it's just the two of you?"

The question triggered a tightness in Tyler's chest. The foray into hiring their first employee had turned her world upside down. She shook off the events of the last two weeks to focus on Syd's question. "We've been picking up more and more clients. So much so that we hired another designer this week. In fact, I recently completed two web pages for The Napa Riverside Hotel and The Green Willow restaurant right here in town."

"Really? We supply wine to both those places. I'll have to check out your designs."

Tyler yawned after taking a sip of her coffee. Her gaze settled on the handful of lights dotting the rolling hills. She longed for a day when she could embrace a peaceful place like this where the busy world didn't exist. But she couldn't. She wasn't whole. She needed enough chaos in her life to keep her pain in the past.

"You must be ready for bed."

"Definitely." Tyler grabbed her coffee mug and returned to the kitchen with Syd leading the way. "I think I'll take you up on that bike of yours tomorrow. I'd like to see more of the area while you and Ethan meet with that secret client of his."

"Thanks for understanding. She wants to keep this issue private." Syd rubbed Tyler's arms. "I'll have one of the crew pull out my bike and have it ready before breakfast. You'll enjoy riding around here. The trails that follow the river are breathtaking. Now, you get some rest. I'm off to grill the men about Francis Boyle."

CHAPTER FOURTEEN

Pulling up to the gate guarding the Barnette Winery this morning came with less guilt today than it had last week. Alex had the access code committed to memory now, and she had the added comfort of not being a stranger in her sister's life—a life she envied. Syd had dared to marry John and buck everything Castle, a boldness Alex had yet to embrace. Castle Resorts wasn't in Syd's blood the way it was in hers, though, which made her cutting daily ties with their father appear easy.

Alex wished the Parkinson's hadn't taken over. Maybe her father wouldn't have put maintaining appearances above her happiness. Some days, more frequently since she was last here, she wished she didn't love him and Castle Resorts so much, so she could cut and run like her sister had. If either wish came true, she'd stop living a life of pretense. Her one solace—William's retirement. It had been eighteen years since his diagnosis, thirteen since their agreement, but when he finally handed over the reins, she swore she'd live her life on her terms, open and proud.

At the main house, the front door swung open to Syd's outspread arms, which pulled Alex into a colossal, welcoming hug. "Two weekends in a row. Maybe you should get yourself into a bind more often."

Alex pulled back, resolve fueling her next words. "I'll take a hard pass on that, but I promise not to be a stranger anymore."

"Good enough, baby sis." Syd glanced at Alex's shoulder. "I see you've brought your camera."

"Since I didn't get any pictures the last time I was here, I thought I give it another try."

"It's the perfect weather for it. Come on in." Syd led Alex into the living room. There, a man with graying, shortly cropped dark brown hair she assumed was John's cousin rose from the leather couch. His golf attire, a collared-pullover shirt tucked into belted dark slacks, accentuated his trim waist and muscular frame. Six feet tall and with chiseled features, he projected a commanding presence. "Alex, this is Ethan Falling."

"It's a pleasure, Alex." Ethan extended his hand and gave hers a firm yet polite shake. Alex respected a man who greeted a woman with a strong handshake. She took it as a show of respect. That he didn't consider her frail or lesser.

"It's a pleasure as well, Ethan. I understand from Syd's call yesterday that your wife is here, too. I'd love to meet her after our consult."

"I'm sorry, Alex. She wanted to respect your privacy, so she went into town to do a little shopping. She should be back in a few hours."

"That's a shame. I can't stay too long. I have to return to San Francisco to meet with the contractor heading up our remodel."

"That is a shame," Syd said. "She's an outstanding graphic and website designer. I checked out some of her work last night. You might want to touch base with her when you're ready to revamp Castle Resorts' website."

"I sure will. Family first and all."

"I'll email you her contact info. We better get right to it." Ethan gestured for Alex and Syd to sit in the pair of easy chairs parallel to the couch. Before retaking his seat, he retrieved several documents from a manilla folder that had been resting on the dark oak coffee table. He handed copies to both Alex and Syd. "I pulled Kelly's phone records for the three months before and after her miraculous stock purchase."

Ethan's tactics surprised Alex. "Was that legal?"

Without a change in expression, Ethan replied, "I cut some corners, and I'm happy I did. We already knew that Kelly purchased almost two thousand nine hundred shares of iQuench at three dollars and fifty cents a share in September 2003. By the end of October, she sold all of her shares at an incredible thirty-eight dollars a share. That's a one hundred-thousand-dollar profit."

"You found a way to connect her to iQuench?" Alex asked.

Ethan's lips curled into a grin. "Kelly telephoned a man by the name of Nick Castor daily for several weeks leading up to the stock purchase. She stopped calling him a few days after she sold the stock. You'll like this part. Castor co-founded iQuench, the small beverage company based in Philly that developed the Neo energy drink in 2003."

"I've heard of that drink. Isn't it part of the PopCo line?" Alex asked.

"It is now. PopCo purchased iQuench along with the rights to Neo in October 2003. Castor is now a marketing manager in PopCo's North America Beverages Division."

Syd shifted in her chair. "Phone calls don't prove insider trading."

Ethan handed each woman a copy of an October 2003 newspaper article. "It seems the acquisition of iQuench was a big deal in the beverage industry. I found this article in *The Wall Street Journal* detailing the transaction. Check out the picture. There's Nick Castor at a charity event, holding hands with and looking rather chummy with Kelly Thatcher."

"So you think Nick and Kelly were doing the nasty, and Nick shared information about the acquisition with Kelly before it went public," Syd said.

Ethan pointed at Syd. "Bingo."

Incomplete thoughts swirling in Alex's head took shape— Kelly, Castor, phone calls, stocks, PopCo. A plan of attack flashed like an atomic blast, forecasting the destruction of one Kelly Thatcher. This was one of the few times Alex was genuinely grateful to be a Castle.

If the confused looks on Syd and Ethan's faces were any measure, her persistent grin must've clued them that she already had formulated a plan.

"What's your plan, baby sis?"

"We need to call Abby."

"Who's Abby?" Ethan asked.

"Abigail Spencer, founder and chairperson of The Spencer Foundation."

"Why her?" Ethan asked.

"Abby is good friends with Indra Kapoor, going back to their college days. Indra is the president and CFO of PopCo." Alex leaned forward, emphasizing her point. "She can leverage Castor to force him to turn on Kelly."

Ethan matched Alex's grin and posture. "We'll need a sworn, notarized statement that he won't be able to back out of later on. We'll also want any pictures, text messages, emails, etc., that would document their relationship and what information he shared with her and when."

Alex pulled out and dialed her cell phone, foregoing her typically more personal greeting. "Hello, Abby. I need your help. Can we meet tomorrow night?" Alex wrapped up her brief and cordial call with the agreement to meet at Abby's penthouse late Sunday night and returned her phone to her jacket pocket. "We're all set. Thank you, Ethan. This is exactly what I needed to get the upper hand."

"My pleasure, Alex. Anything for family." Ethan stood and shook her hand. "I think we're done."

"Agreed. Before I go, though, I'd like to speak to you in private about another matter."

Ethan cocked his head at Syd, who, in turn, arched an eyebrow at Alex. "What other trouble have you gotten yourself into, baby sis?" Syd asked.

"This has nothing to do with me." Alex wasn't prepared to tell her sister that their brother was a thief. At least not until she knew the full extent of the problem.

"Uh-huh." Syd did not appear convinced. Not in the least. "I'll be in the kitchen. Don't leave without saying goodbye."

"Thank you, Syd. I won't be long." After Syd left and Alex and Ethan returned to their seats, she pulled a large folder from her leather satchel. "I need this to stay between you and me, Ethan. Can I trust you won't share any of this with John or Syd?"

"Of course, Alex. You're my client, and in my business, client confidentiality trumps family."

Alex slid the thick folder and a thumb drive across the table. They contained key documents, reports, and receipts Robbie had gathered on the Times Square project. Her heart sank as she weighed the gravity of her next words, but she had to get answers before William anointed Andrew CFO.

"I suspect my brother is embezzling from the company." She couldn't tell if she'd shocked or disgusted Ethan because his expression never changed—the mark of a talented investigator.

"I'm not a forensic accountant, so I'm not sure how I can help."

"I've already done most of the legwork. I believe he's siphoned a quarter-million dollars from Castle Resorts using a contracting scheme. Besides my brother's, one other name kept popping up on the documents, which leads me to believe this guy might be involved too. His name is Victor Padula. I need you to find out who he is and any information you can dig up on the two companies he's associated with—V.P. Construction and something called Suite Hospitality."

Ethan pledged his help and arranged to call Alex in a few days. After the meeting concluded, he excused himself to search for John while Alex found Syd in the kitchen.

"Hey, Syd, I really have to get going."

"You and your secrets." Syd shook her head. *Sometimes family secrets were a good thing*, Alex thought. Despite Andrew's penchant for living on the edge, Syd had a soft spot for him. And in return, Andrew had a soft spot for Syd, despite her abandoning the family business. The last thing Alex wanted was to shatter that dynamic. If she could handle this discreetly, she could put Andrew in his place, make Castle Resorts whole, and salvage the love between siblings.

Alex rubbed her sister's arm and offered her a reassuring wink. "I promise you, if I think you need to know about this, I'll tell you. Okay?" Alex eased the camera case over her shoulder as she had countless times with her first Leica. "I'll keep you updated on the Kelly front."

"Okay." Syd's skepticism manifested in her trademark narrowed eyebrows, but she appeared convinced Alex would keep her word.

After saying goodbye, Alex hopped into her rental car, placed her treasured Leica within reach on the passenger seat, and started her drive to San Francisco. As she approached the town's railroad crossing, the slow-moving Napa Valley Wine Train began its crawl into the station, and traffic came to a halt with her first in line at the crossing arm. On any other day, she'd not-so-silently curse the prospect of being late to an important meeting, but today the delay presented the perfect opportunity to break in Syd's precious gift.

At the blare of the train's horn, Alex raised her gaze to the crowded pedestrian and bike path paralleling the train tracks in front of her car. A single passerby was moving in the opposite direction of the moving train and the rest of the crowd. It made an interesting contrast. The training from her three college photography courses returned like a professional athlete's muscle memory. She opened the aged leather case protecting the Leica and slung the strap over her neck. "Never lose control of your tools," her mother used to say, always securing her cameras around her neck before snapping a single picture.

Alex took a few pictures, alternating the focus between the walkers, bike riders, and the train. When the end of the train neared the crossing, one of the bike riders stopped in the middle of Alex's view and stared curiously at her. Alex snapped a picture, then lowered the camera to get a better view of the cyclist. It was a woman, a beautiful blonde who looked familiar. Before she could figure out how, the crossing arms rose and the car behind her honked. The cyclist, startled by the honking, resumed her pedaling and continued through the crossing, occasionally looking back over her shoulder toward Alex. Alex removed the camera from around her neck, dropped it on the passenger seat, and put the car in drive. As she proceeded over the tracks, she too peeked at the cyclist, gazing at her until she faded from her field of vision.

The drive to Castle Resort San Francisco, fraught with heavy weekend travelers, gave Alex an hour to consider the cyclist. A sense of familiarity fed a desire to find out more; the pictures she had taken held the key. At the hotel, she gathered her purse and camera and headed to the management offices to meet with the hotel manager and the contractor overseeing the renovations. She knocked on the manager's door, and a voice promptly invited her inside.

"Ms. Castle, please come in." George Hammer was, by far, the most efficient manager in the Castle Resorts' stable. He never failed to treat Alex like royalty, though that was a quirk she would have preferred he drop. After all, he was a valued senior employee, not a peasant in servitude. George rose from behind his desk, buttoning his dark suit blazer over the mauve shirt beneath. He repositioned a guest chair to give Alex a perfect view of both his desk and the exquisite view of the bay through the window. "The contractor will be here in a few minutes. He got caught behind a three-car pile-up on the Nimitz."

"No worries, George. I'm glad he agreed to take the meeting on Saturday." Alex brushed off his concern. "I need to fly back to New York tomorrow."

"Of course, Ms. Castle. We have the owner's suite waiting for you," George said. "I hope you find the room satisfactory. I had housekeeping leave fresh peonies, your favorite."

"I'm sure it will be fine, but I do have a question." Alex retrieved from her satchel the roll of film she had pulled from her new-old Leica. She'd snapped only six pictures on the roll of twenty-four, but she wasn't willing to wait to see the images captured there. "Is there any place close where I can get some film developed today?"

"I'm sure there is. Hold on." George pulled out his cell phone and hit speed dial. "Harold, Ms. Castle needs some film developed immediately. Please come to my office and see to it." George smiled as he disconnected the call. "My assistant will be right over. Is there anything else we can do for you before our meeting starts?"

"No, thank you. I'm eager to see the progress of the renovations and how they compare to Times Square. Both projects must be on the same page."

Later, in the owner's suite following a productive meeting and revealing tour, Alex reviewed her notes on the Times Square and San Francisco renovations. She highlighted a few modifications needed to align both projects and jotted down her thoughts on the schedule and budget impacts. A knock on the door interrupted her train of thought. She walked across the sitting area and opened the door.

"Hello, Ms. Castle. I got your film developed." Harold handed Alex an envelope. Last year, Alex had raised an eyebrow at George's choice of his nephew as his personal assistant, but this eager, well-dressed young man right out of high school had turned out to be a gem. "I billed it to Mr. Hammer's account."

"Thank you, Harold. I appreciate you getting this developed so fast."

"My pleasure, ma'am. Will there be anything else?" Following a few more pleasantries, Harold excused himself.

Alex made a straight line to the room's polished tiger maple desk. She sat on the high-back swivel chair, opened the envelope, and sifted through the photographs until she found the one she was looking for. She studied the closeup of the cyclist staring right into the lens of her camera. She resembled the woman she'd bumped into at the Napa riverfront the week before, Alex realized.

"It's her," she whispered. Their short yet intense encounter had left her feeling undone. Initially, she had been embarrassed by causing the woman to drop her package. But then...she'd taken in those intriguing gray eyes, long wavy blond hair, and the smile that had lightened her entire face. They'd turned Alex into a tongue-tied teenager. It was a face she never wanted to forget.

"Who are you?" Alex stroked a fingertip across the image as if the gesture were a prelude to making love.

CHAPTER FIFTEEN

Manhattan, New York

Kelly, Andrew, and crisscrossing the country two weeks in a row had taken its toll. It would've been nice and, in fact, called for to be able to take a catnap in the taxi ride from LaGuardia to Abby's Park Avenue apartment. The constant start and stop at the traffic lights and her cabbie's spirited cursing at the thick flow on Park Avenue, however, kept Alex's eyes wide open.

She focused her stare out the side window at the dark evening sky. Light sprinkles had faded, and clouds had given way to reveal a bright, nearly full moon observable between passing high-rises. Her thoughts drifted to Napa. She calculated the moon would be visible there too by this time and wondered if her mystery woman had her gaze fixed on it at this very moment. Alex didn't understand her obsession. They'd crossed paths only twice and briefly, yet an undeniable connection had sprouted. It was settled. After she'd dealt with Kelly and Andrew, she needed to find her.

Harley came into view the moment the elevator doors swooshed open to the floor of the sprawling penthouse that

Abby shared with her daughter. When she wasn't out on the town, Harley had the role of official greeter.

Harley dropped her smile, exchanging it for a frown. "You look absolutely drained, sweet Alex. Come inside." She ushered Alex past the threshold and took her coat. "Can I get you a glass of wine?"

"Are you kidding? That would put me right in a coma. Something with caffeine and make it a double."

"I'll have Sarah whip up a cappuccino and bring it to the library."

"Is that where Abby is?"

Harley offered a nod fed by blatant curiosity. "Mother didn't tell me a thing, and you've been avoiding my calls." She planted a fist on each hip, arms akimbo. "Spill it, Alexandra Castle."

"Why don't you join us in the library? I'm too tired to go through this twice."

"Fine. Don't start without me."

Harley turned down the hallway leading to the kitchen while Alex took a right to walk to the library. It was her favorite room in the apartment, partly because Abby and Harley had selected every finishing touch. Abby's taste in fabrics and furniture was pristine, but Harley's eye for paintings and sculptures was flawless, born out of her art history major and years of heading the Spencer Foundation's annual art auction fundraiser.

Alex had so many fond memories of that space, but her favorite was a game of hide-and-seek with her mother that had ended in an epic tickling match. That was the last time Alex had laughed with her. She privately hoped Abby never sold this place and handed it down to Harley.

The bones of the room—dark cherry wood floors, matching floor-to-ceiling bookshelves and cabinets, and a rock-faced fireplace—hadn't changed since her mother was alive. The furnishings had several times, though. Polished wood coffee and end tables surrounded an overstuffed cream-colored leather couch and twin chairs to form a cozy seating area.

When Alex knocked on one of the open double doors, Abby looked up from her favorite chair, her smile outshining the logs burning in the fireplace behind her. She had fanned out a hardback book in both hands, and reading glasses were resting low on the bridge of her nose. She placed both items on an end table before waving her in. "Alex, dear. Come. Come. You must be exhausted."

"I am." Alex took a seat on the couch across from her, instantly losing ground in her battle with fatigue. Instead of curling up with her pillow at a decent hour last night, she had spent a good hour or two studying the black-and-white picture of her mystery woman, memorizing her features and her light skin and dark blond hair. On the plane ride, she'd been negligent with her time, too, her mind still fixated on the woman she had to meet rather than working on the looming deadline for presenting a detailed formal plan to put Times Square in the black.

"You were vague on the phone yesterday, but whatever you need, consider it done." Abby's firm tone was precisely what Alex counted on; besting Kelly depended on her helping hand.

"I won't blame you if you change your mind after you hear what I'm asking."

"Nonsense."

"Yes, nonsense." Harley walked in and sat on the couch next to Alex, angling herself to look Alex in the eye. The inquisition was about to begin. "Now, it's late on a Sunday night. What couldn't wait until morning?"

"Kelly Thatcher."

"Thatcher?" Abby cocked her head to one side as if shaking a stubborn memory loose. "Wasn't she the one William almost disowned you over?"

"The worst mistake of my life." Alex rolled her eyes at the memory of the blowout between her and her father sophomore year. He never revealed how he discovered she'd taken a woman as a lover, but she long had suspected he had a security man keeping tabs on her and Andrew when they were out of his orbit.

Harley vigorously rubbed her hands together as if rolling a devious plan into a tidy little ball. At thirty-three, she should be past enjoying teenage-like gossip, but not one nugget ever got past Harley Spencer. "Ooohhh. Did you get what you needed?"

"I think so." Alex shifted her attention. "But that's where you come in, Abby." Alex paused at Abby's inquisitive nod. "I was young and stupid in college and took some photos of Kelly and me. Last week, Kelly used them to blackmail me into giving her a job. I need your help to get her off my back and out of my life for good."

"I see." Abby remained expressionless.

Alex handed Abby the file Ethan had assembled on Kelly. "My private investigator believes Kelly had insider information about the PopCo acquisition of iQuench weeks before the deal and made a sizable profit on the stock. We believe she was involved with the iQuench founder, Nick Castor." Alex pointed to the picture of him and Kelly. "But we have no direct proof of the insider knowledge before the purchase and sale of the stock."

"How can I help?"

"Castor is an executive at PopCo. This might be asking too much, but I know you and Indra were friends at Yale. I need her to intercede and force Castor's hand."

"It's not too much to ask." A distant look commanded Abby's eyes, followed by a faint, satisfied grin. There was a story behind that smile, of that Alex was sure. "It's been too long since I've spoken to Indra."

"Have you spoken to her since Avi's funeral?" Harley asked.

"No, I haven't, and it's about time I correct that. I'm sure Indra will be more than happy to help, and if Mr. Castor values his freedom and his career, he'll cooperate." Abby marched over to her desk, retrieved her cell phone, and dialed. *Interesting*, Alex thought. Abby had Indra's number on speed dial.

"Hello, Indra… I know it's late, but this couldn't wait. I have a favor to ask."

CHAPTER SIXTEEN

Sacramento, California

Tyler blamed cowardice for her longstanding denial. She had not realized how deep that denial was until Maddie had used the word PTSD. Burying her pain had allowed her to live a productive life, yes, but she had recently discovered that a productive life wasn't the same as a healthy one. She hoped Gail Sanders, the clinical therapist Maddie had recommended, would help her change that, starting this morning.

Gail's modestly furnished home office was filled with light and books and its windows offered a picturesque view of the front garden. Two plush leather upright chairs flanked a matching ottoman in the center of the room.

Maybe it was Gail's crisp casual attire instead of the expected stuffy business suit or that they appeared to be about the same age, but Tyler found her as inviting as her office. Her bright smile, firm handshake, and disarming eye contact put her right at ease. Following pleasantries, Gail suggested they sit in the leather chairs. "I'm glad you're here. Coming marks a major first step."

Tyler nodded. In two sentences, Gail had confirmed she'd made the right choice by coming. "It is."

"So, what brings you here today?"

For the next half hour, Tyler recited cursory details about the rape, the bastard's reemergence, Bree's paternity, and her persistent difficulty with intimacy. She left out an important point she wasn't quite ready to address—the mystery woman. Gail listened and took notes. Her probing questions focused on gathering facts, not assessing emotion.

Gail glanced at her wristwatch. "I know we said half an hour for our first session, but I get the sense you don't want to go yet. Am I right?"

Tyler shifted in her chair. If she was that transparent with a person she met half an hour ago, was she the same with Ethan? Like Gail, he was trained to read people and to ferret out deception. A lump formed in her throat at the prospect. She wasn't ready to face the consequences of her feelings, and that worry alone was enough for her to respond with the truth.

"There is something else." Tyler twisted her wedding ring. After eighteen years on her finger, that gold band had become an extension of her. She rarely took it off. Without it, she felt naked. *Sad*, she thought, knowing now that she wore it out of habit, not devotion.

"My next appointment isn't for some time," Gail said. "Let's continue."

Thank goodness, Tyler thought. Everything was begging to come out. With the family court hearing looming in one week, discussing what had her questioning a central piece of herself couldn't wait until Gail could squeeze her in next.

"Three days after I lost it from seeing that bastard, I literally bumped into a beautiful woman in Napa. A week later, I saw her again. I haven't been able to get her off my mind."

"Tell me about the first time you ran into her."

"The encounter with him still had me unnerved, so my best friend took me for a girls' getaway in Napa. After spending all day in the spa, we went shopping and took a stroll along the riverfront. I wasn't watching where I was going and bumped into her. I dropped my shopping bag. We both bent down to pick it up, and then I looked at her for the first time. She was stunning. Exotic. I had never seen anyone like her and couldn't take my eyes off her. Our hands briefly touched, and I felt—I don't know what I felt, but I knew I wanted to feel it again. And her voice. It was mesmerizing. She said only a few words, but her voice was as smooth as silk."

"It sounds like an interesting encounter. What about it bothers you?"

"For one thing, I've been with the same man for twenty-two years. In all that time, I have never had romantic thoughts about anyone else." The term "romantic" tumbled out of Tyler's mouth before she could stop it. Until now, she hadn't labeled her thoughts. Her spontaneous response scared the hell out of her.

"Are you having romantic thoughts about this woman?"

"I'm not sure what I'm having." Tyler left out the dream in which she made love with the stranger. She could only reveal so many embarrassing things in one session. "I just know I can't get her out of my head. Something must be wrong with me because I love my husband."

"Tyler, you've had a lot to deal with the past several weeks. Just because you don't understand your feelings doesn't mean something is wrong with you. It means we have a lot of work to do. How does this woman make you feel?"

"Alive."

"Does Ethan make you feel that way?"

"Not in a very long time."

"That's not unnatural in a long-term relationship. How would you compare the thoughts you have about this woman and the romantic thoughts you have about your husband?"

Tyler gave an uneasy laugh. Gail had successfully steered their conversation to the root of her problems. It would be easy to blame the adage that all life partners eventually fall out of romantic love but stay together out of a more profound one. That, however, wouldn't be the entire truth.

"Since the rape, I have had zero romantic thoughts about Ethan. He's been very patient, but I know he wants more intimacy than I can give. What little I offer is difficult. I'm simply not interested in sex anymore."

"Do you masturbate?"

The question was as jarring as a train whistle outside her bedroom window at three a.m., shaking her from a dead sleep. Tyler's instinct was to ignore the uncomfortable question or lie. She chose the former and remained silent.

"The look on your face tells me the answer is yes. It's nothing to be ashamed of. The fact that you do tells me you still have a sex drive. Here's the big question. Do you miss being intimate with another person?"

Tyler didn't have to think about the answer. The absence of passion was her biggest regret. "I do. It was an important part of my marriage. I miss the skin-to-skin contact. The passion. The emotional closeness. The way I used to feel in sync with another body."

"Do you think you could have those things with a woman?"

"I never considered it before, but I must admit I've never felt so exhilarated by a single touch. My big question is, why do I suddenly feel this way about a woman?"

"I'm not sure sudden is an accurate description. Sexual assault rarely changes a person's sexual orientation, but it can surface latent desires you never knew existed."

"Are you suggesting that I've always been attracted to women?"

"I'm saying that it's possible. We have a lot to unpack, Tyler, starting with your PTSD."

Your PTSD. Those two words strung together made everything she'd gone through real, from the rape to the harm she caused herself by ignoring the trauma. There was no denying it. Her days of turning her back on her pain had come to an end. Lips trembling with overwhelming relief, Tyler was as shaky as her voice. "Okay."

* * *

Next Monday's court hearing couldn't come soon enough for Tyler Falling. Maybe then, she could put the threat of that bastard behind her, along with the fear of Bree finding out he was her biological father. Until then, she hoped, work would keep her mind off things she had little control over. Things like whether that horrible man would show up to family court. Things like the mysterious woman living rent-free in her head.

"Knock. Knock." Shelby, Creative Juice's first apprentice graphic artist, stuck her head around Tyler's open office door. Tyler waved her in. Today, she looked extra-stylish in white slacks and a black and white vertically striped blouse that accented her ebony skin.

"What's up, Shelby?"

"I wanted to make sure you received my mockup for the Micker's Café logo before I head out to lunch. We promised the client a draft by the end of the day."

"I did get it, and I like it a lot. You really captured the owner's vision." Right out of graduate school, Shelby was young, shy, creative, and talented beyond belief and had worked out better than expected. Her best quality: a preference to interact in person instead of email, text, or phone. "I have one or two suggestions that I think would make it pop even more. Look for it after you get back."

"Yes, ma'am."

Tyler scrunched her nose, feeling like the team mom. She'd had this discussion with Shelby almost daily since she came on board last week. "Ma'am" made her feel old. At forty, she had reached the point where avoiding reminders of her middle-age status had become necessary.

"I'm sorry. I forgot. Yes, Tyler. Can I pick you up soup and a sandwich?"

"Thanks for asking, but I'm brown-bagging it today since my appointment this morning had me missing an hour of work."

The moment Shelby disappeared down the hallway, Maddie stepped in. The silly grin plastered on her face made Tyler think she'd spotted JLo at the neighborhood coffee shop. "You won't believe who I have on the phone."

"Do I get twenty questions?"

"We don't have time." Maddie was vibrating with excitement. "Alexandra Castle of Castle Resorts is asking for you. She wants to discuss a contract for us to revamp their web presence."

"I didn't think she'd call."

"Wait. You knew we might get a nibble from Castle Resorts, and you said nothing?"

"Ethan's cousin married a Castle. He said she'd put in a good word for us, but I thought nothing would come of it."

Maddie pointed an index finger at Tyler's desk phone. "Pick it up."

Tyler rolled her eyes. On the outside, she appeared laidback, she hoped. On the inside, she was as nervous as the day she had walked down the aisle. Snagging Castle Resorts as a client would set up Creative Juices for years. She lifted the handset as if she were doing no more than placing a to-go order and pressed the flashing button. "This is Tyler Falling."

"Hi, Tyler. This is Alex Castle. My sister, Syd Barnette, gave me your name."

Tyler hesitated. She had the sense she'd heard Ms. Castle's soft, enchanting voice before, but she couldn't place where. Maybe she'd seen her on the news or something. Right now, the voice didn't matter as much as what Alexandra Castle had said. "Yes, of course. Syd is a gem. She's such a wonderful host. How can I help you, Ms. Castle?"

"First, a woman with a voice as pleasing as yours should never call me Ms. Please, call me Alex."

"All right, Alex." Tyler already liked Alex Castle. She wasn't full of herself. "How can I help you?"

"This weekend Syd sang your praises, and I'm glad she did. I did a little research, and I was impressed. The site you put together that won last year's Webby was spectacular. Sleek, eye-catching, and intuitive to navigate. My company is in the market to contract a new web designer, and your caliber of work is exactly what we're looking for."

"I'm flattered, Alex."

"It's well deserved. I'd like to put you in touch with my Chief Technology Officer. He can go over the specs we'll need for a proposal."

Every dream Tyler ever had about owning her own business was on the verge of becoming a reality. *This is crazy*, she thought. She hadn't forecast nabbing a contract of this size in her long-term business plan until their fifth or sixth year. If she and Maddie played their cards right, Castle Resorts would propel Creative Juices into the big leagues.

Keep your cool, Tyler commanded herself. *Don't gush.* That would be such an amateur move. "Thank you, Alex. We appreciate the opportunity to be in the running."

"I have a good feeling about this, Tyler. If your proposal is half as good as the work I've already seen, I'm sure we'll be in business."

"I have a good feeling about this, too." Call it intuition or a good vibe, but Tyler was sure this was the start of something life changing. She concluded the call with the promise to have a proposal to her within two days. When Tyler returned the handset to its cradle, she reclined in her desk chair. She stared at some nonexistent object in the air, inanely thinking more about Alex's voice at the moment than the prospect of the contract of a lifetime. First, she had admitted her romantic feelings for the mystery woman. Now, she was fawning over Alex Castle. *I must be gay*, she thought.

"Earth to Tyler." Maddie snapped her fingers inches in front of Tyler's face, drawing her out of her trance. "What did she say?"

"She wants a proposal."

Tyler was on cloud nine the rest of the day, accomplishing little beyond Shelby's café logo review. The drive home after she picked up Bree wasn't much better. She was so excited about her company's big break that she had barely absorbed Bree's retelling of the latest rift among her teammates, a clash that stemmed from who had snubbed whom over birthday party invitations—the height of twelve-year-old drama.

"Were you even listening, Mom?"

"Of course I was, honey. I'm sure it will work itself out." No matter the pre-teen disputes between teammates, they always called a truce by the next softball game or practice.

Tyler made the final turn into the driveway of their suburban Sacramento home. One day, she hoped, she and Ethan would clean out the garage and make room enough to house at least one of their cars because the relentless valley heat regularly baked the inside of her sedan sufficiently to cook a soufflé.

Gathering her purse and work satchel, Tyler circled around to the back of the car to retrieve Bree's softball gear. As she did, a faded sedan on the street with a door a different color from the body caught her attention. She wasn't the neighborhood busybody by any stretch, but she knew the neighbors' cars and those of their regular visitors on this quiet court. This wasn't one of them.

A figure sat still in the driver's seat. When she focused on its face, she gasped. The anger and disappointment in the bastard's eyes showed loud and clear from across the street. She felt glued in place, unable to flee to safety. Her painful past and present were in danger of colliding, and that threat was enough to knock Tyler out of her stupor. Her first instinct was to protect her daughter. She slammed the trunk shut without retrieving Bree's things.

"Get inside now." Her uncharacteristic command didn't contain her usual politeness, but her rapid breaths and the tingling down her spine dictated a hasty escape.

"But—"

"Just get in the house." Tyler pushed Bree up the driveway, keeping one eye on the danger behind her. As she reached the porch with Bree in the lead, the bastard's car pulled away from the curb and crept down the street. Her hands shook as she stuck the key in the deadbolt, missing the hole twice.

"Are you okay, Mom?" Tyler hated the fear she had put in Bree's voice, but they needed to get to safety.

"I'll be fine. I just have to pee." A lie was better than the truth. She pushed the door open before glancing over her shoulder.

He was gone, but not her paralyzing fear. She wasn't ready to have her family's dark secret come to light. Inside, she locked the deadbolt and drew the blinds on the entryway window, an extra step she deemed necessary for her peace of mind.

"Can I get a snack, Mom?"

"Sure, anything you want." Tyler rushed her words without the daily qualifier of choosing something healthy and light to not spoil her dinner. Thinking of anything other than her family crumbling at its core was impossible. She dumped her bags on the living room couch before shooting down the hallway, whizzing past framed family photos on the walls. After she locked the bathroom door behind her, the walls closed in. Her world shrank with each passing second. She splashed water on her face to calm her racing heartbeat, but the pressure continued to build. The bastard knew where she worked. He knew where she lived. He knew what Bree looked like. Did Bree see him? Did she piece it together?

The room spun. *Quick, quick, quick.* What did her cardiologist tell her to do if she felt lightheaded? *Think, think, think. Towel.* She turned on the water again, ripped the hand towel from the wall-mounted ring holder, and threw it in the basin. The lights dimmed. She felt wobbly. *No, no, no.* "You can control this." Tyler held her breath and bore down on her lungs to slow her breathing. She lay on the floor, placing the soaked towel over her face.

Minutes passed. Tyler's heart continued to thump dangerously fast. Her chest still rose and fell, gasping for air like it used to do when she ran track in high school. God, she hated running now. Her mind was still fixated on the dangers the bastard presented and how her life would never be the same. Nothing the doctor had suggested calmed her.

Tyler threw the towel on the floor, closed her eyes, and retreated to the one place in her head that calmed her when reality was too much. Going to her safe place, she sat against a mature oak, transfixed by the slow-moving creek. The clear, trickling water threatened to put her to sleep, but sleep was her enemy. If she gave in to it, she feared, she'd never wake up. She stayed, watched, and waited until the water slowed to a micro-drip. When she opened her eyes, the lights were bright again and the room had become stationary. The panic attack had passed.

Pulling herself to a seated position atop the toilet, she determined that her mind and body had stabilized. Now she faced a weighty dilemma. Should she tell Ethan? He would pay the bastard a visit, beat him to within an inch of his life, and lose his job. Only if he showed his face again or appeared in family court would she take that risk. Until then… This. Never. Happened.

CHAPTER SEVENTEEN

Manhattan, New York

Director of Guest Relations at Times Square wasn't the position Kelly had had in mind when she concocted her blackmail plan, but she had to admit she was damn good at it. Over the years, she'd perfected the ability to impress the rich and famous, and that's exactly what this job required. Alex was a genius for placing her here, and in Kelly's book, gifted and hot made for an irresistible combination.

But enough with thoughts of Alex. Kelly needed to concentrate on next week's VIPs by preparing for their written special requests and anticipating the unstated ones. "Above-and-beyond, flawless, upscale, professional service"—that was the phrase Alex had used when she outlined the expectations for Kelly's job, and she wasn't going to disappoint her.

Nearly one week behind an expensive desk, Kelly had yet to convince herself that her scheme was only about paying off her debts. Too many thoughts of the woman she considered perfection in heels occupied her day. She'd rationalized her flirtation was a natural reflex—because what warm-blooded man or woman wouldn't flirt with Alexandra Castle? Sexy, smart, rich, and fun to be around. Only an idiot would've dumped a woman like that to chase a bigger trust fund, as Alex had put it. There was no denying it. Alex was *the* one that got away.

The desk phone buzzed, eliciting a grin from Kelly. On the other end of that annoying sound sat her assistant. Her. Personal. Assistant. The thought still made her giddy. At her previous jobs, neither of which had lasted six months, she had had to share administrative assistants among a sea of entry-level managers. She liked to think since Alex had seen fit to give her one of her own, her job was more important than she initially thought.

She pressed the intercom button. "Yes, Trish."

"Mr. Castle is here to see you."

Kelly sucked in a short, audible gasp. The old man was here? Did this mean her time at Castle Resorts was up? *Damn it.* And just when she'd begun to enjoy the spoils. "Thank you, Trish. Send him in. Oh, and can you bring me the files on Arnault and Bettencourt?"

"Yes, Ms. Thatcher."

A moment later, her office door swung open. She sprang to her feet, straightened her suit blazer, and took sure strides to greet her important visitor. "Mr.—"

"Hello, Kelly."

"Andrew." Kelly stopped in mid-stride, relieved it wasn't William. Andrew's smug expression, though, triggered her survival instincts. This was no social call. "What are you doing here?"

"We need to have a serious talk about your future, Kelly."

"What do you mean? Alex seems happy with my performance."

"Cut the crap. I know exactly why Alex hired you." Andrew plopped onto the leather couch and propped his feet atop the cherry wood coffee table like the arrogant trust fund baby she remembered. "I want those pictures."

Kelly's eyes shot wide open. *How in the hell did he find out?* "What pictures?"

"The ones of you and Alex fucking at Yale."

"I still don't know what you're talking about." Kelly wasn't about to tip her hand until she knew what Andrew was after and she had figured out how to tilt the scales in her favor.

Andrew shifted his feet to the floor and leaned forward. "Personally, I couldn't care less that you two were getting each other off in college, but if those pictures went public, my father would."

"Look, Andrew, I don't know where you get your information, but—"

"I got it from you."

"Me?"

"Around here, the gossip mill is robust, which is why the cardinal rule is to close your damn door. I overheard you sticking it to Alex. I know Alex took pictures and that you dumped her. All I have to do is hint to my father that you two are back at it in the office, and you'll be out on your ear. If you're smart, you'll play ball with me."

"Let's say you're right about Alex and me, and I have some pictures. Why do you want them? And don't give me some line about protecting your sister's reputation. You said it yourself. Castle Resorts has a healthy rumor mill. Word has it that Papa Castle passed you over for CEO and Alex has taken over management of Times Square."

"You have been a busy little bee. All right, Kelly, cards on the table. In William Castle's world, appearing to be the perfect, upstanding family is all that matters. To him, being gay is a sin, but he's willing to turn a blind eye as long as Alex keeps up appearances. Those pictures, as you well know, will blow her out of the water and put me into the CEO seat."

Those pictures had become the hottest commodity in Manhattan. With two rich Castles clamoring to get their hands on them, the price had just gone up. "What can you do for me that Alex isn't already doing?"

"I saw what Alex is paying you. I'll double it."

"That's an interesting offer, but once those pictures become public, my stay at Castle Resorts will come to an end."

"All right, what do you want?"

If Andrew was willing to double her salary, doubling her payday was worth the chance. "Two million in cash."

"Are you fucking nuts? I don't have that kind of cash."

Kelly shrugged. "Take it or leave it."

Andrew's quivering jaw muscles were a sign he was steaming mad, but his silence was even more telling. He'd do anything, give anything for those pictures. Hell, she should've asked for three million.

"Decide now, Andrew, or the price will go up." Two million dollars would go a long way to make up for letting Alex Castle slip through her fingers a second time. But she swore to herself if life ever presented her with a third chance, she wouldn't pass it up.

"All right. It will take me some time to come up with the money. Give me a week."

"You have a deal." Kelly offered her hand, and they shook on it.

* * *

Andrew didn't deserve his father's rebuke, and now he'd found his sure bet to avoid a repeat. Once he got his hands on those salacious pictures and fed them to the tabloids, Alex would be out on her ear, and he'd be the only Castle left standing. All he needed to make it happen was the cash to meet Kelly Thatcher's asking price. That left him one solution. Deep inside Arthur's Alley, peering through the entryway to the private party room, he spotted the man who could make that happen. Conspicuously surrounded by two muscle-bound guards dressed in baggy business suits, that one man held Andrew's future in his hands.

Goon Number One waved him through. With each step he took toward the secluded curved booth, he became more anxious. What he was about to propose represented the greatest risk he'd ever taken, but he'd worked it all out. It didn't matter if he was CEO or CFO. In either position, even if his father delayed his retirement in the aftermath of Alex's public shame, he'd have the access needed to bury the paper trail.

Once seated, he bounced his knee beneath the table, positive scientists would mistake his trembling as an earthquake. "Thanks for meeting me, Victor. I have a proposition for you."

Victor took a sip from his glass of overpriced soda water before picking up and sliding a deadly sharp wood-handled steak knife through a thick filet cut. "Make it quick, Andy Boy. Time's money."

"How would you like to turn two million dollars into four in twelve months? That's twice your normal interest rate."

Victor stopped slicing halfway through. "I'm listening."

"I need two million. If you lend me the money, I will pay you a third of a mil every month for twelve months."

"Why do you need the two mil?"

"A personal issue."

"Tell me this. How are you going to come up with the monthly installments?"

"I'm taking over as Chief Financial Officer of Castle Resorts. It's a fifteen-billion-dollar company, and I'll have total control over the accounting and treasury. I can authorize any transactions under a certain amount myself without having to get the CEO's concurrence. I've figured out exactly how much I can reasonably hide in duplicate contracts at each resort every month, similar to what I've been doing at Times Square. I can then transfer that amount into a shell company I've set up. From there, I can transfer the money to any account you designate, preferably one based in a country without a U.S. treaty."

"Let's say you have my interest. First, I'd like a test run."

"What do you propose?"

"Transfer nine thousand into one of my offshore accounts by close of business tomorrow." *The perfect amount*, Andrew thought. It was a smidge under the IRS reporting threshold in case something went wrong. "You make that happen, and I'll loan you the money next week. If you cross me, you'll be nursing every broken bone in your body."

Andrew offered a timid nod. There was no going back now. The money he'd taken from Castle Resorts before was chump change compared to this. But it would all be worth it in the end. He'd be in the driver's seat, and Alex would be on the street.

CHAPTER EIGHTEEN

If there was one silver lining connected with living in the closet for William Castle's sake, it was the patience that Alex had developed in an age of instant gratification. Days ago, Indra had promised she'd get the truth out of Nick Castor and Ethan had promised he'd get the 4-1-1 on Victor Padula. Having no other choice but to trust they'd come through, she had thrown all her energy into making Times Square profitable. A fundamental pillar in her plan—the task of revamping its web presence to attract both high-end and mid-level clientele—she was about to put in Tyler Falling's capable hands.

While Alex had people to handle calls like this, this was different. Maybe it was the positive vibe that had lasted for hours following their first phone call or how she couldn't get Tyler's voice out of her head. For whatever reason, she wanted to be the one to give Tyler the good news. She dialed the number she'd jotted down when they last spoke. When the phone rang, butterflies came to life in her stomach, making her feel like a lovestruck teenager. *What the hell? This is a business call.*

The call connected. "This is Tyler Falling."

"Good morning, Tyler. This is Alex Castle. I hope you don't mind my calling your direct line." *That's right, keep it professional. She's not gay, and she's married, for goodness' sake.*

"Of course not." Tyler's voice had the same sweet tone Alex detected during their first call. It had a familiar ring, but she couldn't think of who it sounded like. An actress? A radio personality? A sexy encounter at a bar?

"Good because I have splendid news. I've never known our Chief Technology Officer to hand out such high praise over a proposal. He said we'd be crazy to pass this up, so we'd like to offer you the contract with one minor modification."

"What's that?"

"We're increasing your bottom line by twelve percent. I think the family connection may have had something to do with it, but you way underbid the contract."

"To be honest, we're really out of our depth when valuing our work at a corporate level. You're the first major company to consider us."

"Well, then, I'm glad to break in at the ground floor because after word gets out about the caliber of work your firm produces, you'll have the Fortune 500 knocking down your door."

"You're making me blush, Alex. If you have the time, I'd like to ask you a few questions. It's my way of getting to know you better, so I can best meet your expectations."

"For you? Of course. Fire away." The prospect of spending a few extra minutes with Tyler posed a way better option than dealing with Kelly or her brother.

"Great. Some of these questions might sound out of place for a website design, but I like to know what makes my clients tick so I won't waste their time with mockups far afield."

"That's an ingenious approach. I'm impressed." Smart and talented. What were the odds Tyler was pretty, too? Alex opened Internet Explorer, navigating to the Creative Juices website again. When she couldn't find a picture of Tyler, she went to trusty Yahoo!, but the Internet search yielded nothing. "By chance, do you have a webcam? Can we switch this to Skype?"

"I don't. Our customers were all local until now, and we haven't needed one. Is this going to be a problem? Do you prefer to video conference? Because once we set up the test website, you'll see everything that I'm working on."

"No, no." Alex felt more disappointed than she should have for a business call, which should have served as an enormous red flag, but it didn't. She should be chiding herself for fancying a married woman, but she didn't. Appreciating Tyler wasn't horrible, but anything more would cross the line. Maybe it was better that Tyler's appearance remained a mystery.

"It would have been nice to talk face-to-face, but I'm fine with phone calls. What's your first question?"

"All right then. What colors do you hate?"

"Interesting. I'd have to say anything plain or expected. I like pops of surprising color. You should see my townhouse. It's not crazy in terms of color, but one space flows into the next, each featuring its own unique splash of color. One room has pops of purple and there's one with burnt orange."

"Those are some bold choices. I wish I had that kind of daring in my decorating choices."

"I'm sure your home is beautiful." Alex got the sense Tyler was underselling herself. Anyone who could become a graphic designer had to have an artistic flair.

"It's nice but lived-in. My next question is, what does your day off look like?"

"That's a loaded question because I rarely take days off. When I do, I'm catching up on projects around the house or volunteering at The Center."

"What's the center?"

"It's a community of LGBT centers around the country. They put on a leadership boot camp in Manhattan three or four times a year to train new center leaders. I teach financial management, fundraising, and board governance, which is pretty much what I do at Castle Resorts."

"That's wonderful, Alex. Should we put that on the community outreach page?"

Alex hardly knew Tyler, yet she'd already revealed tidbits about herself that would make her father blow a gasket. It felt good but was it too much? Alex didn't think so but thought better of bringing attention to her choice of personal philanthropy. "Oh no. This is something I do on my own."

"The more I learn about you, the more I like you."

"Thank you, Tyler." Alex's cheeks warmed. She felt like a teenager and wanted to say something silly like, "I like that you like me." She settled on something more thought out and intelligible. "It's my way of giving back to the community."

"It sounds like the center is your passion, which answers my next question. Next on the list is, beach or mountains?"

"Definitely beach. The strongest memory of my mother is of a beach vacation on Long Island not long before she died." Alex had two vivid memories of the beach, but the one with her mother far outweighed the one only Harley knew about, one Alex would rather forget.

"I'm so sorry. When did your mother pass away?"

"When I was five, from breast cancer," Alex said. The thought made her nostalgic but not sad. Other than feeling a hole in her life, she had been too young then to appreciate the enormity of losing her mother altogether. Maybe that was why the thought of losing her father as an adult, despite the man he'd become, troubled her more than it otherwise should've. He was her last link to the mother she wished she had over the years.

"That's so sad. She didn't get to see her daughter grow up. Seeing my girls mature brings me such joy."

"How many girls?"

"Two. They're twelve and seventeen."

"That's a bit of a spread."

"Unplanned."

"Sometimes, the best things in life aren't planned." Alex pulled from her desk drawer the black-and-white photograph she had taken when she stopped at the train tracks in Napa last week and rubbed her fingertips across the face of the woman pictured there. She didn't know when their paths would cross again but was sure they would.

"Are you still there, Alex?" Too much daydreaming had pulled Alex from the moment.

"I'm sorry, Tyler. I was distracted." Before returning the picture to its treasured position in her top center drawer, she asked, "Have you ever come across a stranger you couldn't get off your mind?"

"Once." Tyler's voice contained an element of surprise and a layer of pain that still seemed raw.

"What did you do about it?"

"I saw a psychiatrist."

"He must've really gotten under your skin."

"She. And, yes."

This got interesting. And affirming. The vibe Alex felt may have been sparked on a professional level, but personal instinct fanned it. They had a connection, and Alex's gaydar was alive and well. "You surprise me, Tyler."

"I surprise myself by telling you."

"I'm glad you did because I like to get to know the people I plan to work closely with."

"You? I thought I would work with Mr. Cotton."

"For the technical issues, yes, but for the artistic component, I plan on being hands-on. This is my baby, and I want to be involved at every juncture."

"I like that, Alex."

The slight pause before her name told Alex her instinct was right. A connection was growing, but she needed to put on the brakes. Married. Meant. Off. Limits. "I should get going. I'd like to get in my two miles before lunch."

"Are you a runner?"

"I am. How about you?"

"Yes, or at least I used to be," Tyler said.

"What distance did you run?"

"Long distance. I used to love running. It made me feel so free."

"I know exactly what you mean," Alex replied. "Running is the one thing that keeps me sane. It's 'me' time. Despite my hectic schedule, I carve out time to run at least three days a week. Why did you stop?"

"Motherhood. Working and raising two girls left little time for running long distances. How about you? What distance did you run? Were you ever competitive?"

"Long distance like you. I was on the Yale track team but quit my junior year."

"Injury?"

"Heartache. Word of advice: Never get involved with a teammate." Alex half-joked about the doomed sophomore fling that might now be her downfall.

"Well, whoever it was, he or she was crazy for breaking up with you. Their loss."

"She. And, yes, she was crazy." Alex pulled out the Napa photo once more and studied the mysterious woman who had her hooked like a fish. *You'd never hurt me, would you?*

CHAPTER NINETEEN

Sacramento, California

Next Tuesday's therapy appointment was too far off. Tyler needed to understand what was going on in her head before the family court hearing on Monday. Happily, Gail was able to fit her in. There was so much to sort out, including practically fawning over Alex Castle an hour ago and the fact that the bastard had made another appearance. Keeping a secret from her daughter to protect her from feeling like a catastrophe was one thing, but keeping something of that magnitude from her husband was another.

Tyler walked through the front door, hoping to find answers. She let her shoulders slump. This was the one place where she could discard her cobbled-together shell and show her exhaustion. Be her authentic self. Before she could sit in the entryway chair, Gail Sanders peeked her head in from her home office.

"You look frazzled, Tyler. Come in."

"You have no idea. Thanks for working me in."

"That's why I'm here." Gail ushered Tyler into her office. Both took the same chairs in the center as they had for their first meeting, Gail with a notepad and pen in hand. "What has you upset?"

"Where to start?"

"Start with what makes you afraid."

"The bastard parked in front of my house on Monday after you and I spoke. He saw Bree and left without saying a word." The fact that Gail's eyebrows arched dramatically assured Tyler that she hadn't overreacted the other day. That having a meltdown was a natural response.

"That must've been traumatic." Gail placed her notepad on an end table and leaned forward in unmistakable concern. "Did you feel threatened?"

"At first, yes, but when he didn't get out of the car, I knew he was there to catch a glimpse of Bree, not to hurt me."

"That's excellent progress."

"Maybe so, but I didn't tell Ethan what happened. I told myself it was because I was afraid he'd put that man in the hospital and that I didn't want him to lose his job."

"But..."

"But I think I'm still in the rut of avoiding the truth. Of thinking, if I avoid the pain, it doesn't exist."

"The fact you're able to recognize the possibility is proof you're making more progress than you think. Let me ask you this: Does Ethan have a history of violence?"

"God, no." Tyler felt guilty about putting that thought in Gail's head. He deserved so much better. "He's such a gentle man. Though the rape pushed him to his limits. He didn't say as much, but I suspect he"—Tyler used air quotes—"paid the bastard a visit and roughed him up after he reappeared."

"Then I think you should cut yourself some slack about your motivation. As you are discovering, though, secrets in a marriage are never healthy."

"So you think I should tell him?"

"Only you can decide that."

"Well, you're no help." But Tyler already knew the answer. She needed to tell Ethan tonight.

"My role isn't to give you answers but to help you find them."

"Then maybe you can help me sort through another thing." Tyler paused for Gail's affirmative nod. "Today, my small company landed the contract of a lifetime with a multi-billion-dollar international company. That alone should have me bouncing off the walls with excitement, but something happened when I was on the phone with the client."

"Can you describe it?" Gail picked up her writing pad and prepared to take notes.

"She started off by paying me several compliments. I've been on the receiving end of enough male compliments to recognize when they were genuine or designed to butter me up. But one coming from a woman was a different story. Genuine or not, the unexpected attention made me feel desired, like a teenager spinning over a first crush."

Gail nodded again, the kind of nod that telegraphed no judgment. The lack of probing questions meant she'd switched to listening mode. Tyler continued, "While I was asking her a series of questions designed to determine my client's preferences, I felt myself drawn to her. Then, out of the blue, she asked me if I'd ever come across a stranger that I couldn't get off my mind. The next thing I know, I told her I had and that it was a woman. When she told me she once was heartbroken over a woman, a light went on. Maybe it was the way she complimented me or the way her voice lingered on my name each time she said it, but somehow I knew she was gay or bisexual before she said she was once involved with a woman."

Another nondescript nod.

"I know what you're going to ask. How did that make me feel? I'll start by saying it instantly made her more interesting and made me want to know her better. Everything about her screams refined, from the way she speaks and the way she writes her emails to the way she thinks through issues. She's smart, professional, kind, and thoughtful."

Another unremarkable nod.

"I'm losing it. I'm falling for every woman that comes into my orbit. First that woman in Napa, and now Alex Castle. It's like I've let a genie out of a bottle, and now I can't control myself." What if Alex was as alluring as the woman in Napa? She'd have nonstop sex dreams about her too and wouldn't be able to focus on her web design. That settled it. Tyler couldn't afford to find a picture of Alex until their project was done. "I'm turning every compliment into a seductive tease."

"I will stop you right there." Gail placed her notepad and pen on the small end table between their chairs again. She shifted in her seat to look Tyler directly in the eye. "Frequently, victims of sexual assault find it difficult to engage in intimate situations with someone of the same gender as their attacker. Intimacy isn't confined to sex. Intimacy can be a mutual experience or the act of sharing your most personal thoughts. I believe this is why you've pulled away from your husband and why you sought a female therapist.

"Now, the way you described your interaction with Alex sounds like a very intimate experience. It's natural to feel drawn to her. Do I think a genie has been let out of a bottle? In a sense, yes. You are questioning your sexuality. For your own mental and emotional health, you need to see that through. Do I think you are out of control? Answer me this: Do you have romantic thoughts about your business partner?"

"No, of course not." The suggestion seemed absurd. She and Maddie were close friends. In fact, they were best friends, but never once had Tyler thought of her in any other terms.

"How about me?"

"That would be creepy. You're my doctor."

"Then you are not out of control. The woman in Napa was an awakening on a physical level. Your conversation with Alex Castle was an awakening too, but an emotional and intellectual one. Tectonic shifts such as this can be overwhelming, especially when a life partner is in the picture. Now, let's talk about what you think should come next."

"I need to be honest with Ethan."

"That's an important next step."

"This is all giving me hope, Gail."

For the first time in years, Tyler didn't sense darkness looming over her. She saw a glimmer of light. Where that light would take her, she couldn't be sure, but she had to push toward it. Her life would never be the same, but considering how she was living, it couldn't be much worse. It wasn't her fault that brute raped her, and it was about time she stopped living like it was. Her best hope—happiness was on the other side.

"Hope of what?" Gail asked.

"That soon, the rape won't have power over me."

* * *

Courage had followed Tyler home from Gail's office. At the dinner table, Tyler took stock of the family she would turn upside down tonight. Erin, at seventeen, was so much like her. Smart and introverted with an old soul and a similar creative flair. Tyler hoped she'd one day follow in her footsteps and work side by side with her. Bree, at twelve, was so much like her dad, despite not sharing an ounce of DNA with him. Smart, stealthily funny, borderline introverted with the heart of a saint. Then there was Ethan, the man who had been her rock and biggest champion. What she planned to do tonight would hurt him the most, and that would cut her to the core. If she were to heal, though, this was a necessary first step.

Once Erin and Bree were off to bed and she and Ethan retired to their bedroom, Tyler waited for him to finish in the bathroom. She used the time to gather the last bit of strength she needed to have the most honest conversation with her husband she'd had in years. When he finally returned to make his final preparations for bed, Tyler thought, *I should make love to you. You deserve someone who can give you that.*

"Ethan, can we talk?" Tyler's voice cracked from the anger and sadness she was about to precipitate. Her lips trembled, her eyes welled. She was about to turn their world upside down.

"Tyler, what's wrong?" Ethan motioned for her to sit on the edge of the bed. She did.

"That bastard coming back into our lives has messed me up. So much that I started seeing a therapist."

Ethan cupped her hand, gentle and caring. "That's a good thing. Has it helped?"

"I think it has. Gail has helped me recognize the lasting impact of the rape and some critical aspects of myself I never knew."

"Then I'm happy you're going."

"I changed after the rape. I became withdrawn and flinched every time you tried to touch me."

"But that lasted for less than a year. I completely understood your reaction."

"It lasted a lot longer, Ethan. I never got over the trauma, and I've been forcing myself to make love to you, as infrequently as it has been, because I know how important it is to you. Every time we make love, I feel trapped, and no matter what I do, I can't get past it."

Ethan hung his head. She'd handed him a truth, one too heavy to carry. He was silent for several long minutes, then… "I never knew, and I should have."

"It's not your fault. I should have told you years ago."

"There are a lot of sexless marriages. I can accept that. I love you, Tyler." Ethan met her gaze. The strength behind those eyes gave her the courage to go on.

"But that's just it. You shouldn't have to accept it, and neither should I. Ever since the rape, I look at you and all men differently. I love you, but I can't go through the motions any longer."

"What are you trying to tell me, Tyler?"

"When I looked hard at myself, I realized I no longer have romantic feelings for you. I no longer think of you in those terms. God knows I want to. We've spent over twenty years together. We have children. We built a life. But I can't force what isn't there anymore."

"Are you telling me there's someone else?" The hurt in his eyes broke Tyler's heart. The words were coming out so wrong, but she needed to finish what she'd started.

"I'm telling you that I need to find out if I'm even capable of passion again and that I don't feel it can happen with you or with any other man."

"Are you telling me you've fallen for a woman?"

"I'm not sure what it is. When I was in Napa with Maddie, I bumped into a woman. We briefly touched hands, and I suddenly felt alive. As if the rape never happened. When you touch me, I can never get past the trauma."

"Have you been seeing this woman?"

"No. I wouldn't do that to you. I don't even know who she is or how to find her. But for the first time in a long time, I enjoyed being touched."

"What are you saying?"

"I'm saying that we both deserve better. I can't give you the passion you deserve, and you can't do the same for me. We need to face that this isn't working."

"I think I understand. You can't get past me being a man." Ethan slumped, placing his elbows on his knees.

"No," she said slowly. Sadly. "I can't. If I'm ever going to come to terms with this, I have to stop forcing myself to make our marriage work."

"So what now?"

"I don't know. We need to take the time to figure out what we should do next. But I need to be honest with you about one more thing. Now don't get mad, but—"

"I'm not going to like this, am I?"

"No, you're not, and I held back for a good reason." Tyler paused while Ethan rolled his neck, bracing himself for news that would likely rile him up. He gave her a nod to continue.

"Stevens was camped out in his car in front of our house on Monday. I got the impression all he wanted was to see Bree because once he did, he took off." Tyler paused at Ethan's deep intake of air but continued when he appeared to center himself. "I didn't tell you right away because I knew how you'd react.

You'd have a come-to-Jesus meeting with him, and you'd lose your job. Maybe your pension. My gut tells me that bastard will try to sway the judge into granting him visitation."

"That will never happen." Ethan stood up. "I need to think about all of this, Tyler. You've really blindsided me here. I think I should stay in the guest room until we figure things out." He grabbed his pillow and a few belongings from his nightstand and left.

Tyler fell back on the bed. Talking to him was supposed to be the first step to healing. Yet all she'd accomplished was to hurt the man who had loved her unconditionally for half of her life. Rolling over on her side, she asked herself, "Why don't I feel any better?"

CHAPTER TWENTY

Greenwich, Connecticut

The rear passenger door of the town car opened curbside, revealing to its passenger a pristinely kept English-style stone manor. Thirty-four years had a way of fuzzing Abby Spencer's memory, but the mansion was more beautiful than she remembered. The once fledgling vines had grown to outline the windows and the archway over the double-wide front door, making it rival every fairytale castle ever depicted. Now she wished she'd visited when Indra had inherited her family's estate two springs ago, before Avi passed away, to witness the trumpets in bloom and in their full lavender glory.

"Thank you, Richard." Abby accepted her driver's steady hand to help her out of the back seat. He'd offered his hand so many times over the past decade that she knew it almost better than her own. One wouldn't expect a chauffeur to have callouses, but his love of woodworking had left thickened patches at the tips of his fingers. Abby had decided early on, they gave him character. That's why years ago, she had him dump the traditional black suit for his preferred blue in various shades, one for each day of the week.

"If things go well, I might be a while, dear."

"It's all right, Mrs. Spencer. I'll be right here whenever you're ready to go home."

"What would I do without you?" Abby patted his hand with both of hers.

"A lot more walking, I suppose." He winked at Abby's unbridled laugh before guiding her up the two brick steps leading to the front door and ringing the bell.

After Richard retreated to the seclusion of the town car, the front door swung open to a young, smartly groomed butler. Abby stifled her amusement; his attire must've been Avi's choice. The gray striped trousers and vest, white wing-collar shirt, black tie and morning coat, silver cufflinks, and immaculate white gloves screamed tradition. Abby imagined Indra hadn't had the heart to make changes yet.

"Good afternoon, Mrs. Spencer. Mrs. Kapoor is expecting you." The young man couldn't have been older than thirty, yet he carried himself with the demeanor expected of an experienced manservant. "Is there anything I can get you?"

"No, thank you." Abby took in the entry hall of the family mansion. The architecture remained the same, but the décor was untraditionally bright and inviting—obviously Indra's touch and a clear compromise to the costumed servants.

"Mrs. Kapoor is near the stables. I'll take you to her." Abby followed the butler through the primary living room, which had the same familiar structure. Indra had also decorated it with her warm, feminine touch.

Once Abby went through double french doors leading to the rear of the main house, the stables appeared to her left. The building looked as it had in her youth but with an extra coat of paint to freshen its appearance. The snorting of a horse drew Abby's attention toward the exercise pasture where a trainer was putting a stunning, brown Thoroughbred through its paces. Given her refined head, long neck, and sloping shoulders that led to a deep body with muscular hindquarters, she was undoubtedly Indra's prized horse.

Abby nodded to the butler, dismissing him after she spotted Indra leaning against the white four-rail horse fence, her elbows on the top rail. Indra was as beautiful, if not more, as the first day Abby saw her walking across the Yale campus. Her wheat-colored skin, brown piercing eyes, and five-foot-three stature had turned Abby into putty then and still did. Her hair was darker and longer then, but Abby liked how it had started to gray and now ended above the collar. Her jeans revealed curves that weren't there in her youth, the result probably of Indra's notorious fondness for chocolate, a weakness they shared.

Abby paused for a moment and took stock of her greatest regret—saying goodbye to Indra so both could live the lives expected of them in the 1970s. *That was then*, she thought. *This is now.* She made her way across the courtyard and soon she too was leaning against the fence, two feet from Indra, and watching the horse circle the pasture at the pace of a medium canter.

"She reminds me of Athena," Abby said, fondly remembering the summer thirty-four years ago that she and Indra had spent riding the mare and her stablemate in this very pasture. A wonderful time of exploration, experimentation, passion—and love that had ended in eventual heartbreak.

Indra didn't break her stare at the pasture, making her first words that much more intriguing. "Indeed. I named her Moonlight." She shifted to face Abby. The love, longing, and restrained joy in her eyes were breathtaking and matched every overwhelming emotion hitting Abby. "For our first kiss. I remember it like it was yesterday. You were so beautiful in the moonlight that I could think of nothing but kissing those sweet lips of yours."

Indra's Indian heritage had given her a fascinating appeal as a young woman and did even more so now. The girlish features of youth had matured into those of a sexy woman who had lived a full life. Abby raised a hand to graze Indra's cheek. She whispered, "I never stopped loving you." She stroked her face lightly before dropping her hand. "I'm so sorry about Avi's passing. It's been what, ten months?"

"He made me very happy, Abby." The pain in Indra's voice was unmistakable. Abby had felt the same when her husband passed five years ago.

"I know he did," Abby said without hesitation.

"I received your note after the funeral. It gave me hope this day would come."

"You needed time to grieve."

"I did, but it's good seeing you again privately." Indra caressed Abby's arms, starting at the biceps and working her way down until she took both hands into hers. The touch was as soft as their last goodbye as lovers, not like the sterile greetings they had exchanged at charity events over the decades. "It has been much too long." The last time they had seen each other outside of those public events was three years ago during Harley's thirtieth birthday celebration. Abby was free then, but Indra was not. They had shared a drink in the study and carefully limited their reminiscing to their children and nothing more.

"I couldn't agree more."

"Let's get down to business. After, will you join me for dinner?" Indra gave Abby's hands a long, gentle squeeze.

If Abby had her way, she'd never let go. She'd waited years for Indra to be free like she was, imposing upon herself a year's grace to let Indra grieve. Because if she had seen her earlier, like now, she knew she wouldn't be strong enough to resist the pull she felt whenever she was within her orbit. It was plain as day Indra hadn't yet finished grieving the loss of her life partner even if he never had had all of her heart.

"Dinner sounds wonderful," Abby replied. "Can your man let Richard know?"

"Of course." Indra led Abby inside her personal study, a modest room compared to the grand dining and entertainment rooms. The large oak desk there was neither lavish nor cheap but sturdy and functional. The stone fireplace served as the room's focal point, determining the placement of an overstuffed L-shaped couch and adjacent easy chairs. The fireplace's flickering flames provided the room's primary light.

Sitting in a chair would've been the sensible choice to make to conduct their business, but the pull Abby had felt the moment she dialed her phone last night dictated otherwise. She sat on the couch, presenting Indra with a subtle option. If Indra sat on a chair and kept her distance, that would be the sign she needed more time. But if she joined Abby on the couch that would signal she felt the pull too. Or so Abby hoped. Either way, she was prepared to follow Indra's lead.

Indra retrieved a folder and flash drive from her desk before joining Abby on the couch. A promising sign, indeed. "Once you told me about Alex and her failed college liaison, I couldn't help but think about our own summer affair."

"I did the same," Abby replied. Indra's faint smile gave her hope the embers of passion still burned in her long-ago lover.

"I'm sorry hers didn't end as amicably as ours."

"Amicable, yes, but not without heartache." Abby regretted her last words and the sadness that Indra's eyes had held three decades ago. Times had been different when they were young, and they had had little choice but to go their separate ways. Her only solace until now, and she assumed it was the same for Indra, had come in the form of stolen glances.

"I know," Indra whispered. She straightened herself and got right to the matter of Kelly Thatcher. "I was more than happy to interrogate young Mr. Castor. He's been a thorn in my side since the acquisition. Once I presented him with my suspicions of him providing insider information to Ms. Thatcher, he became quite accommodating. The phone records your investigator dug up made my threat to turn everything over to the SEC if he didn't cooperate that much more convincing. The poor lad didn't even care that I fired him at the same time, so long as his freedom wasn't in jeopardy."

"I'm sure you framed the discussion in such a way that left him no options." Abby smiled. Indra could be sweet and loving as she was right now, but she took no prisoners in the boardroom. She listened to her valued advisors, but they knew who was in charge when they walked out.

Indra's grin contained a hint of pride. She handed Abby the file and computer flash drive. "He turned over his cell phone and personal laptop to my techs. They unearthed a treasure trove of text messages and emails that fully document the insider information he provided Ms. Thatcher before and after the stock purchases. I had him sign a full confession and videotaped his admission for good measure."

"I knew I could count on you." The look in Indra's eyes held more than friendship. They contained the yearning Abby had felt since she was free from grieving her own husband. Abby placed the items on the end table next to the couch, hoping she hadn't misread things.

"Don't you know I'd do anything for you, Abby?" Indra paused, her stare fixed on Abby's lips. She scooted closer and placed a hand on Abby's cheek. "I never stopped loving you either." She pressed her lips against Abby's and held the kiss.

Heaven came to mind. Soft lips. Smooth skin. Everything Abby had missed. They moaned in delight when their tongues simultaneously reached for each other and touched. Indra's hand drifted to her breast, the touch awakening desire that she'd kept in check for years. It was as if not a day had passed since they were last in each other's embrace. Thirty-four years of waiting had ended, and Abby's heart had never been fuller.

Indra was the first to break the kiss Abby had waited decades for. She studied Abby's face for several silent beats. "Firelight," she said, earning a questioning look from Abby. "We have yet to name a new foal." Indra caressed Abby's cheek. "Yes, Firelight is the perfect name for her. You are as beautiful in the firelight as you were in the moonlight."

And with those words, Indra and Abby made love as they did in their youth. This time, it came with the promise of spending the rest of their lives together.

CHAPTER TWENTY-ONE

Manhattan, New York

For the second consecutive evening, wine, chocolate, and a laptop were a part of Alex Castle's nightly routine. After arriving home and quietly thanking the three-hour time difference, she poured a glass of Barnette cabernet and filled a small bowl with chocolate-covered raisins. She then escaped to her private courtyard and fired up her office laptop and Internet Explorer before calling Tyler. The main attraction—reviewing the mockups and test site Tyler had set up for Castle Resorts' new web design. The project and their blossoming friendship couldn't have gone better. To her delight, Tyler's first round of content improvements had nearly captured Alex's vision for the site, and her business partner had suggested several technical features that would tie into the long-term plan of attracting a broader clientele. They were off to a promising start.

It was almost too cold to go outside tonight, but Alex couldn't deny herself. She settled into her favorite lounger after adding an extra patio heater. The glow from the half-moon, the laptop, the heaters, and four strategically placed porch lights provided ample illumination. She dialed her new favorite phone number. The call connected. The grin she let grow was surely as wide as the Hudson. So wide that Alex was relieved Tyler wasn't able to see how smitten she'd become. It wouldn't be professional.

"Hi, Alex."

As it had last night, her heart fluttered at the sound of her name. She was embarrassed to admit that the first spark she sensed during their first two calls had swelled into a full-blown infatuation. Tyler's sweet tone, subtle humor, shared interests, and the way she put Alex at ease had blurred the lines to the point she almost forgot Tyler was married.

Almost, but not quite.

"Hi, Tyler." Those two words came out sounding way too seductive—low and slow—but she couldn't help the involuntary reflex. It was like breathing. She couldn't have stopped it if she wanted to.

"Did you have time to look at the revised layout of the home pages for the resorts?" Tyler asked.

"I did, and as an amateur photographer, I love the addition of the camera icon for the photos."

"You're a photographer, too?" Tyler's voice buzzed with excitement. "I took photography in college."

"Me, too." First running, now photography. *Could our interests be more in sync?* Alex asked herself.

"Oh, my gosh. I still have the first camera I ever had. For my tenth birthday, my parents bought me a new Nikon F2. I've loved photography ever since."

"I've loved it since I was a child, too. My mother was a professional photographer. I remember little about her, but I have one vivid memory. I was sitting on her lap, and she showed me how her favorite camera worked. She died not long after, and I've had a fascination with cameras ever since. When I was old enough, my father gave me her 1957 Leica M3. I took my first photo with that camera and used it until I lost it in a move."

"That's a shame. I'm sure that camera meant a lot to you."

"Losing it devastated me. For my birthday this year, my sister gave me a 1965 M3. It looks and functions like my mother's."

Alex teared up. Her voice cracked as she opened the picture of the mystery woman she'd scanned and now stored front and center on her desktop. "It made me feel connected to her again."

"That's a wonderful story, Alex. I'm sure you'll cherish it for the rest of your life. Have you used it much yet?"

"I have. In fact, I'm looking at one of the first photographs I took with it right now. It's of a woman, and the clarity is amazing. It fascinates me, and I look at it every day."

"Is it the picture that fascinates you or the woman in it?" Tyler asked.

"To be honest, it's the woman. I want to meet her, but I don't know how to go about finding her."

"Have you gone back to the place where you took the picture?"

"I haven't. I took it in a city thousands of miles away. It would be like trying to find a needle in a haystack."

"You never know. This woman might show up when you least expect it."

The sliding glass door leading into the kitchen whooshed open. That meant one thing. "I hate to cut this short, Tyler, but I have a visitor." Alex lowered the phone and mouthed, "You're early."

"No problem, Alex. I still have to finish the revisions on the booking pages I promised. I know it will be Saturday, but would you mind me calling the same time tomorrow? I want to get those done while they're still fresh in my mind."

"I wouldn't mind at all. It's a date." Alex cringed. She shouldn't have phrased it that way, but at some level she wished their next meeting *was* a date. A woman like Tyler deserved dinner of her choosing, followed by an experience of a lifetime. She deserved Paris in the spring, Aspen in the winter, serene beaches in the summer, and a canvas of turning leaves in the fall.

"A date." Tyler repeated those words as if Paris were in her future.

The moment Alex disconnected the call, Harley, dressed for a hookup night in a stylish dress that hit at the knee, asked, "Was that Jordi?"

"The redhead? No." Alex eyed Harley's glass. "I see you've helped yourself to my wine again."

Harley plopped down in the neighboring lounge chair, legs crossed at the ankles. "Of course. It's a Barnette. Now, tell me about this date."

"It's a work date."

"I saw the look on your face when you were talking to her. You may work with her, but you don't have spreadsheets on your mind. Bedsheets, on the other hand…"

"You won't give this up, won't you?" The smirk on Harley's face confirmed Alex's suspicions. "All right. Her name is Tyler. I hired her firm to redesign the company web pages, and we've spent several days working together over the phone. What started out as a business relationship has blossomed into an instant friendship." Alex sighed. "Now I want something more."

"That's great."

"Not great. She's married to John's cousin."

"Ooohhh." Harley sipped her wine before forming a devious grin. "Alex Castle fell for a straight woman."

"Not straight." Alex sipped her wine before forming an equally devious yet imprudent grin, considering what could be if Tyler weren't married. She shook her head. This fantasizing had to stop. She'd be better off finding the mystery woman than thinking of "could be's" with the unobtainable Tyler Falling.

"This just got more interesting."

"Which makes it hard not to go there."

"You won't. You may be a lot of things, Alex Castle, but you are not the other woman."

"You're right. I'm not. I should concentrate on the mystery woman."

Harley swung her legs off the lounge chair and turned to face Alex. She leaned in, her eyes narrowing as if she were about to sink her teeth into a thick, juicy steak. "What mystery woman?"

Alex turned her laptop screen toward Harley. The photo of the woman on a bicycle was still on full display. "When I was in Napa two weeks ago, I literally bumped into this woman. She dropped her package of shoes, and when I helped her pick it up and looked into her eyes, we had this moment."

"What kind of shoes?"

"A cute pair of Aquatalia woven sea metallic Donnie flats. Why?"

"You noticed and remembered. That means this woman made an indelible impression."

"She did. It was like time slowed down. We exchanged only a few words during our chance meeting, but it left me exhilarated. There was nothing remarkable about her dress or appearance, nothing that would make her stand out in a crowd, but something about her gray eyes drew me in. I felt a connection. Last weekend, I returned to Napa. On my way out of town, I saw her again and snapped this photo of her. Now I can't get her off my mind."

Alex turned the screen back around and ran her thumb across the outline of the mystery woman's body, thinking of what she'd do if their paths crossed a third time. She'd do all the things she'd wanted to do with Tyler. She'd sweep her into her arms and tell her she wouldn't let her slip through her fingers again. She'd look into her eyes and tell her no one had occupied her mind as she had. She'd kiss her sweetly and tell her she never wanted to let her go. Alex didn't understand how she could simultaneously have powerful feelings for her mystery woman and Tyler, so for now, she settled on, "I'm going to find her one day."

"I've never seen you like this, Alex, and I have to say I like it. It's bold, unrealistic, and immensely romantic."

"Enough about this." Alex shook off her melancholy and focused on the last phone call she had with Abby. She had said she was on the way to retrieve a treasure trove of evidence that would put Kelly Thatcher in her place, but that was two days ago. "Did Abby say what took so long to get the information from Indra?"

"Not a word. All she said was to meet her here before eight for some exciting news."

"Well, then. We better head upstairs." Alex stood and gathered her things. "Unlike you, she doesn't let herself in."

"Am I supposed to take offense? Because I don't." Laughing, they teased one another until they reached the main floor. Soon afterward, the doorbell rang.

"Abby. Indra? I wasn't expecting both of you. Please come in." Pleased that Indra had personally come to deliver the results of her digging, Alex settled them onto the couch and got drinks for everyone. "I can't thank you enough, Indra, for lending a hand. I found myself boxed into a corner, and you were my only option."

"You're quite welcome." Indra's extended glance at Abby, combined with a soft smile, affirmed decades of friendship.

"You seem rather happy today, Mother," Harley said. Her observation was accurate. Abby seemed to be smiling at nothing and everything.

"I am, dear, but first, let's dispense with business."

Indra laid a folder and flash stick on the coffee table. "You'll find everything here that you need to counter Kelly's blackmail threat, including a written and videotaped confession. Mr. Castor is thanking his lucky stars that he's in the unemployment line and not behind bars."

"Thank you, Indra." Relief washed through Alex, lifting the weight of a crashing world from her shoulders. "You don't know how much this means to me."

"Anything for a dear friend of my Abigail."

My Abigail? Alex suspected a story behind those words, and the way Indra patted Abby's hand, one was more than likely.

"Girls, I need to tell you about an extraordinary time in my past, the summer of 1973." Abby returned Indra's loving touch with one of her own. "It was weeks after Indra and I graduated Yale. She and I had several months before we were expected to marry our fiancés and start working in the family businesses. She invited me to spend the summer with her at the Greenwich estate. We spent many lovely days sailing, horseback riding, and picnicking. And falling in love."

"Mother, I never knew." Harley's tone contained only surprise.

"It was a long time ago, dear," Abby said. "By the time August rolled around, we both had to return to our lives and do what was expected of us. She married Avi, and I married your father."

"Did Father ever know?" Harley asked.

"Much later." Abby squeezed Indra's hand, and Indra met her questioning look with an affirmative nod. Her gaze bounced between Alex and Harley. "It's time to be completely honest with both of you. Especially you, Alex."

"Me?" Alex pointed to herself.

"Yes, dear. Your father stumbled across your mother's diary not long after his diagnosis. My guess is that one had to do with the other." Abby scrunched her nose as if reliving a distasteful memory. "When he read it, he learned that after your mother had exhausted all treatment options and came to terms with her prognosis, she and I had acknowledged our feelings for one another. That our affair was short-lived yet beautiful. And that she died loving me, not William." Abby directed her attention to Harley. "That's when I opened up to your father about Indra."

The earth shifted beneath Alex. Abby's confession not only shed light on her father's launch of a bitter war against Abby but also clarified Alex's longstanding dysfunctional relationship with him. By extension, it also illuminated her own sexual journey. Her life for the last thirteen years suddenly made sense. The genesis of her father's homophobia wasn't his disease but his personal contempt for her mother and Abby. It all became clear. Alex's sexual orientation was a stinging reminder of his wife's betrayal.

Her jaw clenched. She had forgiven him so much because of his Parkinson's. Too much apparently. She'd lived a lie for nothing.

Abby's soft caress on her arm woke Alex from her reverie. "You're worrying me, Alex. Say something."

"This explains so much." Alex couldn't tell if she pitied her father or hated him more now. The only thing she knew for sure was that discovering this changed everything.

"I should've told you sooner, but out of respect for your mother's dying wish, I remained silent. She wanted to protect both of us from a cruel world. But times have changed, and I no longer need that protection. And now that I've reconnected with this wonderful woman"—Abby glanced at Indra with love in her eyes—"I can honestly say I never stopped loving her. Two days ago, I discovered she felt the same. Indra and I are giving it a go, and hopefully this time, for the rest of our lives."

CHAPTER TWENTY-TWO

Sacramento, California

For the past year, Ethan had used his twenty-minute commute to and from work to plan his retirement from the force. But for the last two days, he'd spent that time sorting through his nightly talks with Tyler. Tonight's drive home in bumper-to-bumper traffic was particularly troubling. During their last conversation, she brought up divorce. That was a topic he wasn't ready to embrace yet. He needed one final push. While he better grasped the depth of her pain, he still hadn't come to terms with the idea that their marriage was over. For her sake, he wanted her to take whatever steps she needed to heal, but for his own, he hoped their marriage would weather the storm.

The chime of his cell phone alerted him to an incoming call. Recognizing the caller ID, he answered it. "Hi, Alex. I was planning to call you tomorrow. I have some information on Victor Padula."

"That's good news, but that's not why I'm calling. How soon can you fly out here? Indra Kapoor came through tonight, and I have what I need to counter Kelly Thatcher's threat. I want you there when I confront her so you can retrieve the photos."

So much was on his plate—Tyler, Erin's college applications, family court to get Stevens out of their lives—how could he fit in a trip to the East Coast? "I have a lot going on, Alex. I couldn't—"

"I'll double your fee."

"You sure know how to tempt a guy."

"I hate to press, but I need to put this issue to bed before Kelly gets too comfortable. If that happens, her demands will never stop. I can make this easy. Abby has offered the use of the Spencer corporate jet. We can fly you back and forth at your convenience."

"You drive a hard bargain, but I can't leave until Monday evening. I have to be in court that morning."

"Thank you, Ethan. This means a lot to me. As long as I have you in the agreeable mood, I'd like to hire you to do one more thing for me."

"You know, Alex, you're becoming my personal retirement plan. At this rate, I won't have to start a private detective firm after I retire from the department."

"You're worth every penny."

"Flattery gets you everywhere. What do you need?"

"I want you to find a woman. I ran into her in Napa two weeks ago and again last weekend, but I don't know her name. All I have is a picture of her."

"That's not much to go on. Can I ask why this woman is so important?"

"Let me ask you this. Have you ever come across a stranger you instantly connected with and knew she was something special?"

"Once, and I married her."

"Well, there you go. I need to find this woman to see if the connection I felt was real or an aberration."

"All right, Alex. I'm a romantic at heart. Send me the picture. I have a friend in the FBI who owes me a favor. I can ask him to run it through their facial recognition program."

"Thank you again. This means more to me than putting Kelly Thatcher in her place."

By the time he wrapped up the call, he'd pulled into the driveway. His phone dinged, alerting him to the photo Alex had promised to send to him. He remained in the driver's seat and navigated to the picture. Its quality was sharp, but the black and white tones made it challenging to discern hair and attire colors. He zoomed in on the woman's upper body. The bike helmet hid some of her features, but she looked familiar. He studied the slope of her jawline and the curve of her neck. When his focus landed on the swell of her nose, it hit him.

"Tyler?"

This can't be. Tyler is Alex's mystery woman? When did she take this? He inspected the photo. Tyler was on a bicycle. It all made sense. That was Syd's bike. This must've been the day he briefed Alex on his Kelly Thatcher findings and when Tyler went into town alone. But when and where did they meet before? Alex had said something about Napa two weeks ago. No. It couldn't be. Tyler and Maddie's spa day? Was Alex Tyler's mystery woman? Was she the catalyst for his wife's sexual reawakening?

A burning built in his stomach at the thought it was Alex whose single touch had made Tyler feel alive when he couldn't. Somehow the notion of someone else doing that for Tyler was easier to accept when the chance meeting with a nameless and faceless other woman had had no possibility of repeating itself. But Tyler and Alex were working together, for God's sake. They were bound to meet in person at some point. How they hadn't pieced it together was beyond him, but…

Tyler had been telling the truth when she told him about not taking her infatuation beyond mental consideration. The truth stared him in the face. Tyler still loved him, just not in the way he'd hoped.

When Tyler said their situation wasn't fair to either of them, he didn't want to believe it at first. He'd be lying if he said a sexless marriage was what he wanted, but he had accepted it because that was what Tyler needed. On their wedding day, he'd promised to always be there for her and provide whatever she needed to be her best self. She needed this. On reflection then, this was the best sign he could've hoped for. Something to provide that final push.

Ethan dragged himself to the front door. This would be the last time he'd walk through it knowing he had a marriage. He thought he'd feel the weight of the surrounding walls when he stepped inside, but he didn't. Instead, the roof seemed to blow off, allowing the disinfecting rays of truth to warm his home. Letting her go and pushing her in the right direction would be his greatest act of love.

Tyler was sitting at the dining table, intent on work on her laptop, likely the Castle project. The hint of oregano and garlic in the air meant she'd fixed her grandmother's spaghetti sauce—his favorite. This beautiful creature whom he'd loved for twenty-two years and built a family and a home with for eighteen deserved the freedom to explore who she really was. His heart ached at the thought of waking tomorrow, knowing they were no longer a team. But for her happiness, heartache was an insignificant price to pay.

"Hi," he whispered.

Tyler tore her gaze from the computer screen, and their eyes met. The first time he saw those eyes on campus, he knew she was the one. They sparkled back then with infectious joy. But now, even behind the same grin he'd seen for decades, they seemed empty. He had no right to hold her to the commitment they'd made to each other long ago. The woman she was then no longer existed, and it was up to him to free her of her vows.

"Hi," she said, turning her complete focus on him. "I hope you're hungry."

"Starved." He sat in the chair next to her at the table for four.

"Good. I'll start the pasta. Dinner should be ready in about twenty minutes."

Tyler placed both palms atop the tabletop to push her chair back. Before she rose to her feet, he placed a hand atop hers. "Wait. Got a second?"

"Sure." She returned to her seat.

They'd talked more openly and honestly in the last few days than they had in two decades. Ethan had finally come to know the real Tyler Falling, ironically someone whom he liked even better than the person he'd been living with all that time. Now he was about to let her go.

"You were right last night. I wasn't ready to admit it then, but I am now. It's time."

Her eyes welled with tears but not with the heartache that should come with the agreement of a divorce. Instead, those eyes sparked alive for the first time in years, reassuring Ethan this was the right choice.

"Are you sure?" she asked.

"This is the hardest thing I've ever done, but yes, I'm sure. I'll talk to Scott after the family court hearing on Monday."

"Does this change—"

"No." He gave her hand a reassuring squeeze. "I'm going to adopt Bree. She's my daughter. Our divorcing doesn't change that."

She turned her palm and closed her fingers tight around his. Her voice cracked like his had. "You're such a good man, Ethan Falling. I'll always love you."

"I'll always love you, Tyler Falling." He released her hand. "Now, if you don't start that pasta, I might faint from starvation."

As Tyler filled the pot with water and placed it over the lit burner, Ethan retrieved the plates from the cabinet to set the table.

"By the way, I have to go to New York for a Tuesday meeting with Alex Castle about some P.I. work I've been doing for her. She's sending a company jet after the court hearing and setting me up in their Times Square resort for a night or two. You've never been there before. You should come with me. I'd like to take one last trip with you before I move out."

"If anyone should move out, it's me. I'm the one who's walking away from this marriage."

He put the plates on the table and gently placed his hands on her upper arms. "Get this straight. Neither of us is walking away from one another. We don't have to live under the same roof to be a family. Say you'll come. Erin can watch Bree, or Bree can stay with Maddie. You can explore the city while I'm working. Plus, you can finally meet Alex in person and properly thank her for the contract."

"First, I need to be honest with you about my work with Alex." Tyler's hard swallow confirmed everything she'd been telling him. He'd never affect her the way Alex Castle could.

"You feel something for her, don't you?"

"I'm not sure, but I feel close to her."

"Then you owe it to yourself to find out."

"You are a good man, Ethan. Let's go tell the girls we're going to New York."

When a smile bright enough to blind oncoming traffic formed on Tyler's face, Ethan knew her life was about to change for the better. Never in a million years did he think he'd play matchmaker for his wife and Alex Castle, but despite the improbable odds and how much he'd miss Tyler, he had to bring those two together.

CHAPTER TWENTY-THREE

A few weeks ago, Ethan's call to Scott Campbell, his college buddy and lawyer, had been a simple one. He'd used Scott's services at the "friends and family" rate with no glitches to form an LLC for his one-man private detective firm. Though family law wasn't Scott's expertise, Ethan had also asked him to help strip Stevens of his parental rights. That would clear the way for Ethan to adopt a child he'd considered his own since he learned Tyler was pregnant.

"State law has changed," Scott had told him. "Convicted rapists no longer have automatic parental rights over a child born from rape. Tyler will need to petition family court and appear at a formal hearing."

"Will that bastard know?" Ethan had asked.

"Unfortunately, yes. Tyler will have to serve him a petition to give him a chance to respond."

On Monday at ten a.m., Ethan, Tyler, and Scott ascended the steps leading to the second-floor hallway of the Ridgeway Building, home of Sacramento County Family Court. A handful of shouting matches and one brief scuffle were occurring among emotionally charged litigants, but nothing big enough to gain the attention of the deputy sheriff assigned to keep the peace. Ethan pulled Tyler to a stop when he spotted Stevens standing outside the last courtroom door on the right. Ethan's eyes zeroed in on him like a fighter pilot locking his sights on an enemy plane. "I can't believe he had the guts to show up today."

"He has a right to make a statement and ask questions before the court renders its decision. In cases like yours, though, it shouldn't make any difference in the outcome," Scott said.

"Do you think he'll fight this?" Tyler asked. Ethan heard the uneasiness in her tone. He'd heard it every evening since Stevens reappeared.

"There's nothing to fight, Tyler," Scott reassured her. "The law is clear about Stevens' parental rights. He has none, so this hearing is more pro forma than anything else. My primary focus is to convince the court to issue a restraining order against him and move on Ethan's adoption petition."

"I don't know, Ethan." The fear in Tyler's eyes was palpable. "I have a bad feeling."

"Scott, will you excuse us for a minute?" Following a quick nod from Scott, Ethan ushered Tyler to a quiet corner in the hallway. "I know this is scary, Tyler, but we'll get through it."

"I'm not scared of him anymore, at least in terms of what he could do to me. I am, however, worried about Bree."

"I am too, but it will be all right, trust me." Ethan liked this bolder version of Tyler, a woman who faced her demons head-on instead of ignoring their existence. In his peripheral vision, he tracked her tormentor's movement as he entered the men's room. He decided he needed to follow Tyler's lead but in his own particular way. "I have to use the bathroom before we go in. I'll be right back."

He walked away before waiting for a response. Inside the restroom, Stevens and another man stood at the wall of urinals. A floor-level scan of the three stalls told Ethan they were unoccupied. This was a public place, so time wasn't on his side. He needed to act now.

The man next to Stevens zipped up his fly. Before he made it to the bank of sinks, Ethan flashed his police badge in its leather case. "Wash up somewhere else." His stern tone gave the man no option, no leeway. The stranger left.

Ethan approached, too close to respect a man's personal space in a public restroom. Heat surged up Ethan's neck as Stevens zipped up his pants.

"I don't want any trouble." Stevens turned around. Other than dropping weight, that once pimpled-face little fucker hadn't aged well. Five years in prison, likely as someone's bitch, would do that to anyone. *Good*, Ethan thought. Unfortunately, Stevens opened his mouth again. "I'm here to listen to what the judge says."

"He'll say you're a dirtbag who has no rights when it comes to *my* daughter. He'll also say you're to stay away or your ass will be back in prison."

Ethan paused, took a step closer, and stared directly into Stevens' eyes. "But prison won't be necessary because after the stunt you pulled in front of my house last week, if you come within a mile of us again, you'll be in a coma. If you even think about trying to sweet-talk the judge, I'll make it my life's mission to make sure you never see sunlight again. And the way you screw things up, it won't take long."

Another man walked in, and Ethan took a step back. "Am I making myself clear?"

Stevens fixed his suit jacket and walked out without washing his hands. *Typical*, Ethan thought. At least that animal wasn't holding his shoulders high in defiance, which gave Ethan hope that he had gotten his message across.

The court was in session when he entered. He quietly took a seat beside his wife on one of the eight hardwood benches in the gallery. Why courtrooms clung to tradition and refused to transition to theater-like seating was beyond his comprehension. During twenty years on the police force, he'd spent countless hours on benches like these, waiting to testify. Every time, he walked away with a butt that felt like he'd biked five miles following a six-month hiatus.

Tyler squeezed his hand when his thigh touched hers. He had room to shimmy an inch or two away and give Tyler her space, but he wanted the connection. This might be the last time he'd feel her leg against his like this. The last time her arm would rest over his with their hands entwined. As much as he hated these damned benches, he willed the Honorable Samuel Beckwith to take his sweet time with things so he could savor the feeling for a while longer.

Ethan kept one eye on Stevens across the aisle as one case after another was heard. If his fidgeting and rapid breathing were any measure, he was planning to do some song and dance in front of the judge. Either that or he was constipated.

"Falling v. Stevens," the court clerk finally announced. Scott motioned for Tyler and Ethan to join him at the petitioner's podium near the front of the courtroom. They stood to his right.

"Your Honor, Scott Campbell, counsel for Petitioner Falling." Scott explained the legal basis of their petition. He presented supporting documentation, including sworn statements, Bree's birth certificate listing the child's biological father as unknown, and the court record of Stevens' rape conviction.

The clinical tone of Scott's presentation was professional and appropriate, but it made Ethan's skin crawl. Those items weren't only evidence. They represented the worst and best things to happen to his family. His wife had been assaulted and raped, her soul beaten into something unrecognizable. But out of that brutality had come Bree, one of the brightest parts of Ethan's life. She was a constant, living reminder of an unthinkable act, yet her tight hugs and sweet kisses on the forehead erased the darkness of how she came into the world. DNA didn't matter. Bree was in his blood. Under his skin. In his heart. She was his, and nothing a court of law said could change that undeniable fact.

"Is the respondent present in court?" the judge asked.

"Yes, he is, Your Honor," Scott replied.

The judge scanned the gallery. "Mr. Stevens, please step forward."

Paul Stevens reluctantly rose and walked up the aisle until he was several feet behind Scott at the podium.

The judge addressed him. "Mr. Stevens, are you represented by counsel today?"

He shook his head. "No, sir."

"Do you wish to seek counsel in this matter?"

"No, sir."

"Do you have any statement or evidence to present in your defense?"

Stevens glanced at Ethan and gulped noticeably. "No, sir."

"The petition is so approved." Judge Beckwith signed and handed a piece of paper to his clerk seated several feet away. "I hereby grant full custody of the female child Falling to Tyler Falling."

Those were the words Ethan and Tyler needed to hear. They were one step closer to preserving what was left of their family.

"Thank you, Your Honor. Next, you'll find our petition to grant Ethan Falling stepparent adoption of the same child. I've attached a copy of the Fallings' marriage certificate, demonstrating they were both legally married in California at the time of birth. In addition, you now have Mrs. Falling's declaration, attesting that both Mr. and Mrs. Falling were married and domiciling together at the time of the child's conception and have co-parented the child since birth."

Judge Beckwith glanced at the documents Scott presented before signing and handing a piece of paper to his clerk. "The petition is so approved. I hereby grant Ethan Falling stepparent adoption and joint custody of the Falling female child."

Ethan looked over his shoulder, locked eyes with Stevens, and mouthed the words, "She's mine." He had every reason to spike the football, but he remained calm. Despite the DNA connection, Stevens had no claim over Ethan's daughter. Not before. Not now. Not ever.

Scott continued, "One more item, Your Honor. You'll find our petition to restrain respondent Paul Stevens from contacting or attempting to contact Tyler Falling, Ethan Falling, the Falling female child, and the Falling's other minor child. The petitioners fear the respondent may attempt to contact the child and reveal details of her paternity. You'll note an incident last month where the respondent made such a statement to Mrs. Falling at her place of business."

Ethan had witnessed enough reluctant judges to know one incident might not make a convincing argument. He couldn't chance not putting the last nail in Stevens' coffin. "And last week, Your Honor. He was parked in front of our family home when my wife and daughter returned. He's demonstrated a pattern."

Judge Beckwith redirected his attention. "Mr. Stevens, do you have any statement or evidence to present in your defense?"

Stevens lowered his head. "No, sir."

"All right then, the petition is so granted. Mr. Stevens, you are hereby restrained from contacting or attempting to contact all Falling family members in any form, including by proxy, for a period of five years. Do you have questions?"

"Yes, sir, I do." Stevens looked directly at the judge. "What happens after five years?"

"That's usually a question for your attorney, but since you have none today, I'll address your question. Let me ask you first, why are you asking?"

"At some point, I might want her to know I'm her father," he said.

"Let me be frank with you, Mr. Stevens." Judge Beckwith shook his head in impatience. "Rape is an act of violence that often has a lifelong impact on its victim. In this case, your abhorrent act, for which you were convicted and, in my opinion, served an inadequate prison term, resulted in the conception of an innocent child. I ask you, years from now, do you want this young woman to know that she was the product of your violence and to look you in the eye, knowing you raped her mother?"

Stevens hung his head, chin to his chest. It was thirteen years too late, but the bastard finally was showing an ounce of regret. "No."

"You'll have about six years to think about it. After this restraining order ends in five years, either Mr. or Mrs. Falling may petition the court to issue another restraining order that will extend until the child turns eighteen."

Would this be enough to keep Stevens at bay? Enough to keep the truth from Bree? Time would determine if they'd done the right thing. Ethan glanced at Tyler. He required no other reassurance than the tears streaking each of her cheeks and the relief on her face. The judge had lifted the weight of the world from her shoulders. This was what she needed.

Letting Tyler go would be the hardest thing he'd ever done, but, oddly, knowing Alex Castle was likely waiting in the wings took away most of the sting. What little he knew of her, he liked. Some might consider her weak or greedy for striking the bargain she had with her father, but Ethan saw something different. He saw a strong, giving woman who refused to deny who she was but recognized that love sometimes required compromise and sacrifice, especially with someone with a debilitating disease. Alex was precisely the life partner Tyler needed and deserved.

CHAPTER TWENTY-FOUR

Manhattan, New York

On rare occasion, Alex beat her assistant and most of the headquarters' staff into the office. She'd never arrived before the construction workers in the lobby nor seen the floor this vacant in the daylight on a weekday, however, preferring to work well into the evening hours. Maybe her sister had rubbed off on her. Getting an early start had an unexpected appeal now. Finishing the day's work with enough daylight remaining to still enjoy it, she decided, was a lifestyle she wanted to try.

First, though, she had to get through the ambitious day she had planned. By its end, she hoped to have rid herself of Kelly Thatcher, gotten to the bottom of her brother's betrayal, and been officially named her father's successor. But the thing she was looking forward to most was meeting Tyler Falling in person. She was off-limits, and Alex would respect her marriage, but putting a face to the voice that had brightened her day for weeks would serve as the icing on today's cake.

Placing her satchel and purse atop her desk, she stepped over to the panoramic windows of her twenty-third floor Madison

Avenue corner office. The treetops of the southernmost end of Central Park swirled in light gale winds, forcing pedestrians to clutch their jackets and hats as they shuffled down the city streets in an amusing dance.

A rap on the door, followed by the words, "Knock, knock," tore her attention from the urban entertainment and to the start of a busy day.

"Ethan, you're early. Come in."

"Good morning. I hope you like sugar and light cream." Ethan joined her at the window. He handed her a steaming cardboard cup imprinted with the logo from the café around the corner from her office. He'd traded the golf attire he'd worn during their first meeting in Napa for a tailored dark suit and an impressive pair of wingtips—a style that looked good on his fit body.

"You're a lifesaver. My assistant won't arrive for another half hour, and I don't know where he hides the key to the office kitchen."

He gazed out the window. "I'm not sure which view I like better, this one of Central Park or the one we see of Times Square from our suite."

"Both are quintessential Manhattan. I hope you and Tyler like the accommodations."

"Are you kidding? Hands down, it's the best room we've ever stayed in."

"We" was a stinging reminder that Tyler was married and unobtainable—a fact Alex accepted without hesitation but not without deep regret.

"Yes, well." Alex gestured toward the leather couch. "Shall we get started?"

Ethan pulled a folder from his briefcase and spread its contents on the coffee table. "Victor Padula is not a good guy. He has quite the rap sheet—three assault cases pled down to misdemeanors and one bookmaking conviction, a Class E felony, for which he served one year on probation. But all of those were a decade ago. He's either gotten a lot smarter or is better connected now. My contact on the NYPD said his name has come up in several gambling investigations. He is Manhattan's bookie to the city's rich and famous."

Alex sighed. Ethan had confirmed her suspicions. The year's worth of irregularities she'd traced to the Times Square remodeling project all made sense now. His having a Manhattan elite bookie meant Andrew had amassed an enormous gambling debt.

"I need to find out how deep Andrew is into him without involving the police. Andrew's embezzling, not to mention the bad PR, would send my father on a tirade. Can you find Victor? I want to meet with him."

"You can't be serious."

"I am. I need to put a halt to whatever business arrangement Andrew has with this man, but I won't risk him getting hurt in the process. I may not be a fan of my brother at the moment, but he's still my twin. And with his history, Andrew might end up with broken legs or worse."

"Let me make a phone call, but there's no way I'm letting you meet with him alone. I'm coming with you."

"Thank you, Ethan. I really appreciate your help, but I have to ask. Have you had any luck finding the woman in the picture?"

"I'm sorry, Alex. I haven't had time yet to look into it."

She sighed. If she had to choose between putting Kelly in her place or finding her mystery woman, despite the consequences, she'd go with the latter every day of the week. "I understand. Before you make that call, we should talk about the photos I need you to retrieve from Kelly."

Ethan shifted on the couch, smoothing his tie. "I'll need to inspect them to ensure they're the right ones. Does that make you uneasy?"

"Yes, but it's the only way we can bring this to an end."

"I can do a cursory examination. The date stamp on the back will confirm when they were processed."

"Unfortunately, I printed them myself in the university darkroom. You're looking for twenty-four three-by-five black and white photos, compromising ones, of me with Kelly." Alex shifted to face Ethan. "I trust you, Ethan. I know you'll do the right thing and look only as much as you have to."

He confirmed that with a strong nod, then went off to make a phone call.

During his absence, Alex prepared for Kelly. Over the next half hour, she printed and neatly compiled copies of emails, photographs, and transcripts of voice mails and text messages between Kelly and Nick Castor and placed them into a flip folder. She also spooled up a copy of Castor's videotaped confession to play on her laptop. She was ready for a full-on counter-blackmail.

Ethan returned after learning the location of Victor Padula's hangout. Later today, he'd take her there and she'd be one step closer to cleaning up her brother's mess.

Her office intercom buzzed. "Ms. Castle, Kelly Thatcher is here to see you."

Alex sat in her executive desk chair, the seat of power. She would remain there until Kelly turned into a quaking pile of Jell-O. Since her assistant never used the speakerphone and she could tell from the clearness of his voice that he was adhering to that practice, Alex added, "Thanks, Robbie. Please have security standing by my office. My meeting with Ms. Thatcher will not be cordial. Send her in." She drew in a long breath of focused determination and nodded at Ethan, who responded with a confident wink.

"You got it," Robbie replied.

Moments later, Kelly strutted through the door, smiling in her off-the-rack dark gray pencil skirt, matching boxed jacket, and tasteful black heels. At least she'd finally learned to dress the part.

"Close the door and take a seat," Alex directed.

"O-kay." Kelly's shaky voice told Alex she suspected this wouldn't be the friendly meeting Alex had led her to believe it might be. She closed the door and took a seat in the guest chair facing Alex's desk.

Alex gestured to her side, where Ethan stood tall, a sturdy wall of defense. "This is Ethan. He's here to make sure you don't make any trouble because I'm about to change the terms of our arrangement."

Alex turned her laptop, giving Kelly a perfect view of the close-up shot of her former lover, Nick Castor. The nervous gulp Kelly gave was the reaction Alex wanted. She pressed the spacebar, unleashing video evidence that would cut Kelly off at the knees. Within the first thirty seconds, Castor had thrown her under the bus, detailing the information he shared with her regarding iQuench before its acquisition went public.

Alex stopped the video before sliding the folder across her desk. Kelly flipped through the pages, biting her nails as she digested the mounting evidence. When she looked up, Alex asked, "Do you know the punishment for insider trading?" Kelly offered a slow headshake in the negative. Reality was apparently sinking in.

"Twenty years in prison and a fine of two million dollars," Alex continued at Kelly's hard swallow. "Despite her millions and an army of high-priced lawyers, Martha Stewart was convicted on much less evidence and still went to jail. How well do you think you'll fare after PopCo's CEO, who is a friend of mine, presents this information to the Securities and Exchange Commission?"

Kelly shrank like a cornered chihuahua. "What are you proposing, Alex?"

"First, you're fired. Second, if any information about our affair comes to light, including those pictures, I'll make one phone call to PopCo, and the game will be over. Third, after you turn over all copies of those photos to Ethan here, I never want to see or hear from you again. Do we have an agreement?"

Kelly straightened and tugged on her bunched blazer. "Fine, Alex. You win."

"Good. Security will help you clean out your office and escort you out. After that, Ethan will take you wherever you need to go to retrieve those photos." Alex directed her attention to Ethan. "I gave her one set, but look for extras."

"That won't be necessary, Alex."

"Oh, I think it will be."

The last time Alex felt this good, she was hugging Syd for giving her the perfect birthday present. Kelly would no longer be the albatross hung around her neck. She had her life back. And after tonight, she would be the captain of her own ship. Besides seeing Tyler, the only thing that could make this day better would be coming face-to-face with her mystery woman. *If only*, she thought.

* * *

New York City had been on Tyler's bucket list for years. As far back as she could remember, she had compared it to Dorothy's Oz, the magical, shining city on the hill where all of her dreams could come true. With Alex Castle covering most of their expenses, she had no excuse for not making the most of her time here.

The two days she and Ethan had weren't nearly enough to explore the city, so Tyler had started early with shopping in the West Village. She weaved in and out of trendy and hip local shops in the charming tree-lined streets and blocks of historic brownstones. The winds calmed after lunch, making her afternoon street exploration more palatable. Passing a camera shop, she focused on the eye-catching window display of antique cameras. The thought of Alex's story drew her inside.

The shop carried the entire spectrum of modern cameras, accessories, and supplies. In a glass counter in the back, though, the store displayed a collection of antique cameras for sale. She instantly focused on a particular model and got the attention of a clerk. "That's a Leica M3, right? What year is it?"

The clerk peeked at the information sheet nestled below the camera. "It's a 1959."

"That's a shame. I was looking for a '57."

This is crazy, thought Tyler. Alex had mentioned her mother's lost Leica in passing, and now here she was, in the middle of Manhattan, trying to find one for her. What was she thinking? Alex Castle was out of her league—rich, cultured, Ivy League-educated, and heir to an international resort chain worth billions. How could Tyler impress a woman like that with an old camera?

If Tyler's mother were still alive, she'd tell her, no doubt, that when it came to taking the measure of someone, money, looks, and education meant nothing compared to what was in his heart. Or, in this case, hers. She gave the camera one more look and decided if it had been a 1957, she'd have thrown caution to the wind, bought it, and taken her chances—because Alex Castle had a good heart.

She'd bet her last dollar that she was beautiful too. A part of Tyler now regretted not scouring the Internet for a picture of Alex, but there was no sense in looking her up now. That mystery would reveal itself tonight.

* * *

Alex was walking the last block to Arthur's Alley after the cab dropped her off when she spotted Ethan walking from the subway station. Light afternoon drizzle left the streets of the Flatiron district smelling fresh and earthy into the early evening. The cool temperature combined with a barely there breeze, sending what she hoped was the last chill of the season.

"I love New York, but I wasn't expecting it to be this cold." Ethan had flipped up his collar and his shoulders were slightly raised to combat the cold. Periodically, he looked behind them and scanned the crowd of pedestrians, likely a habit born of years of detective work. Given his keen awareness of his surroundings, he'd make an excellent bodyguard, Alex thought.

"If you think it's cold now, you should experience the city when it snows." Alex tightened the front of her coat around her torso. "Mission accomplished with Kelly?"

He handed her a thick letter-sized envelope. She stopped in her tracks. She'd put some thought into how she could confirm the authenticity of the photos. Several options had come to mind. She'd trust Ethan's cursory assessment if he said those were *the* photos, but she would always doubt if he'd gotten them all. For her own peace of mind, she had to look.

Alex stepped to the side, somewhere neither he nor passersby could see the contents of the photos. The last time she'd laid eyes on the pictures was when she burned her copies at Abby's beach house after Kelly dumped her. She wanted to forget everything about that horrible weekend, but if she hoped to get past this untenable situation, she had to relive what had brought her to the brink all those years ago.

Thankfully, the first picture wasn't one of the money photos, the ones the tabloids would pay top dollar for but couldn't publish unredacted. Neither was the next nor the one after that. Partial nudity wasn't as frowned upon today as thirteen years ago, but the images nonetheless sparked Alex's regret.

Then she came to the most embarrassing pictures. Embarrassing not because they were titillating enough to cost her her job and her relationship with her father—after Abby's revelation, she couldn't care less about what William thought—but because Ethan had seen them. He was a professional detective and had likely come across photos like these dozens of times before, but that didn't take away the sting that a man she respected, a man whose wife she'd been crushing on for weeks, had seen her naked and engaged in sex.

She jammed the prints back in the envelope. The next stop for these reminders of that abominable time would be her home shredder. She'd destroy them as soon as she went home to dress for tonight's festivities.

"No other copies?"

"I don't believe so. I don't think she wants to cross you. Kelly was shaking so much, I thought she was having a seizure."

"Then consider this matter closed." Alex shoved the envelope deep into her coat pocket, and they resumed their walk to Arthur's. When they got there, Ethan pulled her to a stop.

"When we get inside, we'll get a table, and I'll scan the room," he said. "If Victor is here, he'll likely have one or two guards around him for security. I'll flash my badge. Let me do the talking. These guys are all about the money. We have to convince him that talking to us is in his best interest."

"And how do you plan to do that?" Alex asked.

"Four letters. R-I-C-O." Ethan spelled it out for emphasis. "That would get any bookie's attention."

Ethan strode confidently to the sports bar entrance and held the door open for Alex. "That's the plan." Minutes later, the hostess led Ethan and Alex to a table in the center of the noisy, jam-packed main dining room. Ethan scanned the crowd. "At your three o'clock."

Alex slowly turned her head to the right. She spied a large, muscle-bound man dressed in a black suit guarding the entrance of what looked like a separate dining area. "The gorilla?"

"See the bulge under his left arm? That's likely a .45." Alex nodded. "I'll scout. Stay here."

What had her brother gotten himself into? Alex had expected brass knuckles, maybe, but not guns. Armed thugs meant Andrew was in a lot more trouble than she thought. She needed to put an immediate stop to his schemes and pay off his debts, whatever they amounted to. One thing for sure, she was glad Ethan, with his years of professional law enforcement training, was on her side.

She watched while he asked a question of a server, who then pointed toward the rear of the building. Ethan gave a polite nod and walked in that direction at a pace designed not to attract attention. When he passed the tree stump with legs, Padula's likely bodyguard, he glanced into the secondary room, so briefly it was barely noticeable even to Alex. He was good.

After a few minutes, Ethan returned to their table. "Victor's in the back room with someone who I assume is a client. Let's wait for that guy to leave. The last thing we want is to piss him off by disrupting a business transaction. Then we can make our move." He picked up a menu and flipped to the first page. "Do you like nachos?"

Ten minutes later, Ethan and Alex were diving into cheesy nachos and sipping on sodas while keeping an eye on Victor's cave. Eventually, a man carrying a briefcase exited the private room. Alex instantly recognized the expensive haircut and jacket. "Shit. It's my brother." She picked up her menu and buried her head in it, hoping Andrew wouldn't spot her. She wanted to eliminate all plausible deniability before she confronted him. That meant talking to Victor Padula first.

She glanced at Ethan. "Did he see me?"

"I don't think so." Ethan's eyes followed him toward the front. "He's gone. Do you want to leave? He may come back."

"No. We need to strike now. I may not get another chance."

Ethan took the lead. He stopped shy of the secondary entrance and flashed his detective badge at the goon guarding it. "I'm here to see Victor." The burly man, large enough to knock Ethan into next week, looked at the badge but remained expressionless. "This can go one of two ways. You can let me see Victor, or I'll come back in an hour with food inspectors who will shut down this place for several weeks after they conveniently find a rat or two in the kitchen. Your choice."

"Stay here." The guard walked the few steps to Victor, whispered in his ear, then returned. After giving Ethan a stern look, he jutted his chin toward the private room's interior, signaling that Victor would talk to him.

When they reached the gaudy, red leather couch, Ethan gestured for Alex to sit first. "Hello, Victor. I'm here in an unofficial capacity. My friend here needs some information from you, and I'm here to negotiate." Victor remained silent. "We need to talk to you about Andrew Castle."

"I don't know him." Victor's unblinking response was less than convincing.

"May I call you Vic?" Ethan didn't wait for an answer before he continued, "Listen, Vic. Andrew walked out of this room not five minutes ago, looking like he'd pissed his pants. Cards on the table. You and I both know what you do for a living. You have a lot of rich, stupid customers. I'd hate to see them have to go somewhere else because you're doing a twenty-year stretch for racketeering. You already have one conviction for gambling, one more and you become the poster child for the RICO statute. Also, you've heard of the Patriot Act, right? I say 'possible terrorist ties' to the FBI, and they'll tap every phone you and your goons have ever called. How long do you think it would take me to flip some Wall Street wuss into giving you up?"

"I'm listening," Victor replied, remaining expressionless.

"We want to know how much Andrew Castle is into you and what the payment plan is."

"Why is this important to you?"

"He's my brother." Concern that Andrew might return had sapped Alex's patience.

Ethan put a hand over Alex's, signaling her to keep quiet. "It's a family matter. You're a smart businessman who wants to make a profit. I get that. Let's say my friend is willing to settle his debt in a way beneficial to both you and her family. You negotiate with us, and I don't scream 'terrorist' to the FBI."

"If this is a negotiation, I want more than money in return," Victor countered.

"How can I sweeten the pot?" Ethan asked.

"One of my competitors has been drawing away some of my long-term customers. You take care of him, and I'll negotiate."

"What's his name?"

"Sammy Bastain."

Ethan pulled out his cell phone and dialed. "Hey, Jimmy, it's Ethan… You know a bookie by the name of Sammy Bastain? Good. Can you do me a solid and disrupt his business for a month? Thanks, buddy. I'll let you know when it's a go."

Ethan closed his flip phone and then returned his attention to Victor. "If you play ball with us, my contact in the Seventeenth Precinct will have a patrol car sitting outside Sammy's place of business for the next month. Are we good?"

Victor laughed, the kind that suggested respect but little more. "I like you, Ethan. You get right to the point and get things done. Andrew still owes me two million."

Alex's eyes shot wide open. "He lost two million dollars gambling?" She couldn't believe her brother had accumulated debt that large to a bookie. And, to top it off, that he had planned to embezzle from the company to pay it back.

"Not gambling. Borrowed."

"You said *still*," Ethan said. "What was the original debt?"

"A double on two mil, payable in twelve months. His first payment is due next Friday."

"So you've already received your principal back?" Alex asked.

"He returned it tonight. Tried to weasel his way out, but a deal is a deal. I need to make a profit."

Ethan leaned over to whisper into Alex's ear. "If you want your brother in one piece and this out of the papers, offer him something. Can you handle half a mil?" Alex slowly nodded yes.

Ethan continued, "I understand that. Considering the extra business you might roll in after we shut down Sammy, I think twenty-five cents on the dollar is a fair profit."

"Fifty," Victor countered.

"Vic, my friend." Ethan pulled out his cell phone again and flipped it open. "You control the next call I make. If you insist on fifty, I call the FBI, and you're counting down the days in a medium-security prison. If you agree to twenty-five, I call the Seventeenth, and you're counting your half-million-dollar profit by the end of tomorrow. What's it going to be?"

"All right, Ethan, I'm a reasonable businessman, and a profit is a profit." Victor gave him a disarming smile. "You have a deal."

"One more thing. You cut off her brother. He's a bad risk now. As of tomorrow, he'll no longer have deep pockets."

"He isn't worth the headache. I expect payment by five p.m. tomorrow."

"You'll have it sooner than that." Ethan stood and offered his hand to Alex.

They silently walked out of the sports bar, Alex struggling to process how far her brother had fallen. They turned the corner, and Alex doubled her pace, seething anger fueling her stride.

"My God, Ethan. I can't believe what Andrew has gotten himself into and how much he would've embezzled from the company. I knew he liked to gamble, but this is beyond the pale."

"The question now is, why did your brother need that much fast cash? Until we find the answer, I'm glad I recorded everything." Ethan patted his breast pocket, where he'd hidden his recording device. He halted mid-step in front of a restaurant entrance and began studying the menu displayed in the window, pulling Alex to a stop beside him. "At your nine o'clock."

Alex furtively glanced in that direction. Two unmistakable, brawny, tough guys in suits had paused a half block down on the sidewalk, failing to appear nonchalant. "Victor's men?"

"We ruffled some feathers. The sooner we pay Vic, the better. If you courier the cashier's check to the Times Square hotel today, I'll personally hand it to him before tonight's party." Following Alex's nod of agreement, Ethan hailed a cab and ushered Alex into its backseat. "I'll take the subway. See you tonight at your father's."

CHAPTER TWENTY-FIVE

When William Castle finally passed, Alex wanted no piece of the Castle mansion, family home or not. Her father had followed the example of a long line of elite Manhattan families—the Carnegies, Rockefellers, Roosevelts, Kennedys, and Dukes—and relocated the household to the Upper East Side when she was six. It had a zip code her mother would've never approved of. Judging by the tales Abby had told, her mother would have called it too pretentious and favored the artsy vibe of Chelsea or Greenwich Village.

Her father was a different story. His stylish limestone mansion on Fifth Avenue, facing Central Park, spoke of money and status, both of which he'd spent decades accumulating. Tonight, family, friends, dozens of business associates, and a member or two of the New York press were assembled in the main room for a "celebration," as William had ambiguously designated the festivities. During the day, the room was lit by two floor-to-ceiling picture windows that opened to the lush trees in the property's back garden. But this evening the place was illumined by the room's massive crystal chandelier, strategic floor lighting, and a glow from the décor's dramatic centerpiece, a black marble fireplace.

Alex usually was a master at "working" a room. Tonight, though, the daggers her brother was shooting her way and the prospect of meeting Tyler Falling in person were throwing her off her game. Between the champagne, cocktails, and hors d'oeuvres, she nevertheless managed to mingle among the list of who's who in two-thousand-dollar suits and dresses. Her preferred drive-by greeting before moving on to the next guest comprised a firm handshake, accompanied by a "So glad you could make it. We should talk next week. Give my assistant a call." If he hadn't been debating the international stock market's finer points with a Rockefeller, William definitely would've labeled her greetings as inadequate.

Alex glanced toward the entry hall again. The party had been underway for almost an hour, but Ethan and Tyler hadn't yet arrived. She should've insisted they accept her offer of a town car.

"Whoever she is, she should be ashamed for keeping you waiting," Abby whispered into her ear. Her tone was one of confidence, not conjecture. Alex's sympathies and envy went to the woman by Abby's side. Abigail Spencer had a way of reading people and zeroing in on their emotions. Indra would have no chance to hide any irritations that might arise, but neither would she have to beg for the attention she craved. Abby would sense Indra's need and respond with grace and passion.

"I could say you're seeing things, but that would be a lie," Alex said.

"She must be special if she has you this distracted on the occasion of your 'coronation.'"

Alex stared at the front entrance again, disappointed that Ethan hadn't yet walked in with a cute blonde on his arm. At least she hoped that was Tyler's hair color. She shook her head. She had to stop this. A fascination with the wife of someone else, especially someone she respected as much as Ethan, was unhealthy and dishonorable.

"What little I know of her, yes, she's special, but she's married."

"I haven't seen you this smitten since that awful experience at Yale."

"Don't remind me." Alex's stomach shuddered at how her youthful infatuation had turned her life upside down then and now. "Thank goodness, she's nothing like Kelly Thatcher."

"That is a definite plus." Abby scanned the room. "Have you seen my daughter? William appears ready to make his announcement. She'd never forgive herself if she missed your big moment."

Alex didn't have to guess who Harley was with, only where. A delicious brunette had arrived dressed in a tight little dark-blue number, and after a single drink, Harley had her under her spell. Which meant Harley would have wanted absolute privacy. With the family and guest wings closed off for the event, that left her one option—the playhouse.

"I'll find her." Alex gave Abby a reassuring pat on the hand. "Stall my father for ten more minutes."

"Me?" Abby pointed at herself with an expression suggesting that Alex had just asked her to go over Niagara Falls in a barrel. "He might insist on dueling at twelve paces if I initiate a conversation."

Indra kissed Abby on the cheek. "Darling, I've got this." She pushed both sleeves above the elbow and marched toward William.

Slipping out to the lush back garden, Alex followed the pathway to the guest house her father had converted into a teenager's dream, equipping it with televisions, video games, air hockey, and a fully stocked pantry and fridge. The central feature, a plush sectional and ottoman big enough to host an orgy, was likely Harley's location.

Muffled soft music and the dim glow seeping through the drawn blinds confirmed Alex's suspicion. More proof came in the form of the faint moan from behind the door. She knocked loud enough to pull Harley away from her evening snack.

"You need to wrap things up, Harley. Father is about to make his big splash."

The moaning stopped, but not the music. Moments later, the door was flung open. Harley wiped the corner of her mouth, looking as if she'd been through a hurricane. "Holy hell, Alex. You have horrible timing."

The sight deserved a proper belly laugh, but Alex restricted herself to a snicker. "You better freshen up, but don't take too long. We can't keep William Castle waiting."

The door opened wider to reveal the luscious brunette, perfectly put together, who was taming her short, straight hair by merely running a hand through it. "I better go find my husband before he notices I'm gone."

Harley whipped her head around so fast she'd need a neck brace for weeks. "Wait. You're married?"

"I thought you knew."

Alex inspected the woman's left hand, noting the bare ring finger. "Who's your husband?"

"Blake Ward. We eloped to New Orleans last month."

That explained the sudden vacation of Castle Resort's interim CFO. Alex racked her brain to recall the details of Blake's costly divorce earlier in the year. She remembered hearing rumors of him trading in his fifty-year-old wife for one half her age. This little number fit the bill.

Harley's disappointment in herself was likely visible from space. Player or not, like Alex, she had one rule: no cheaters.

"All right, whatever your name is. Your husband works for me. If you want your sugar daddy to continue raking in the Benjamins, you better forget this ever happened and forget you ever saw my friend." Alex folded her arms across her chest. "Do we understand one another?"

"That's a shame. I rather liked you, Harley. I guess this is goodbye." She moved to kiss Harley on the cheek but received a brush-off.

"Just go."

The woman shrugged, took a few steps down the pathway, then stopped. She looked back over her shoulder and winked. "You really should get a talent agent, Harley. With a tongue that talented, you could star on Broadway."

After the woman walked out of sight, Harley hung her head. Though it had been unintentional, she'd broken her primary rule. Like Alex, she'd been cheated on and dumped. That had led to their mutual pact to never contribute to another person feeling that devastated.

Alex had to lighten the mood. She gave Harley a shoulder nudge. "A talent agent, huh? Shall I call William Morris?"

Harley's lips parted, exposing a satisfied and apparently well-deserved grin in the dim light. "I gave her my best service." The smile faded as quickly as it appeared. "I feel horrible."

Alex slung an arm across Harley's shoulder and squeezed tight. "You did nothing wrong, at least not intentionally. I, on the other hand, am actively struggling with our cardinal rule. At least on an emotional and intellectual level."

"John's cousin's wife?"

Alex nodded.

"Is it one-sided?"

"I don't know, and that's the most frustrating part. I'm both glad and sad that Tyler might not feel the same way. It would mean she's faithful, yet also mean I'll never know if she's as special as I suspect."

"You have it bad." Harley snaked an arm around Alex's waist. "My advice is to take your mind off things you can't have by finding 'Miss Donnie Flats.' The way you described your mystery woman, you owe it to yourself."

"You're right." She needed to rein in her fascination with Tyler and treat Ethan with the respect he deserved. The first thing she'd ask of him tonight would be to drop everything else and find her mystery woman.

"I'm always right. Now, let's go watch you assume the mantle of Castle Resorts."

Alex and Harley made their way through the sea of guests, packed shoulder to shoulder in the main room to hear William's announcement. Speculation had reached high tide, most attendees throwing pretense to the wind and trading guesses about the nature of tonight's "celebration." Alex's favorite was that her father was about to announce his engagement to a long-term mistress. She couldn't help but laugh. Her father loved only his company and his children, in that order. He had no emotion left for anyone or anything else. Castle Resorts was his mistress.

Alex joined her father at the fireplace, the room's focal point. Next to her stood her brother. Andrew's anger, jealousy, and envy were as palpable as the vibrations generated by a cranked-up bass speaker. He was immature, selfish, cut corners, and had an unhealthy sense of entitlement, but he was also her twin. That connection could lead her to forgive almost any misstep. Forgiving, though, didn't include forgetting. As long as she was in control of Castle Resorts, he'd never hold a senior position of trust.

William clinked a silver spoon against his champagne glass, bringing conversation in the room to a slow, murmuring hush. Alex scanned the crowd. Abby, Indra, and Harley filled the front row, friendly faces whose support she welcomed as she prepared to step into the next phase of her life. Syd would have been among them if not for a problem with aging wine barrels.

William returned the spoon to the mantle behind him. Taking in what Alex would characterize as a proud breath, he faced the collection of friends and colleagues. "Thank you for coming tonight. I apologize for the vague description given for tonight's festivities, but…"

Alex's attention swung to the crowd on the side near the entrance to the room, where people were shifting to make room for a late arrival. Ethan stood out with his broad shoulders and chiseled features. As he settled into a position, her heart sank. Where was Tyler? Had she come? Then the crowd shifted again, and a woman a half-foot shorter than Ethan slipped in front of him.

"It's her." The words tumbled from her lips before she could make sense of what she'd seen.

Everything and everyone in the room blurred and fell away as if swallowed by a black hole. Nothing existed except for Alex's mystery woman. It was sophomore year in high school all over again and the day Coleen Haskel had walked into the classroom and made her heart jump out of her chest. Seeing the mystery woman's face in her childhood home was a thousand times more intense, though, than what had happened in high school.

It *was* her. It *had* to be her. Alex couldn't make out the blue-gray eyes she'd peered into for less than a minute weeks ago. Yet she was confident a day would come when they'd smile at her every morning. The hair was identical, dark, golden strands of delicate ribbon drawing her in like a magnet. The scooped neckline exposed creamy, light tones and a hint of cleavage that had Alex captivated. But it was the button nose and cleft chin that had her addicted like she was to dark chocolate and red wine. They were the sweet, satisfying indulgence she craved every night.

Then the mystery woman locked her gaze on her. Nearly three thousand miles and three weeks later, the pull was the same. Palpable. Powerful. Earth-shifting. She must feel it, too. Her breasts rose and fell in a rapid rhythm that matched Alex's feeble attempt to gather enough air to keep her from succumbing to this craziness. How had Ethan found her? If him saying he hadn't begun his search was part of a planned surprise, she'd forgive him in a heartbeat. This was a month of Christmases and birthdays all rolled into one.

Wait.

When Ethan placed a hand atop her shoulder in a familiar, practiced manner, the woman didn't flinch. She seemed to not mind the friendly, almost loving touch. Two explanations popped into her head, but neither made sense. Ethan didn't seem the philandering type. But if that was the case…

It couldn't be. Was that why Tyler's voice sounded familiar? Why Alex couldn't explain the connection she felt with a woman she'd never seen? That was the only coherent narrative.

Tyler was her mystery woman.

"Alexandra?"

A shoulder shove brought her out of her trance. The not-so-gentle nudge was Andrew's childish method of commanding her attention.

"What?" She ripped her stare from the mystery woman. How long had she been standing there with her mouth wide open? Andrew's nudge meant it had been too long to brush it off as a momentary lapse.

Alex turned toward her father. William greeted her with the same sour expression he had given Syd when she announced she was quitting Castle Resorts to make wine with her husband. This time, anger clearly outstripped his disappointment. Her next words needed to deflect his attention from her potentially career-ending blunder.

"I'm sorry, Father. Your vote of confidence had me recalling the first day I walked through the doors of Castle Resorts Headquarters. I remember that magical and awe-inspiring day like it was yesterday. It made me dream of walking in your footsteps and being worthy of stepping into your shoes one day. Today, that dream has come true."

Alex pulled out her widest smile and focused her stare on Harley, her eyes begging for a bailout. "Would someone please pinch me and remind me this is all real?"

"I'll do it." A loyal friend, Harley raised her champagne glass to a chorus of laughter. Alex could always count on her best friend for an unqualified rescue. She raised her glass in appreciation.

Alex turned her attention back to her father and raised her glass to him. His expression had softened. Disease or not, homophobic resentment or not, the moisture pooling in his eyes reflected the love and pride she'd always thought was there for her. "I hope to live up to your example and trust every day."

"Here, here," someone called out, and in unison, the room concurred with raised glasses and a loud buzz.

Alex had turned a potential disaster on its head. Everyone, including her father, was solidly behind her. All but one, that is. She didn't have to look at Andrew to know he was seething. His negative energy battered at her like rain in a hurricane.

"I'm sure you will, Alexandra." William clinked his glass against Alex's before turning his attention to the crowd. "Now, please, enjoy the rest of the food and champagne."

As the applause died down, Alex returned her gaze to the entrance, but the mystery woman wasn't there. Alarm bells went off. Had she not felt the electrical charge that still lingered from their single touch weeks ago? She scanned the room from one corner to the other. Thankfully, Ethan was taller than most and easy to recognize, even from behind.

She started to weave her way toward the buffet table where he was filling a plate, but smiling front-row faces held her up. Abby extended her arms for a welcomed, albeit poorly timed, embrace. "We're so happy for you, dear."

Alex accepted Abby's hug but pulled back before giving it the appreciation it deserved. "Thank you, Abby, but I have to find someone."

Abby gently grasped Alex's elbows, her eyes filled with concern. "The one you spoke of earlier?"

"Yes. Or I think so." Alex kept an eye on Ethan, reluctant to let him out of her sight. "But things have changed. I have to find her."

"My dear Alex, you're playing with fire."

"Maybe so, but I need answers." Alex softly brushed off Abby's hold, but Harley pressed a hand against her chest, preventing her escape. Frustration mounted as precious seconds ticked away. "It's her, Harley."

"Tyler?"

"No. I mean, yes. It's *her*, Harley."

"Mystery woman?"

"Yes, and I'm not letting her slip through my fingers again."

Alex dismissed Harley's hold and stepped toward the buffet table. Her heart thumped faster at the prospect of coming eye to eye with her mystery woman again. Two guests politely congratulated her as she zigged through the mingling crowd. She was steps away from her target and getting the answers she wanted when a hand fell on her shoulder. She stopped and turned. "Father."

Always a hard one to read, William could've had in mind giving her a new Mercedes or a public flogging. She hoped the room filled with people he wouldn't dare make a scene in front of would give her a reprieve from an inquisition, but she braced for the worst.

"Alexandra, do you have a moment?" William's expression and body language gave no sign of which way this conversation would go. His businesslike tone, however, gave her the impression she was in the clear.

"Of course, Father." She kept one eye at the buffet table, tracking Ethan when he stepped away. "But I have some late-arriving guests I should greet."

"This won't take long. We should meet with Blake Ward first thing Monday morning to discuss the transition of Andrew to CFO."

"Did I hear my name?" Blake appeared from behind Alex with his wife draped on his arm. "Ms. Castle, I'd like to introduce you to my wife, Veronica."

"We've met." Alex made no move to shake her hand. She had an inkling where that thing had been recently and doubted whether Veronica had time to wash up. "I understand Veronica has a fascination with Broadway."

"I had no idea." Blake turned toward his two-timing, guilty-as-shit wife.

"Yes, well, I hate to cut this short, but I have more guests to tend to." Alex hoped that would be enough for Blake's new toy to pull him away.

"We need to meet soon to discuss Andrew's transition," William repeated.

Twin or not, her father's wishes or not, Alex couldn't give Andrew the keys to the candy store. Her best tactic was to stall her father from appointing him until she took over. "I had an overlap in mind, with Andrew learning the ropes first. We should minimize disruption at the top."

Blake's face lit up at the prospect of delaying his demotion from Interim CFO. "Grand idea, Ms. Castle."

"Let's discuss this later. Say Friday?" As she stepped toward Ethan, she patted Blake on the shoulder. "Good luck with that marriage of yours."

Alex locked her sights on Ethan. He was occupying himself by scanning the crowd and his surroundings. *He's always on alert*, she thought. Two more well-meaning guests tried to detour her, but nothing would stop her this time.

After ten more confident strides, she reached her target. "Ethan, you made it."

"Thanks for inviting us. I'm sorry we didn't arrive in time to chat before your big moment, but detouring to pay off Victor took a little longer than I anticipated."

"No worries. I'm glad we're done with Victor and that you came. Did Tyler?" Her question came out a little too fast and with a little too much zest for him to consider it casual curiosity. Under any other circumstance, she'd regret her haste, but the confusion hitting her from all sides dictated her reasoning.

"She did."

"The woman I saw with you earlier, that was Tyler?"

"Yes."

Alex's legs wobbled beneath her. It was true. She'd found the woman she'd been searching for, yet she was still out of reach. Alex had built up in her head a movie-like happily ever after with her mystery woman, and now, Ethan had shattered the fantasy.

"It's a shock, isn't it?"

What did he say? "You knew and didn't tell me?"

"I figured it out after you sent me the photo."

Alex felt like scum. Lower than that. Whatever they called the muck and algae at the bottom of the East River, that was her. She'd asked an incredibly good man to hand over his own wife so she could fulfill a fantasy. Yet, he had said nothing and had continued to give her his full measure with Kelly and Andrew. She hung her head, ashamed of her selfishness, of putting her wants and desires above Ethan's.

"Ms. Castle. Matt Crown, *Daily News*. Care to make a statement on your father's plan to appoint you as CEO and not your brother?"

Alex wouldn't give Matt Crown the time of day, let alone insight into her family dynamics. Tonight's clean-cut appearance didn't fool her. He'd shaven his trademark three-day stubble, slicked back his greasy black hair, and traded in his wrinkled rolled-up sleeves and mustard-stained tie for an off-the-rack pressed suit. If past was prologue, she fully expected him to twist anything she said into a shocking narrative to drive up sales.

"No comment."

She turned to Ethan. "Come with me." Guests were confining themselves to the main room, so she led him to the well-lit, unoccupied back patio. As an added precaution, after closing the double french doors there, she ushered him to a lounge area with cushioned chairs and an above-ground metal firepit. "I'm so sorry, Ethan. I didn't know until you two walked in tonight."

"She didn't either."

"Why didn't you say anything? I would've walked away and forgotten all about it."

"Now, that's a lie. If you've been feeling half of what Tyler has, you'd rather cut off your right arm than walk away."

So Tyler felt it too? But why would Ethan tell her that? This was so complicated and confusing. The connection she had sensed while working with Tyler wasn't all in her head. She could see it now. The seed they'd planted weeks ago along the Napa walkway had blossomed into hope.

But Tyler was Ethan's wife. Despite how drawn Alex was to her, she couldn't go there. Wouldn't.

Ethan's reaction confused the hell out of her. Why hadn't he blown his top yet? Everything she knew about him told her he was a devoted family man. He should've given Alex a "what for" with a stern warning to stay away from his wife.

"As hard as it will be, I'll walk away. I can't do that to you," Alex said.

"You're too late. I beat you to it," Ethan said without batting an eye.

"No, no, no." Without more than the single touch during their chance meeting in Napa, Alex had become the "other woman." She was a homewrecker, the one thing she and Harley had mutually sworn to never become. She turned and placed her hands on her hips, unable to face what she'd done. "I wanted none of this to happen. It's all my fault. I should've never hired her company."

"Look at me, Alex." He waited until she turned and looked at him squarely. Sadness had enveloped his eyes, not the rage she expected. After nearly two decades of marriage, he should be mad as hell that his wife was attracted to someone else on more than a physical level. "As much as I'd like to lay blame at your feet, this is not your fault. It's not even Tyler's. This was a long time in the making and was something I should've seen coming."

"I don't understand."

"Tyler should explain the rest. She's waiting for you."

"Where is she?"

"I'm right here, Alex." Those four words cut through the cool night with the warmth and softness of a summer breeze.

Alex turned. She'd broken up a marriage and needed to know why Ethan had accepted it without a fight. Tyler's chest rose and fell, matching Alex's own struggle to calm the jitters of this surreal moment. She approached, reeling Alex in with each step. Alex lay captive to her pull. She didn't have to see her to confirm its existence. It was there, invisible, like stars hiding in a noon sky.

Alex felt her heart hammer to the beat of the hundred questions flying into her head. Only one fell from her lips. "How?"

"I don't know."

Tyler was the bold one. She reached out with the hand that had set all of this in motion, her eyes begging Alex's hand to do the same. Alex took it into hers. Soft. Smooth. Familiar. This second touch outstripped the first. Sweeping tingles dwarfed those that had coursed through her in Napa. This was the pinch she needed. She wasn't dreaming. Weeks of wondering, wanting, and hoping had come to an end.

Without giving a thought to who might see them, Alex curled their hands against her chest. "This is so much to take in." Motion behind the windows lining the main room caught her attention. She shifted her gaze. The crowd had yet to thin, but one figure stood out. Her father stood near the window, rigid, his haughty stare aimed at Alex as if she had a bullseye painted between her eyes.

Surprisingly, she didn't care. For thirteen years, she had denied herself a full life in deference to his feelings. Now that she knew the real reason behind his close-minded way of thinking, she had had enough. Refusing to let go of Tyler's hand, she broke her stare at her father, initiating a standoff.

"I think we're making a spectacle." Tyler's voice contained a hint of embarrassment.

"I don't care."

"Can we go somewhere more private? He's making me uncomfortable."

"Come with me." When Alex turned, she discovered Ethan had vanished. She couldn't blame him. Walking away from a wife of some years was one thing, but seeing her infatuated with someone else was another.

Alex fast-stepped toward the playhouse with Tyler in tow. Though the rush she first felt had faded following that jolt of reality, her determination hadn't. Holding hands for everyone to see never felt so right. With each step she took, she became more resolute. She'd never go back into the closet. When she reached the door, she gave Tyler's hand an extra squeeze.

* * *

Alex's touch made Tyler's heart pound like a teenager's. When she'd held a woman's hand before—in a moment of frivolity or due to family connection—she'd never given it a second thought. This was not frivolous, and Alex was not her cousin. This was an overture, as welcoming as a refreshing spring rain.

Alex pulled her inside something she called the playhouse and hit a switch on the wall, bringing the room's lighting to life. This must be a media or game room. Alex straightened the disheveled pillows on the sectional before sitting on one corner and inviting Tyler to do the same on the other. Sitting three feet apart was Tyler's compromise—close enough to smell the woody fragrance of Alex's perfume, yet far enough away to curtail spontaneity.

"Talk to me, Tyler. Ethan said he's walking away from your marriage. I'm so sorry if I did anything to cause this. I had no intention of interfering." The regret in Alex's voice was unmistakable. She clearly blamed herself.

Tyler resisted the urge to reach for Alex's hand. She'd held it but for a few minutes tonight, and already her skin longed for it to touch more of her. She needed to ease Alex's feelings of guilt, though, and that meant sharing a painful past only a few people knew of.

"You have nothing to be sorry for. This isn't your fault."

"That's what Ethan said, but I don't understand. Is there someone else?" Alex's averted eyes told Tyler she hoped it wasn't true.

"No, Alex, there's no one else. Since I met Ethan, I've never considered acting on an attraction. Before you came along, that is."

"Then it is because of me." Alex shot up from the sectional and paced in front of it. Tyler had only one word to describe her: cute. "This feels horrible. I swore to never wreck a marriage."

"And you still haven't. Will you please sit back down?" Tyler waited.

Alex paced the length of the sectional once more for good measure before reclaiming her seat. Definitely cute, especially the way her knee was jiggling up and down. Alex could recharge a cell phone with all that nervous energy. "Fine."

"Your self-loathing is chivalrous but unnecessary." When Alex opened her mouth to say something, Tyler raised an index finger to shush her. "I'm going to tell you about something that is still very painful, but I need you to listen until I'm done. Can you do that for me?"

"Of course. Anything for you." Alex stilled her knee.

"Thirteen years ago, a man I knew beat and raped me." Tyler paused when Alex knitted her brow in reassuring but quiet concern. "Ignoring the trauma was easier than dealing with it. Once the man accepted a plea, Ethan and I never spoke of him. Until last month when he showed up at my office. His appearance resurfaced the trauma I thought I'd buried. I was wrong. I was never the same after the attack. My marriage and the way I reacted to intimacy were never the same. Love was there, but nothing more. I had no desire. No passion. No attraction. Then I bumped into you, and all of that changed."

Alex reached out her hand, and Tyler took it. Warmth. Strength. Compassion. And, dare she imagine, love? It all radiated from Alex's touch. Tyler gave her hand a firm squeeze to send the same message and then let go.

"There was something about your touch that brought to life that part of me I thought was long dead. I couldn't get you out of my head, so I started seeing a therapist. She's been helping me work through my PTSD and see the truth about myself. I've always been attracted to women. And for the first time, I was honest with Ethan about everything. My trauma. My attractions. That I'll never be able to give him the love life he deserves. That a woman's single touch made me feel more alive than I had in years. And that I felt close to you."

Tyler had to stop. This was the first time she'd summarized everything she'd been through, and she needed time to process the account of her transformation. She exhaled the pain of her past and inhaled the hope of her future.

"Are you all right?" Alex asked, following a lengthy pause.

"I'm fine. It's still a lot for me to take in."

"Tyler." Alex took Tyler's hand back into hers. "I'm so sorry for what happened to you. No one should ever go through what you have. I'm so relieved you're getting the help you need to come to terms with your trauma, but…"

Alex trailed off. She seemed hesitant to voice her next thought, so Tyler guessed. "But you still think you're the reason for our separation. You're not. I asked him for a divorce because we both deserve better, not because I have feelings for you."

Alex dipped her chin. If Tyler had to guess, she was hiding a blush. "You have feelings for me?"

"Yes." A surge of boldness hit Tyler like a tidal wave. This was her chance to validate the energy she felt between them. "Don't you feel it, too?"

"Yes, I do." Alex raised her gaze to meet Tyler's. The desire swimming in her eyes was all the confirmation she needed.

Alex leaned closer at an agonizingly slow pace. Tyler tensed. All the self-examination and weeks of fantasizing soon would come to a head. What would it feel like to kiss a woman? This woman? Would it feel as soft and luscious as she expected? Would Alex's lips taste sweeter than breakfast in bed on a Sunday morning?

Kisses with Ethan had long lost their appeal. Habit had replaced passion, and obligation had replaced desire. Tyler's shallow respirations were proof that passion and desire had not wholly left her. She wanted this first kiss like she wanted colorful sunsets. She hoped it would last for hours.

At six inches, Alex's moist breath mixed with hers, a hint of champagne tickling her nose. At three inches, Tyler couldn't inhale. The energy flowing between them would've pegged every meter known to humanity.

This slow dance was more excruciating than her first first kiss. Worse than waiting for the final school bell before summer break began.

She froze. Having only been the recipient of a first kiss, she hadn't the courage to close the final inches. Doubt flitted into her head. When did she last brush her teeth? She should've popped a mint before she walked through the front door of the mansion.

Alex pulled back a foot. "Are you sure you want this?"

"More than anything." She cursed to herself. All that ground lost over the thought of a damned breath mint.

Alex's smile returned, one meant only for Tyler. The anticipation grew more substantial, the desire more palpable as the slow march forward resumed. Alex's focus on Tyler's lips awoke a dormant part of her with a throbbing roar.

Seconds later, the door flew open, and the moment was lost.

She and Alex turned toward the racket and sat straight. A man teetered in the doorway, the one who had stood by Alex's side during her big moment, the one who was a shorter-haired version of her.

"You're drunk, Andrew." Alex's words had an edge to them.

"Polishing off Father's twenty-five-year-old JP bourbon will do that."

Slurring his words, Andrew staggered toward the sectional. He plopped down, thigh to thigh with Tyler, and twisted his neck toward her. The ugly smell of whiskey hung from his breath. "You must be my sister's next conquest, though you're not her usual type. You're much more...pedestrian."

"That's enough, Andrew. You need to go back to that pencil-thin model you brought with you tonight."

Tyler's muscles tensed at the nauseating, memory-triggering odor emanating from him. If he was close enough to smell, he was close enough to be a threat. Her breathing grew labored, and her heart started thumping harder than it had before with Alex. If she didn't get things under control, she'd have another panic attack like the one she had had when Stevens came to the house. Tyler closed her eyes, trying to meditate as Gail had taught her, but the rolling stench of whiskey made it impossible.

"Are you all right, Tyler? You're pale and trembling." Alex's voice was a shelter in a storm, but one that Tyler couldn't reach. "You scared her, you asshole."

"Just ribbing her a little. Is she that fragile?"

"You have no idea what she's been through." Alex's voice raised to a roar like that of a mama bear protecting her cub. Tyler flinched at the touch on her hand, but the gentle rub that followed was the life preserver she needed. Her heart and breathing slowed to the rhythm of Alex's hand stroking back and forth on hers.

"If that double-crossing Kelly Thatcher hadn't left town already, I'd suggest you go back to tapping her." Andrew sneered. "I hear she's *very* photogenic." He gave Alex a smug look.

Tyler's eyes shot open when Alex ripped her hand away. The fire in her eyes could've burned down the city.

"What do you know about that?" Alex's words were sharp enough to pierce metal.

"I know if I had those pictures, it would be the end of you."

"Then it's a good thing those pictures are in safe hands. Victor Padula, however, will be the end of *you*."

"What do you know about him?" Andrew's slur cleared a fraction.

"I know you're still into him for two million dollars and that you've been skimming from the company coffers to pay up. That, my dear brother, stops now. I'm cutting you off. You'll no longer have signature power for as much as a square of toilet paper."

"What do you want?"

"For you to tell Father you're declining the CFO position first thing tomorrow morning."

"And when he asks why?" Andrew asked.

"That's your problem. Tell him whatever eases your conscience."

"Are you telling Father? The police?"

"You're my brother, Andrew. I love you. That's why I've agreed to pay off your mark. This is between us at this point, but don't push me."

"You're paying Victor two million dollars?"

"No. This is where you and I are different. I'm a smart businesswoman who knows how to negotiate a deal. Victor accepted my offer of half a million and agreed to put you off-limits to every bookie in town in order to avoid a federal investigation."

"Fine, Alex, you win as usual. You can have the damn company."

Andrew lurched up and out, taking his whiskey breath and bad vibes with him. Tyler's anxiety had subsided, but Alex's anger had not.

Alex rubbed her temples with both hands. "I can't believe I had it out with my brother in front of you."

Tyler wasn't sure how to react. Juicy tidbits about gambling, stealing, and compromising photos aside, she had two critical questions: Who the hell was this Kelly Thatcher, and why did she feel jealous of her?

"It's really none of my business," Tyler said.

"After the way he treated you, it became *your* business. I love my brother, but you needed to see what kind of man he is, and he needed to be embarrassed in front of you." Alex's temper disappeared. She reached for Tyler's hand, her expression softening. "But enough about my scheming brother. Are you all right? Did he frighten you?"

If Tyler were with Ethan, she'd brush off the incident as nothing, return to the main house, and fix them a plate from the buffet table. But Alex wasn't Ethan. She wanted to share the good parts and the bad with her and wanted Alex to do the same. Always.

"He did." Tyler accepted Alex's reassuring hand. "The smell of whiskey triggered me."

"Why that?"

"My rapist was drunk on it. I remember that smell like it was yesterday."

Before Tyler had started her work with Gail, she wouldn't have said the word rapist. She would've tucked away the memory and busied herself twenty hours a day with work and family, ignoring the pain. But those days were behind her. Her heart condition meant she needed a low-stress lifestyle. In turn, that meant facing the bad head-on with the support of family and friends.

"I'm so sorry that he scared you. I never want you to feel afraid when you're with me."

Tyler squeezed Alex's hand to stress her next words. "Your touch pulled me back. It made me less afraid. There's so much more I want to tell you, but I need to rest first."

"When can I see you again?"

"We have a meeting scheduled for three o'clock tomorrow at your office."

"A business meeting? That won't do." Alex scrunched her nose, forming the cutest grin. "Consider it canceled. I want to buy you dinner. How about the hotel restaurant at seven tomorrow night?"

"It's a date." Tyler hadn't been on a date since she was twenty-two. She should be nervous or at least anxious, but strangely the idea calmed her. A date with Alex Castle was simply meant to be.

CHAPTER TWENTY-SIX

A summons was Alex's best descriptor for the no-notice meeting William's secretary had scheduled on her behalf. Gretchen didn't offer the meeting's topic when she informed her of it, and experience had taught her not to press. Under no circumstance, not even with the offer of her favorite danish, would that loyal woman betray her boss's confidence. Gretchen was more secure than Fort Knox.

Alex suspected the meeting would center on one of two topics. Her father would either chastise her for her public display last night, as he'd classify it, or he'd bemoan Andrew's declination of the CFO position. If he were in a particularly sour mood, he'd do both.

Stepping down the hallway, Alex approached William's grand office suite. She was done with compromise. Done with putting her love for him first. Because the consequences of doing so weren't as significant as they once were. She knew the truth about the root of his hatred and how he'd taken it out on her. She'd spent the night tossing and turning and had come to a satisfying conclusion: she had found a future she wanted more than the throne of Castle Resorts. She wouldn't let her father keep her from living a life with someone she loved, and that person was Tyler Falling.

Alex pushed open the double glass doors to the faint scent of fresh lavender—her mother's favorite. Over the years, William had erased many of her mother's touches, both here and at his home. All but the lavender. The sweet, floral scent with herbal undertones had remained a constant, giving Alex the sense that her mother was continuing to look over her. Today that sense of support gave her the strength and courage to do what she should've done years earlier.

William's secretary, coifed in shortly cropped blond hair with hints of gray and garbed in fashionable attire, was sitting at her desk. If not for the gentle crow's feet and barely-there creases along her neck, no one would've guessed Gretchen was a grandmother of five. Her stately posture and piercing dark blue eyes made her a formidable sentinel.

"Good morning, Gretchen. Is he ready for me?" Alex spoke with growing self-assurance. Her malleability to her father's wishes had never been driven by fear, and she wasn't about to let it start doing so now.

Gretchen lifted her stare from her computer screen. This woman had been Alex's greatest ally in this fortress for a decade, warning her of power plays among the upper echelon. She had never, though, betrayed her father's confidence with as much as a warning frown or a wink—until now. Her silence spoke volumes, as did her sympathy-filled eyes.

"It will be all right, Gretchen. One question." A barely perceptible nod signaled her ally's continued support. "Has my brother been in to see my father this morning?" Gretchen shook her head. So, this was how it would be—a power play between twins. The next few minutes with her father would tell her everything she needed to know about Andrew and dictate her next moves.

Gretchen pressed the intercom button on her desk phone. "Mr. Castle, Ms. Castle is here, as you requested." After a voice through the line said to send her in, Gretchen's posture sagged. "Good luck, Ms. Castle. I'll be here if you need anything."

Alex had no doubt those few, carefully selected words were Gretchen's hidden pledge of loyalty. It was an act that wouldn't go unrewarded once the reins of command changed hands. Alex stepped forward and gave her a grateful pat on the shoulder. "Thank you, Gretchen."

Alex squared her shoulders. No matter what happened in the next few minutes, she controlled her destiny. As she walked through the office's custom-milled doors, she realized that idolizing this office had been a waste of her youth. So many pointless years, working to occupy her father's oversized, intricately carved mahogany desk. She wanted that now only if she acquired it on her terms, not William's.

Her father's stiff posture behind that desk telegraphed this would not be a pleasant visit. Not a hair was out of place. Not a single wrinkle besmirched his blazer. He was the very image of power and money. "Take a seat." Neither his tone nor his eyes showed an ounce of affection.

"I'd rather stand." Standing up to her father required standing. She wouldn't let him make her feel small.

"All right." He raised his chin before adjusting his silk tie. Her defiance had clearly gotten to him. "Have you forgotten our agreement?"

"I have not."

"Then explain last night."

Alex inhaled the sweet, herbal scent of the fresh flowers atop a nearby table, as well as a dose of her mother's courage. She planted her feet in front of her father's desk. "Forgetting and disregarding are two distinct things."

"I see. And you think last night's public announcement nullifies our agreement."

"I do not."

His lips formed a rigid line. Once before, a child of his had exhibited such defiance and had moved to Napa to lead a happy, fulfilling life. Apparently, the possibility of a second doing so didn't sit well either. "Then why did you choose to embarrass me in front of my guests."

"I did not choose to embarrass you, Father. This is 2007. Only close-minded people would let the sight of two women holding hands embarrass them. I have no regrets for showing her the affection I feel for her, and I will not apologize for it."

"Even if it costs you the position you've always wanted?"

There it was, his ultimatum, one she wasn't willing to accept.

"Yes, Father." Alex straightened. She'd never been so sure of herself and of her next words. "I love you, but legacy or not, illness or not, I will no longer deny myself my full measure. I am proud to be a Castle. You have raised me to be strong and independent and to be worthy of the name. Except for my sexual orientation, I have measured up in every respect. I bowed to you on this one issue out of deference to your Parkinson's, but I can no longer keep my promise. I have found something I want more than to walk in your footsteps, and I owe it to myself to pursue it."

"A dalliance is no reason to throw away your future." His eyes narrowed.

"What I have found is not frivolous. I'm not sure where it will go or even if she'll have me, but I need to find out, and I refuse to do it behind closed doors as if having a courtship with her is a shameful thing. It is not. If you can't accept that, do what you must."

"So you intend to embarrass me more."

"I intend to follow my heart. If it embarrasses you, that is on you. I challenge you to find another person in that room last night who was offended by my holding hands with a woman. I know everyone who was there. You'll find none of them cares who I sleep with as long as it's not their wife."

William jerked his head back. The intended sharpness of her response had hit its mark. "Your crassness is unbecoming."

"Bigotry and homophobia are the most unbecoming things about you. I wish you could see that."

"Your mother would be disappointed in what you've become."

"You're wrong. Mother would've been proud of the woman I've become, not the one I settled on for the last thirteen years."

Alex inhaled another dose of her mother's strength. "I only wish she'd had the time to do the same before she died."

"What does that mean?"

"I know the truth, Father. Abby told me about her and Mother and what they meant to each other."

"Humph." William rose from his chair, trying to erect a commanding defense against Alex's revelation. It was no use—she knew his deepest secret. He straightened his jacket and stepped to the wall of windows overlooking Central Park. It offered a beautiful view, one she would have enjoyed seeing daily, but not at the price he demanded. "At this point, your brother might make a more suitable successor."

What was it with the Castle men? Both entitled. Both shiny on the outside and ugly on the inside. One out of bigotry, the other out of greed. She'd had enough of them.

"You might want to conduct a full audit of Times Square before you make any changes."

He wheeled in her direction. Only a threat to his true love—Castle Resorts—could overshadow his homophobia. "What do you mean?"

"You may not like what you find. Fire me. Don't fire me. Appoint someone else in my stead. But do not give Andrew the keys to the kingdom without due diligence. Have Gretchen pass along your decision."

And with that, Alex walked out. The weight she'd carried for years was now gone, a burden she should've never let her father place upon her. She breathed in the scent of lavender again, reminding herself that her mother would've been proud of her today.

Gretchen's eyes begged for an inkling into what transpired behind that door, but Alex wasn't about to place her in the awkward position of having to choose loyalties. She patted her on the shoulder and offered a reassuring smile. "It will be all right, Gretchen. No matter what happens now, I'll be happy."

* * *

Andrew's word of the day was "regret." He regretted the gambling addiction that had led to him draining his trust fund and mortgaging his loft to the hilt. He regretted his need to please a father who didn't know the meaning of unconditional love. He regretted his jealousy of a sister who had rightly earned her accolades, leading to him taking shortcuts to get their father's attention. At the moment, though, his biggest regret was the drumline stomping in his head, brought on by polishing off William's treasured top-shelf stock last night.

Despite a bathtub full of regrets and the worst hangover of his life, Andrew had no intention of caving into Alex's demands, not while he still had a chance of avoiding two broken legs. No matter what agreement Alex had made, Victor would want his pound of flesh if he didn't get all the money promised. Fear of that had Andrew skipping work today, staring at the neon sign of Arthur's Alley, and reviewing his plan to retrieve those pictures Alex had said were in good hands.

The early evening crowd inside was small yet. In a worst-case scenario, that could be in Andrew's favor. There wouldn't be a room full of roaring sports fans to drown out the sound of his bones cracking and his screams of agony.

The man he feared the most after Victor Padula was standing guard outside the private lounge. With biceps as big as anvils, he clearly could snap a leg like a toothpick. Oddly, it was his help that Andrew was going to need to get out of this mess. Andrew tucked away his jitters and approached Bone Breaker with a bold flair. "I'm here to see Victor."

"You're not a very smart man."

"Tell Victor if he wants to see the other mil and a half, he'll want to see me." Andrew used language he hoped even a vacant-between-the-ears brute could understand. His sole chance of avoiding a lengthy hospital stay was to show Victor he was a man of his word. Andrew needed to present him with the opportunity to get the rest of his money. He was counting on Victor's greed to turn the tide.

The guard disappeared into the bowels of the lounge, returning a minute later looking as if he'd suckered another gullible soul into buying a chunk of the Brooklyn Bridge.

Andrew got the distinct impression the guard hoped Victor would give him the green light to teach Andrew a badly needed lesson. He jutted his chin toward the private room. Andrew strode by, confident on the outside, Jell-O on the inside.

Sitting at his usual booth, Victor seemed particularly intimidating today. Nothing about his appearance had changed, but Andrew's outlook had. He was as nervous as a caged dog.

When Victor's eyes met his, Andrew stiffened his posture. "I have an offer."

"You've become more trouble than you're worth. I'm not naturally a violent man, but Rocko there is." Victor nodded toward the entrance and the muscle-bound guard. "Give him one reason to not break your legs right here."

"I have a way to get the rest of the money."

"Word has it that your deep pockets have dried up."

"The only thing between me and those deep pockets is my sister. Has she delivered your negotiated price?"

"Yes. It and a repeat of her threat of triggering a federal investigation if I renege on the deal."

"I know how to neutralize her."

Andrew's jaw tightened at the memory of his call yesterday with that double-crossing bitch, Kelly Thatcher. "*It was your offer or my freedom,*" she had said. "*So I gave the pictures to her large guard dog.*"

"That could solve both of our problems," Victor said.

"There are some pictures she doesn't want to go public. If they do, our father won't appoint her as CEO. I borrowed the money to buy those pictures, but a private investigator got his hands on them before I could. A guy named Ethan Falling. We get those back from him, and we're back in business."

"So? What's stopping you?"

"The guy who has them is big. If he doesn't want to hand them over, someone bigger will have to supply the motivation."

Victor sneered. "That's definitely not you."

"I need to borrow Rocko for an hour. If he gets the pictures, I get access to the company coffers, and you get your money in full."

"And if you don't?"

"I still have a job. I can go on a payment plan and pay you the rest over three years. It's a win-win. You'll either get your money in a few months or a few years."

"All right, Andy, but if this goes sideways, don't expect another bailout."

"Thank you, Victor. You won't regret this."

"For your sake, that better be true." Victor snapped his fingers, and Rocko approached, his hands clasped together at the waist, accentuating his brawny shoulders. "Go with him. He has a job for you."

Rocko narrowed his eyes at Andrew. Clearly, he wasn't happy being Andrew's errand boy. It didn't matter, Andrew decided, because whoever this Ethan Falling guy was, he'd be no match for Rocko. If this P.I. was half as smart as Kelly had made him sound, he'd hand over the photos without so much as a whimper. Thanks to Andrew's access to the registration records at the Times Square hotel, he knew exactly where to find him. Everything was set.

CHAPTER TWENTY-SEVEN

As Tyler slipped into the V-neck, navy blue sheath she'd bought at a boutique a few blocks from the hotel that morning, she agonized over whether she and Alex would finally kiss tonight. Her last first kiss had happened on the second date with Ethan when she was a freshman in college.

She'd thought after she said "I do" that first kisses were a thing of the past. After all, when her mother was on her death bed years after her husband's death, she had said that she still felt married.

Marriage was forever. Or so Tyler had thought. She hadn't counted on experiencing a trauma so deep that it would turn her vows into a prison. It wasn't her fault, but being unable to follow her parents' example made her feel like a failure.

A knock on the bathroom door pulled Tyler to the present. "Come in."

"You look beautiful." Ethan would probably appear to be being playful to anyone else in the world, but Tyler recognized the sadness in the eyes reflected in the bathroom mirror. She felt it too—a meaningful, twenty-two-year journey was coming to an unanticipated end. She turned around.

"Long goodbyes are hard, aren't they?" she said.

"Yes, they are, but this is what we both need."

"I feel like such a failure." Tyler flung her hands onto the shoulders of the man she didn't deserve.

He wrapped his arms around her. When she let a tear drop to Ethan's shirt, he pulled back enough to look her in the eyes. "Don't think for one minute that you've failed. If anyone is to blame, it's that bastard. There's no checklist on how to deal with what you've been through. Though we won't be under the same roof, we'll still be a family."

"That's exactly what I needed to hear."

"I wish I could kiss you right now." His eyes spoke to a time when kisses at moments like this had been as natural as breathing. But that time had passed.

"I wish I could too, but that would make it harder," she said with a heavy heart.

"I know." He brushed back whatever emotion had him blocked and turned playful again. "You should add that single pearl necklace the girls got you for Mother's Day. It would go perfectly with that dress."

"You're right." Tyler dug the necklace out of her small jewelry pouch but struggled to put it on.

"Let me." In a surreal moment, Ethan stepped behind her and carefully secured the clasp. Her husband of eighteen years, lover for about half that time, put the finishing touches on her outfit for her first date with a woman who had infatuated her for weeks.

Surreal or not, this was the moment Tyler truly let go. The joy in Ethan's eyes said he had too.

"Thank you. It looks perfect." She patted the pearl pendant against her chest and cleared the emotion from her throat. "Are you sure you're comfortable with this?"

"Go before I change my mind. I'll be fine. The hotel comped room service dinner and drinks at the bar tonight."

For the first time in their marriage, Tyler left without kissing Ethan. Her obligation there had ended. She walked out the door and toward a new life.

During her long elevator ride down to the restaurant, Tyler's anxiousness turned into jitters. She had forgotten how thrilling a first date could be. This wasn't a date night with Ethan when they'd go to their favorite little restaurant and order the same dishes they had the last time they were there and the time before that. Or when they'd go to the movie theater at the local mall, get tickets for whatever blockbuster movie was out at the moment, and select seats about two-thirds of the way up as close to the center of the row as possible—the optimum viewing location according to Ethan.

Tonight was all about the unknown. Would she be over- or underdressed for tonight? Would Alex like the dress she picked out? They had talked little about their favorite foods. What if Alex wasn't a meat eater? Tyler would have a hard time giving up her steak. Would she order wine or a cocktail? If Alex were a whiskey drinker, would that be a nonstarter? What would they talk about? Tyler had no idea what Alex's version of casual dinner conversation was. And when the talking was over, what would Alex's lips taste like if they picked up where they left off last night?

She stepped up to the host station at the hotel restaurant's entrance. The tourist guide in her suite had given it five stars and made it sound like a dream with its fine American cuisine and modern ambiance. At first blush, Margo's lived up to the hype. Bright accents, abundant pendant lighting, contrasting woods, and abstract artwork combined for exceptional ambiance. The groomsman-gray tuxedos on the staff completed the modern feel.

"Good evening, ma'am. Welcome to Margo's. May I help you?" The host's three-day black beard, chiseled features, and tanned complexion would've made for delicious eye candy in Tyler's younger days, but her attractions had permanently shifted. Out of the corner of her eye, she spotted Alex seated at a table near the fireplace. Dark cherry red was definitely her color. The straight-line collar that exposed a clavicle on one side was sexy as hell. Long, dark waves cut to hit at the shoulder made her look like a movie star.

"I'm so out of my league," Tyler mumbled. Andrew had said it last night. She wasn't his sister's type, utterly pedestrian compared to her typical conquest. Tyler imagined the women Alex must have been with before—blonde, brunette, redhead. They all had one thing in common: a beauty far surpassing her own.

"Miss?" The tuxedo-clad male model snapped her out of her misery. *Well, almost.*

"I'm sorry." Tyler shook off her cobwebs. "Castle. Party of two."

"Yes, the rest of your party is here." He stepped from behind the podium and gestured toward the dining room. "Follow me, please."

"I see her, thank you. I can find my way."

As Tyler glided past tables, she kept her gaze on Alex. Eyes fixed on the flames dancing in the nearby tiled fireplace, she lifted her wine glass to her lips and let it hover there for two, three, and then four beats before sipping. One word came to mind: elegant.

"Yow!" A sharp pain shot through Tyler's big toe, bringing her to an abrupt stop. She'd jammed her foot into the leg of a guest chair, brushing against a seated elderly man in a white suit. "I'm so sorry, sir."

"No harm, miss," he said in a kind tone before returning his attention to his table partner.

She resumed her course, limping to a throbbing beat. When she looked in Alex's direction again, her stomach flip-flopped. Alex had her gaze trained on her and her lips were failing to fight back a grin. A sudden rush of heat made Tyler's neck impossibly hot. Not since a home perm gone wrong at the age of twelve had she been this embarrassed. *Way to impress somebody*, Tyler thought. Somehow, she'd become a slapstick act.

Alex waved her over, mouthing, "Over here."

Tyler decided she wouldn't let a misstep prevent her from taking a mammoth leap of faith. She shook off the diminishing pain, took the remaining steps to Alex's table, and forced a smile that instantly became voluntary. "Hi."

Alex stood and pulled out a chair for Tyler. "You sure know how to make an entrance."

"It's a gift." Tyler sat, hoping humor would rule the moment.

"One of many." Alex returned to her seat, exposing as she did the silver zipper running the length of her dress. Every inch of the fabric hugged a curve, a sight that sent Tyler in search of more air. Alex placed a hand atop Tyler's, putting her more at ease. "You look beautiful tonight."

Her words vanquished most of Tyler's jitters and assured her that nothing had changed since last night. Alex appeared as enamored as she had been when they said goodbye at the playhouse. "You're stunning."

"Thank you." Alex averted her eyes and blushed. Surely she'd been told that a thousand times. Tyler took Alex's bashfulness with her as an excellent sign.

"I took the liberty of ordering a bottle of my sister's cabernet. If you'd prefer—"

"I love Barnette wine. If it's anything like the one Syd served at her home last month, it'll be perfect because I'm a little nervous about tonight."

"Well, that makes two of us," Alex said.

"You? What do you have to be nervous about?"

"You're very important to me, Tyler. I don't want to screw this up."

"You mean a lot to me, too, but I'm not sure if I'm ready for—"

"Before you finish that thought, I assure you, whatever this is, we'll take it at your pace." Alex squeezed Tyler's hand. The soft yet firm gesture reassured Tyler that she was in control. "Are you hungry?" Alex asked.

"I'm starved. I was too nervous to eat lunch."

"Let's get you fed. We have a wonderful menu here. Or if you'd prefer, I can have the chef prepare just about anything you'd like."

"Thank you, but the menu will be fine." Tyler picked up the rectangular menu from the table, its hardback cover thicker than most she'd encountered. The smooth gold cursive print matched the stylishness of the restaurant and that of her table partner. "What do you recommend?"

"I'm partial to the filet and asparagus."

Two of her favorite dishes.   Tyler closed the menu, encouraged by the promising start. "That sounds perfect."

Midway through dinner and more wine, the conversation drifted to family. "Has Erin applied for college yet?" Alex asked. "From what you told me, with her GPA and SAT scores, she'd be an asset to any university."

"Oh, yes, and it scares the heck out of me."

"How's that?"

"She got accepted to Berkley, Stanford, and her dream school, Yale."

"That's wonderful. I'm a Yale alum."

"Not wonderful. We'll have to take out a second mortgage if Erin accepts Yale's offer."

Alex patted Tyler's hand. "You're an exceptional mother. I'm sure you'll make it work."

"Enough about my family. What about yours?" Tyler asked.

"You met my half sister, Syd," Alex said.

"Half?"

"Father divorced her mother before marrying mine two years later. Syd became my role model after she stood up to our father to marry John and head off to make wine in Napa. No one had ever defied him like that."

"I get the impression you and your father have a tense relationship."

"That's one way of putting it. He loves his company and his children, in that order, and has a very dated way of thinking. He's homophobic, for one thing."

"Ouch."

"We had an agreement until today—he'd ignore my sexuality as long as I kept it out of the public eye."

"What changed today?"

"You."

"Me?" Tyler pointed to herself.

"Yes, you. I told him I'd found something I wanted more than to follow in his footsteps." Alex took Tyler's hand into hers, but this time, she didn't let it go. "I won't deny who I am any longer."

The idea that Alex would give up everything she'd worked for all her life left Tyler speechless. Only this week, Tyler had walked away from a marriage because she couldn't give Ethan the romantic life he deserved. She hadn't a clue if she could give that to Alex.

Tyler's heart speeded up. What if she had the same reaction to intimacy with Alex as she did with Ethan? Alex would've given up her legacy for nothing. She felt lightheaded, a sure sign she was on the verge of another episode.

Tossing her cloth napkin on the table, Tyler rose from her chair. "If you'll excuse me, I have to use the restroom." Without waiting for a response, she wound her way to the back of the dining room. Once inside the ladies' room, she decided lying on the nicely polished tiled floor was out of the question. Ruining her makeup was the only other option. She splashed water on her face, hoping to slow her heart rate and avoid an embarrassing scene on their first date.

Several splashes in, Alex appeared behind her in the mirror, standing in quiet concern. Tyler grabbed a paper towel to dab away the smears and runs. "Waterproof makeup is a must until I figure out this dating thing."

Alex's shoulders slumped. "I've made a mess of things, haven't I?"

"It's just… I mean… It's not every day someone gives up billions to go on a date with me. That's a lot of pressure."

"My share is only millions."

"Only millions. Well, that's different. I feel much better." Tyler gave a wry smile. A billion. A million. It made no difference.

What Alex was walking away from wasn't merely money. She was walking away from a way of life.

Alex leaned a hip against the counter to look Tyler in the eye but kept her distance. "We're a lot alike, you know."

"How do you figure?" Tyler returned her stare to the mirror and dabbed at her face with a paper towel she'd plucked from a mesh tray atop the counter. Alex was even more beautiful with worry lines etched between her piercing eyes. "You're younger, seven years according to your bio. Not to mention rich, polished, and worldly. And you're so damn gorgeous. I'm none of those things."

Alex gently nabbed the paper towel Tyler had been holding before she could finish wiping away evidence of her insecurities. She tossed it in the nearby trash bin and turned Tyler by the elbows to face her.

"Get this straight, Tyler Falling. Unless you're under eighteen, age means nothing to me. I won't lie and say money doesn't either. Having things is nice, but it's not as important to me as you might think. I've always lived within my means, not within my trust fund's. Worldly is an illusion. I much prefer the solitude of my garden than traveling to oversee these damn hotels. As far as polish and beauty, you've never seen me when I first wake up in the morning. I'm a wretched sight."

"I can't believe that."

"Believe it." Alex activated the sink faucet and scrubbed her face with one handful of water after another. After drying her face with a fresh paper towel, a natural beauty emerged—one of vulnerability. Her skin was smooth but uneven, with red spots on her nose and cheeks. Minus the mascara and shadowing, her eyes had lost their sexy allure but gained a friendly warmth. She ran both hands through her perfectly styled hair, creating a windblown appearance. "I'd take this dress off too, but I don't want to risk being arrested for indecent exposure."

"You're still beautiful." Tyler couldn't hide the grin that was insisting on making an appearance.

Alex glanced at herself in the mirror. "You're too generous." She turned until she faced Tyler. "Now that you've seen the real me, can't you see we're very similar? We're two women, ready for change. Ready to face who we are and live life on our own terms, without fear.

"Now, don't take this the wrong way. I'm risking everything I've spent a lifetime working toward because you gave me the final push, but I'm not doing it for you. I'm doing it for me. Breaking free of my father was long overdue. You came along at a time when I faced losing it all, and the more I got to know you, the more I realized that living my life to please my father was no way to live. I no longer wanted what he had to give if it meant denying myself the opportunity to find love."

Tyler inched closer until the heat from Alex's body warmed her like the sun's rays. Alex's jasmine scent had her wanting more. "That was the nicest thing anyone has ever said to me and the hottest thing anyone has ever done for me."

"I stand ready to expand your horizon." Alex leaned teasingly close until her warm breath mixed with Tyler's. Another inch forward and their lips would touch, but then the anticipation would be over. The thought of taking this moment to its natural conclusion had Tyler taking rapid, shallow breaths.

Alex pulled back. "As much as I want to kiss you, I won't have our first kiss in a bathroom."

"I'm aching for this." It took every ounce of strength to not seize the moment and learn if her fantasies were only wild supposition or if she was meant to be with a woman, this woman.

Alex stepped back. A sly grin signaled she had something in mind. She grabbed Tyler by the hand. "Come with me."

* * *

Taking full advantage of Alex Castle's generosity and show of goodwill wasn't in the cards for Ethan tonight. He was on the road to accepting his changed circumstances, but the knot in his stomach over losing an eighteen-year marriage made eating impossible. Drinking, however, was a viable, if not critical, option.

When he went to the hotel bar, he quickly discovered that even though there was a lobby buffering it from the restaurant where his wife was discovering her true self, it wasn't putting nearly enough distance between him and the hard truth—he was still in love with Tyler. Even though he could now, he supposed, he couldn't bring himself to order what was once his go-to drink. He'd given up whiskey when Tyler mumbled in the emergency room after the rape that the one thing she remembered was the smell of it on that animal's breath.

Ethan caught the attention of the bartender and signaled for a third shot of tequila. He was pushing his personal drink limit for one reason: he wasn't emotionally prepared to deal with it if Tyler made tonight's date a sleepover. This drink would be his last. Any more after this one and he wouldn't be able to walk back to his room in a straight line.

While waiting for his drink, Ethan unwisely let his mind drift. He'd done his professional best and didn't look too long at the blackmail photos, but damn his training. As a cop, he was groomed to recall details. To pick one eye-catching, minute point from which to build a lasting and more complete memory. Even two drinks in, his memory still was working fine. It was all too easy to picture Alex and Tyler in similar poses.

He couldn't decide if his lack of anger made him the best husband in the world or the most pathetic. That assessment was probably best made sober. Looking for a distraction, he focused on the television screen behind the bartender. Thousands of protestors had marched to the Pentagon in Washington, DC, to mark the fourth anniversary of the start of the war in Iraq. Another decades-long quagmire, he predicted.

When his third and final drink was delivered, Ethan downed it in one swig. Its burn didn't compare to the sting of his new reality. After returning to Sacramento tomorrow night, he and Tyler would get the ball rolling on their divorce. He'd have to start looking in earnest for a place to live. Other than his clothes, toiletries, and golf clubs, he didn't think he could live with daily reminders of the life they'd built together. That meant living like a minimalist until he could afford proper furniture.

Numbed and better able to accept whatever was going on across the lobby, Ethan threw sixty dollars down atop the bar and made his way to the bank of elevators and up to his floor. Tyler was probably just halfway through her date. That meant he had time for the last of the tequila to do its job and help him fade off like his marriage.

Surprisingly, his key card worked on the first swipe. As he entered the main suite, the hairs on the back of his neck tingled. Something wasn't right. The drawer in the desk next to the windows overlooking Times Square was askew. He distinctly remembered it being closed when he left. He turned toward the door leading to Tyler's bedroom; it was slightly ajar just as she had left it. He turned to the door leading to his bedroom and bathroom. Its door was ajar too, and a light was on within. He and Tyler always shut the lights off when they left a room. His defensive instincts kicking in, he reached for his waistband and his nonexistent service weapon. *Damn it!* He'd locked it in the room safe in the bedroom before he went drinking. Why did he always have to be such a rule follower?

He slid toward the lit doorway, positioning himself against the frame. A quick peek inside revealed nothing unexpected. Perhaps he was being paranoid. Or maybe Tyler had returned to retrieve something? His heart sank at the thought of her hastily collecting overnight necessities and then scurrying off to the owner's suite. *Stop it*, he chastised himself. Tyler needed the freedom to explore her sexuality. To finally be happy.

He shook off his suspicions and stepped into the bedroom. On his second stride, something hard and cold pressed against the back of his neck. Though he'd never been in this situation on the job, he'd been through enough self-defense training to recognize what the muzzle of a gun felt like. Based on the angle of the pressure, he guessed the assailant was taller than him by a good half-foot. He remained calm, aided perhaps by the tequila he'd consumed earlier.

"Don't move," a deep voice from behind him ordered. "I want those pictures."

"What pictures?"

"You know what I'm talking about. The ones with the two skanks."

Ethan assessed his situation. This thug wanted Kelly's blackmail photos. For whom and why were answers he'd have to find out later. The room was generously sized, but its extra-large furniture also made for narrow passageways. The most prominent hard surfaces to throw this guy against were the armoire or the walls.

"I don't have them." *Thank God.*

The man clubbed him on the back of the skull. Sharp pain was followed by the sense that the room was spinning, whirling too much to attribute it solely to the tequila. The thug pushed Ethan onto the bed face first. Continuous blows to his kidneys with what he assumed was the gun sent his pain level skyrocketing. He needed to get the upper hand, but given his alcohol buzz and head injury, that would require having a weapon. "Wait, wait, wait," he spat out in agony.

The blows paused. "Pictures."

"In the safe." Ethan's best hope of getting out of this alive was to get to his service weapon. Once he opened the safe, he'd need a distraction to level it on this asshole.

The man lifted him to a sitting position, giving Ethan a first good look at him. Holy crap, he was huge. Ethan's vision was blurred, but he recognized the gorilla as Victor's main goon. Whatever Victor wanted with Kelly's blackmail photos, Ethan was sure Andrew was behind it.

"Get them." The bruiser waved the gun toward Ethan, leaving no room to negotiate.

"Okay, give me a second. You cracked my head, idiot." Ethan placed a hand on the wound. It was wet. He didn't have to look at his palm to know blood had covered it. He focused on concocting an escape plan. Overpowering a man of this size was out of the question. Surprise and close combat training would be Ethan's only advantages.

"Move," King Kong insisted, waving the gun this time as if he were deciding whether to shoot Ethan in the face or chest.

Ethan rose from the bed, exaggerating his disorientation. The closet door leading to the shelf-mounted safe was already open, as were the dresser drawers. This gorilla had been in his room for a while. At least Tyler was safe with Alex.

He entered the custom code on the safe panel. Once he opened it, he'd only have seconds to effect a distraction. When the panel beeped, he positioned himself between the thug and the safe, blocking it from view. He cranked the handle, pulled the door open, and slid his fingers around the butt of his Beretta.

In one synchronized move, he pulled his gun out and stomped on his attacker's foot, hoping he'd broken at least one of its twenty-six bones. The man pulled back, yelping in pain. That was Ethan's cue. He wheeled around. He fired twice. The goon dropped, but not before he got off a shot of his own.

Pain. Searing heat.

Ethan hit the floor next to the other guy. The room went black.

* * *

Despite the pristine condition of Margo's restrooms, Alex couldn't allow their first kiss and Tyler's first lesbian kiss to be cliché. She had no time for candles, but she had the perfect location for soft lights and romantic music. Guiding Tyler up the lobby's grand staircase to the mezzanine level, she zigzagged them through the last vestiges of the construction materials being used for the remodeling project on this floor.

"Where are you taking us?" Tyler asked, doing an impressive job of keeping up while wearing three-inch heels.

"You'll see." Alex offered her a suggestive wink. At the end of the hallway, she stopped and released Tyler's hand. "Wait here." She slipped through a set of double doors.

The grand ballroom renovations had turned out better than expected. Gold and silver accents completed the sleek metropolitan look that would make this room the number one sought-after venue for New Year's Eve and other special events. She quickly accessed the utility room and set the room's lighting to event mode before cueing music on the state-of-the-art sound system. This was a setting worthy of a first kiss.

Retracing her steps, she opened the main door and extended a hand to Tyler. "Dance with me."

Tyler took her hand and stepped inside the dimly lit ballroom. Slow music and accent lighting along each wall combined to produce a romantic glow. She gasped. "Oh, my."

It was the reaction Alex wanted. She guided them to the center of the room and raised her left hand to lead. Alex had danced with a handful of women, but none had her heart racing like it was now. In the past, dancing had been a prelude to sex, filled with erotic teasing. This was different. This was the prelude to a tender, loving first kiss. She had to do it right.

Tyler's soft hand tentatively slid into hers. Sensing a building desire tempered by trepidation, Alex waited for a sign to move forward. Her patience paid off. Tyler raised her arm and placed her left hand on Alex's right shoulder. Slowly, gently, Alex slid her arm around Tyler's shoulder blade and pulled their bodies close but not touching. Tyler would have to take the last steps on her terms.

Alex glided them into a simple two-step to the slow beat of Van Morrison's "Someone Like You." The words rang true. Her soul searching had led her here, hoping to find someone who could make all her choices worthwhile. Hoping for someone like Tyler to come into her life.

During the second verse, Tyler dropped Alex's hand and wrapped her arms around her neck, pulling their bodies together. The lavender scent of Tyler's perfume confirmed the rightness of the moment. Alex's search was over. With Tyler in her arms, she was at home. She paused her slow sway, hoping to glimpse in Tyler's eyes the emotion she was feeling. She found it. If Tyler had doubts, Alex couldn't tell. From her breathing to her posture to the longing in her eyes, everything said she was ready.

Tyler craned her head to enable a first light brushing of their lips. Stomach flutters. Chest tingling. As Tyler had earlier said, Alex was aching for this. Never had the lead-up to a first kiss been packed with such dizzying anticipation.

Then it happened. Tyler pressed their mouths together in a soft, luscious kiss. Unlike Alex's previous female partners,

Tyler didn't load the kiss with rabid hunger, drunken delight, or, in Kelly's case, a deceit-filled agenda. This kiss was languid and gentle, designed to slowly turn up the heat on a simmering passion. Alex's lips parted, offering a path for curious exploration.

Alex dug deep, resisting the urge to take the lead. For the first time, she surrendered herself when Tyler sent her tongue searching. A moan escaped, first from Alex and then from Tyler. The contact lingered as if Tyler were memorizing the shape of her mouth, savoring its taste and its texture.

How many kisses had Alex wasted? So many had been exchanged in haste, given in quest for gratification rather than romance. Kisses that titillated revved her engine when speed was of the essence, but this couldn't be more different. It was unhurried, charged by the deep connection that had first drawn them together, not just sexual attraction.

Alex had almost forgotten to breathe until Tyler pulled back. Silence and a relaxed look of pure satisfaction fed the moment. She ached for more but reminded herself to let Tyler make the next move.

When Tyler opened her eyes, she whispered, "So, that's how a kiss is supposed to feel."

"I was thinking the same thing."

Damn. The cellphone in the pocket tucked into the back of her dress's waist buzzed to an incoming call. The ringtone told her it was from one of the hotel emergency lines. Of all the inappropriate moments for a call, this topped the list. She pressed the button to silence the phone. "I hate to say this, but I have to take this."

Tyler stared at lips that were still tingling. "Can it wait? Because I can't." Tyler captured her lips again, this time with unmistakable swelling confidence. She cranked up the heat, her hands wandering the length of Alex's back.

Quaking muscles and the growing ache between her legs made it impossible for Alex to maintain her restraint. She let her hands drift to Tyler's bottom. When another moan escaped from this beautiful creature's throat, Alex couldn't contain her hunger. Her ache needed relief. She pressed firmly, bringing their centers together in an instant. The resulting moan and her ache intensified, urging her to press harder. The heat between them swelled enough to set off fire alarms.

Her phone buzzed again with the same damn emergency ringtone. For the first time, she hated her job. Moments ago, she had experienced the perfect first kiss and she was now beginning a searing hot make-out session with a woman she'd waited a lifetime to meet. Castle Resorts' long reach, however, had her tethered like a ball and chain.

Alex reluctantly released her grip, the resulting lack of contact making her ache increase tenfold. She pulled her lips from Tyler's, which were strikingly plump from that incredible second kiss.

"I'm sorry, but I really do have to take this. It's the company emergency line."

"Damn, and just when I thought you couldn't beat that first kiss."

"Hold that thought. I'll make it quick." Alex retrieved the phone from her pocket and brought it to life without shifting her eyes from Tyler's luscious lips. "This is Alex Castle."

"Ms. Castle, this is David Mitchell, Head of Security at Times Square. We have an active Level One emergency."

The hairs on Alex's arms prickled. A Level One emergency involved fire, natural disaster, active shooter, or death. "What is it?"

"We had a double shooting in a suite on the fourteenth floor. One victim is dead. EMTs have arrived to tend to the other."

Alex's stomach twisted, her eyes flying to meet Tyler's. That floor had nothing but VIP suites, including Tyler and Ethan's. "Which suite?"

"Fourteen-o-two."

Alex's heart skipped a beat. That was Tyler's suite. Dreading the answer to her next question, Alex grabbed Tyler's hand. "Do you have any names?"

"No, ma'am. Both male. Unidentified at this point."

Alex's knees weakened at the unbearable thought that Ethan was one of them. She'd never forgive herself if anything happened to him in her hotel. "Thank you. I'll be right up."

After she disconnected the call, Alex's first thoughts were for Tyler. She'd already undergone tremendous pain, and she was about to endure more. Her husband likely was either dead or shot. Either possibility would set her world into a tailspin.

Alex took Tyler by the elbows and searched her eyes, seeking evidence of the strength she'd need to hear the news. Without a doubt, it was there.

"Tyler, something has happened in your suite."

CHAPTER TWENTY-EIGHT

Whoever said change was a good thing never had it coming at them from all sides at once. As if coming to terms with her PTSD, her sexuality, and her crumbling marriage weren't enough, Tyler now had to contend with the biggest challenge her family had yet to face. The onslaught should have been enough to send her over the edge, but Alex Castle was there. That was the only thing keeping her from caving into the chaos.

For the last hour, Tyler had been sitting with Alex by her side in the overcrowded emergency room at Empire State Hospital, waiting for news. Alex seemed to sense what she needed—silence and handholding to give her strength. The unruly crowd, though, wasn't cooperating. Ten rows of ten chairs each were filled, and a dozen other people were standing waiting for treatment or news. Though the older ones quietly slept, they were outnumbered by the gangbanger types and families with youngsters who were paying no attention to the concept of indoor voices.

Tyler's immediate concern was what to tell the girls. From birth, they'd faced the possibility their father might never come home every time he walked out the door wearing a badge, but they couldn't have prepared for this. The news had blindsided Tyler. It would devastate the girls if he didn't pull through.

Alex returned from a quick trip down the hallway and knelt in front of her, holding a full plastic water bottle with her hands. "You need to drink." She unscrewed the cap and offered Tyler the bottle.

"Thank you." Tyler's hand shook as she raised it to her lips. She hated waiting. It gave her too much time to think about worst-case scenarios, especially after seeing the blood covering Ethan's head and leg when the EMTs wheeled him out on the stretcher.

"You still look rattled." Alex rested a hand on Tyler's knee. "I found an empty area down the hallway and let the reception nurse know that we'll be there."

"You've thought of everything. Thank you."

Once she was in the sanctuary of the small waiting area outside another department, the quiet closed in on Tyler. She and Ethan had built a life that she couldn't deny was good. Their marriage may have been ending, but she still loved him. Seeing him near death's door had hit her as hard as a fully loaded Mack truck. If one thing went wrong in the operating room, her girls would be without a father, and she would be without the man she had loved half her life.

"I love him, Alex."

"If you didn't, you wouldn't be the woman I think you are." Alex wrapped an arm over Tyler's shoulder and pulled her chin toward her with the other hand. "We haven't known each other long, but I already know you love deeply. You can't easily turn that off."

"I don't know what I'd do if we lost him."

Alex's eyebrows narrowed in concern. "We'll get through this—together—no matter what happens, Tyler. I promise."

Tyler averted her eyes. Before that phone call, she'd hoped the connection between her and Alex would lead to something more profound tonight. But Ethan's life was hanging in the balance. She couldn't think past his surgery. If he survived, he'd need weeks, if not months, to recover. She wouldn't leave him when he needed her the most.

"I can't—"

Alex placed an index finger lightly on Tyler's lips. "I'll wait."

Tyler found that putting a label on her feelings at the moment was like trying to solve a Rubik's Cube on the first try—it couldn't be done. Tyler had been hooked on Alex long before she laid eyes on her yesterday. As they worked together from opposite sides of the country, she'd gotten to know the woman below the surface, and she was sold, sight unseen. But, my God, physically, they were on fire. In that ballroom tonight, she'd never felt more brazen, more alive emotionally and sexually.

Tyler pressed her forehead against Alex's and closed her eyes. Strength, comfort, affection, and love flowed between them. Whatever the future held for Ethan, Tyler wasn't prepared to let Alex go. She caressed Alex's cheek with a hand. "Thank you." She drew back and kissed Alex on the lips, lightly, sweetly, and full of gratitude.

"Mrs. Falling?"

Tyler turned toward the voice and found a weary-looking, ebony-skinned woman in maroon surgical scrubs. A matching cap hid most of her finely weaved dark hair. "Yes?" Her voice was shaky.

"I'm Doctor Slater. I have news about your husband."

Embarrassment flushed her cheeks. The doctor had interrupted her kissing Alex to give her potentially shattering news about her husband. How fucked up was that?

There was no time for excuses. Tyler stood. "How is he?"

* * *

A pungent antiseptic scent, beeping monitor, and collection of tubes and wires underscored how close Tyler had come to losing Ethan. She'd seen her children through flu, bloody mouths, many cuts and scrapes, and one heart-wrenching broken arm, but the worst she'd nursed Ethan through was a thrown-out back. Seeing him in this hospital bed bordered on excruciating.

She touched his leg below the bandage covering his wound and let the relief settle in. Another few inches up and to the left, he would've bled out in their hotel room before the EMTs arrived. She would've never forgiven herself if he died while she was making out like a hormone-fueled teenager. Her hand drifted up to squeeze his. Countless times that strong, masculine hand had provided reassuring comfort when she was down. It was her turn to do the same for him.

"He looks so weak." Tyler struggled to keep the tears welling up behind her eyelids from falling.

"He's strong." Alex caressed her back in gentle circles. "The doctor said he should make a full recovery. After a month of physical therapy, he should be good as new."

Tyler failed to shake off the guilt of being moments away from asking Alex to take her to a room while he lay on the floor in agony. "I'm so relieved he'll be okay."

Ethan stirred from the anesthesia, moving first his hand and then his uninjured leg.

"It's Tyler, Ethan." Tyler squeezed his hand again. His eyes fluttered open with a look of confusion. "I'm right here. You're going to be fine."

He returned the squeeze with one of his own before shifting atop the clunky hospital bed. His voice croaked, "You're safe?"

A tear dropped to his arm as she leaned forward. "I'm fine. I was with Alex."

He struggled to scoot himself further up the bed and grimaced. "Is she here?"

"I'm right here, Ethan." Alex stepped from behind Tyler.

"You're not safe." He strained to push his torso up a few inches. "Can you raise this damn thing?" Tyler set the bed to a more comfortable, reclined position. "The other guy was Victor's man."

"Victor?" Alex's voice ended in an uptick. "I thought we had an arrangement."

A knock on the doorframe. Two men in cheap suits and one-day stubble walked in. They carried themselves with the same look of official business as Ethan had worn for years and flashed their gold detective's shields. While Tyler understood their presence was necessary, she didn't welcome it at the moment. The smaller, blond detective said, "NYPD. We need to ask Mr. Falling some questions."

Tyler gave them her best glare. "He just woke up, for God's sake."

"It's all right, Tyler." Ethan shifted taller in the bed. "This should only take a few minutes."

"Thank you, Mr. Falling. Can you tell us what happened?"

"I returned to my suite, and it looked as if someone had rifled through it. When I went into the bedroom, someone hit me on the back of the head. Then this big guy threw me on the bed. He had a gun and said he wanted the pictures. I asked him what pictures because I didn't have any. He got pissed and threatened to shoot me. I stalled and told him I had them in the safe. That was where I had stored my service weapon. I'm an off-duty police officer from Sacramento. I retrieved my weapon and shot. He shot too."

"Had you seen him before?" the other detective asked.

"Yes. I saw him at a place called Arthur's Alley. I was there for nachos and to watch some sports. He must've followed me."

"Why would he think you had these pictures he wanted?" the first one asked. "Did he say what was in them?"

"He said something about some skanks." Ethan shifted again and winced. His skin had turned several shades whiter, nearly matching the bedsheets. "Beyond that, he didn't say much after waving that damn pistol around."

"Look, fellas." Tyler stepped forward, placing a hand on Ethan's arm. "My husband needs his rest. He's obviously not going anywhere soon. Can you finish this later?"

"Sure thing." The bigger officer handed Tyler a business card. "If he thinks of anything else, call us."

Once they left, Ethan's voice became more gravelly. "Alex, this is important. He didn't want money. He wanted Kelly's photos."

"How in the hell did—" Alex stopped in mid-sentence. "Andrew."

"Your brother did this?" Tyler didn't like where this was going. Her first instinct had been right. He was trouble.

"No." Ethan shook his head, exhausting what appeared to be the last bits of his energy. "He wasn't there, but I suspect he had something to do with it."

"Andrew knows about the pictures," Alex said. "He said so last night."

Tyler recalled her brother's tone when he mentioned something about pictures and Kelly. She got the impression he thought they were his golden ticket. "You need to tell the police."

Alex rubbed her temples and took several steps back. "For all we know, he told Victor about the pictures, and Victor went after them on his own."

Tyler's facial muscles tightened. Why was Alex making excuses for him? She wanted to find who was responsible for nearly killing her husband and make them pay. "What does that matter? Let the police sort it out."

"He's my twin, Tyler. I can't sic the police on him if we have no proof that he did anything."

Ethan groaned in pain, prompting Tyler to adjust the bed position again and his pillow. "Let's not argue about this. You're my client, Alex. I won't volunteer information that's not in your best interest, but I won't lie. It won't take them long to figure out who that guy works for. If Victor talks, they'll be knocking on Andrew's door."

"If?" Tyler's blood boiled. Neither of them was going to help the police? "This is absurd. Andrew needs to pay."

"I'm tired." Ethan rested his head against the pillow and closed his eyes. "I need to rest."

"Thank you, Ethan." Alex's gratitude was the last thing Tyler wanted to hear.

"I think you need to leave." Tyler's words were razor sharp, as intended. Leaning on Alex to get her through this was now out of the question. Realizing that hurt as much as seeing Ethan shot.

Alex's face went slack. The magical feeling Tyler had had on that ballroom floor now seemed like a distant memory. The comfort she had taken from Alex since then had evaporated, along with the hope she had for a bright, new future. Alex dipped her head.

"May I call you later?" Her voice was meek but hopeful.

"I need time, Alex."

After absorbing those four words, the future Tyler had hoped for walked out the door.

CHAPTER TWENTY-NINE

Fury built in Alex as she left the hospital, one so hot all the water in the Hudson couldn't put it out. With proof or without it, she was certain Andrew had a hand in the debacle that almost cost Ethan his life. As horrible as she felt for Ethan, she couldn't help but ache for her own loss too. She'd stood up to her father, telling him she'd found something she wanted more than to follow in his footsteps. That something might be slipping through her fingers now because of her devotion to her brother. Calling the police was still out of the question, but Tyler was right. Andrew needed to pay.

She arrived at his sleek Manhattan loft, carrying a leather satchel full of documents she'd picked up at her office. The final damning piece of evidence was a voice recording. After she rang the bell and knocked several times, Andrew answered the door, looking disheveled in his T-shirt and plaid pajama bottoms. "It's one o'clock in the damn morning."

"Stop your whining." Alex pushed her way through the front door and made her way down the hallway where her brother had hung his collection of autographed sports memorabilia. The living room was a veritable man cave, decorated with more of his collection. Leather movie seating for six, as many flat screens tacked to the wall, a built-in bar, and enough lighting for a sports stadium finished the look.

Andrew poured himself a glass of twenty-five-year-old Jefferson's Presidential straight bourbon whiskey before plopping down in one of the oversized chairs. "What in the hell do you want this time of night?"

"Enjoy the JP while you still can because after I'm done with you, you won't be able to afford Jim Beam." Alex placed her satchel on the coffee table. Retrieving the portable recorder, Alex gritted her teeth to maintain the cap on the volcano threatening to blow. She pressed PLAY.

"Andrew still owes me two million." Victor's voice was unmistakable.

"He lost two million dollars gambling?" she heard herself say.

"Not gambling. Borrowed."

Ethan broke in. *"You said still. What was the original debt?"*

"A double on two mil, payable in twelve months. His first payment is due next Friday."

"So, you've already received your principal back?"

"He returned it tonight. Tried to weasel his way out, but a deal is a deal. I need to make a profit."

Alex stopped the recording. "That's me with Victor Padula and the private detective who was shot tonight because of you." Andrew spat out his liquid gold security blanket. Alex estimated that was a five-hundred-dollar reaction.

"Shot?" Andrew's darting eyes said the news was unexpected but not a complete surprise. He downed the remaining liquid in his glass.

"Yes, shot." Alex tapped an index finger on the recorder. "And this tape links you to the man who did the shooting and was killed for it."

"I had nothing to do with any shooting or killing." His less-than-convincing, shaky response meant Alex had him on the ropes.

"Maybe you didn't intend to have it happen, but Victor's thug, the one you obviously hired, shot a good man while looking for Kelly's photographs. The same pictures you were whining about losing out on last night."

"A coincidence."

"The police might think otherwise. Now, unless you want the cops knocking down your door today, two things will happen." Alex pulled from her satchel a piece of paper. "First, you are resigning from Castle Resorts. Here is your resignation letter. All you have to do is sign it." She pulled out more documents. "Second, you will repay me every penny: the five hundred thousand I gave to Victor to pay off your marker, plus the two hundred and fifty thousand you stole from the company. It's all documented right here."

"I don't have that kind of money." Andrew moaned. "I'm already mortgaged to the hilt."

"Only you could turn Father's graduation gift for earning an MBA into a mountain of debt. You sell everything you have, this loft, your motorcycle, and your prized memorabilia."

"And where am I supposed to live?"

"That's your problem. Try couch surfing. I hear it's all the rage these days. You have one month to put the money together or everything goes to Father and the police."

Andrew steepled his hands together, his tell that he'd been one-upped.

"By nine o'clock this morning, you will walk into Father's office like you were supposed to do yesterday. This time, you will tell him you're resigning."

"What excuse am I supposed to give?" Andrew asked.

"Again, not my problem. Tell him whatever you want. You're lucky we're family, because if you weren't, you'd be sitting in a holding cell tonight, waiting for a public defender to show up."

"Fine, Alex. You can have the company, my loft, my motorcycle, and all of my things. But mark my word, you haven't seen the last of me. I *will* pick myself up, and I *will* be a thorn in your side for the rest of your life."

"Whatever helps you sleep at night, Brother. I sent a message to Gretchen to put you on Father's calendar. Don't be late."

* * *

Once before, Alex Castle had experienced the devastation of a broken heart. She considered herself a child the first time around and since had carefully avoided a repeat performance. Until tonight.

She could tell herself that she should've known better and brush off Tyler's stinging rebuff as a bump in the road, but who was she kidding? Before tonight, she never considered surrendering herself to a woman, but after two hot-as-hell kisses, she couldn't think of anything better. She wanted to be the one who made Tyler feel alive and desired again, but she had blown it. The only thing keeping her together now was her belief in second chances. If Tyler was half as compassionate as she suspected, her second chance would come.

Her optimism didn't extend to a desire to be alone. Swooshing open, the elevator delivered her to Harley, a much-needed friendly face, and to Abby's penthouse, the place she'd considered her private refuge since she was five. Abby hadn't hovered over her or coddled her after her mother's death. She'd nurtured her. She'd also called her out when she failed to do her homework or clean up after herself. In short, she became the mother she needed. She needed her now.

Alex followed Harley into the penthouse and hung her coat on the wall peg reserved for her.

"I'm glad you called. Mother and Indra are up and waiting for you in the study. I'll get you a drink," Harley said. Those were the first words she and Alex had spoken since she stepped off the elevator. For friends of thirty years, exchanging words was unnecessary.

Moments later, Alex entered Abby's study. She paused, contemplating the scene in front of her. A scene that she had envisioned achieving for herself someday and had possibly lost. Indra was curled up in Abby's arms on the couch in front of a roaring fire, sipping brandy. She had wanted that for her and Tyler, but considering their last words…

"Cabernet or pinot?" Harley settled beside Alex, holding two glasses.

"Pinot." Alex accepted the more prudent choice. She didn't need a reminder of the wine she shared with Tyler only a few hours ago.

Abby turned and patted the empty seat cushion next to her. "Sit, my dear. Harley has told us of your horrifying night."

Alex sat, realizing suddenly how exhausted she was. As she sank into the deep cushion, her arms went limp. "It was a horrible end to the best evening I'd ever spent with a woman."

"How are you holding up?" Indra asked.

"Not well. I thought I'd found something as special as you and Abby have, but after tonight, I'm not sure where we stand."

"Is this the woman you spoke of the other night?" Abby paused at Alex's confirming nod. "I'm guessing her being married complicates things."

"I won't betray her confidence with the details, but I can say with certainty that her marriage is amicably over. Her husband confirmed as much at the party."

"He was the one who was shot, Mother," Harley said.

"Oh, dear. This woman must be beside herself." Abby frowned. "How is the poor man?"

"He suffered a leg wound but should make a full recovery."

"Thank goodness." Abby frowned again. "I'm confused. If things appear to be manageable, why do you think you've lost her?"

The time had come to reveal what she knew about Andrew. In her mind, he and Kelly were now inexorably linked. Both had the potential of wreaking havoc on Castle Resorts.

"The man who shot her husband, Ethan, was there looking for Kelly Thatcher's photos."

"Not the ones we maneuvered around with young Mr. Castor's confession?" Indra asked.

"The very ones. I think Andrew is to blame. His gambling has gotten worse, and he's been pilfering from company coffers."

If you could call two hundred and fifty thousand pilfering. This wasn't padding his expense account, Alex. Call it what it is: embezzling.

She wasn't ready to do that yet, refraining out of love and the guilt she felt for not protecting him. Though that was waning.

"That boy has yet to grow up," Abby said. "Does William know?"

"Not yet, but I was so angry at him, I put Father onto his scent. That's just the tip of the iceberg."

Harley plopped down on a nearby armchair and rubbed her hands together with the glee of a six-year-old on Christmas morning. "I knew I'd hear a juicy story tonight."

"May I continue?" Alex shot Harley the stink eye until she settled down. "Anyway, in a fit of desperation, he borrowed a sizeable amount from a bookie. Ethan helped me strike a deal with the thug to square Andrew's account."

"How exciting." Harley perked up again. "What kind of deal?"

"If you must know, twenty-five percent of the agreed-upon profit to avoid Federal agents dissecting the financial records of him and his clients."

"Ooh, this is stuff of The Sopranos," Harley said.

"Will you stop?" Alex generally appreciated Harley's way of turning misery into delight, but she needed to get all of this off her chest. Harley relented.

"I pieced together last night that Andrew planned to buy Kelly's photographs to force me out of the company, but I got to Kelly first. Here's where it gets interesting. The man who was killed tonight worked for Andrew's bookie. My guess is that Andrew tried to make good on his debt and suggested those photos would make for a generous payday."

"I'm not following. If you have the pictures, why would they go after this Ethan fellow?" Abby asked.

"After I confronted Kelly with Castor's confession, Ethan retrieved the photos from her. She must've told Andrew about Ethan. She wouldn't know he passed the photos to me at first opportunity."

"Oh, my. What has this boy gotten himself into?" Indra asked.

"The type of trouble Castle Resorts can't afford to associate itself with. I'm forcing him out of the company, but I can't bring myself to turn him in to the police."

"Ah, and there's the rub," Abby said. "This woman you're so fond of can't forgive you for protecting the man who may be responsible for nearly killing her husband."

"Yes. Tyler is an amazing woman who's been through more than anyone should. I hope she'll forgive me. In the meantime, I need Indra's help again."

"I'm happy to help," Indra said.

"Tyler's daughter has been accepted to Yale for next fall. It's her dream school, but her parents can't afford the tuition. I don't want money to be a disqualifier for her accepting the offer of admission. I want to fund the expenses, but if Tyler knew I had a hand in this, even as a way of making amends for Ethan being shot while working for me, she likely would not accept it."

"Then how can I help?" Indra asked.

"PopCo offers several college scholarships, doesn't it? I'd like you to set up a special scholarship for Miss Falling for her entire stay at Yale, which I will anonymously fund."

Abby and Indra quietly consulted, whispering back and forth into each other's ears.

"Consider it done." Indra smiled.

CHAPTER THIRTY

Sacramento, California

Walking into Gail Sanders' home office came with its own particular brand of guilt. Since that fateful trip to New York City nearly four weeks ago, Tyler had left most of Alex's messages and phone calls unanswered, citing the commitment she'd made to stay with Ethan until he was back on his feet. One that she answered was to thank Alex for handing off the now completed Castle Resort website project to her Chief Technology Officer. While the unpredictable schedule of working, parenting, and playing caregiver was accurate on its face, she could've, and in her heart, should've made the time to talk to Alex or at least Gail before now, but something had held her back. She had succeeded in tucking away her conflicted feelings until she read today's news article, the one she now clutched in her hand.

Gail poked her head into her little waiting area after Tyler had walked in. "Come in, Tyler. It's good to see you."

"Thanks for seeing me on short notice again." Gail gestured for her to sit in her usual chair, but Tyler's rapid-fire thoughts had her wound up like a spring. She paced to work off the nervous energy. "Thanks, but I'd rather stand."

"Whichever makes you comfortable." Gail sat in her chair and followed Tyler with her eyes. "It's been a while. What brings you in today?"

"This." Tyler handed Gail a printout from *SF Gate Online* that detailed this week's grand reopening of the Castle Resort hotel in San Francisco. She subdued her frustration long enough to sit on the edge of her usual chair, bouncing a knee up and down. "Alex Castle is the most exhilarating and aggravating thing to happen to me."

"How is that?" Gail jotted something on her notepad without as much as a muscle twitch. Her training made her a hard one to read. Why couldn't she be more like Maddie, whose facial expressions telegraphed every emotion? Maybe then Tyler could decipher when her end of the conversation had gone off the rails.

"She and the mystery woman from Napa are the same person."

"Interesting." Still not a single tell.

"Understatement of the year. Imagine my surprise when I meet Alex Castle for the first time in person, and I realize she's the one who set all of this in motion."

"How did it make you feel?"

"Like everything made sense. The way I felt connected to the mystery woman with a single touch. The way I felt drawn to Alex after a handful of phone calls. They were both linked."

"But?"

A seething boiled inside Tyler with growing intensity. Even if she wanted to, she couldn't bottle it back up again. She clenched her fists. "But her brother was involved in Ethan's shooting. She refuses to tell the police anything, and since she's Ethan's client, he won't either."

"And why is this a problem?"

Tyler flung her hands in the air and screamed. "I almost lost Ethan because of him, and that bastard is getting away with it." Heat engulfed her. Her heart raced out of control, but this time she didn't get dizzy. She got furious.

"And it bothers you when a man hurts you deeply and pays little to no price for it."

254 Stacy Lynn Miller

"You're damn right it does!"

Tyler buried her face in her hands, giving herself permission to surface the pain from that life-changing night. As Gail let the silence linger, she realized that the fear that it could destroy her was gone. Darkness had finally turned into light. Pain was no longer a beast to keep at bay. Instead, it had become the thing that made her stronger.

After a few more moments, Gail put her notepad down. For the first time during a session, she leaned forward, her expression changing from unreadable to clear and present delight.

"That's it. The breakthrough you needed."

Tyler slumped in her chair, arms limp as if her tears had zapped every bit of strength from them, beginning to process the enormity of what she'd just said.

"I haven't felt this drained since I had the flu."

"That's what beginning to heal feels like," Gail said.

"I've been such a fool." How could Tyler not have seen that her anger was misdirected?

"How so?" Gail asked.

"I've been avoiding Alex because I thought I was mad at her, but in reality, I was furious at Stevens." Gail nodded. Tyler ran her hands through her hair, regretting the way she'd left things at the hospital. Regretting not responding to Alex's calls, texts, and emails since returning to Sacramento. "I need to fix this."

The elation Tyler had gotten from finally breaking through her PTSD didn't last beyond the drive home. Before she tried to make things right with Alex, she knew she needed to end her commitment to Ethan. That, she expected, would come with heartache for both of them.

She walked inside her home, and the odd silence had her antenna up. Ethan had started driving short distances this week and should've picked up Bree from school by now. Tyler had expected to be faced with one of the two scenarios that she'd come home to every day since she and Ethan told the girls they were divorcing. Either the TV should be blaring or Erin and Bree should be yelling at each other at the top of their lungs, arguing about who took what personal item from the other's room without asking. This silence meant something was amiss.

Tyler called out, "Ethan? Girls?" No one responded. Disposing of her purse and jacket in the entry hall, she walked toward the heart of their home. Ethan, Erin, and Bree were sitting quietly at the kitchen table. They grinned when she walked in.

"What? Did we win Publishers Clearing House?"

"No, but someone has won the lottery." Ethan wagged his thumb toward Erin, who pushed a large envelope across the tabletop. The distinctive blue and white crest in the upper left corner emblazoned with *Lux et Veritas* meant one thing—Yale. Tyler felt her eyes widen with a mix of excitement and dread.

"I thought you still had another few days before you had to decide. Did you accept and not tell us?" A pit formed in Tyler's stomach, imagining the second mortgage payment she and Ethan would have to take on.

"Not yet, but Yale just upped their offer." Erin handed her the envelope.

Tyler pulled the two-page letter from its casing and read the opening paragraph to herself.

Congratulations on your acceptance for admission to Yale University for the fall semester, 2007. We are pleased to inform you that PopCo International has selected you to receive its Friends of Yale Scholarship. In addition to a monthly stipend, the scholarship covers tuition, books, and room and board. The total shall not exceed seventy-five thousand dollars for each year of undergraduate study as long as you remain a student in good standing.

"Holy crap."

"Well put." Ethan's grin appeared permanent. "Our girl is getting a full ride to Yale."

"So, UCLA, Berkley, Stanford, and UC Davis are out?" Relief didn't come close to describing how Tyler felt. She had long suspected that Erin's pragmatic side had been what inspired her delay in accepting an admission offer. The California colleges' art schools were as impressive as Yale's, and the in-state tuition at the public universities was a fraction of its tuition, making them more rational propositions. It had saddened Tyler, however, that Erin would settle on her second choice for one of the most significant decisions of her life simply because of money. Thankfully, her procrastination paid off.

"Duh. Yale is the only school to offer a full scholarship, and we're talkin' Yale here." Erin leaned back in her chair, beaming with pride. "A full scholarship! I still can't believe it."

"Well, believe it." Ethan walked toward the hallway with a limp considerably less noticeable than he had last week. His hard work during physical therapy was paying off.

"Where are you going?" Tyler asked.

Ethan smiled. "I'm going to order myself a Yale sweatshirt. What else?"

Once the excitement died down and Bree was off to do homework and Erin off to celebrate with her friends, Tyler joined Ethan at the computer. She considered tabling her next discussion and letting him revel in his fatherly pride, but if her sessions with Gail had taught her anything, it was to take care of herself first.

She caressed his shoulder as he perused the online Yale Bookstore. "Can we talk for a minute?"

"Sure." He continued his hunt for the perfect proud parent apparel.

"This is about Alex."

He released the computer mouse and spun his chair to face Tyler. "I've been waiting for this talk." His expression suggested he welcomed it.

"You have, huh?"

"It's obvious you two belong together. I hate the fact that you put your life on hold to take care of me."

"We're divorcing, but I still love you. I couldn't abandon you."

"Which is why I signed a lease today on an apartment downtown. I move in on the fifteenth."

"So soon? That's not even three weeks away."

"I knew you'd never pull the trigger, so I did. Since I can take care of myself now, there's no sense in delaying this."

"It's all coming so fast."

"We need to make a clean break, and I need to start over. Which is why I also put in my retirement papers today, so I can start doing the P.I. thing full time."

"I'm happy for you." Tyler wiped away a single tear. So much change, but all for the better. She hoped the phone call she was about to make would mark a fresh start for herself too. "Thank you, Ethan."

"For what?"

"For letting me go."

* * *

San Francisco, California

She was seventy-five miles away from Sacramento, but Alex felt Tyler's pull as strongly as if she were sitting next to her in the back seat of the town car she was riding in. She imagined her asleep with a cheek pressed against Alex's shoulder, softly exhaling onto her neck. Alex would have an arm wrapped around Tyler's torso, keeping her in place as the driver took the swooping off-ramp from the Bayshore Highway. She'd gently nudge her awake when the car came to a stop at the Castle Resort entrance and whisper into her ear, "We're here, T." Then she'd take her up to the owner's suite and make love to her until the sun came up.

"We're here, Ms. Castle." The driver had opened the rear passenger door and offered his hand to help Alex out of the back seat.

"Oh, thank you. I must've been daydreaming." Alex let him assist her out of the car at the exquisite, brass-trimmed hotel entrance.

"I wish I had daydreams that could make me smile like that." He maneuvered to one side and gestured for a twenty-something male bellhop to gather Alex's lone suitcase, which he'd already placed curbside.

"Sometimes, the fantasy is more palatable than reality." She handed him a twenty-dollar tip. "If you have no other fares this evening, please be my guest at our new restaurant. Tell them to put it on my tab."

"Thank you, Ms. Castle. I think I will."

Once she was inside the hotel, reality replaced fantasy. Alex's life was in limbo, personally and professionally. Tyler had occupied her dreams and every waking thought when she wasn't throwing herself deep into work. Her father had put his retirement on hold and, along with it, her transition to CEO. For a month now, William, Andrew, and Tyler had refused to talk to her. If not for Harley, Abby, and Indra, Alex would have had only her disappointment and regret for company.

Her phone buzzed to an incoming text from her childhood friend. *At Pegu. Jordi asked about you. What should I tell her?*

The thought of sliding between the tasty redhead's legs or between any pair other than Tyler's had lost its appeal. Each time Alex turned down Harley's invitation to hit the Pegu Club and its sea of beautiful women, Harley accused her of being an excessive optimist. Alex knew better. This had nothing to do with optimism. The moment she thought she'd lost Tyler, Alex was sure she loved her. Jordi would have to move on because the only woman Alex wanted to curl up next to was two hours away, caring for a husband who took a bullet to the leg because of the foolishness of her youth and her brother's treachery.

Tell her I'm taken, Alex typed.

Thanks to the coast-to-coast flight she'd just undergone, Alex didn't have the energy to explore the completed renovations as she'd intended. The tour would have to wait until morning. She retrieved the keycard to the owner's suite at the registration desk and shooed off the bellhop. Even dead tired, she was more than capable of toting a single overnight bag.

The suite was as she'd left it a month ago. Seeing it brought back heartening memories. After dropping her luggage, she sat at the desk where her journey began. She pulled from her jacket pocket the photo that had set all of this in motion. She rubbed a thumb across the image of Tyler. She refused to believe the best thing to happen to her was over.

Her phone came to life again, this time a custom ringtone that made her breath hitch. She'd waited a month to hear the opening line of Van Morrison's "Someone Like You," and now that she had, her hand shook. This could either be a good sign or the final goodbye, an ending she wasn't prepared for. Her voice croaked when she answered.

"Tyler?"

"Alex." Tyler's breathy voice was a slice of heaven. Its longing undertone gave Alex a glimmer of hope.

"I hoped you'd call when you were ready."

"I'm sorry I didn't return your calls until now." Tyler paused as if searching for the right words. "I had a lot to work through."

"You have nothing to apologize for. I'm the one who needs to apologize for how I handled things with my brother."

"You were conflicted. I get that now."

"Thank you for understanding." Alex slumped in the chair, the weight of uncertainty now gone. Tyler's forgiveness foreshadowed the possibility of a long-awaited second chance. "How is Ethan?"

"Doing well. He has two more weeks of physical therapy, but he's already walking and driving."

"That's such a relief. I worried he might have permanent damage. And your girls. How are they coping with their father being home all day?"

"As well as expected after we broke the news about the divorce. They've been going through their own grieving process. They're past denial and anger and are well into the bargaining stage."

One word Tyler said sparked a rush of optimism. If Tyler was moving forward with a divorce, that left the door open for—

Don't get ahead of yourself, Alex silently chided herself. "I'm so sorry."

"We're getting through it." Tyler paused again, but the silence wasn't awkward. It gave Alex time to let the enormity of the call soak in. "Alex?"

"Yes?"

"I've missed you."

Those three words had Alex's arms aching to hold Tyler. Her lips quivered at the prospect of kissing her again. "I've missed you, too."

Tyler audibly exhaled. "I want to see you."

"I've waited a month to hear those words." Her heart wanted to shout the words she'd known were true for a month, but saying "I love you" would have to wait until she was sure Tyler felt that too.

Tyler sniffled. "I don't want to wait any longer. I can fly out on the weekend, and—"

"Tyler, wait. I'm in San Francisco."

"Of course, the grand reopening. I read about it in the paper. The hotel looked beautiful in the picture." Joy filled Tyler's voice.

"You saw that, huh?"

"I did." Tyler's tone turned serious. "Reading about you made me realize what a fool I've been, blaming you for something you had nothing to do with. I need to make it right."

A boldness overcame Alex, one that she couldn't keep bottled up. "Come here tonight. Stay the weekend with me."

CHAPTER THIRTY-ONE

Tyler's sweaty hands had a death grip on the wheel as she turned off the busy Bayshore Highway and into the wide circular driveway of Castle Resort San Francisco. Several aspects about tonight had her wound up tight, but at the moment most of her jitters could be attributed to the damn drive over. As much as she wanted to see Alex, she first needed a drink.

Still shaky, Tyler tossed her key fob to the valet attendant, who was sporting a maroon jacket, black pants, and matching tie, receiving a ticket stub in exchange. She said, "Long drive. Where's the bar?"

The young man winked as he accepted her tip. "Through the lobby and up the escalator to the next level. You can't miss it."

Tyler mouthed a sincere, "Thank you" and grabbed her bag. The ride up the escalator revealed a spectacular nine-story atrium in the hotel center flanked by guest rooms on three sides and a wall of windows on the other. The ceiling opened to a skylight system through which twinkled the night sky.

At the escalator's top, Tyler spotted the bar. A dozen televisions along a far wall were broadcasting everything from sports to news. A late evening crowd had packed that place. She took the only vacant seat, tucked between two suited businessmen in boisterous conversation and an elderly couple staring at the screens. The news crawl on one screen mentioned the first Democratic Party presidential debate in South Carolina and how Senator Obama made a strong appearance but that Hillary Clinton was still the frontrunner. Women's and men's golf, auto racing, sports shows, and several baseball and basketball games were featured on the others.

Tyler was anxious. No, more than that. She was on the verge of another panic attack as she conjured up images of the beautiful woman waiting for her in a room a few floors above. She desperately needed to calm her nerves. A bartender dressed in a uniform similar to the valet's placed a napkin on the bar in front of her. "What can I get you?"

After scanning their happy hour specials, Tyler eyed a drink that contained her preferred ingredients but added an item that would offer a novel experience. "I'll try your Delayed Connection. It seems fitting."

"Excellent choice. Coming right up," he said.

Moments later, he returned with a colorful cocktail made of vodka, grapefruit juice, and a surprising splash of rosemary simple syrup. The drink's uniquely sweet, herbal spin invited a faster than fashionable consumption rate. Within minutes, the alcohol took the edge off. Tyler was almost ready. She flipped her phone open to check the time. She still had twenty minutes until when she'd agreed to meet Alex in her room.

While swirling the ice cubes in the near-empty cocktail glass, Tyler considered the circumstances that had brought her to this hotel. Two months ago, she was a suburban wife and mother who co-owned a small business with her best friend. Now, following a rocky period full of crisis and near-tragedy, she found herself in a hotel bar, one elevator ride away from a luxury room where she would likely make love to a woman who had her spellbound at first sight.

"This is insane," she said to no one, shaking her head in disbelief.

She downed the last of her drink. Its bittersweet combination, she thought, was appropriate for the weekend that lay ahead for her—one part of her life was coming to an end while another was coming into its own. She picked up her phone again and dialed Alex's number.

Alex answered after two rings. "Hello." Several uncomfortable moments of silence passed. "Tyler?"

Tyler's heart thudded, asking herself one vital question: Was she ready for intimacy? In her heart, the answer was yes, but in her head, she feared she'd freeze or, worse, shut down. She uttered, "Hi."

"You're not coming." The disappointment in Alex's voice was palpable.

"I'm downstairs at the bar." She signaled the bartender to send her a second round. "I'm nervous as hell, Alex."

"Nervous about what might happen tonight?"

"Partly, yes."

"Tyler, if you're not ready—" Alex sounded out of breath.

"It's more than that."

"Then what is it?" Alex's voice took on a faint echo. She must have moved into a different room.

Tyler sensed her jaw beginning to tighten as her nervousness magnified. "I just drove over the longest fucking bridge in my life."

"I didn't know you're gephyrophobic."

"I'm what?"

"You're afraid of bridges."

"I never knew it had a name."

"Well, it does. Turn around."

Tyler turned on the barstool to find Alex approaching at a steady clip. Ending the call, Alex slipped her cell phone into the back pocket of her formfitting jeans. Tyler followed her curved hips down to where the fabric narrowed tightly at the calf. Lord, she was sexy in those pants. Did she look as good from behind? Alex's dark brown hair was loosely gathered at the back like it had been the first time they met, and her loose, three-quarter-sleeve, low-cut blue silk tunic blouse revealed a hint of cleavage.

Alex closed the distance, her serious expression transforming into a warm smile. She placed her hands on Tyler's cheeks and pulled her face closer. Tyler inhaled the now familiar and intoxicating jasmine scent of Alex's perfume. The warmth of Alex's breath gently caressed her lips as Alex whispered, "I missed you."

Tyler had been thinking about kissing Alex ever since their first kiss on that dance floor a month ago. Those wispy words were all the encouragement she needed now. She captured Alex's lips in a kiss hot enough to melt her bridge- and anxiety-induced tension. As they parted ever so slightly, Tyler didn't have the strength to open her eyes. She wanted the fiery sensation to linger. After a few beats, she mustered a faint, "Wow."

Alex leaned her forehead against Tyler's, stroking her arms. "Still nervous?"

"Not as much." All those weeks of pent-up anger and misdirected blame now seemed like a colossal waste of time. Being in Alex Castle's arms was where she was supposed to be.

As they parted more, they smiled and gazed into each other's eyes. Alex's expression told Tyler she would remain patient but, like her, wanted more than one kiss. She looked at Tyler with apparent concern. "Have you eaten?"

"Not since breakfast."

After glancing at the empty cocktail glass on the bar, Alex suggested, "How about we enjoy a less liquid snack while you unwind?"

"Good idea. I think that drink affected me more than I expected."

Alex captured the bartender's attention and asked that he send two Pellegrinos, a cheese board, and a side of fresh fruit over to the lounge. She helped Tyler off the stool, grabbed her overnight bag while Tyler grabbed her purse, and led her to a more secluded couch area.

After they sat, a comfortable foot apart, Alex posited, "You said this isn't only about a bridge."

Tyler blew out a deep sigh, biding her time as she tried to figure out how to address her hesitations without having Alex turn tail and run. "I'm nervous about tonight."

"I am too."

"I'm more than a little nervous, Alex. I'm worried about how I might react when…" Tyler's voice trailed off.

Alex sighed, and then in a soothing voice, said, "I understand. With your history, intimacy can be difficult. How about we do this? I want you to think about what things might trouble you: a smell, sound, word, object, or a certain touch. Tell me whatever you're comfortable revealing, so I can avoid triggering a bad memory. I can do something similar by sharing my dislikes and areas I consider out of bounds."

Tears formed in Tyler's eyes. Her voice shook. "You understand."

"Since you told me what happened, I've been researching how partners can best help survivors overcome the trauma." When the first tear dropped, Alex caressed her arms again. "Tyler, please know, no matter what may happen, I am foremost your friend. I want to do this right, so our first time won't be our last."

A server brought their food and drinks, and they put their conversation on hold to sample the delicious food, filling the time with small talk. After they had their fill of artisan cheeses, jams, and a tropical fruit mix, Tyler said, "I hate the smell of whiskey. My rapist reeked of it. That's why I reacted so strongly to your brother."

"I'm so sorry you had to go through that again. I never was much of a whiskey drinker, but from now on, it's off my list."

"I can't stand feeling trapped. He had pinned me down lengthwise across the bed, and I couldn't get free." The more Tyler disclosed, the more at ease she became. This back and forth was developing into a revealing exercise that made Tyler want Alex that much more. One vital question remained unanswered.

"Alex, I need to ask before this goes any further. With all your money, you can have any man or woman you want. Why me?"

Alex scooted closer to Tyler on the couch, so the length of their thighs touched. As she leaned in, her breast lightly grazed Tyler's. They both shivered at the contact. Alex lifted Tyler's chin with one hand and searched her eyes.

Alex dropped her hand. "I spent years searching for someone with whom I would feel a connection. I felt it the moment we bumped into each other at the riverfront, and though I didn't realize you were her, I felt it while we were working together. Money, looks, status—they meant nothing. What mattered was how you made me feel. And there's nothing more I'd like to do right now than to take you upstairs and show you."

Alex pulled Tyler into their second passion-filled kiss of the night. Every bit of her tension melted away into Alex's lips. She was ready for whatever came next. She let Alex lean her to the back of the couch. They kissed with abandon, not caring what type of audience they might attract.

Tyler's boldness grew, every ounce of inhibition dissolving. Her hands began a search, moving first to Alex's thick, alluring mane and then to her smooth cheeks, velvety neck, and defined shoulders. She slowly drew a hand down and gently caressed the side of Alex's breast, the one that had teased her earlier. Moans escaped from both at the sensation. Both explored, touching and caressing, until Alex suddenly halted.

"We need to stop before we get arrested." Alex received a well-earned chuckle from Tyler. "Would you like to go upstairs?"

With one finger, Tyler traced Alex's jawline. "More than anything."

Alex helped Tyler grab her things. They made their way down the escalator to the elevators in comfortable silence, giving Tyler a chance to slow the pace and gather her confidence.

At the bank of elevators, a handful of guests patiently waited for the next car to arrive. Alex and Tyler joined them and stood close, side by side. After a few moments, Alex's pinky softly rubbed the back of Tyler's hand. Tyler kept her gaze focused forward but smiled at Alex's stealthy show of affection. In response, she shifted her hand and rubbed Alex's hand in the same manner. A quick glance at Alex revealed a delightful grin.

When an elevator arrived, they entered along with three other guests. As they maneuvered to the rear of the car, Alex politely requested, "Nine, please." After a guest left at the first stop, Alex leaned in and whispered in Tyler's ear so only she could hear, "I'm already wet."

Tyler's eyes shot open. Her center instinctively clenched in reaction. A little louder than intended, she replied, "Damn."

In unison, the two remaining guests turned and gave Tyler a questioning look. Alex grinned and offered a quiet smirk. Tyler liked this playful side of Alex. In truth, it was quite a turn-on. The last guests exited on the next floor, leaving the two of them alone. Tyler not-so-gently pushed Alex against the elevator side wall and gave her a quick, passionate kiss. "I'm drenched."

Alex replied, "Damn."

The elevator bell dinged, and the doors opened to their floor. Halfway down the hall, Tyler slowed until Alex was a full step ahead. She needed an answer to the question that had arisen at the bar. She eyed Alex from behind. *Lord!* Tyler had thought the view couldn't get any better, but Alex's formfitting jeans provided a tantalizing preview of experiences to come.

She stopped dead in her tracks, listening to the voice screaming in her head as if trumpeting breaking news. *I'm so gay.* It was so clear to Tyler. This was not a bi-curious experiment. She was definitely a lesbian.

After a few steps, Alex stopped and turned with a quizzical look. "Having second thoughts?"

Tyler gave her a flirtatious grin. "Nope, just enjoying the view."

Alex smiled, extending a hand. They interlaced their fingers and held hands the short distance to the owner's suite.

Tyler was surprisingly calm when she entered the room. The ceiling-to-floor windows revealed an expansive view of San Francisco Bay that took her breath away. She dropped her purse and walked over to them. "Beautiful."

Alex came up behind, wrapped her arms around Tyler's waist, and pulled her tight. "Yes, you are."

Tyler expected the sense of being encircled to alarm her as it frequently did with Ethan, but this felt natural. Caresses soon joined light kisses on the neck. The touch to her breasts ignited every nerve ending. Shallow breaths turned ragged as all the memories that had kept Tyler up at night evaporated, leaving a blank slate. No one else but Alex existed, and nothing mattered but how Tyler was coming undone. She whispered, "Please…"

"Please, what?" Alex continued to massage Tyler's breasts.

"Please touch me."

"All in good time."

"Fuck." Tyler's frustration set in.

"That too, but all in good time."

Tyler couldn't help but grin. She let Alex's hands roam her body, but they avoided the place where she needed them the most.

"I know what you don't want," Alex whispered. "Now, tell me how you do want me to touch you."

Tyler's center pulsated with need as one fantasy after another flashed in her mind. She wanted to live out all of them. "I want you to touch everything."

Alex paused her exploration to remove Tyler's sweater, exposing her sleeveless magenta silk blouse. She traced Tyler's triceps, leaving goose bumps along her path.

"Lift your arms." After removing and discarding Tyler's blouse, Alex kissed the newly exposed skin of her shoulders and neck. While those kisses left Tyler tingling, they weren't what she wanted. In the past, before the rape, she would've waited patiently until Ethan worked his way to the thing she craved. Here she had no preconceived notion of who took the lead. She wanted more contact, so she pressed their bodies together and directed Alex's hands to her bra-covered breasts. "I love black lace." Alex reveled at her discovery.

Tyler turned around to face Alex and took a step back. "I got it for you."

The hunger in Alex's eyes meant her emergency stop at the mall had paid off. When she had seen the bra hanging on the rack, Tyler had envisioned Alex's breasts encased in the seductive network of french embroidered flowers dancing over sheer rounded cups. She had hoped it would elicit the same breathtaking response in Alex that it had in her. Her hope came true.

"You're irresistibly sexy in it." Alex glided her hands across Tyler's breasts, stopping to use her thumbs to tease each nipple into a hardened state. Pleasure exploded, bringing a moan to the surface and snapping Tyler's head back in ecstasy.

Tyler kicked off her shoes and Alex unbuttoned Tyler's slacks. Bending at the knees, Alex slid Tyler's pants to the ground, revealing matching black lace bikini briefs. The sight of Alex on her knees had Tyler licking her lips in anticipation. Alex inhaled, taking in the scent of Tyler's damp center. "I love the way you smell."

Tyler closed her eyes and groaned. "Fuck."

Alex let out a small chuckle. "That seems to be your favorite word."

"It is today," Tyler croaked.

Alex stroked Tyler's outer thighs before hooking her thumbs around the thin lace waistband and pulling the briefs down. "It's becoming mine, too."

She lowered the lace garment to the ground and helped Tyler to step out of it. She rose, skimming her fingertips along the outside of Tyler's legs as she went, stoking one fantasy after another. Once she was standing, Alex moved her hands around to Tyler's back and found the clasp holding in place the lace bra she'd admired earlier. Within moments, it too dropped to the floor. Alex retreated a step to take in the entire length of Tyler's naked body. "My God, you're beautiful."

Tyler reached up with one hand and cupped Alex's cheek. "So are you, but you're wearing way too many clothes." She grasped the hem of Alex's blouse and lifted it over her head, revealing a sheer white lace bra that contrasted with Alex's vibrant, tanned skin. Tyler traced a single fingertip a fraction above the line of fabric, down one breast and up the other. "So beautiful."

She reached for the top of Alex's jeans. After several futile efforts to unbutton them, she looked up, the heat in her cheeks telegraphing her embarrassment. "I'm not good at this."

Alex placed her hands over Tyler's. "Let me." After Tyler took a few steps back, Alex relieved herself of her slim-fitting jeans, exposing toned legs and the sexiest lace thong Tyler had ever seen. She gasped.

As Alex reached around her back to release her bra, Tyler stepped forward. "Let me." She reached behind her and undid the clasps before pulling the bra from Alex's body. Before this year, she had never envisioned a day when an exquisite pair of breasts would elicit such a visceral response. Every inch of her skin tingled. She ached to touch them. She desperately wanted to hold them in her hands, to test their weight and suppleness. And so she did. Alex tossed back her head and moaned, lost in the caress. Never had a partner's response stimulated her more.

Tyler captured Alex's lips in a searing kiss hotter than all the kisses she'd ever experienced combined. When she wrapped her arms around Alex's neck, Alex urged her back toward the bed. Two steps in, Tyler broke the kiss, drawing a concerned look from Alex.

"Are you okay? Do we need to slow down?"

"God, no." Tyler smiled before looking at her feet. "I got tangled in your bra." She paused at Alex's grin and then dove in for another long kiss, starting a slow dance with their tongues. Alex guided her backward until Tyler's legs hit the mattress.

This time, Alex broke the kiss. "I…" She paused, searching Tyler's eyes. Her brow creased, followed by a visible swallow. "Are you sure?"

"I've never wanted anyone more than I want you right now." Tyler fell to the bed, pulling Alex down beside her.

Tender and patient, Alex explored Tyler's body exhaustively, eliciting pleasure and burying Tyler's past. It had been years since Tyler had wanted to be filled. Now she begged for it. Her body's response to each kiss, caress, stroke, and lick convinced her this was how lovemaking was supposed to be—all-consuming. What a climax was supposed to be. How giving pleasure could come from a deep-seated need to please the one you love, not from obligation.

She wanted to know the musky scent and feel of Alex's damp core. Wanted to know the sweet and salty tastes of her body as she prepared her for the ultimate pleasure. Wanted to memorize every look and sound Alex made as she writhed under her in ecstasy.

By the end of the night, Tyler had experienced it all. She felt connected with Alex—physically, mentally, and emotionally. And when exhaustion finally set in, she discovered another gift—her nightmares, it seemed, had become a thing of the past.

CHAPTER THIRTY-TWO

Movement nudged Alex awake from a deep sleep, perhaps the best sleep she'd had in years. The warm body pressed against her breasts and abdomen played a significant role in that achievement. The arm she'd flung over Tyler's body gently rose and fell in cadence with Tyler's rhythmic breathing, a sure sign her lover was still sleeping. She inhaled, searching for the lavender perfume that had helped fuel her desire last night, but found only the tangy mixture of sweat and arousal. It served as a convincing, concrete reminder that last night wasn't a dream. Her only regret about their first time together was failing to say, "I love you." Her hesitation stemmed from concern for Tyler, not doubt. Impossible as it seemed, she loved Tyler with her every fiber, but Tyler was not only letting go of an eighteen-year marriage, she was also evolving sexually. She had to be the one to say the words first.

Alex remained motionless until the ache in her core built from a whisper to a roar. She soon had no control over her hands and lips, finding herself unable to keep them from caressing the sweet body next to her. A moan escaped Tyler's lips—the response Alex wanted. Tyler arched her back and raised a leg to give better access to what had become Alex's favorite place in the world.

"Good morning, lover," Alex whispered.

"Good morning." Tyler shifted more, but before Alex could slide her hand down, she said, "I have to pee."

Alex flipped back the white Egyptian cotton sheet, exposing Tyler's luscious, spellbinding, naked body. "Hurry back."

A glance at the nightstand clock told Alex she had less than two hours before the hotel manager would send out a search party for this morning's grand reopening ceremony. Eager to see the result of the renovation project that had taken her a year to complete, she would welcome a private tour ahead of the festivities, but that would have to wait. She wanted more time to drink in Tyler and the magnificent way she made her feel.

Minutes later, Tyler reappeared from the bathroom. The search party might have to be dispatched after all. Alex lifted the sheets. "Come back to bed. I need my morning fix."

Their bodies quickly entwined, hands exploring every inch of inviting skin. Their tongues caressed the other in a slow sensual dance, taking turns leading and following. Sheets rustled as their legs desperately sought more contact. Low moans of erotic pleasure filled the air. Could Alex ever get enough of this woman? One thought permeated her head: *Where has she been all my life?*

A pronounced gurgle interrupted their intimate embrace. Alex pulled back. "You're hungry."

"Famished, actually."

"Would you like to go downstairs and get something, or should I call room service?" Alex caressed Tyler's bare bottom.

"I could spend all day in bed with you," Tyler said, emphasizing her point with a naughty eyebrow waggle.

"I like the way you think." Alex kissed Tyler on her neck. "But I have a ceremony to attend."

"In that case, I'd like to see the results of your hard work. Would you mind going to the new restaurant?"

"I was hoping you'd say that."

* * *

To savor the renovation's full grandeur, Alex suggested taking the elevator to the lobby and riding the escalator to the atrium level. Her strategy didn't disappoint. Standing on the same stair as Tyler for their ascent, Alex wrapped her arms around her waist, resting her chin on her shoulder. The morning sun filtering through the full-ceiling skylights bathed the nine-story atrium in radiant light. The live vegetation outlining the balconies on each floor reached for the sun, creating a utopian atmosphere.

"Oh, my," Tyler said. "I thought it was beautiful at night, but this is breathtaking."

"It ended up so much better than the architect described." Without caring who might see, Alex tightened her hold and kissed Tyler on the neck.

The bar and lounge at the top had a different vibe in the morning, with cascading natural light turning them into something resembling an outdoor cantina. Turning to the left, Alex discovered the new restaurant measured up to the atrium's splendor. Her vision and the hard work of making San Francisco their showcase resort had come to fruition. No matter how her father felt about her private life, he couldn't deny she was the best choice to succeed him.

During their meal in a corner booth, Alex's thoughts drifted from work to the woman next to her. Yesterday morning she had been in a perpetual limbo state, waiting for Tyler to work through her PTSD and the changes that came with it. Little had Alex known that before the day was over, her wait would come to an end and her life would change for the best. She realized she wanted Tyler Falling for life.

"Tyler?"

"Yeah, babe?"

"Babe, huh?"

Tyler put her fork down, scooted closer on the bench, and inched her mouth dangerously close to Alex's. "After you called me T last night during the throes of passion, I put some serious thought into a pet name. Babe fits you."

Alex was nearly thirty-three years old, and this was the first time a woman had given her a pet name. Besides Kelly, who never cared about someone beyond their checking account balance, she had let no one stay long enough to coin one. Now that she had her own private moniker, it felt like the best thing in the world.

"I like it." Alex gave Tyler a short yet passion-filled kiss. Whether she became Castle Resorts' next CEO no longer held importance. The only thing that mattered was that she loved this woman. Only one question remained: Did Tyler love her too?

* * *

Lively jazz music—one of Tyler's secret pleasures—from a band set up on the hotel's circular driveway added to the festive atmosphere. Over a hundred guests dressed in suits and thousand-dollar dresses and dozens of media types with both video and still cameras were milling about the exterior of the main entrance. Champagne and hors d'oeuvres flowed while the crowd waited for the VIPs to appear for the ribbon-cutting ceremony and official grand reopening of the resort.

Tyler only cared about the VIP who had given her back her life. She could barely believe her own boldness of the last twelve hours, but the main lesson she had taken from her sessions with Gail was that burying her feelings caused more harm than good. Based on the euphoria she was still feeling, she had to admit that was the most profound lesson of her new life.

Almost on schedule, a man dressed in the hotel uniform walked up to the microphone near the entrance. He invited everyone to gather in front of the twelve-foot-long red ribbon stretched across the main entrance on stanchions. Minutes later, the crowd cheered as San Francisco's mayor and his wife appeared through the sliding glass doors. Alex, and the hotel manager Alex had pointed out earlier, followed. As they all lined up behind the red ribbon, the jazz music stopped, replaced by the clicking of dozens of cameras.

"Good morning. I'm George Hammer, manager of this magnificent hotel. I'd like to thank everyone for coming out this afternoon for the grand reopening of Castle Resort San Francisco." George waited through the polite applause. "It's my pleasure to introduce the mayor of San Francisco, Gerry Vines."

Following more applause, Mayor Vines approached the microphone. "Thank you, George. How is everybody doing? Is this a great day or what?" He paused a few moments as the crowd cheered. "Castle Resort has been one of the finest hotels in our city since it opened its doors in 1992. But as all of you are about to discover once you walk through these doors, the new Castle Resort has rightly been named 'The Jewel of the City.' I'd like to thank Alexandra Castle, the Chief of Operations of Castle Resorts, for her vision and dedication. She has made this hotel the best place to stay in the city and a center of art and culture featuring many sculptures and paintings from local artists. Now, if we're all ready, let's cut this ribbon."

After the ceremonial ribbon-cutting, guests and media filtered into the hotel, eventually making their way to the atrium level that was now the heart of the resort. As Alex cordially spoke with George, the mayor, and their wives, Tyler busied herself at a buffet table that offered elegant finger food.

Someone tapped Tyler on the shoulder. She spun around to find Syd and John, nicely dressed for the special occasion. "It's good to see you here, Tyler," Syd said. "Did Ethan come too?"

Tyler gave Syd a quick hug, stalling while searching for the right words. Other than the girls, Alex, Maddie, and their lawyer, she and Ethan hadn't announced their impending divorce. Whether Ethan had told John was a mystery because those two never betrayed a confidence.

"Um, no. I'm here as Alex's guest."

"That's a shame. How is his recovery coming?" Syd asked.

"Better than expected. He's back walking and driving."

"That's great," Syd said. "When does he go back to work?"

John popped a watermelon cube in his mouth and mumbled, "He put in his retirement papers yesterday."

Tyler's spidey sense heightened. If John knew about Ethan's retirement, she guessed he knew the rest of it. Yet he said nothing more. Based on his relaxed posture and friendly expression, she surmised Ethan had done an excellent job of explaining the circumstances.

"And I might as well tell you," Tyler said. "He's taking his own apartment because we're divorcing."

"He's leaving you?" Syd flew a hand to her chest and shuffled a step back. "But why? You two seemed so happy."

"It's a long story, but—"

"Syd? I didn't know you were coming." Alex placed a hand on Syd's back. Her bright smile stretched across her face, and if Tyler had to categorize it, it was sexy as hell.

"You would know if you'd answer your phone once in a while," Syd said in a playful tone.

"Shoot. I forgot." Alex pulled her cell phone from her front jacket pocket. "I put it on silent last night."

"Uh, huh." Syd raised an eyebrow in outward skepticism. "I hope she was worth it because Father was trying to reach you all night. He didn't sound happy."

Alex glanced at Tyler, giving her a subtle wink. "Yes, she was."

"What was that?" Syd's question came out sharp as she wagged a finger between Alex and Tyler.

"Syd, I need to tell you something about Tyler and me."

John finished chewing on a section of roast beef crostini. "They're a couple, and Ethan is okay with it. In fact, he pushed them together when he realized they belonged together."

Syd spun her head around to look her husband in the eye. If a look could slice and dice that crostini—or the man eating it—into a purée, Syd's could. "You knew and didn't tell me?"

John shrugged. "It wasn't my story to tell until Tyler was ready to spill the beans."

"You and your damn man code," Syd said.

"It hasn't been easy for Ethan." Tyler grabbed Alex's hand. She'd hidden her true self for too long and wasn't about to lose ground now. Tyler would face whatever backlash was in store. "The truth is, I love your sister." She turned toward Alex and met her eyes. "And I hope she loves me too."

Alex's eyes danced the words back to her. The smile behind them said they were true.

"This will take some getting used to, especially on Father's part." Syd tugged on Alex's arm, dragging Alex's attention back to her before she could voice the words Tyler achingly wanted to hear. "I thought he was furious with you last night. Wait until he finds out about this."

"Did he say what it was about?" Alex returned her gaze to Tyler, joy stretching across her beautiful face.

"Nope. All he said was that you are to see him in his office tonight. You're supposed to call Gretchen for the time and your new flight reservations."

"How mad was he?" Alex asked without breaking her stare at Tyler.

"Remember how pissed he was that time you took his new Mercedes out for a spin when you were fifteen?" Syd paused at Alex's nod. "Worse."

Whatever memory Alex had conjured up, it was enough to break the trance they'd been in since Tyler said, "I love you."

"Shit." Alex squeezed Tyler's hand. Her expression turned somber. "I'm not ready to leave you. Come with me to New York."

Alex's invitation was temptation on steroids. For thirteen years, companionship had replaced desire in Tyler's marriage, but last night, Alex had flipped Tyler's world upside down, one caress at a time. "I'd love to, but—"

"It's too soon." The disappointment in Alex's eyes was palpable and required immediate reassurance.

"It's not that. I have a conference with Bree's teacher tomorrow." Tyler knew their relationship had a long way to go before it no longer resembled a daytime soap opera, but they were on their way. Once Alex did as they had discussed last night and left her brother's fate in William's hands, Alex would walk away from Castle Resorts forever, paving the way for a life with Tyler. It was a journey Tyler looked forward to. Tyler drew Alex into an embrace and whispered in her ear, "Otherwise, I'd never leave your side and we'd be card-carrying members of the mile-high club before we landed."

EPILOGUE

Manhattan, New York

Waking up this morning to an empty side of the bed had Alex in a sour mood. She had missed having Tyler's body warming her throughout the night. Missed caressing her smooth legs and kissing the sensitive little patch of skin behind her ear. The three-hour time difference meant it was too early to call her. Hearing Tyler's voice would have to wait until she got out of this cab and finally put Castle Resorts behind her. The only solace: she was finally done with her father, following last night's contentious meeting with him. Once she packed her personal things from her office and said a few goodbyes, especially to Gretchen and Robbie, she'd leave the building and never look back. A fresh start was exactly what she needed. She had enough money, and with her skills, she'd be in high demand.

The taxi pulled to a stop well short of Castle Resorts' Madison Avenue offices. The driver looked over his shoulder toward Alex. "I'm sorry, miss, but police activity has traffic detoured."

"It's fine. I can walk the rest of the way." After thanking and tipping him, Alex proceeded on foot. The rain clouds that had rolled in overnight had finally cleared, leaving the city smelling fresh. As she got closer, she expected to see the usual plethora of construction vehicles connected with the never-ending refurbishing of the building's lobby and stairwells. Instead, several police cruisers, a fire truck, an ambulance, and other city vehicles were blocking the southbound lanes. Alex thought at first they might have been there for a fire alarm or gas leak, but no, foot traffic was still moving in and out of the building.

Finally inside, Alex walked straight to the elevators, passing three police officers. The usual clamor of construction was mysteriously absent, making it easy to hear the squawk of a radio, though not audibly enough to decipher what was being said. Though curious, she entered the elevator car and began her ascent to the twenty-third floor. When its doors opened, she expected to hear the usual buzzing of power tools. She was greeted instead by the bustling of several police officers and technicians. They appeared to be dusting surfaces for fingerprints or other evidence.

Worry flooded her. Castle Resorts occupied the entire floor, so something must have happened at her corporate offices. She picked up her pace as she walked toward the reception desk, but a uniformed officer stopped her short of it.

"I'm sorry, miss, but you can't go in. It's a crime scene."

"I'm Alex Castle. I'm the Chief of Operations here." Or at least she was until last night. "What happened?"

"Wait here, miss. I'll get the lead detective." The officer retreated to the inner offices.

"Detective? Why are there detectives here?" Alex shouted as another officer continued to block her entrance.

Several minutes later, a tall, well-dressed man with close-cropped inky hair emerged from the interior offices' reception area. "Good morning, Ms. Castle. I'm Detective Greg Sterling. Will you follow me?"

Alex nodded without saying a word, knowing somehow that Sterling wouldn't answer her questions until she did as he asked. He led Alex to one of the smaller offices, where Gretchen was sitting in a guest chair. Her eyes were red and puffy, and it was apparent she'd been crying.

Alex's pulse raced. She darted toward Gretchen and knelt on the floor in front of her. She placed her hands on Gretchen's arms. "My God, Gretchen, what happened?"

Gretchen continued to sob. She leaned forward, buried her head in Alex's chest, and cried uncontrollably. Alex wrapped her arms around her and turned her head toward Detective Sterling. "Will you please tell me what happened here?"

Sterling cleared his throat and then said in a flat tone, "Ms. Castle, I'm afraid there was a suspicious death here last night."

"What? Who?" Alex looked back at Gretchen, who continued to cry.

He said, "Your father, William Castle."

Bella Books, Inc.

Women. Books. Even Better Together.

P.O. Box 10543
Tallahassee, FL 32302

Phone: 800-729-4992
www.bellabooks.com